Tyranny of Fortune

Donovan Hoult

Publishers:
Inspiring Publishers
P.O. Box 159 Calwell ACT 2905, Australia.
Email: inspiringpublishers@gmail.com

National Library of Australia Cataloguing-in-Publication entry

Author: Hoult, Donovan

Title: **Tyranny of Fortune**/*Donovan Hoult.*

ISBN: 978-1-925908-50-3 (pbk)
        978-1-925908-51-0 (eBook)

Subjects: Inheritance and succession—Western Australia—Fiction.
        Models (Persons)—Fiction.
        Murder—Fiction.
        Suspense fiction, Australian.

Cover pic: Jack Poplawski
        Warrawagine Station
        Western Australia

1

'Hi there, you must be Andrew Hanna?'

Andrew looked up from the brief he was reading at the muscular figure with heavily tattooed forearms attached to bulging biceps barely constrained within the tailored suit. 'You know who I am, don't you?'

Andrew was well aware of who he was looking at, but feigned ignorance. 'No, I don't.'

'Ron Ratsakis.' The big man sat down opposite with a beaming smile spreading across his face. 'You were recommended to me by one of your associates too busy to take my case. He told me where to find you.'

'And who was that?' Obviously, whoever it was did not want to represent the likes of *Ronnie the Rat*. He quickly glanced around the court foyer to identify who it might be, but there were too many lawyers and individuals in the hurrying throng, to identify anyone in particular.

Ratsakis ignored the question as he grinned and thrust his giant paw across the table to shake Andrew's hand. An equally dangerous looking associate pulled up a chair and sat motionless, his tattooed arms resting on the table. Andrew knew by reputation Ratsakis was a thug and a criminal and guilty as charged with whatever alleged crime he was in court to defend. A member of a notorious motor cycle gang into drugs, burglary, prostitution, extortion and murder. Mess with Ronnie or members of his gang and it was highly likely you would get beaten to a pulp or simply disappear. There was only one warning, there were no second chances.

Andrew cursed himself for not immediately going back to his office instead of sitting in a discrete corner of the coffee bar waiting for a client he was due to meet in an hour, or for that matter, anyone in-between looking for representation. If they had the money he would plead their case, no matter how guilty or hopeless he perceived their chances to be. But in this case it was an exception. It was simply too dangerous.

'What do you want Mr Ratsakis?'

'It's Ronnie. I've been charged with possession and dealing. All bullshit of course, but the cops reckon they've got me nailed. I want your assistance.' The expression was not that of a plea for help, but one of demand.

Andrew had tried to restrain his shock and adopt the composure of the professional counsel able to deal with any situation. 'I'm too busy to represent you Ronnie. I'm booked out for the next two weeks, so you'll have to make an appointment.'

'You are going to help me Hanna, so don't hand me the line you're too busy.'

'You don't understand Mr Ratsakis. If you're in court today I can't possibly read the charge sheet and form a defence.'

Ronnie guffawed softly, leaned over and slapped him on the shoulder. Andrew recoiled at the familiarity. He was there to defend, not to make friends with the likes of Ratsakis.

'Then you'll just have to re-arrange some appointments. My problem takes priority. Do you understand?'

Andrew understood perfectly. He could get up and make a run for it, or call for one of the security staff evident in the foyer. The merciless expression opposite was reading his mind.

'Don't even think about it Hanna. You can't hide from me. Now, let's get down to business. I'll give you three grand now and two more if you can get this bullshit dismissed.'

'I've already told you I'm too busy, but what's this about? Maybe I can refer you to one of my colleagues.'

Ronnie outlined the charges and the circumstances surrounding them. The more Andrew listened, the more he was convinced Ratsakis was going down for a stretch. 'So that's it. What are my chances and don't give me any crap?'

'Mr Ratsakis.....I'

'It's Ronnie.'

'Mr Ratsakis, I'll give it to you straight. It's pointless me representing you. I believe your position is hopeless. And anyone I refer you to would advise the same.'

'But what about the fucking cops. They were in on it. You see that fat turd of a detective who's just come through security.' Ratsakis nodded his head in the direction of the entrance. 'That's detective bloody Connors. He and his mates were getting too greedy and wanted a bigger cut. I refused, so this is the result.'

'You can forget about trying to implicate him. The magistrate is not going to be moved by anything you may claim without some form of proof.'

'Proof? The whole bloody force knows he's bent. I've been paying him off for years.'

'So why's he turning against you now?'

'A rival with a bigger spread of members – more distribution, both here and interstate, therefore larger profits. Connors said it was nothing personal, just business, but if I was prepared to cut him in for a larger slice to match what they were offering, then he would allow our arrangement to continue. I told him to get fucked.'

'Obviously not a wise business decision,' Andrew replied pulling a wry expression. 'You're undoubtedly going to serve time.'

'Have a look at this.' Ratsakis pulled a photo out of his jacket pocket and pushed it across the table.

Andrew studied it. He could see the clear features of Ratsakis handing a bundle of cash to the partially obscured face of a person taking hold of it. 'What am I supposed to be looking at?'

'That's a photo of me handing cash to Connors in my car last month. The camera was concealed in the radio. I would say that's strong evidence Connors is bent.'

Andrew pushed the photo back. 'You'll have to do better than that Mr Ratsakis. It doesn't confirm a crime is being committed. That may be Connors, or may be someone who resembles him.'

Ratsakis pulled another photo out from his jacket and dropped it in front of Andrew. It clearly identified both men and the money.

'You're still cooked unless you've got some real proof of what you two were transacting. Connors can claim he was slinging you a few bucks for acting as his snitch. The photo doesn't prove who was handing who the money. As a detective, Connors testimony would weigh heavily against you with the result you are still going down for the count. You can't win, you must realise that?'

'Oh, I have a full video of the whole transaction and Connors demands.' Ratsakis produced a USB drive with a grin of satisfaction. 'It shows a meeting in my car.'

'But can't you get it into your head this evidence just confirms you are going to jail if it contains what you purport it does. From what you've told me, Connors is the king-pin in the drug squad so he's setting you up for a long stretch. What did he nail you for?'

'While I wasn't looking he slipped a packet of meth under the passenger seat. I was pulled over while on the way home and guess what the cops found. That's why I'm here.'

'You're still going to be flushed down the pan if you produce this. You've got a real problem, don't you understand that?'

Ratsakis smiled and nodded. 'You've got it in one, so I'm tossing it in your lap, so now it's your problem. You're going to have a word in his lily-pink ear before we get into court?'

'And wind up in the same cell as you?' Andrew hissed angrily. 'What you're suggesting is both blackmail and perverting the course of justice. I certainly can't be party to that. Now get lost and I'll forget your approach.'

'Can't you get someone to just hand him the stick and the photos? I have copies. I want him to drop the charges before he goes into court.'

'Connors would be too smart for that. I can't be party to it. I suggest you give it to him and call his bluff. It just might work.'

'I can't take that risk. There must be a way of getting at him.'

Andrew's mind was elsewhere when he caught sight of the person who had just walked up to Connors. He recognised him immediately, "Iggy" Ignatius McQuire, an overbearing individual who made it very clear he wanted to become a Supreme Court judge, just like his father. Alex had always treated him with deference, never addressing him by his nickname. Unlike his fellow alumni, he never believed in creating antagonism. Iggy had the talent with ruthless intent and there was no doubt in Andrew's mind he would eventually succeed. With Iggy prosecuting there was no chance of Ratsakis escaping jail and there was no way Andrew was going to defend him and suffer the inevitable defeat. It would only confirm to McQuire he was penniless and hanging around the court taking on hopeless cases. Suddenly a thought entered his head as his ethics jumped a cog. He was desperate for income without compromising himself. 'Tell me, what was the exact location and time of your meeting with Connors?'

'It's all there on the video. Problem is, it blows us both away.'

Andrew picked it up and tapped it on his other hand. Obviously, the contents were damaging, too damaging to be ever produced in court.

'Mr Ratsakis, I want you to immediately get up and leave. I must decline to represent you. I want to think about it, but I'll meet you in the coffee bar just down the the street in half an hour.' He watched anxiously as Ratsakis and his minder swiftly departed unobserved by Connors or the prosecutor.

2

McQuire had not noticed Andrew when he walked in and ordered a coffee. He turned and was balancing it in one hand while the other clutched his change and briefcase when he saw Andrew and walked over. 'Hi there, how's it going? Getting any work?'

'Unbelievable,' Andrew beamed. 'More work than I can handle.'

'You're a lying sod Hanna.' McQuire gave a cynical laugh as he sat down opposite. 'There's no money in defending criminals who haven't got the money to pay, or won't pay you. Why not join me and apply for a position in prosecutions?'

'I just might do that, but I thought I'd work this side of the fence first. It will give me an idea of what to expect in the way of excuses if I ever move over to your area of expertise. Are you handling anything interesting at the moment?'

'Just the usual lying bums and stiffs claiming their innocence, although there's a more entertaining one on in the next thirty minutes.'

'Oh, anyone in particular? Do they need a good defence lawyer?'

'Forget it Andrew. He'll need someone more experienced than you.' McQuire held up his hand and laughed. 'No offence mate, but this guy is going down. The demons have been after him for ages and now they've got him cold, possession and trafficking drugs big time. Typical motorcycle gang modus operandi, but this guy is the kingpin.'

'What's his name?'

Ronnie the Rat – Ronald Ratsakis – have you heard of him?'

'The name sounds familiar. You reckon you've got him in leg irons already do you?'

'Not me, I'm only the prosecutor. It's Detective Connors who reckons he's got him going down for ten.'

'This Connors is a friend of yours is he?'

'Only in a professional sense. I don't drink or socialise with him, if that's what you're suggesting. However, I get a real buzz when I help him send one of these low-life's to the can. It's a feather in both our caps.'

They chatted idly while McQuire finished his coffee and made to leave. Andrew had been fighting his internal turmoil. He could see his moment of decision was about to vaporise unless he made the move. He was risking his career and reputation. He pulled a pad and envelope out of his satchel and started to scribble a note. He turned his back and slipped the photos and stick inside the envelope. 'Would you do something for me Ignatius?'

McQuire gave him a suspicious look. 'If I can.'

'Can you give Connors this letter please?'

'Why don't you give it to him yourself?' McQuire's face hardened. 'Hold on, this has something to do with Ratsakis hasn't it? Are you representing him? If you are, you can present this to the court yourself. If you are attempting to compromise me in some way I'll be compelled to report this to the magistrate. You'll be in deep shit man.'

'No, I'm not representing Ratsakis, so you can rest your mind on that matter. And I'm not compromising you? I'm well aware of the risks and your position. However, I am aware of certain information that should be brought to Connors' attention.'

'That's not good enough. I want to know what you have.'

'Ignatius, all I'm asking you to do is hand this envelope to Connors. When he's read it, you can ask him if he wants to share it with you and I don't mind you telling him from whom, and how you acquired it. Believe me, Connors mightn't thank you, but I believe he will be very grateful.'

'And if he wants to talk to you?'

'I'll be right here. I'm always here on the lookout for some poor miscreant looking for representation.'

McQuire stood and took the envelope. 'Okay, against my better judgement I'll do it, but if you've set me up, I'll tip the bucket on you. And make sure you stay right here.'

'I'm not going anywhere. And thanks Ignatius. I really appreciate it.' He watched as McQuire strode off. He had the feeling sometime within the next five minutes he would see Connors striding towards him, or it would be an angry prosecutor who confronted him.

McQuire walked up to the detective where he was talking with some of his colleagues and handed him the letter.

'What's this?'

'I've been asked to hand you this. I'll wait while you read it.'

Connors opened the envelope and stuffed the stick into his pocket before moving to the side of the corridor. He unfolded the note while glancing at the photos. McQuire watched as Connors face screwed up in anger. 'Who gave you these?'

'Just an acquaintance.'

'Does he have anything to do with Ratsakis. He's in deep shit if he does. This is attempted blackmail – perverting the course of justice is not some trivial offence.'

'If it's to do with Ratsakis, can I read it? Can I see the photos?'

'No, you can't.' Connor folded the page back into the envelope along with the photos and shoved it inside his jacket.

'Ratsakis is due to appear this morning. Am I still prosecuting?'

Connors shook his head. 'No, Ratsakis has escaped down a rat-hole for now, but I'll get the bastard some other time.'

'But, you just can't abandon it surely? He's got no defence.'

'You heard what I said McQuire. We're not offering any evidence so you can withdraw the case.'

McQuire was fuming as he watched Connors swing on his heel and walk off shaking his head in anger. What was the damning evidence Hanna had given him? Andrew was still sitting at the same table, stirring a coffee and pretending to read a paper when McQuire stormed up.

'I don't know what was in that envelope Hanna, but that's the last time I'll ever do you a favour. You set me up you bastard.'

'So, Connors has dropped the case?'

'Hanna, I should report you to the court and the Law Society. We had an iron-clad case against Ratsakis and you just blew it for me. I'm bloody furious.'

'I can see that Ignatius, but before you self-immolate with rage, sit down and I'll explain a few facts to you. Whatever you may think, I'm not representing Ratsakis. I came into possession of some evidence that would have made you look a complete fool if it had been tendered to the court. No doubt Ratsakis would have been convicted, but your favourite detective would have been sharing a nearby cell. Connors is a criminal, he's into the drug business and I don't mean that as an enforcer of the law, but rather as an active participant in the distribution of drugs of all classes.'

'I don't believe you.'

'Wake up Ignatius. I saw Connors' reaction when he read the letter and I noticed he didn't give it to you to read. He nearly had a stroke when he saw the photos. I saw him follow your glance in my direction when he asked you something. And I can only assume he was asking you who gave you the letter. I'm right, aren't I?'

'I don't believe it. Sure, I know he's a hard-nosed cop when it comes to catching crims, but I wouldn't have guessed he was in on the business?'

'Well, now you know. I saved you from a very embarrassing situation. My advice is to steer clear of any cases he's involved with. Connors would have been doing time along with Ratsakis if the contents of that letter, photos and video had been revealed in court. You start getting into bed with scum like Connors and you'll never follow your father to the Bench.'

'You're an officer of the court Hanna. I've a mind to report you for withholding vital evidence. You just destroyed an important case which would have done much for my reputation putting that scumbag away.'

'Don't try that bluster and bullshit with me McQuire, I just saved your backside and reputation, not to mention your friendship with Connors. Despite your denial, I know you often drink with him, so you would have some awkward questions to answer if you decide to take your complaint about me any further. And I'm sure Daddy wouldn't be pleased his son was consorting with a crim.'

'What was in that letter, and don't forget you wrote it in front of me? And I did see you slip the photos and stick inside. You must be representing Ratsakis.'

'Yes, I have spoken to him, but when I saw the implications of your involvement I decided not to accept his case. I was only thinking of you.'

'Jeez, you're all heart. You mean to say you did that for me? Why am I adopting a cynical attitude towards your pleadings?'

'You can take it anyway you like Ignatius. I've done you a favour and you did one for me, so we're square. Look at it this way. I ran the greater risk if Connors had decided to call my bluff and have me charged with blackmail or perversion. I had to have a messenger, banking on the fact he would not shoot the messenger. He's seen me around the courts as a destitute young attorney looking for work. He would not have thought twice about taking me aside and shaking me down, but you are a court appointed prosecutor. He didn't know what you knew, but if he threatened you he would have realised his whole day would likely turn to crap.'

McQuire smiled and sighed. 'So there goes my shot at glory, putting one of the biggest drug dealers behind bars. But I agree, it would have been embarrassing to have my chief witness indicted on Ratsakis' evidence. That would have been a real coup for you Hanna. I can't understand why you didn't represent Ronnie? By the way in what form was the evidence?'

'All I'm prepared to say is, it was damning. You can't afford to prosecute anything Connors wants to drop in your lap in future. Find some other dope to do it.'

The insult was ignored or not heard. McQuire stood and held out his hand. 'I don't know whether to thank you or report you. I still can't figure it out.'

'Do me one last favour Ignatius. Don't ever divulge to Connors what I've just told you. And if you want some sound advice, find another pub and friend to drink with. And don't bother to deny it, because I'm aware of your association.'

McQuire nodded and looked sheepish. 'I can see that, but I'd be watching my back if I were you. Detective Connors is obviously a very dangerous person.'

Andrew nodded as he watched McQuire walk away. What was the real reason he had just done what he did? It was simple justification. If he'd accepted Ratsakis' case he would have been imprinted as being mixed up with the mob, the notorious motor cycle gangs who controlled drugs, the most lucrative crime of all. He would have been marked by the police as a defender of those criminals and the perpetrator of the downfall of one of their colleagues, no matter how tainted he was. The ranks would immediately close. He had dodged both bullets. McQuire was in the clear because he was appointed by the Court. However, his reputation would have taken a nasty hit when the case blew up in his face. It was time to collect.

Ronnie the Rat was deep in conversation on his mobile, but signalled Andrew to sit down. The accompanying goon remained expressionless.

'Yeah, yeah, well just get the bloody business done. Nah, I won't be going to bloody jail. I've got the best lawyer in the State on my side. Get those goods organised.' Ratsakis was smiling as he turned off his phone and gave Andrew a steely look. 'Tell me that's correct counsellor, isn't it? I'm free and clear?'

'Yes, you are Mr Ratsakis. The charges have been dropped.'

Andrew pulled back to avoid another pat on the shoulder – there were too many eyes around – the sign of compliant affection had to be avoided. 'It's Ronnie from now on. I knew you could handle it. But tell me, what did you do?'

'I won't go into that and I don't think you need to know.'

'But you must have shoved it right up Connors keister. Oh, what the hell. It doesn't really matter. You know Andrew, I want you on my side from now on. If you act for me I'll put you on a retainer. How does that sound?'

'Mr Ratsakis, I told you I would not act for you and I confirmed to the court prosecutor that was indeed the case. I merely tendered a letter and items outlining what you intended to tell the court which would have involved a detective sharing a cell with you.'

'Don't be so bloody moralistic with me Hanna. You had established I was guilty and likewise Connors. There was nothing in it for you. If either I or Connors went down you were going to be pissing me off or pissing off the cops. It was a no-win situation. By doing what you did, you have guaranteed my gratitude and ongoing patronage. You're my legal counsel from now on. Look at it this way – I'm the only one with money to pay your tab in cash, the cops haven't.'

'Mr Ratsakis, I've no intention of accepting a retainer from you. You see, the prosecutor is a professional colleague, termed a friend of the court. I didn't want to see him make a fool of himself when the case exploded ten minutes from the commencement of proceedings.'

'Yeah, yeah, we both know that's bullshit, but I'll accept your explanation. The real reason is you believe I'm too dirty to be associated with.' Ratsakis nodded to his associate who pushed an envelope across the table. 'That's for your help. There's five grand in there.'

Andrew didn't touch the envelope. 'I cannot accept that. I told the prosecutor I was not acting for you and cannot accept payment. How do you know one of Connors' associates is not filming this meeting. That would be the end of my career, and a likely jail term if I pick that up.'

Ratsakis nodded. 'I'll have it dropped in your letter box this evening. You'll know it's there when your intercom is pushed three times. But look, I want you to consider acting as my legal counsel. I can put a lot of work your way if you want. We buy a lot of property, we're into a lot of legit businesses, and you could really set yourself up if you agree to work for me and only me. You won't have to worry about Connors. He won't come near me again now he knows I'm holding all the cards."

'I prefer to reject that offer Mr Ratsakis.'

'No hard feelings then.' Andrew felt dirty as he shook the extended hand. 'You just saved me from at least five years behind bars. Sure, Connors would have gone down as well, but I was going to make sure I took him with me. I don't know how you pulled it off, but I'm grateful you did. I'll never forget that.'

3

'Who owns Ironstone Park?'

The secretary hurriedly opened a file and studied the particulars. 'The Ironstone Park Pastoral Company from what I can see Minister.'

'Christ man, can't you just answer a simple question. Who the hell owns the company?'

'It's… it's owned by Chloe Boyce,' the secretary stammered in reply as he flipped over another page.

'You're telling me that some bloody woman holds title to a billion tons of iron-ore? How did that happen?'

'She also owns Baracool, an adjoining property with another billion tons.'

'Who the hell is she and why haven't I heard of her before now?'

'Minister, with all due respect you must be the only person in the State who hasn't heard of Chloe Boyce.'

'I'm the Minister of Mines, I'm only interested in mining, not the bloody social pages register and I don't appreciate your cheap cracks Harrison. How the hell am I supposed to know who Chloe Boyce is?'

Michael Harrison realised it was a short-fuse morning. It was going to be a tough day until Jack Gibbs' hangover began to wear off. In the meantime he would have to persist and endure the abuse and verbal bullying. His boss was always in a foul mood when he had been dining and drinking in some private club late into the night. He should have picked the mood and condition before he opened his mouth and made the facetious remark about his apparent ignorance. If he had been standing closer he would have caught the rancid fumes of stale alcohol. He suppressed a grin of contempt. The mood would have been the opposite if he had spent the night with his mistress. In that event he would have stormed into the office acknowledging everyone with a loud greeting of goodwill and cheer.

Harrison had been ten minutes late when he entered and saw the light on his direct extension to Gibbs' office glowing. 'How long has he been paging me?' He glanced over at one of his staffers.

'It's only just come on.'

'Any idea what he wants?'

'I think it's to do with the file on Ironstone Park. He asked me to retrieve it late yesterday. He said he wanted to study it overnight. However, he didn't pick it up as it's on your desk where I left it.'

'What's the mood sign, red or green?'

'I don't know Mr Harrison. The Minister got in early today.'

'Okay, who is this Chloe Boyce?'

'She's a former international model sir. She inherited the properties from her father Henry Boyce a few years ago. Ask Christine in reception about her. I'm sure she can fill you in on her background before she retired to take up running cattle stations.'

Gibbs gave him a quick look to see if he was being subjected to another cheap shot, but Harrison's expression was blank. 'Oh, now I do recall something. She's that darkie isn't she?'

'If you mean, is she coloured sir, yes she is. But there's not a man in the country, including you sir with all due respect, who wouldn't be prepared to be seen in her company.'

'That good eh?' Gibbs sat back in his chair and searched his memory. 'I wonder if it's the girl my son Oliver was trying to bed when he was at university years ago. He brought her to my birthday party. She was a real smasher and I'd have given anything to be years younger and in my son's place. However, Audrey made it clear she wasn't going to have her son bedding an abo, no matter how beautiful, charming or acceptable she may be. She could envisage the piccanninies biting her ankles even as Oliver was introducing the girl. I was given the order to knock the liaison on the head immediately. I think the girl must have heard me giving him the message, because she apparently just walked out on him. Come to think of it, he did mention it some time later she became a model and had gone to Europe.' Gibbs sat back in his chair searching his memory. 'She's not the same person who had something to do with diamonds, is she?'

'That's correct sir. She was known to have a fabulous red diamond given to her by her grandfather, but she would never reveal where it came from.'

'What happened to it?'

'She said it had been returned it to a sacred place she swore she would never reveal.'

'Probably stolen from the Argyle mine if the truth be known.'

'No, a diamond merchant here in Perth subsequently arrested and jailed for handling stolen Argyle gems, testified he had been shown the gem by Walter Boyce, the adopted son of Henry Boyce and it was not from Argyle.'

'Boyce senior was part abo, was he?'

'No, he was white. Not a trace of colour in him from what I read in the papers.'

'So, old Henry Boyce was a gin jockey and afraid to acknowledge he'd been playing in the chocolate box? Mind you it's common knowledge plenty of that was going on in years gone by. Even the clergy in the outback missions failed the temptation test.'

'Apparently he was her natural father, although he was married to someone other than her mother at the time. He never acknowledged Chloe while he was alive, but it all came out in his Will when she inherited everything. Apparently, he had an old aboriginal elder on the station pose as her grandfather and adopt her so his wife wouldn't be suspicious when a pretty little coloured child arrived at the homestead. Also, it got around the problem of having to acknowledge to Child Welfare authorities he was her natural father, as it was highly likely they would never have granted him custody. He should have waited and saved himself all the potential trouble as his wife up and left him a couple of months later.'

'How do you know all this?'

'The media had a field day when he died. They really did the full dirty laundry bit on her with all the embellishment they could muster.' Harrison threw his arms wide as he described the imaginary headlines. *'International model and the secret of her parentage. Chloe inherits millions. Beautiful model the result of secret liaison. Model's mother found violated and dead in Darwin motel after U.S. marines leave. Chloe knows secret of fabulous diamond mine.'*

'You don't have to explain it to me anymore Harrison. I get the picture. You say she had a brother. What happened to him?'

'She had two brothers, Carl and Walter, but they were a couple of feral twins adopted by old Henry. Whether or not they were in someway related to him or just a couple of strays he took pity on is not known, but they certainly weren't his natural sons, nor were they coloured. Carl was gored to death by a bull and Walter simply disappeared somewhere on Venus Downs, one of the Boyce cattle stations.'

'So that's how she inherited the lot?'

Harrison nodded. "That's correct sir.'

'How many stations does she own?'

'Five at last count, although she has partnership interests in at least another six when I looked up her register of holdings. She owns Venus Downs, Romulus Park, and the giant Ascot Downs in the Kimberley and Ironstone Park and Baracool in the Pilbara out-right. In addition, she owns a huge beef processing operation which supplies into the Asian market. She also is the largest shipper of live cattle to the Indonesian abattoirs and feedlots. She owns trucking companies. Her whole operation is vertically integrated. You name it and she's in it.'

Gibbs whistled softy. 'Very impressive. How does an abo control an operation that size?'

'She may have aboriginal blood in her sir, but she is one smart lady and I would advise you if I may be so bold, to refrain from using the pejorative abbreviation. She's of part aboriginal descent, and not an abo as you describe her. Why not be more understanding and refer to her as indigenous?

A flash of anger crossed Gibbs' face. He resented Harrison's censure, but knew it was correct. He waved his hand in guilty dismissal. 'Yeah, I know it's not politically correct and I know the established protocol, but they give me the shits. They're the most privileged indigenous nation on earth. We spend billions on them every year and all they do is whinge about theft of their land, so-called past massacres and the stolen generation. It's all bullshit, but while they can incite the bleeding hearts to fight their cause, there's nothing we can do about it. Those Canberra politicians are a pack of cringing pissants who don't want to jeopardise the black vote, or upset the guilt-ridden cringe-fringe of this country. Anyway, how much is Chloe Boyce ripping out of the system?'

'What do you mean sir?'

'By that I mean, how much is she getting by way of government grants and assistance because she is one of the privileged ab……. aboriginal class?'

'Not a cent sir.'

'I don't believe she's that bright. Models are all air-heads in my book, or is she unique? I don't believe it. And as for abo's having any skills other than blowing didgeridoos and rounding up cattle, well I'll just leave it at that.' A sudden thought crossed his mind. 'Is she married?'

'I don't think so, but I can easily check. She does live with a fellow by the name of Andrew Hanna and they have a son. She was married to a Lebanese by the name of Marcel Faroud, a real shady character who got his throat slit by an Afghani refugee. Apparently Faroud was into people smuggling, but he made the mistake of shipping this particular Afghani's family in a leaking boat from Indonesia. The boat foundered and the Afghani father was the only survivor.'

'And he caught up with Faroud?'

'Correct, but that wasn't the full story. Apparently Faroud was out to murder Hanna because he believed he'd stolen his wife. He almost succeeded in that he knifed him in the lungs. But who should be hiding in the next room, the Afghani who promptly slit Faroud's throat.'

'I remember something about this. Didn't some police sergeant then blow the Afghani away with a shotgun?'

'Not only the Afghani, but the wealthiest and most despised person in Wyndham. The cop claimed self-defence as the guy was standing behind the Afghani as they were coming down the stairs. He told the coroner he feared for his life and just instinctively fired. Rumour has it the cop and money-bags, a guy by the name of Shulman, along with Henry Boyce and a couple of others were partners in a huge cattle duffing operation. The result was the cop retired and the police buried the case along with the victims.'

'So Boyce was mixed up in this?'

'I appears Henry most certainly was, but he's dead. His daughter may have been aware, but I don't think she could have been involved. She would have been too young and then she was in England and Europe for a number of years. However, there is an area of doubt in my mind in that she now owns Ascot Downs, the cattle station from which the duffing supposedly took place.'

'But surely cattle duffing is a peanuts operation. So what if someone knocks off a few hundred head and flogs them? Those big properties wouldn't know how many head they were carrying and wouldn't even know if they'd lost a few thousand.'

'Ascot was owned by an absentee English landlord. It carried in excess of fifty-five thousand head. The manager, who is now dead, was rumoured to be shifting between five and ten thousand clean-skins off Ascot onto the adjacent Venus Downs for branding and ear-tagging every year. Boyce was rumoured to be up to his ears in debt to the bank before the duffing started. Shulman acted as agent for the stolen cattle and was potentially in the clear as he was not directly involved, although he most certainly was behind the scenes. Everyone got a piece of the pie, including the cop.'

'So when Henry snuffed it, his daughter inherited the lot?'

'On the face of it, that would appear to be the case, but apparently there was some arrangement between Shulman and Boyce which gave Shulman some sort of pre-emptive rights he tried to cash-in on. He intended to exercise those rights and deprive her of everything.'

'Then how the hell did she wind up with Ascot Downs and the other properties she now has? Surely, she's not that bloody smart?'

'Boyce bought Ascot after her father died, but I don't know how she did it. International models make big bucks, but Ascot would have been way outside her credit card limit. It would have run into tens of millions.'

'So who's the brains behind her? No doubt she's smart, but to amass what you've just told me is obviously not all her own work. Who is this Hanna fellow?'

'I don't know sir. He very much remains in the background.'

'Well, I want you to find out all you can, where he comes from and what his trade is.'

'I very much doubt he's a tradesman.'

'Everyone's a bloody tradesman Harrison. I don't care if you're a proctologist, a high court judge, the Pope, or a plumber – you learn a trade and you apply it.'

Obviously that definition did not apply to politicians, Harrison observed to himself. They were on a pedestal far above the tradesmen class, or assumed they were. He had watched successive governments come and go, their fate determined by the fickle nature of the voters and what the politicians could promise to enrich their lives. Elections were nothing more than an auction of stolen goods with the biggest liars, cheats and thieves hustling the public to believe their spiel. Gibbs was just another self-opinionated buffoon in a continuing parade of incompetent ministers he had served under. They came in with their inflated egos and determination to change the world. The majority invariably went out exhausted with the voters shoe firmly imprinted on their backsides, but safe in the knowledge they were entitled to a fat parliamentary pension for life, fully indexed for inflation with attached benefits.

'I'll make some enquiries about Hanna. Now in reference to your original enquiry, is there something in particular you want to know about Ironstone Park and Baracool?'

'Yes, I want to know when the permits for mineral rights were first granted. I want to know if all the conditions of the permits have been complied with. I want to know if Boyce intends to develop them and when. I can't allow such valuable assets to be left in the ground thereby depriving the government of taxes and royalties, not to mention the employment such development would entail.'

Harrison nodded. What was Gibbs really up to? What was his motive? Why the sudden focus on the two properties? 'I'll look into that sir and get back to you in due course.'

'I want a report on my desk by next week. No later. And also dig out all the articles concerning Boyce and the red diamond. It's preposterous she won't reveal where it came from because of some mumbo jumbo about a sacred site.'

'Despite major programs by diamond exploration companies, nothing has been found. Although dozens of potential diamond pipes were located, none contained anything other than a few micro diamonds. The source of the red diamond is unique and unless Boyce can be persuaded otherwise, there's only a vague chance of locating it. Diamond exploration is a very expensive business. It was concluded the diamond must have come from somewhere in the vicinity of the Venus Downs station, but that's one huge area to search in. And without Boyce's co-operation the search was abandoned as being futile.'

'Everyone's got their price Harrison. I wonder what hers would be?' Gibbs was lost in thought as he swung his chair around to face the view over the city and river.

'Unlike politicians, some people cannot be bought," Harrison murmured as he picked up the file and made to leave.

Gibbs slowly snapped out of his reverie as his subconscious reconstructed the comment. Furious, he swung around in his chair only to see the door being closed behind his assistant. He made to shout and then restrained himself. Harrison was a public servant on contract and it was not in his power to terminate him arbitrarily. There would be an appeal which could drag on for months before Harrison was finally re-instated without loss of pay or benefits – it was a no-win situation. If he won and Harrison was sent packing for gross impertinence, then he would feel the full stonewalling wrath of the Public Service Union. He would get no co-operation and achieve very little in his limited time in office. If he lost, he would most certainly feel the silent rejection. It would be no use pushing Harrison aside into another department as his replacement would be under firm direction from the union as to how he or she should co-operate and comply with the Minister's bidding. Gibbs knew he was treading on eggs when dealing with public service personnel. He may be the person in charge with the big office, retirement benefits and position, but he realised the limitations of his power. Many a Minister had been binned in a re-shuffle of cabinet by Angus McDonald, the Premier of the State - the result of an embarrassing leak of a confidential memo or document appearing in the media, or the salacious rumour of a Minister's private life beginning to circulate. Gibbs was well aware of his vulnerability to the latter. McDonald had already warned him about his rumoured dalliances. So, he wasn't doing it in office hours any longer, but he was now sure from whom and how the snippets of gossip were finally channelled into McDonald's ear. He shuddered at the thought if another divergence were to come to light. He would have to be careful, bloody careful in future. To hell with Harrison, he would just have to tolerate the dangerous pillow-biter's sniping. However, if he ever got the chance to get him in his sights with a clean shot, he wouldn't hesitate to figuratively pull the trigger. Gibbs could feel his anger subsiding as he reached into a drawer and took a swig of brandy from small leather-bound flask.

'Oh, fuck him and fuck them all,' he muttered to himself as he felt the liquor take effect. He knew he had only scraped into parliament by the slimmest of margins and he would have to work hard to impress if he was to be re-elected in three years time. He was confident he would make it. He had been successful in business before selling out at a handsome profit. He intended to repeat the exercise in politics. His appointment as Minister of Mines was exactly the position he had aimed for. It pays not to step on anyone's toes, and he had always made sure of that. Go with the flow and pick up any flotsam and jetsam that drifts your way was his motto. He'd been handed the keys to a fortune if only he could find a way of availing himself at every opportunity. He took out his mobile and pushed in a speed-dial number.

'Hi, what are you doing for lunch?'

'Have you got something of interest?'

'Working on it. I'll see you at the usual place in half an hour.' Gibbs pushed his chair back, got up and walked through to his private bathroom. He relieved himself and rinsed his hands before running them through his meticulously barbered hair. He studied his face from side to side in the mirror. It was losing its firmness as he stretched and patted the emerging loose folds on his neck. Nothing he could do about that although, it did not seem to repel the steady stream of women who submitted to his charm and wit. He adjusted his tie and tucked his shirt into his taught waist.

He had never let himself go like many others his age with their over-hanging bellies, the result of long lunches and no exercise. No wonder women lost interest in them. He patted some Kouros after-shave on his cheeks and neck, took a final look at his appearance and walked out.

'I'm out to lunch and out of contact unless it's the Premier,' he said as he walked past Harrison's office. He winked and smiled at Christine Morley. Tonight is your turn darling. Sure, the derriere was of over-generous proportions along with her shape from the waist up. Her breasts were fighting to stay contained within the loose blouses she wore to cover the embarrassment. It was the smile that portrayed her personality, but the real attraction was the magnetism of the hidden depravity in the depths of those soft brown eyes. No man had ever got close enough to read the signal, that was until Gibbs ran his hand over her rump when she was bending down beside him to put something on his desk some months before. It was an irresistible action. He realised in an instant he had overstepped the mark and quickly withdrew his hand. His career hung on a knife edge. A complaint of harassment would end his career within the hour. Angus McDonald would make sure of that. The sanctimonious god-botherer only believed in strict Calvinistic principles.

'Please forgive me Miss Morley,' he stammered. 'I, I really wasn't thinking.'

'That's not a good enough excuse Mr Gibbs. We both know exactly what you were thinking and the consequences if I make a complaint. Why don't you take me out to dinner so we can discuss what we both have in mind?'

Gibbs let out a sigh of relief. She had him trapped and in no position to object. It would have to be somewhere quiet, obscure and out of the way where no one would recognise him. The rumours would spread like a bush fire if one of his parliamentary colleagues should spot them dining together. He could hear the comments, '*Gibbs is off with his secretary.*'

'Where would you like to go?'

'Why not come around to my place. I'll cook something nice. Do you have a favourite?'

'No, not really, although I do like Italian.'

'Tomorrow night then. I'll see you at eight.' She scribbled her address on a post-it and stuck it on the back of his hand.

Christ, what was he thinking? He'd committed the cardinal sin of getting involved with his staff. She had blackmailed him without any trace of guilt or shame. How the hell was he going to break it off without committing himself to political oblivion?

He knocked quietly on her door. He was in full view of the other three doors of adjacent apartments. He felt exposed as he waited. '*C'mon, c'mon,* he muttered under his breath. He impatiently knocked again. It was a minute before her door opened. She was wearing a long black chiffon number with her hair loosened and flowing over her shoulders. The smile and eyes said it all. There was no hope of escape from the entrapment. Gone was the appearance of the demure office frump. Here was one statuesque, solidly built woman with clear evidence of desire.

The saltimbocca was excellent, matched by the fine bottle of Classico Chianti. The constraints of their inhibitions disappeared with the second bottle as he took off his tie, kicked off his shoes and lay back in the lounge suite with his arm around her. She suddenly got up and pushed a disc into the player. The strains of the Righteous Brothers *You've got that loving feeling* filled the room as she pulled him to his feet. The rest took its natural course, as the barriers disappeared and she danced him into her bedroom. The primal animal emerged and no carnal depravity was out of bounds. No plain vanilla for her; no missionary position and then rolling off satisfied and exhausted. She said she'd never had sex. Her mother had always told her to save it for the person she fell in love with and married. To hell with mother. She had been dead for a year. She was intent on making up for what she'd missed out on.

Gibbs was looking at the ceiling, cursing himself for getting into this situation. One peep from her and he would be out of a job, consigned to the backbench as a nobody. And once Audrey got wind of his indiscretion, he'd be out on the footpath. His wife knew he played away from home, but as long as nothing became public, she was content to live her own life away from his demands. He slowly turned towards the sleeping figure. She was really quite pretty despite the makeup having long disappeared. He slowly slid out of the bed, picked up his clothes and went through to the lounge where he dressed. He opened the front door as quietly as he could and let himself out. Christine Morley had heard the movement, but did not move as she heard him dress and leave. She smiled to herself as she turned over and went to sleep again.

4

'No Sal, not my usual table today. How about the private dining room in the back.'

Salvatore Fiorini suppressed an expression of surprise. Jack Gibbs liked to be seen and acknowledged with a table near the window now he was a powerful politician, but not today. It was not a *to be seen* day, but an unobtrusive meeting where serious business could be discussed without observation or being overheard. The restaurateur welcomed the continuing patronage and was quite happy to oblige Gibbs' request. It was none of his business what was discussed in private, but it was. Gibbs was a good customer and always ordered the best steak and fine wine. Sal did not query that sometimes he paid in cash and other times he used a credit card, depending on who he was dining with. Today it would be cash. No paper trail linking him to a particular day or meeting.

'Sal, I'm expecting someone to join me. Would you show him in when he arrives please?'

'Will do Mr Gibbs,' Sal replied as he closed the door behind him.

Gibbs gave a derisive chuckle. It was strange how people treated you when they observed your status. Normally, Sal would have greeted him as plain Jack as he had done over the years, brought on by the familiarity of long association, but now it was Mr Gibbs. Was it in deference, or was it a veiled insult? It had to be deference. Sal was not going to jeopardise his patronage with any smart remarks.

Gibbs felt good as he lay back in one of the large lounge chairs and looked around the room. He looked at his watch. His contact was running late. Just as he was about to ring for a drink the door opened and Sal ushered in his lunch appointment.

'Hi Tony, what would you like to drink?'

'A beer please Jack. Sorry I'm late, but I couldn't find a parking spot.'

'Make that two beers Sal.'

Tony Chan flopped down in a chair. 'Give me the good news.'

Gibbs held up his hand. 'Let's wait until we have a drink and order.'

They made small talk until a couple of minutes later a waiter arrived with the drinks and menus. He was about to leave when Gibbs glanced at the menu. 'Hang about a moment - I'll have a rare rib-eye with mushrooms and salad. Also a bottle of fine pinot noir.'

'Make that steaks by two.' Chan had not bothered to look at the menu. The waiter nodded, poured the wine and departed closing the door behind him. They raised their glasses to each other. Chan reached inside his jacket, took out an envelope and slid it across the table.

Gibbs opened it and flicked the bills before stuffing it into his jacket. 'I might have something for you Tony. I'm having it checked out at the moment.'

'What is it?'

'Iron-ore deposits stretching across two cattle stations in the Pilbara - hundreds of millions of tons of high-grade ore - probably closer to billions of tons.'

Chan nodded. 'Sounds interesting. It would have to be high-grade to get my contacts excited and as you well know they don't get excited easily. Prices are soft now the Chinese are becoming more conscious of pollution and shutting down older steel mills close to major cities. However, if the profit margin's there, I'm sure it would be of interest. How soon will you know?'

'Give it a couple of months.'

'Are the cattle properties up for sale the ore is on?'

'Not that I know of.'

'My contacts would be interested in buying a couple more large spreads in the Pilbara or Kimberley. They're very pleased with your assistance to date.'

'Tony, as you're well aware, there's a lot of opposition to foreigners and particularly the Chinese, buying cattle stations. It's a bit of political hot potato.'

'But iron-ore isn't a problem?'

'No, that's portable. It's just a matter of digging it up and shipping it out. It's the land beneath that creates the problem. In one instance you're just buying a commodity, but in the other you take physical ownership of the land. Foreigners can't buy land or property in China, so why would we allow the opposite to happen here? However, there could be a way around it, but I won't go into that now.'

'Who owns these properties?'

'A certain Chloe Boyce. I don't know much about her, but she appears to be one very smart lady, or has some savvy advisers.'

'And she's not developing any mines on the properties? How's she able to hold onto the exploration permits?'

'That's what I'm looking into. She may lose title if I can determine she's not carrying on any serious exploration or development. She can't just sit on them and do nothing.

That's not in the interests of the State. My job is to ensure mines are developed and revenue is received from royalties, taxes and employment.'

'You say if she doesn't commence work on developing the mining permits she can lose them? How long before that happens?'

'She's got two years left.'

Chan laughed. 'Two years Jack and you expect me to keep paying you? We could both be dead by then.'

'I plan to take them off her very soon. At the moment I can't do that because Angus McDonald would veto any such move. However, he's just getting over his second heart attack and doesn't look too healthy. If he dies or retires I'm in line to inherit his position as Premier. When that happens, I'll just confiscate her permits.'

'But surely she'd mount a legal action?'

'Undoubtedly, but all she could do is sue for compensation and she would win. The State would be forced to pay her a hundred million at the most, but you would have iron-ore worth tens of multiples of that figure. And I could justify the expense by pointing out the State would recover the awarded damages through royalties, employment and infrastructure quickly, rather than waiting on the never-never for Boyce to comply.'

'You seem sure of yourself Jack?'

Gibbs took a long draught of his beer. 'I am. McDonald is not going to last another six months. He'll either retire or his heart will give out. You just keep those payments coming Tony.'

'Does Boyce live on the properties in question?'

'From what I understand she lives on Ascot Downs in the Kimberley. It's a real showcase developed by an English company which she purchased some years ago.'

'The English could, and still can buy anything they want, but the Chinese can't? Is that the way I read it?'

'Precisely. Australia used to have a white Australia policy which was supposed to have been repudiated years ago. It stems from when the Chinese gold miners overran the early goldfields. They could find gold where no European could. The government was petrified the *yellow hordes,*' as they termed them, would take over the country. The politicians are in denial of that fear, but it's alive and well today in the minds of the voting public. And that's who the politicians fear most.'

'So you go along with that?'

Gibbs was caught off guard. He pulled a face and shrugged in resignation. 'I don't agree with it, but I have to go with the flow if I'm to hold my job. It's only natural I'll protect my source of income. Being a politician and a minister with such an important portfolio as mine, I'll do everything I can to protect it.'

'You and your countrymen put great emphasis on honesty and probity, don't you?'

'Of course, but let's face it Tony, we both know that's pure bullshit. When it comes to money and graft, everyone adopts their own set of morals and standards. Everyone is flexible, depending on the degree of temptation and the financial rewards corrupting them.'

Chan smiled. 'Yes, in China I suppose we could call it free enterprise. You know I could set up a bank account for your in Hong Kong using trusts and nominees. No one would ever be able to trace it back to you.'

Gibbs slowly shook his head. The thought of an offshore bank account where he could hide funds was enticing, but he did not trust Chan at this stage. 'I'll take it in cash for now. I can put it under my mattress.'

Chan gave him a querulous look. 'Mattress?'

Gibbs ignored the question. 'There's nothing like cash Tony. I don't have to account for it and I can spend it without questions being asked.'

'You're going to have a problem Jack. Over the past year I've already given you a hundred and fifty thou. We start doing serious business and you're going to have to bury it somewhere. You can't have that much cash just lying around someplace and certainly not in a local bank. I've read the Tax Department relies on tip-offs. You get investigated and charged and I'll go down with you as an accessory to bribery. I rather like it here. I don't want to have to catch the next plane back to China.'

Gibbs snorted dismissively. 'You don't have to worry about that. I can look after myself.'

Chan did not reply as he studied the man opposite – a vain, avaricious, self-important, unworldly individual who did not understand the rules of the game, his intelligence a thin veneer, his loyalties non-existent. Money and power were the only things motivating him. Gibbs would squeal like a pig about to be butchered if the heat was applied. He was making no attempt to cover his tracks or take precautions. Kickbacks and money-laundering were serious offences that would inevitably lead to public humiliation and a stretch in prison. Gibbs had only one loyalty and that was to himself. Chan would have to be careful. He was playing a highly dangerous game he would have to extricate himself from at some point. If the warning bells started to ring it would be Gibbs who would have to disappear. He was the weak link and it would be simple to have him vanish. In fact Chan was sure he would have to arrange it when the time arose. And exposure to Gibbs was one half the danger, the other was the syndicate financing his activities. He was assigned the task by his Hong Kong superiors, but he knew full well the real entity in control was across the border. He was paid well and could expect much more if he delivered, but fail and he would be abandoned immediately. He was expendable and he knew the rules. It had taken him some time to make contact with Gibbs, the softly, softly approach, while he worked out the man's weaknesses and strengths, contacts and haunts. Was he a politician devoted to serving his constituents with the honesty and integrity he'd projected on the hustings, or was he like every other politician seeking a position of power and self-aggrandisement? He realised now he should have been more reactive and established the game-plan earlier. Sex and money were the prime motivators of all crimes across the total spectrum of mankind. And Gibbs fell into that category on both points.

A restaurateur gave Chan the tip-off he'd been waiting for. The first time he mentioned the name and showed the photo, the owner smiled and nodded – that was all it took, a nod and a few quick words. Everyone goes for a Chinese meal now and again, some more than others. Gibbs was in the latter category. His favourite was a restaurant and bar in Fremantle, but it wasn't only the Peking Duck he savoured along with a good bottle of red. It was the club in the rear contained in the converted century-old stables, complete with high-stakes gambling and imported hostesses. The walls were sound-proof thick sandstone. An outer door was opened by a sumo-sized Chinese bouncer as he let someone in, closed it behind them and checked their credentials. He would pick up a phone and check inside before opening the inner door of the sound airlock.

Chan had sat in the corner watching his mark finishing his meal. He'd already been told Gibbs was not a gambler.

A couple of hands of blackjack or stud poker and he was out. He would sit in one of the large lounges, order a drink and adopt the affected attitude of a connoisseur as a hostess opened the cigar box in front of him. He would indicate his choice, never too large as he associated size with ostentation, an impression he did not want to transmit. The majority of Chinese in the room only smoked the biggest. After all the biggest had to be the most expensive? They were all high-rollers where observed status was paramount. The hostess would clip the ends and hold the gold lighter as the client sucked the cigar into life, before settling back to concentrate on the cards. The scotch was complimentary with hostesses hovering, watching for an empty glass.

'Good evening. Do you mind if I sit here?' Chan indicated the empty lounge chair alongside Gibbs.

'Not at all. Help yourself.'

Chan ordered a drink, but declined a cigar. He noticed Gibbs' eyes fixed on her firm rump clad in tight black trousers.

'A very pretty girl, don't you think?'

'Most appealing and very pretty,' he replied with a grin. He didn't have to hide his intent from the Chinaman - he was obviously here for the same reason.

'You like them younger?'

'I like my scotch aged and my woman young.'

Chan held out his hand and smiled. 'My name's Tony Chan. You're Jack Gibbs aren't you?'

Gibbs' face hardened a he glanced at Chan. He was suddenly alert and on his guard, but compelled to shake the out-thrust hand.

'Don't look so worried Jack, I recognised you from a TV interview you gave the other night. You're a very high profile politician from what I gather.' The compliment worked. No politician, not even from the most obscure minority fringe party, could resist a compliment. Whether it was genuine or a sycophantic quip was consigned to the all important *look at me* file. What the hell if they didn't vote for him? At least they knew who he was.

Gibbs' tension eased. This was no ordinary businessman looking for a bit of relaxation. His English was excellent. He was smartly, but casually dressed, nothing inscrutable about this oriental. His manner was open and smiling in contrast to his fixed-expression countrymen crowding the gambling tables, all intense and silent as they watched the cards fall.

'So you've recognised me, but what do you do Tony?'

'I'm an agent looking for investment opportunities.'

'Found any yet?'

'Not yet. I've been offered some rubbish I could never present to my principals.'

'What are you looking for in particular? Maybe I can assist.'

'Cattle stations, real estate suitable for large scale investment, hotels and mining projects such as iron-ore, gold, copper, lead and zinc. They're also very interested in lithium and cobalt – you name it and I'll look at it. The only criteria is that it's got to be big. Any contacts or assistance I can get, my principals will gladly pay a commission in any nominated jurisdiction.'

Gibbs gave no indication he'd received the message loud and clear. Chan was clearly saying any kickbacks would be in cash, or in an offshore bank account. Gibbs was not that naïve as to rise to the bait, not yet anyway. He took out a card and handed it to Chan. 'Give me a call on my direct number next week and I'll see what I can dig up for you in the meantime. But you must excuse me. I'm going upstairs for a massage.'

'Just a minute Jack. I'll see if I can't organise something special for you.' Chan signalled to the floor manager, who instantly walked over to him. The manager listened to the rapid-fire delivery, nodded and smiled thinly at Gibbs.

'All arranged Jack. It's on me and it's young and very exclusive. She's one of the elite reserved for the very high rollers and I mean high rollers. You'll feel more than relaxed when she's finished.'

'I can't accept that. I don't even know you. What are you after?'

'Jack, you know well enough this establishment is illegal. It's operating right under the cops noses and yet here you are completely immune to being busted. So why don't you loosen up and enjoy the evening.' Chan indicated the waiting manager. 'Fong is a busy man, so don't keep him waiting. I'll phone you next week.'

5

ndrew was sitting on the beach watching Charlie taking a surfing lesson along with a dozen other children of similar age. Charlie had listened and grasped the concept of balance quickly, although it would take practice to master. Within half an hour he was attempting the small waves rolling in from the Indian Ocean. Andrew's face broke out in delight as he watched him lose his balance time after time, only to quickly retrieve his board and paddle back out to the breaker line, eager to catch the next wave.

'Which one's yours?' She already had him marked as one of two people she was going to destroy.

Andrew didn't turn to the voice as he pointed. 'That one there, just starting to stand on his board.'

'He's a natural by the look of him. What's his name?'

'Charlie.' He turned to face the person in profile. She was looking out to sea and laughing.

'That's my son Anton beside him, but he hasn't got the hang of it yet.' She turned towards him and held out her hand. 'Hi, I'm Helen Gould.'

'Andrew Hanna.' He shook the extended hand. She was about his age and strikingly vivacious with flaxen hair tied back in a pony-tail. The dark sunglasses hid her eyes, but there was no hiding the form of her body moulded by the sheer swim suit. He watched as she stepped back and dropped the towel onto the sand and sat down beside him.

'I hope you don't mind me joining you?'

'No.....not at all,' Andrew stammered. 'The pleasure's all mine.'

There was nothing equivocal about her approach. It was just an open spontaneous reaction by a stranger with an obvious common interest in mind – watching two children learning to surf.

'You were here last week, weren't you?'

'Yes, and it looks as though I'll be here next week. There's no keeping him away now.'

'Anton's the same.'

The conversation lapsed as they watched the boys competing with the other nippers, each vying for positions on an inviting wave. Andrew was attempting to resist developing a friendship or showing any real interest. He had a partner and he was happy, but it was hard to rebuff the apparent innocuous friendship of the chance encounter. He preferred the isolation, pressures and comfort of Ascot Downs, far removed from the metropolitan bi-weekly boredom. The only highlight was picking Charlie up from boarding-school on a Friday afternoon and returning him exhausted on Sunday night. Their weekends were over in a moment with Charlie's football, cricket or surfing commitments according to the season. Andrew felt guilty he had not succumbed to Chloe's constant pleadings they should move to Perth permanently and put an experienced manager into Ascot Downs to oversee the vast cattle stations. He loved being with his son, but resisted moving to the city on a permanent basis. The isolation Dond timeless beauty of the Kimberley and Pilbara was where he wanted to be, although he knew it wasn't the real reason he preferred the vastness and social contacts of the region in contrast to the anti-social climate of the city where everybody made it their business to know everybody's personal and business affairs. Outback people were open, their conversation guileless, simply because they depended on one another and were well aware of the hardship and unrelenting toil involved in running their cattle stations. At first Andrew had resisted it, but as the years passed he fell into the rhythm of the common interrelated interests and subjects of conversation.

Charlie rode a wave right to where it touched the foaming beachfront and jumped off closely followed by Anton. They started talking, laughing and frolicking together as they walked up the beach towards them.

'Looks like Anton's found a friend.'

Andrew nodded. 'Looks that way.'

'I promised Anton a gelato. Would Charlie like one?'

'I think you know the answer to that.'

'That's settled then,' Helen laughed as she got up, threw her towel at Anton and took his surfboard. 'Why not join me for a coffee? I've banned him from eating in the car. It was gelato all over the seat last time.'

'You buy the ice-cream and I'll get the coffee. What's your preference?'

'Straight black.'

'Noir for two it is then.' As he waited for service he could see Helen taking a particular interest in Charlie. He got the impression there was an interrogation being carried out. He felt uneasy. Anton was sitting to one side looking out at the ocean not paying any attention other than to his gelato. The questioning stopped abruptly when Andrew returned within earshot. 'I don't know whether you take sugar?' He handed

Helen the paper cup and dropped sugar sachets and wooden stirrers on the table.

'Yes, thank you. I was just asking Charlie what school he goes to and whether he likes it. I think he and Anton have a lot in common in that regard. Unlike most kids their age, they both seem to think it's okay. Charlie said you live on a cattle station in the Kimberley and you and his mother take turns to be close to him.'

'That's correct. I don't have much time for the city life.'

'You don't look like a cattleman to me.' She smiled followed by a subdued laugh meant to draw him out. 'Are you married?' He could feel the start of the inquisition.

'A lot of people are not what or who they appear to be. But I can assure you, I am a cattleman and no, I'm not married.' Before she could load the next question Andrew finished his coffee and stood up. 'Hey Charlie, let's get going. It's been a pleasure talking to you Helen, but we've got a few things on this afternoon.'

She nodded and tried to hide her disappointment. She realised she was moving too fast. 'The pleasure was mine Andrew. And thanks for the coffee.'

'Likewise the gelato.'

The two boys gave each other a high five. 'See you next week Anton,' Charlie shouted back as he followed his father. Andrew could feel her eyes following him. What was it about her? He didn't need or seek a relationship outside the one he had, but there was something about her he found hard to resist.

'Yes Andrew Hanna, I will be seeing you next week and as often as I can after that,' she muttered to herself as she watched him open the hatch of the Mercedes SUV and toss in the surfboard and towel. She watched as he waited for

Charlie to buckle himself in before slowly driving out of the parking lot. *'Although you don't know it, I'm going to get real close to you. A lot closer than you can imagine and for a reason you'll not realise until it's too late. I'm going to destroy you.'*

'Are you talking to me mum?'

She looked down at the boy, realising he had overheard her. He was giving her a querulous look. 'No Anton, I was just talking to myself.'

'Don't you like him? I like Charlie. I think he's a lot of fun - I promised I'd see him here next Saturday.'

'Oh yes, we'll be here. I promise you that.'

'Anton's mum is okay, isn't she dad?'

'Is that because she bought you an ice-cream?'

Charlie screwed up his face and nodded in an expression of agreement. 'Yeah, but I could see you liked her.'

'What did she ask you while I was getting the coffees?'

'Just the usual all grownups ask, what school did I go to, what class was I in, what did I want to do when I left school. You know, all that sort of garbage. She also wanted to know where we lived in Perth and our phone number.'

'Did you give them to her?' He could feel the prickle of alarm in his subconscious.

'Yeah I did. Why, did I do something wrong?'

'No Charlie, no problem with that.' It was a lie. Why did a perfect stranger approach his son for his address and phone details? Why didn't she ask him? And she made no mention of it when they were talking over coffee. He was on the defensive. Who was Helen Gould?

'I've got another surf lesson next Saturday and that's it until Spring. I've been picked in the school football team, so Saturday's are out and there are no surfing lessons on a Sunday. I want to join the nipper lifesaving club when footy is finished.'

'Hey, that sounds great. The whole world will hear about Ironman Boyce in a few years. Or do you want to join so you can get to know all those girl nippers?'

'Girls suck. They're too bossy.'

Andrew laughed as he pulled into their driveway and the automatic gate started to slide open. 'I'll ask you that question again in a few years. You'll change your mind.'

6

He pulled up in the parking lot and sat there while Charlie retrieved his surfboard and ran off down the beach to join his group. He could see Anton waving and shouting at him. He glanced around, but there was no sign of Helen. Maybe she had just dropped him off. He would be perfectly safe with the instructors and lifeguards hovering around the group of young enthusiasts. Andrew got out and wandered across the car-park to the beach, spread out a towel and propped up with his back against the seawall. He had brought a book, but he wasn't really interested in reading. In between watching Charlie gaining confidence as he ventured further to get a larger breaking wave, he would close his eyes and drift off for a few minutes. Then he heard her voice and looked for her from under his beach hat and screen of his dark sunglasses. She was amongst a group of women further along the beach talking loudly and laughing. He wondered how long it would be before she broke away and approached, as he had no doubt she had seen him. She could not have failed to have seen Anton and Charlie together. He saw her glance in his direction a couple of times, but she remained where she was apparently totally engrossed with her group. He was broken out of his intrigue by Charlie and Anton standing in front of him. It was clear the surf lesson had finished.

'Dad, can you buy us a gelato?'

Andrew slowly sipped his coffee as the boys licked the overflowing cones. He positioned himself so he could look straight at her. Likewise, she was facing him, but the distance, the sunhat and sunglasses made it impossible to determine whether she was watching him. Finally, as though noticing him for the first time, she smiled and waved. The women she was with turned to see who she was acknowledging before returning to their gossip. Obviously she was treating him as a casual acquaintance and not someone she was really interested in. To his relief he started to form the same opinion, but there was still something about her that made him feel uneasy.

'Okay, that's me done.' Anton sucked the last of the gelato through a hole he'd nipped in the bottom of the cone. 'Thanks Mr Hanna. See you next week Charlie.' A high-five was exchanged as he turned to run off.

'Hey, hang about Anton. I want a coffee.' She was walking up the beach towards them. She sat down as Andrew got up and returned minutes later with two cups. He had been listening for any questioning, but it had been all laughter and joking between her and the boys.

'Thanks Andrew. You should be out there with the boys, or don't you surf?'

It was her infectious smile and challenge in her voice softening his doubts. 'No, I've never been on a surfboard and have no interest in taking up the challenge. Do you surf?'

'Sure, but not as much as I used to. The salt and sun plays hell with the skin and I just seem to be too busy.'

'What do you do that you're always busy?'

'I'm a busy mother would you believe?'

'A busy mother? I'd never have guessed it.'

'I would never have guessed you're a cattleman either. So there you are, you can't just stereotype people by their looks. Why didn't you come down and join us?'

Andrew laughed. 'No way. I wasn't going to get involved in a hen's session and the resulting interrogation.'

'Yes, they can be a bit boring, but I feel I have to join in as Anton has got friendly with other kids from these sessions, so I just can't completely withdraw. It's his birthday tomorrow and I'm throwing him a party. You can't get out of it as I'm sure he will have already invited Charlie.'

Andrew knew he could not avoid the commitment although he detested the thought of having to make small talk and fend off the never-ending questions from inquisitive wives and spouses, all probing for snippets of information as to his background and possible financial status. It was the standard seemingly harmless questions that would quickly establish whether he measured up to their standards, or was to be politely acknowledged, but avoided in future.

'I'm sure Charlie would enjoy that. We'll be there.'

The house was set back from the road down an avenue of trees in an expensive suburb. Helen Gould was well-heeled. He wondered what Mr Gould did for a living. Charlie as usual, had opened the door and gone as Andrew rolled to a stop behind a RangeRover. He scanned the line-up. Impressions were being made with the guests all driving their trophy car, the everyday hack left at home. He pushed the doorbell and walked through the open entrance. It opened into an expansive forecourt with rooms either side and a wide stairway leading upstairs. He walked towards the sound of loud talking and laughing and the overriding shouting of children. Helen appeared wiping her hands on a cloth.

'Oh, hi there Andrew. I saw Charlie flash past so I knew you couldn't be far behind. Come and meet a few people while I pour you a glass of champagne.' Helen shouted their names above the clamour of discussion and laughter while he acknowledged them with a smile and a nod as they returned to their familiar groups. She handed him a flute and touched hers against the rim. 'Here's to life.'

'And to Anton. May it be a long and happy one for him,' Andrew replied as he took a sip of the wine.

'That's a nice gesture. I can see you're a very sensitive person.' She let the statement hang for a second before breaking the thread to her subconscious. He felt a momentary reciprocal vibe. 'You'll have to excuse me Andrew. I must find out what those kids are up to in the pool and I've got to organise the caterers.'

Andrew nodded as he strolled out onto the terrace. It wasn't going be too much of an outdoor party. The clouds were rolling in off the Indian Ocean followed by a cold breeze which drove everyone inside, the children to a games room and the adults into a scattering of rooms and an enclosed verandah. Andrew wandered into a large lounge where a number of photos were arranged on the mantelpiece of an open fire-place. He was looking at one with no real focus on the subjects when he felt the presence beside him.

'That's Joe and I with Anton when he was about six months. You're wondering whether I've got a husband, aren't you?'

'It's none of my business, but it had crossed my mind.'

'Joe died about a week after that photo was taken. He was killed in a helicopter accident in the goldfields north of Kalgoorlie.'

'I'm sorry to hear that. Can I ask what he did?'

Helen gave a shallow laugh. 'Don't be sorry. You had nothing to do with it. Joe was a financier and broker and a very successful one. I don't know what he was actually looking for, but it must have been some type of mineral, copper, nickel or gold or the like.'

Andrew was not really listening as he studied the striking features of the young Helen Gould in the photo. He could see why Joe was attracted to her and she to him. His eyes started to run along the line of photos. He caught a glimpse of an older man holding a young girl of about ten on his knee. He was about to pick it up when Helen reached over and turned it face down before shoving it in a drawer.

'That's me and Dad. He used to call me pudding, so for that reason it's not for public viewing, especially with me showing off the new braces on my teeth.'

Andrew laughed along with her, but it was something about the father that caught his attention. A flashback or one of those observations where you see similarities in a person to someone you know? He wasn't sure, but there was something about the person he recognised.

'Is your father still alive?'

'No, he died some years ago, also as the result of an accident.' She could sense Andrew was about to ask another question. She took him by the arm to guide him out of the room. 'Come on, Anton's about to blow out the candles and cut the cake.' She closed the bi-fold doors and hurried off. He was sure she had seen his reaction to the photo. What was it about her father that triggered something in his memory? His recall was a blank. He had been warned he was likely to suffer cognitive impairment following the attempt on his life those years before, short periods when everything went blank, the result of a brain injury. He had consulted a neurologist recently who viewed scans and confirmed the blackouts were caused by a mini-stroke. He had asked for a prognosis and got it without equivocation – he was likely to suffer similar occurrences.

'You fly helicopters – you present a potential danger to anyone who travels with you. I should really report you to the relevant authorities and have your licence cancelled.'

'I only ever fly by myself doc, I never take passengers. Please don't report me as I need my flying licence to get around in the Pilbara and Kimberley. I would be like a blind man in a desert if you did that.'

The medico looked at him contemplating his ethical position. 'Okay, just this time, but I want you back every six months and be warned, if you don't comply I will be forced to act. This is very much against my better judgement – you should be nowhere near the controls of any aircraft.'

Andrew was stunned – he had not expected the rebuke in such abrupt terms. 'Thank you for your understanding doctor.'

'My understanding is you're going to kill yourself which I don't have a problem with as long as it doesn't involve anyone else.'

The guests started to disperse an hour or so later when Andrew summoned Charlie. 'We've got to leave lad. You're due back at school for roll call by five.'

Helen followed them out to the car. 'I'll see you next Saturday then?'

'No, I'm afraid not. Charlie's got football so it won't be until later in the year when he joins the lifesaving club he'll be next at the beach.'

Andrew waved as he turned the car around and drove out the long driveway. It was a beautiful house in a beautiful setting. Either Joe had struck it rich before he departed for the afterlife, or Helen had money, and plenty of it. There was nothing reticent about her, she was open and outgoing towards him, inviting his friendship, only he had the strong feeling it was more than a friendship she sought. The invitation and opportunity was there.

He was leaning back in the comfortable seat of the Falcon jet late the following morning when a facial form and features slowly coalesced in his brain. It was vague, but certain idiosyncrasies started to match and fall into place. It was Helen's eyes and gesticulating hand movements – they were common to the form he was recalling. And there was something about the tone of the laugh. He would have very little time in the next two weeks to give it much thought and in any event it could be of little consequence. It was probably just his memory playing tricks on him. He dozed off and put the image out of his mind.

7

They were sitting on the verandah in the small hours before the emerging heat of the day drove them indoors to the comfort of the air-conditioning. They heard the approaching vehicle and watched as it pulled up in front of the homestead. An unfamiliar figure got out. Andrew rose and opened the fly-screen door.

'Hello there. My name's Martin Cresswell.'

Andrew returned the open smile and shook the outstretched hand. 'Come in and sit down. I'm Andrew Hanna and this is Chloe Boyce.'

Chloe rose and shook Cresswell's hand, indicating a squatter's chair opposite Andrew and herself. 'You must have started early to get here at this hour? Have you had breakfast?'

'Yes, I had breakfast at the hotel. Please call me Martin. May I call you Chloe?'

Chloe smiled and nodded. 'What brings you out here?'

'I'm looking for cattle stations that maybe on the market, or could be if the price was right.'

'I don't know of any for sale. Do you know of any Andrew?'

Andrew gave a thin smile. 'Martin, what you really want to know is whether Chloe is interested in selling any of her properties, aren't you? I've no doubt you've already done your homework by contacting all the leading agents and found there's next to nothing available. Times are good, beef prices are up with strong demand for both the live cattle trade and export chilled product.'

Cresswell looked at Andrew and nodded. 'You are correct. I represent a group of investors interested in securing future food sources. Asia has a growing population and increasing demand for beef.'

'Well, the properties are not for sale Martin. This is our home and Chloe has no intention of leaving the Kimberley.'

'You also have properties in the Pilbara. Do they fall into the same category?'

'What are you really after – beef or iron-ore?'

'Both Andrew. I believe Ironstone Park and Baracool contain significant iron-ore resources we would be interested in.'

Andrew shook his head. 'They do, but once again the exploration and mining permits covering those deposits are not for sale.'

Just then the screen door from inside the homestead was slowly pushed open and a small head appeared, looking at the stranger, first with trepidation and then with confidence and assurance. 'Hello, my name's Charlie Boyce,' he said thrusting out his hand.

'Hi Charlie, I'm Martin.' He shook the firm hand. The boy started to bombard him with questions until Chloe cut in.

'Charlie, would you go and ask Violet or Rosebud to bring out some cold drinks please?'

Martin smiled as he watched the boy disappear inside. 'How old is he?'

'Just turned twelve, but going on twenty,' Chloe replied with a laugh. 'Never a dull moment with him around.'

'Only the one?'

'One's enough,' Andrew interjected as Chloe was about to say something. Cresswell noticed the momentary sharp look Chloe directed at Andrew.

'Would you consider selling any of your properties if the price was right?'

'And exactly what are you talking about? Is it the Baracool and Ironstone iron-ore, or the beef operations?' Andrew was asking the questions.

'Either, but the iron-ore deposits are of particular interest.'

'Well let's assume for the sake of an academic exercise, how you would value the ore and what would your associates be prepared to pay?'

'The norm is an upfront payment and then a trailing royalty on tonnage extracted. By the look of the potential size of the deposits, Charlie's grandchildren will be still receiving royalty payments.'

'And how much do you think the upfront payment would be?'

Cresswell laughed, diverting his attention to Chloe. 'I really don't know at this stage. If you were interested I would have a letter of intent exchanged and then I would arrange for an assessment of the commercial value of what was on offer. At this stage I'm really only trying to establish whether there is any interest on your part?'

Andrew nodded. 'None of the beef operations are for sale. We are buyers not sellers of cattle stations. As you are no doubt aware, we have an abattoir supplying beef to the Asian markets. We also have a live cattle export trade we cannot satisfy.'

'That leaves the iron-ore.' Cresswell noted Chloe had not said a word as she let Andrew do all the talking. He knew Chloe and Andrew were not married, but Charlie was theirs. Searches showed hers as the ultimate beneficial name on all the property titles. She owned everything including the abattoir along with an extensive portfolio of real estate, including a mansion in Perth. She was one extremely wealthy woman. He had checked her background and although it had been some years since she had walked the international fashion runways, she had lost none of her striking features. She was an instant magnet to any man, the flawless deep olive skin, the soft brown eyes and guileless smile dispelled any thoughts of a hidden adverse intent. Her features were a complete melange of local native, Timorese and European influence, where one veneer overlapped the other in perfect harmony, stripping away any imperfections. She was devoid of any of her father's features and heavy build. It was though his seed had been completely eradicated by a gentle, but dominating precursor of femininity and manner.

Hanna was a lawyer who had bought into a small legal practice in Wyndham. Not a lot was known about him and no one was inclined to make any enquiries. He was a lawyer who had assumed Chloe Boyce's legal affairs on the death of her father and saved her from the total loss of her ill-gotten inheritance. Hanna appeared to be the brains behind her wealth. But why wasn't he married to her? Why was everything in her name? Was she just a brainless trophy he was intent on exploiting? Despite what he had been told, Cresswell did not accept the proposition now he had met her. He sensed a sharp calculating mind behind that aura of demure deferment to Hanna.

'We haven't given the iron-ore much consideration The deposits are situated on ground which Chloe is reluctant to see disturbed. And I agree with her in that it encompasses surroundings which are timeless formations of natural beauty and significance.'

'Have you complied with your exploration commitments on the tenements? You are aware the titles can be forfeited if the government considers a potential valuable resource is not being developed?'

'We are, but we've carried out minimum exploration and filed the results to comply with the conditions of grant.'

The screen door was pushed open and held by Charlie as Violet appeared with an ice-filled pitcher. 'Lemon, lime and bitters,' she said as she sat the tray down and poured out three glasses and handed them around.

'Thank you Violet.' Chloe looked across at Cresswell. 'You will stay for lunch won't you Martin? You're most welcome.'

'I would enjoy that,' he replied as he held the glass up in salute and took a mouthful.

'C'mon Charlie, you can help me with lunch,' Violet said as she ushered him inside.

'Who exactly is the syndicate you're representing Martin?'

'A mixture of Hong Kong Chinese, Singaporeans, and Malaysians - basically all of Chinese origin, and all committed to large investments.'

Andrew nodded. 'Even if Chloe was interested, have they got the funds to put such a huge project into operation? You're talking about billions for a large scale mining project.'

'I believe they could handle that, but as you know, I would imagine there would be a consortium of banks involved with their exposure guaranteed by off-take agreements for the ore.'

'What are their other projects?'

'You name it and they're in it. Everything from hotels, apartment blocks to construction, engineering, gambling casinos in Macau and agriculture.' Cresswell looked at Chloe. 'Does a proposition interest you?'

'My initial reaction is I'm not interested. Ironstone Park and Baracool cover a magnificent area of unspoiled beauty and scenery in the Pilbara. Have you ever seen the two properties?'

Cresswell was about to deny it, but realised Chloe was reading his mind. 'Yes, to be honest I have. But surely it's no more than a no-man's land of wilderness no one pays any attention to or cares about? It's only suited for cattle and mining, surely?' He trailed off when he noticed the smile disappear. He made a vain attempt to recover the situation. 'I can see I've expressed myself poorly and I apologise.'

'Martin, I suggest you spend some time in the Pilbara and soak up some of it's beauty.'

'Do I take it you have an objection to mining?'

'No, not mining per se. It's vital for the economy of the country. Andrew and I are not religious conservationists – far from it. However, when it comes to the patch of ground covered by two pastoral properties and mineral permits, we are fiercely protective. You only have to look at the giant mining operations tearing the iron-ore out of the Pilbara - mining that has been going on for the past fifty years – giant pits and scars in the earth that will never be rehabilitated. They will be scars on the landscape for all time.'

'With that attitude, aren't you liable to have the government take them off you? All politicians are agnostic as regards conservation when it comes to royalties, taxes and the creation of employment.'

'We've not heard from the authorities. We maintain our commitment to keep the mining tenements in good standing and that would appear to be enough.'

'I wouldn't be too sure about that Chloe. Never stand between a politician and a revenue source.'

'Or a bunch of voracious mining entrepreneurs with no consideration for the environment, intent on adding another scar to the wilderness?'

'You can't stop progress Chloe."

'I accept that, but there are any number of major companies with iron-ore mining operations in the Pilbara – giant multi billion dollar projects. The Pilbara is the world's largest producer of iron-ore. The commodity is in over-supply and yet you maintain there's room for another mine. The way I see it, iron-ore is in a boom and bust situation at the moment and only the strongest lowest-cost producers will survive.'

'My syndicate is thinking long term. They know your two adjoining properties contain high-grade ore which is always in demand. They're prepared to wait as long as it takes to justify their investment.'

'Maybe so, but I would invite you to drive in or fly over them in a helicopter to take in their natural beauty. They are pristine, walked over by ancient man for tens of thousands of years and still held sacred by their descendants. The only trace of their existence is the countless cave paintings, hieroglyphs, petroglyphs, bora rings - the significance known only to them. The two properties consist of magnificent ironstone escarpments and gorges which take on every hue of the rainbow depending on what time of the day the sunlight hits them. Plants yet to be identified, with birds and animal life that deserve to be preserved; waterholes and ancient streams that will immediately disappear under the tread of earth moving machinery and yet your syndicate has only one motive in mind. And that is to desecrate formations that have been in place since time began.'

'But Chloe, from what I understand cattle can be very destructive to the environment.'

'They can be. Overgrazing has a very detrimental effect, but once the cattle are removed, the ground only takes a few years to recover. With mining, the destruction is irreversible. Nothing is left but a hole in the ground and the scars of exploitation. The point I'm making Martin, is there are enough mines operating to last the next hundred years. The world and most certainly the Pilbara does not need excess production. Would you like a tour of the two properties? I can fly you around in my helicopter, or Andrew will be happy to do so. You will see first hand what I seek to preserve.'

Cresswell smiled and raised his eyebrows. 'You fly helicopters. I'm impressed?'

'I take it you don't think I'm capable? Is it because I'm a woman, or is there a combination of concerns?'

He noted the brittle tone of her questions. 'I....I didn't mean it that way,' Cresswell stammered. 'I apologise, I'm sure you're very capable.'

'I'll accept that excuse Martin, but in my experience the slip-of-the-tongue remark is exactly what the author was thinking. Don't you agree?'

Cresswell tried to think of a rebuttal, but realised he had been caught out. It was exactly what he was thinking. This woman had a very sharp mind behind that benign exterior. He would have to be careful. It was easier to agree, rather than attempt to further explain his remark and dig himself in deeper. 'I can't argue with that Chloe,' he replied with a weak smile. 'Once again I apologise.'

Chloe nodded, but said nothing. She was happy to let him stew in his discomfort.

He recovered quickly. 'Getting back to the Pilbara; it covers a huge area. The development of mines on either of your two properties would only represent disturbance to a fraction of your holdings.'

'You've flown over them then?'

Cresswell nodded. 'Yes I have.'

'And I take it, so have the members of your syndicate?'

'Yes, we were invited on a government sponsored aerial tour of mines in the Pilbara some months ago. The Mines Minister was on the flight and it was he who diverted the flight over Ironstone Park and Baracool.'

'Was that Jack Gibbs? What was his reason for doing so?'

'Yes, it was Gibbs. His explanation was he just wanted to show visiting foreign dignitaries and potential investors what iron-ore deposits looked like in their natural state.'

'And no doubt the buzz was they were looking at huge deposits of high-grade iron-ore just waiting to be exploited? You did see the beauty of the place didn't you, and the reason why I don't want to see it disturbed?'

'That was obvious, but there's only so long you can stand in the way of progress. Your title to the exploration and mining tenements is somewhat tenuous from what I understand. Isn't that so?'

'The permits have some years to run and I will certainly be looking to renew them. All conditions have been complied with and I don't see any impediment to renewal.'

'But renewal isn't automatic, is it? The government could decide to grant the tenements to another party.'

'Where is this leading?' Andrew had been silently observing the body language. Cresswell was attempting to make a subliminal point, by sowing the seeds of doubt. However, the attempt did not register any reaction from Chloe. She had been approached many times over the years and was well aware of offers, threats and insinuations in all their forms and guises. 'Did Gibbs suggest something along those lines?'

'No, no. He was just filling in a day by giving us a tour.'

Andrew could see he was lying, but decided not to pursue it. Cresswell was relaying an unmistakable message. Andrew knew Chloe was too astute not to have also heard it.

'Well, Chloe won't have to concern herself for awhile yet. And who knows what's going to happen after that? Conservation is a growing and very powerful lobby politicians are well aware of. There is also the question of the native aboriginal claims to ancestral land and their voice is becoming more strident and powerful. They simply cannot be overlooked or ignored. Ironstone and Baracool cover some of the most spectacular iron formations in the Pilbara and for that matter the whole world. I'm with Chloe – I don't want to see them ever disturbed.'

'But you've got to accept the fact they may be and it could be sooner than you think. Of course, I'm only making a hypothetical comment. I know nothing to the contrary.'

Andrew gave a derisive laugh. 'Why do I get the impression you know more than you're letting on?'

'I resent that insinuation Andrew. What I've said is the truth.'

'We'll just have to accept it then. Do you know Jack Gibbs socially?'

'I've met him a couple of times. Do you know him?'

'Only from his image on TV and what I've read about him. I've never actually shaken his hand. However, Chloe has had the pleasure of meeting him.'

'Oh, and when was that?' Gibbs had referred to Chloe as being the owner of Baracool and Ironstone, but did not mention they were acquainted.

'Is that relevant?'

'Andrew, you know what politicians are like. They'll tell you they're on first name terms with the barber's cat if it projects their image and influence. When did you meet him Chloe?'

'A number of years ago now. It doesn't matter when and where.'

'By the sound of that, it wasn't an occasion to remember?'

'You may assume that.' She could see he was about to pursue the subject when the screen door opened and Charlie announced lunch was ready. Chloe got up and patted her son's head as she walked in. Andrew ushered Martin in as they followed her through to a dining room.

Andrew was aware Cresswell was taking in the vast expanse and opulence of the surroundings. 'What a magnificent homestead. Did you build it?'

'No, it was constructed by the previous owner who used it as his getaway from the stress and pressure of London. Unfortunately for him, he didn't live long enough to truly enjoy it. I bought the station off his estate.' Chloe indicated a chair for him to sit down.

Cresswell whistled softly as he looked around. 'It must have cost him a fortune, but I suppose money was no object. Can I ask you what you paid for the privilege?'

'I don't think that's any of your business, other than to say I could afford it, so I bought it.'

Cresswell smiled, unfazed by the curt reply. He shrugged. 'Chloe, I apologise for any offence, but I've learnt that if you don't ask, you won't receive.'

'No offence taken Martin. Andrew and I are in business and this is a very competitive business, so we like to keep our commercial affairs to ourselves. I'm sure you do the same.'

Cresswell was about to reply when Violet and Alice entered with plates and a large bowl of salad. 'My, I was only expecting a corned-beef sandwich. What do we have here?'

'Thai beef salad with noodles, lettuce, red onions, tomatoes and my special olive oil dressing,' Alice beamed as she began to place some onto Cresswell's plate.

'We may live in the back of beyond Martin, but we're not ascetics. Can I get you a beer or a glass of wine?'

'A beer thank you Andrew.'

Over lunch Chloe could see he was uneasy as Andrew tried to ply him with what on the surface appeared to be innocuous questions about his Chinese connections and his knowledge of the mining industry. Finally, Cresswell pushed his chair back and dropped his napkin onto his plate. 'That was a fine lunch, but I really must be on my way.'

They followed him out to his vehicle. 'I take it I can tell the syndicate you are neither interested in selling your pastoral interests, nor your mineral rights. However, can I tell them you may reconsider at some point?'

'No Martin. I think you can see from my reaction Ironstone and Baracool are not for sale and I completely reject the idea of mining.'

'Okay Chloe, thank you for your time and you too Andrew.'

They stood there and watched him drive off. 'Do I smell trouble?'

Chloe pulled a face as she turned to walk back. 'I don't like the sound of it, but we're on safe ground for now.'

'I'm not as confident as you. I think Gibbs could be up to something, Cresswell was merely the forward scout and messenger.'

'Well, I've got complete confidence my lawyer will be able to handle any problems.' Chloe laughed as she slapped him on the shoulder. 'Maybe it's a good thing you didn't cancel your practice certificate.'

'I've got the feeling my experience won't be good enough if Gibbs gets serious. It will be a case of high-powered barristers with full wigs and gowns, with bloated egos and daily charge rates to match, if this gets out of hand. Gibbs wouldn't be worried as he can hire the very best counsel in the knowledge the government is footing the bill.'

'You worry too much Andrew. We have plenty of time.'

Andrew put his arm around her waist as they walked back inside the verandah and sat down. Charlie came out and sat beside Andrew. He tousled the boy's hair, before Charlie laughed, pushed Andrew in the chest and strode off outside towards a row of sheds. Minutes later they heard a motorbike and watched as the helmeted figure propped the machine into a wheel-stand with a burst of power before riding off in a cloud of dust.

Chloe looked horrified. 'I thought you'd forbade him doing that?'

'I did, but as you can see it hasn't worked. Anyway he's off back to school next week so you can stop worrying until the next holidays.'

Chloe nodded in resignation. Andrew was a good father but hopeless disciplinarian. She turned to him. 'I still can't understand why you don't want to move down to Perth? We could shift the whole administration down there and make it our home.'

'Chloe, I thought we'd settled this. The nerve centre of your whole operation is right here in the north. It's taken us years to attract the right staff and managers who understand the complexities of this business. You can't simply just up sticks and move administration two thousand kilometres to the south and control all this from there. That's just wishful thinking. You now have an interest in more cattle stations than you can count. You wouldn't have a clue to the nearest twenty thousand how many head of cattle you own and....' He gently grabbed her arm as she was about to snap an angry protest. 'Don't take me literally. I'm just making the point you cannot run this business from Perth. It's important we maintain the office and staff we have in Perth as that's the initial contact point for our foreign markets, but one of us has to be hands-on here at all times.'

'Why did you make the crack about one's enough to Cresswell? It hurt me.'

Andrew looked puzzled for a moment, and then broke into laughter. 'Oh you mean Charlie, I was just joking, you know that. I would love another couple of kids, but it ain't for the want of trying. You know I love you.'

'Then why don't we formalise it and get married? What are you worried about?'

Andrew took her hand. 'Hey, we agreed when Charlie arrived on the scene we would maintain the status quo and forget about marriage. What the hell does a piece of paper mean anyway? Look, you haven't mentioned this subject in ages, so why now?'

'Because you are entirely responsible for where I am today. Without you, Ike Shulman would have wiped me out. I want to share it with you.'

He leaned over and kissed her. 'You're forgetting in the eyes of the law I'm already a shareholder. We have a son together and everyone knows we're joined at the hip. We do everything together. Isn't that enough? Don't spoil the wonderful relationship we have. I knew from the first minute you walked into my office you were going to be the only person in my life. I fumbled and stumbled and thought I'd blown it and was going to be sacked as your lawyer.'

Chloe laughed. 'Yes, I did play it a bit off-hand, but didn't want to show any interest until I got to know you a bit better. And when you drove up uninvited that weekend, I thought, here's someone who doesn't take rejection easily.'

'I was desperate for work and desperate to see you and it worked, didn't it? You can imagine the dilemma when I found out your father was involved in a criminal syndicate and you appeared to be perpetrating the crime. My whole world started crumbling before me. By not reporting it, I was complicit in the theft.'

'Forget about the history lesson darling. You know, if I didn't know better I would think you're hiding something from me – something in your past?'

'My past is a clean slate. You know it all.'

Chloe threw her arms around his neck and pulled him towards her. 'Why don't we try for another Charlie tonight?'

'God no, not another Charlie, but I'll go along with a Charlene.'

'No, no, you got to name Charlie so it's my pick next time and a girl won't be saddled with Charlene. I would love another Charlie and I know you love him too.'

'Of course I do. I miss him those weeks we alternate.'

'Why do you call him Alex sometimes?'

'Do I?' Andrew tried to hide his surprise. 'I wasn't aware I did that. Maybe it's because my father's name was Alexander.'

'You don't do it often, but when you're both fooling around and engrossed in what you're doing, it just comes out. I find that strange. Charlie sounds nothing like Alex.'

'Yes, I agree. I have no other explanation.'

8

'Well, how did it go? Any success?'

Cresswell was sitting opposite Jack Gibbs in his ministerial office. 'I think you can forget that one Jack. She's got no intention of selling her cattle properties or iron-ore permits.'

'I can't believe she'd throw away millions of bucks in royalties every year. She's adamant she's opposed to mining. Is that what you're saying?'

'She made it very clear to me she's not interested. She thinks the Pilbara stations cover an area of unique natural beauty and wants it to stay that way.'

'What about her bloody cattle? Overgrazing causes just as much ecological damage as mining,' Gibbs exploded.

Cresswell tried to suppress a restrained laugh as he shook his head. 'She touched on that point. Mining leaves a scar for all time, whereas cattle can be moved off to let the landscape recover.'

'Mining is what the Pilbara is all about – royalties, employment and taxes. I can't let her stand in the way of that revenue stream while she runs a few head of cattle.'

'She's running in excess of forty thousand head on Ironstone and Baracool at the moment according to my enquiries. That's not an insignificant contribution to the economy of this state. She can sell all the beef she can produce, both slaughtered and live. That's one hell of an integrated operation she controls, combined with her holdings in the Kimberley which would account for another ninety thousand head. And her interests in other partnerships would account for another hundred thousand.'

'And she controls this by herself? She's got a bit of darkie in her hasn't she? In my experience they haven't got a clue how to run a business. How the hell has she accomplished it?'

'She may have a bit of colour in her, but she's one very smart lady. She's got it all, stunning looks and a brain to match. I take it you've never met her?'

'I've got a vague recollection I may have, but that was years ago.'

'She also has a very smart partner. An ex-lawyer by the name of Andrew Hanna. Apparently he started as her lawyer, but gave the law away when he joined her full time.'

'They're not married?'

'Apparently not, but that doesn't mean a thing today.'

'Yeah, I don't suppose I can draw any conclusions from that. Different in my day – they had to have the ring on the finger before you were even allowed to touch the forbidden garden. What I would give to turn back the clock thirty years.'

'How good's her mineral title to those properties?'

Gibbs pulled a face and shook his head. 'Under the system I inherited the titles run for another two years. If they don't carry out a registered exploration and development plan, I can forfeit them and put them up for tender. I changed the legislation last year enabling me to grant exploration permits at my discretion. This stops the chancers and carpetbaggers obtaining tenements and then flogging them to the highest bidder for a massive profit. The State missed out on its appropriate share of that profit. Under her old title grant she can just sit on those tenements for the next two years and not do a damn thing. I'll make sure she loses them, but I don't want to wait that long. I might not be sitting in this chair. There might be a change of government or McDonald might decide to move me into another portfolio. It's a dog-eat-dog political system in this State, there's no glue holding me to this chair. I've got to act while I have the position and power.'

'By the look of it you don't have a choice Jack. Those properties cover a massive high-grade iron deposits. I indicated to Boyce I represented a syndicate prepared to pay big money to acquire the mineral rights. Can I ask you if that's correct? I was only wasting my time if it's not.'

Gibbs was annoyed at the frustration and Cresswell's question. 'Of course it's bloody true. Why would I bother to commission you to go up there and sound her out if it wasn't?'

'Do you want me for anything else, or can I go and look after some of my other clients?'

'Yeah, but keep this one as your priority. I want you to get the background to Hanna. I want to know where he graduated in law, where he practised, whether he's been married, whether he's ever run a red light, you know what I want, the full rundown. I've already got someone on it, but you may find a hidden skeleton.'

'Apparently from my enquiries in Wyndham, he just blew into town and bought a desperate law practice previously owned by an alcoholic who had his hand in the clients cookie jars.'

'How did he strike you?'

'Very bright and switched on. He's certainly no country hayseed.'

'I'll bet there's more to Hanna than is apparent. Why would a bright lawyer go to a backwater like Wyndham to practice law – it doesn't add up. Boyce must have been his only client and he wiled his way into her pants. And I still don't understand, despite his input and advice, how she managed to obtain the business interests and vast land holdings she has.'

Cresswell smiled as he raised a finger to get Gibbs' attention. 'Oh, there is a little bit of scuttlebutt on that score. You may be aware that Boyce was one of the highest earning international models. She just went by the name of Chloe. Anyway, she tossed it in and returned to Venus Downs in the Kimberley owned by her natural father, Henry Boyce.'

Gibbs held up his hand. 'Yeah, I know all about that. I'm not interested in hearsay of how she acquired her wealth. I'm only interested in her Pilbara holdings. I find it strange they're not married. You'd have thought Hanna would have made a move to certify a more legitimate claim to his share?'

'You should see the Ascot homestead where they live. It's magnificent. It must have cost the English mob a fortune.'

'Any kids?'

'Son of about twelve or thirteen.'

'And they think they can sit on a vast pile of iron-ore without developing it? I'll have to work on that,' Gibbs replied as he spun around and gazed out the window lost in thought. *Why don't you have another health problem McDonald and retire. I can't move to confiscate Boyce's permits until you're out of the scene.* Gibbs snorted under his breath. *Maybe if I did it would precipitate another heart attack and I would then become Premier?*

'You've obviously got someone knocking at the door wanting to develop it. Can I ask who would that be?'

'No you can't,' Gibbs replied acidly as he spun around. 'I think that will be all for now Martin. Send me an invoice and I'll authorise the department to pay it. Justify it as an official study regarding a tour of the Pilbara. By the way, I don't want you putting anything on paper about meeting with Boyce or any scuttlebutt you may have heard. This is all to be kept completely confidential and off the record.'

Cresswell nodded as he got up to leave. 'Understood Jack. You know where I am if you need anything more.'

Gibbs did not look up as he waved his hand in acknowledgement. 'Hey, don't forget about Hanna. See if you can find anything.'

Cresswell smiled at Christine Morley and nodded to Michael Harrison as he walked through the outer offices. Did Gibbs really think he would not write a detailed report from the minute he first called him to his office, to the meeting with Boyce and Hanna and discussions with the various rumour-mongers he'd met, complete with his own observations and conclusions – the meetings with Gibbs would certainly get a mention. Trust no one, not even your closest colleagues as they will invariably turn on you to save their own hides. It was a lesson learned through personal experience – dated diary notes would always be believed over someone's verbal personal recollections. He couldn't envisage it happening with his current client, but if some enquiry was launched for whatever reason, he had no doubt Gibbs would attempt to label him the scapegoat and deny he'd ever commissioned him to follow up on Boyce and Hanna. What was Gibbs up to? If the Pilbara iron-ore tenements had two years to run, what was the premature interest now? Why had he instructed the charter flight to circle them a number of times during the recent aerial tour? It was supposed to be a tour of the established mines, not a tour of the wilderness. He shrugged it off as he entered the lift. Why should he be concerned about Gibbs' agenda? He got paid well for his time to be bothered showing any personal interest.

9

'Rangemoor and Lucy Plains are on the market. I think you should buy them. They're not big, but combined they'd add another twenty thousand head and more to the point they would close a gap in your holdings.'

Chloe looked across at Andrew where he was reclining in his usual lounge chair looking out over the Swan River. He was studying a copy of the Rural Gazette. She shook her head imperceptibly and smiled. Why did he always use the singular when they were clearly partners.

'That is a surprise. I don't know how many offers we've made to buy them from old Stan Rogers, but have always been knocked back. They'd certainly be a real coup if we could get hold of them.'

'Stan has been in hospital for the past month. He fell off a windmill he was servicing and broke his back. The prognosis from what I hear, is not good. He must be in his late eighties. Tough as an iron-bark, but it looks as though he's finally realised time is running out. No family to take over and the hired help just won't stick around on the wages he's prepared to pay.'

'That's sound thinking Andrew. Those two properties are run down through poor management, but they're situated in good country. Plenty of water and feed. You've already looked at them then?'

Andrew turned to her as he tossed the paper down. 'Yes, I took a tour over them last week. I reckon you'll get them at a good price.'

'What about the Chinese syndicate Cresswell referred to? Wouldn't they be interested?'

'They could be, but with the present government attitude towards the Chinese taking control of large landholdings, I'm sure we'd be successful.'

'I thought you said you were just going to take it easy while you were down here with Charlie. You were going to put your feet up and vege around for a couple of weeks you said?'

Andrew laughed. 'You know I can't do that Chloe. I like to be moving.You're off back to Ascot tomorrow, so I can amuse myself by organising the purchase and arranging the finance. I only see Charlie on the weekends when he's allowed out, so I've got the whole week to fill in.'

'I've been thinking about Charlie. I think we should take him out of boarding school. After all, one of us is here permanently now things have settled into a steady rhythm business-wise, so he could be home every night. What do you think?'

'Have you broached the subject with him? By the look on your face I can see you have.'

'I have. At first he was in agreement, but the last time I suggested it he was not so enamoured. He reckoned he would lose touch with his housemates. Apparently there's a rivalry divide between the day-boys and the boarders.'

'Well, that's the end of it then. If he doesn't want to change the present arrangement, I suggest you drop the subject.'

'Would you see if you can change his mind?'

'Chloe, Chloe, why do you want me to do that? The boy is happy, so why change it?'

'You don't want him around? Is that it?'

Andrew got up and walked around the back of her chair. He leaned down and threw his arms around her neck and kissed her gently on the cheek. 'You know that's not true. I love him just as much as you do, but I don't see the point in trying to disturb him. He's got a mind of his own. You've seen that haven't you?'

Chloe patted his hand. 'Yes, he certainly takes after you in that regard. Nothing changes his mind when he sets a course of action.'

'So, it's okay if I add to your beef cattle empire?'

'What ever you say is okay by me. I don't know what I'd do if anything happened to you.'

'Now look here Chloe Boyce. Don't get so maudlin. You're the most capable woman I've ever met. The operation runs like clockwork with you in charge.'

'That's only because you've set it all up for me. Besides, Ascot is an empty shell when I'm there by myself, although I do keep busy. I hate just sitting around the homestead and I do enjoy getting around in the chopper everyday. You know, rctaining Ray Massie and not firing him was an excellent call on your part. I've got no doubt he'll take the addition of Rangemoor and Lucy Plains in his stride.'

Andrew nodded in agreement. Massie had quickly risen to the position of general manager of the rapidly expanding cattle and property holdings. Andrew had realised when he first met the man he could not fire him for his part in the cattle duffing syndicate. To do so would have exposed Chloe to condemnation by public opinion, despite the fact she was totally innocent and in no way implicated in the crime. It would not have taken long for Massie to start the gossip mill turning by exposing the true connection between Venus and Ascot Downs. It would have been a natural act of revenge at being party to a crime he was economically forced to comply with. It would not have taken him long to realise he could make a few unguarded comments for the chain reaction of damage and innuendo to commence without it being sheeted home to him. Andrew had at first been intent on firing the man because he'd been knowingly complicit in the crime. He was on the point of doing so when he realised the error he was about to make. Massie fully expected to be fired with his wife already packing and making to leave the station when Andrew promoted him and gave him a pay rise. He had just ensured Massie's gratitude, loyalty and silence. Chloe had not realised at the time why Andrew had adopted the course he had and wondered why until he explained his motive the following day.

'So, you're off in the morning? I'll take you out to the airport.'

It was dull and overcast as he used his pass key to open the private entrance gate and drive around and away from the commercial terminal towards the general aviation ramp. The Falcon's engine fans were already turning over as he pulled alongside. Chloe leaned across and pecked him on the cheek.

'Behave yourself. I'll see you in two weeks, but I want to hear from you every night.'

He watched as she was greeted by the pilot who took her bag and quickly raised the door. She waved to him from the cockpit right hand seat and then bent down intent on reading through the checklist with the pilot. The Dassault Falcon was a relatively new acquisition and she had already gained her rating licence. She had determined the turbo Pilatus was just too slow for the distances being travelled and the time taken. She announced one day she had ordered the Falcon. Andrew was amazed how quickly she grasped and mastered any technical situation. First it was the Robinson R22 copters used for mustering cattle. She applied herself and within six months became licensed to undertake the dangerous occupation. Then it was the bigger brother R44 and finally the Eurocopter Squirrel with its range, endurance and ruggedness with which she could get around the vast cattle stations. He had implored her to give away mustering at tree-top level and below as she drove out cattle from where they were hiding. There was no need for her to do it, no financial necessity whatsoever, but she ignored his pleas. It was as though she was in her element facing the danger as she dipped, swerved, reversed and swung the light R22 on its axis in a moment as she herded the cattle before her. Engine failure at that level, or for that matter anything below five hundred feet was known as the - *dead man's zone* – a zone from which there was only a split second to react to retain the rotor blade inertia and prevent it plunging into the ground. At best, failure meant the acceptance of quadriplegia with a crushed spine and the worst, a few moments while the pilot experienced terminal fear as death approached. She ignored him. It was an adrenaline rush she could not resist. Andrew had also qualified, but had quickly abandoned the notoriously dangerous mustering in the light choppers. He did not have the touch, nor reflexes and preferred the Squirrel.

Within minutes the aircraft had turned and moved off down the taxiway. He watched it turn onto the main runway and quickly gather speed before lifting off.

10

He did not look up as he heard the voice of the criminal he had erased from his memory. It was a meeting he'd hoped would never happen, as the previous one flashed back. There was no mistaking *Ronnie the Rat*. He had the distinct feeling this was no chance encounter.

'Where have you been hiding counsellor?'

'I haven't practised law for more than ten years Mr Ratsakis. What about yourself?'

'Oh, I've got very respectable since I saw you last. Still in the old business, but no longer at the sharp end where someone can point the finger at me. I just stay in the background counting the money and paying off the right people.'

'A good move I would say, but one day it's going to catch up with you.' Andrew let the conversation hang. What was Ratsakis really after?

'I see you're married to that former model Chloe Boyce. She's one smashing looking bird. I would say you did alright for yourself.'

Andrew did not bother to correct the statement about being married.

'She's a very powerful person with all those cattle stations. She's a real cattle baron from what I've read.'

Andrew nodded. Was the thread of this chance encounter beginning to emerge? 'Mr Ratsakis what is the point of this meeting. It's not casual, so why don't you tell me where this is leading?'

Ratsakis slowly shook his head. 'Very astute Andrew. No, this is not a chance meeting. I've been following the growth of the Boyce operation for a number of years. Chloe Boyce may be one smart operator, but I have the feeling you're the real brains behind it. You saved her arse when she could have been up on cattle duffing charges when her father died. She's built a marginal cattle operation into a powerful empire since that time. She's got her fingers into everything and she couldn't have achieved that without some expert help. That manoeuvre you engineered in buying Ascot Downs and screwing Ike Shulman was a masterclass example for any business school to study. That's got you rattled hasn't it? You're wondering how much I actually know about you?'

Andrew could not hide his shock. He took Ratsakis to be an uneducated criminal, but it was now apparent that might not be the case. 'You're clutching at straws Mr Ratsakis....'

'Don't get formal with me Hanna. It's Ronnie, because despite what you may think we are going to become friends or at best, business associates.'

'I don't think so Ronnie.' Andrew tried to adopt a repulsive tone, but deep down he was wondering what was to come next. How much did this man know? 'We have absolutely nothing in common and I've no intention of getting involved by way of friendship or business.'

'But we are involved and you will assist me.' He shook his head as Andrew was about to protest. 'I wasn't aware of it at the time we first met you would eventually cost me a great deal of money. I can see the incredulous look on your face so let me explain.'

Andrew made to rise, but was blocked by someone standing behind his chair. 'I've heard enough Ronnie. I'm out of here.' The iron-hand on his shoulder thrust him back down.

'I could see your surprise when I mentioned Ike Shulman. Ike was the perfect fence to launder my excess income from sources you can now imagine. How do you think he was able to become so wealthy? A person of stature and influence who owned a string of cattle stations and controlled a busted-arse town in the Kimberley? He came up with the perfect crime of duffing cattle off Ascot and channelling them through Venus Downs. It was a multi-million dollar scam until you came along and fucked it up. I wasn't aware of your involvement and assumed it was an accident when Ike got blown away by the cop. It took me sometime before I established what happened. However, it was too late by then as Boyce, with your help, had taken control of everything Ike had worked for. I lost a great deal of money.'

'Well, I can hardly be held responsible for those losses. It's only now I've learnt you were involved.'

Ratsakis gave a hollow laugh. 'I've got to admire you Andrew. I thought Ike had the sharpest mind I'd ever come across, but you outwitted him. I could use a mind like yours.'

'I'm not for hire. I don't practice law and I'm content with what I do, so I can't be of any assistance.'

'Does Chloe Boyce know anything about your past?'

'Of course she does. There aren't any secrets that would impinge on the business.'

'That maybe so, but I'll bet you haven't told her everything? In fact, I believe I know of a nasty little secret you're hiding.'

Andrew had he feeling his world was about to drop out from under him. He realised it was a stab in the dark by Ratsakis, but the taunt hit home.

'I thought not. It probably wouldn't make any difference if she's really hooked on you, but I'm sure it would raise the seeds of doubt and distrust if she was made aware. And you've got a son together. Charlie Boyce isn't it? Why didn't you name him Charlie Hanna?'

'What the hell do you want Ratsakis?'

'First, I want us to be friends and then we're going to get involved in business. I insist you call me Ronnie from now on.'

'*Ronnie the Rat,*' Andrew hissed in barely controlled anger. 'I don't want anything to do with you.'

Ratsakis remained calm and unfazed by the outburst. 'The last person who used that tone had a serious accident. I suggest Andrew, you adopt a more respectful attitude. You know, when I finally found out how you had brought Ike's world crashing down around his ears costing me a fortune, I was going to have you disappear for good – taken for a one-way ride in the outback. I wanted revenge. Then I was going to subject Boyce to so much discomfort and pain, she would sell out to me. But, I changed my mind. I decided to check you out and see what made you tick. You've got a rather dubious past from what I can gather. You solved the problem I had with Connors, but apparently he got at you in regard to a murder you witnessed. The word was Connors had fallen out with another of his dealers, just as he'd done with me. No doubt some other gang was offering a bigger share of the pie, which was what happened to me. Only somehow you unknowingly got involved. Tell me how that happened.'

'It's too long ago to remember.'

'It's not too long for the guy you and Connors stitched up. I'm sure Carl "Maggot" Evans would like to track you down to settle a score. Theo behind you there could snap your neck right now with a simple twist and I know Maggot would gladly reward him for doing it.' Ronnie laughed at Andrew's shocked expression.

'So you're in Perth now, thousands of kilometres away from where I last saw you in Sydney. Maggot and I were mates before he was sent down for murdering some creep who failed to pay for a consignment of goods. However, he's due out in six months. The sentence for murder is life, but with good behaviour you're out in ten. Anyway he's going to kill you when he finds you and find you he will. You were the chief witness for the prosecution. You identified him as one of the two people you saw go into Angelo Basili's apartment the night he died. You had been warned not to testify, but you ignored the warning. You had a price on your head, a failed marriage and no money when you shot through. And the only way you could have got out of town was if you had a deal going with Connors. And look at you now. Here with not a care in the world.'

'I don't know what you're talking about.'

'Crap you don't. We both know it's the truth. One of our finest of the force got a little over-juiced in a pub and someone overheard him boasting how a detective Connors, with your help, had nailed Maggot for the murder of Basili. The boast was Connors couldn't believe his luck when you happened on the scene. He was going to charge Evans because he had set up the murder and was watching from down the street. Evans would go down for life, but he would quickly work out who'd organised the hit. The result would be that Connors would be forever watching his back, although he was prepared to take that risk as there was too much money involved. And there was always the possibility Evans might not survive to be released. The fact he was locked up would not have stopped Evans from putting a price of his head. However, you did the right thing and identified Evans as the culprit. We both know you would never have come forward in normal circumstances. Which leads me to the obvious conclusion, Connors must have had some compelling influence over you for you to do what you did. And I know you were warned several times by Maggot's associates that if you testified your life was over. The end result was that you testified, Connors was in the clear and he put you into witness protection before you disappeared.'

Andrew was about to get up and walk away, but the large hand restrained him. 'Don't be in such a hurry Hanna. I won't be disclosing your whereabouts if you do as I ask. I'm sure Evans would be in my debt if I disclosed where you had buried yourself all these years.'

The accusation hit home. What Ratsakis was alleging was true. It was a nightmare that would not recede. He'd abandoned his principles. It all began at law school when he and another student became best friends, graduated and then drifted apart for a number of years. That was until he got a desperate phone call pleading for his help. They arranged to meet at the friend's apartment. Andrew instantly recognised a hopeless drug addict, an unrecognisable derelict living in filthy conditions in a very expensive apartment. He was about to turn and walk out when the Angelo grabbed his arm and started to spew out his problems.

'Please help me Andrew. I'm a dead man when Evans catches up with me.'

Andrew didn't need to hear the details, he knew it involved drugs and Angelo was both a dealer and user – a fatal mistake. He listened, but knew there was nothing he could do to help. He had no option but to walk out. The lift doors opened just as he arrived. He could not hide his shock as the two ugly looking characters slowly emerged. They said nothing as he nodded, stepped in and hit the down button firmly in the hope it would descend faster. It was obvious who they were intent on visiting. He felt sick. He hesitated on the ground floor when the doors opened. He should go back, but decided the situation was hopeless. He sat in his car observing the entrance to the block of units from down the street. Half an hour later the two thugs emerged and drove off.

He slowly pushed open the door. Angelo was sprawled on the floor, his face a pulverised mess. The place had been ransacked for hidden drugs and cash. He felt for a pulse in the neck. It was there, but faint. He picked up Angelo's phone and made two calls before wiping it clean and quickly leaving.

The ambulance arrived first, followed soon after by a police car and a dark blue Mercedes. He recognised the person who alighted and hurried after the paramedics. It was Angelo's father, a construction multi-millionaire, an indulgent generous man who had been witnessing the destruction of his only son. Andrew knew him well. He had been to his house countless times for social engagements, dinners and gatherings of an extended family, of which he was considered a member. Marco Basili had contacted Andrew many times over the past two years asking if he'd seen or heard from Angelo. Marco was in despair. Andrew never told him he had seen Angelo from a distance on several occasions, but refrained from making contact. He had been given word his friend was heavily into dealing drugs.

He kept watching until half an hour later the paramedics appeared with a gurney carrying an inert, covered figure. They were in no hurry as they loaded it into the back of the ambulance. One of the medics was about to close the door when Marco restrained him and climbed in. The ambulance pulled away without lights or bells ringing. It was in no hurry. This wasn't an emergency. It was a delivery to the city morgue.

Andrew had seen enough - his friend was dead. He started the car and was about to drive off when the offside door opened and a heavy figure lurched into the passenger seat.

'What the....'

'Turn off the ignition Hanna. I want to talk to you.'

'What do you want Connors?'

'Your co-operation. I've been sitting just up the road watching Basili's joint. You can imagine my shock when I saw you go into the building, followed by Maggot Evans and a mate minutes later. You came out in a hurry and just waited until Evans finally exited and took off in a hurry. The next thing I see you go back in and then leave with a very worried look on your face. And then an ambulance and the police arrive closely followed by some old guy in a Merc. What's your connection to Angelo Basili?'

'We graduated from law together. We were close friends until he got into drugs. Now, where's this going?'

'You know very well you've just witnessed a murder. I want you to report it.'

'Knock it off Connors, you're the detective. You know very well who killed Angelo and why. You go and arrest Evans and his mate.'

Connors turned and gave him an evil grin. 'It doesn't suit me to do that Hanna. Let's just say it's payback for that shit you caused me when I had Ratsakis within minutes of going behind bars. And now you're going to help me fit Evans with murder.'

Andrew screwed up his face trying to pick apart Connors line of thinking. It came in a flash. 'Oh Christ, you've fallen out with Evans. You can't arrest him as he'll tip a bucket on your involvement in his drug dealings, so you expect me to do my civic duty and report what I've just witnessed. My answer is, go to hell.'

'You're a smart lawyer Hanna, but dumb. One phone call and Maggot will suddenly have an address for the person who can pin him to the murder. I don't like your chances of surviving.' Connors took the Glock out of his shoulder holster and tapped it on Andrew's chest. 'You're going to contact Homicide and report what you witnessed. If you don't they'll get a anonymous tip off and then you'll be in all sorts of trouble. Perverting the course of justice, by not reporting what you witnessed will ensure a conviction and disbarment as a lawyer. If you attempt to implicate me, I can assure you this pistol will be used. On the other hand if you testify against Evans, I'll put you into witness protection. You can change your name and get lost in another State. I would suggest you move to a different climate – go practice law in England. Meanwhile Evans will be cooling his heels for at least ten years and may forget about you by the time he gets out. You've got to disappear in any event. I can't have you hanging around as Maggot is sure to contract one of his thugs to knock on your door if you stay here. What's it to be?

Andrew had the feeling either way he wasn't going to survive. He could feel death pressed into his ribs now. In the case of Evans he stood a chance.

11

'So what are you after?'

'I want to recover what I lost when you rubbed Ike out financially. My operations generate a lot of cash I can't possibly explain if the tax boys or cops get too inquisitive. I want to get back into the beef industry and I want you to manage it. You're going to set it all up for me just as Ike did. I provide the funds, you oversee it and employ suitable managers to run things.'

'You're nuts Ronnie. Why should I get involved in a money laundering operation that will surely be discovered in time?'

'Ike got away with it. There was never the slightest hint of an investigation.'

'That maybe the case, but the cops and taxation have developed some very sophisticated money tracking software in the past few years. Foreign tax havens are being tied into the data base because too much revenue is being lost to people like you. It's a worldwide problem no country can turn a blind eye to.'

'My contacts tell me you're looking at buying Rangemoor and Lucy Plains. I'm aware you've been trying to buy the stations for some time, but you refused to meet Stan Rogers' asking price. The old bastard realises how vital they are to combining them with adjoining Boyce properties both north and south. However, my enquiries tell me Stan's close to winding up in a wooden box, hence the sale. I think you should start with those two as the new point of re-entry for me into the industry. You've inspected them and are undoubtedly going to try and purchase them by way of tender. However, with your help, Boyce is not going to get them, I am.'

Andrew could not conceal his look of surprise. It was not possible Ratsakis knew about his interest in the two stations unless his phone was tapped and that was highly unlikely. It had to be the agent handling the sale. A healthy cash payment would overcome the agent's ethics and Ratsakis would know exactly who had the money, who had inspected the properties and who was at the top of the list of potential buyers.

Ratsakis laughed. 'I got lucky. I met someone who wants to settle a score. A person with a real grudge against you and Boyce that goes back a long way. I know you think it's the agent handling Rogers properties who told me of your interest, but it's not. But it is someone close to him. I'll give you that much. I'll leave it at that for the moment. However, as I've already said, it took me awhile to unravel just how Ike had stuffed things up. It was a brilliant manoeuvre on your part in acquiring Ascot Downs which caused the domino effect of Ike losing everything. But I couldn't figure out how you managed to trip the first tile that set the whole sequence in motion. At that point I wasn't thinking straight. I was furious with Ike and the cop who'd blown his head off. I knew they were in cahoots because Ike had told me, so it became obvious the cop wanted to shut Ike up and bury the crime and his involvement. That was until I saw a gossip column photo of Boyce and you talking to a banker by the name of Geddes at some charity event. At first it didn't register, but the more I thought about it, I realised there could be a connection. Sure enough, my informant remembered Ike mentioning the name Geddes.

It didn't take long to establish the Boyce empire was heavily involved with Geddes' bank. No wonder Boyce has become one of the largest landholders in the State. Unbeknown to her, the source of easy finance and the bank's strong patronage is not because of her charm and beauty, but due to your cunning and manipulation. You put any purchase, or business proposition up and Geddes signs off on it. Mind you, you haven't put a foot wrong to date, so the bank's happy to go along with it. And that's why you're going to assist me. And please don't deny you blackmailed Geddes, because it's obvious you snookered Ike by Geddes giving you prior information Ascot Downs was for sale. If Ike had known, we wouldn't be having this conversation today and I wouldn't have lost millions.'

'So if I don't go along with it, you'll attempt to dredge up some history which you won't be able to prove. I admit, it will be very damaging image-wise to Chloe and myself, but aren't you forgetting one thing?'

'And what's that?'

'What if I tell you to go to hell, I'm not interested in any dirt you may care to dish out.'

'Yes, that could be a flaw in my thinking. But your assumption is based on you still being alive. Have you ever thought you could be hit by a cattle train on an outback road? You could walk out onto the street today and be involved in a fatal hit and run, with you the fatality of course, or Maggot could find out where you're living.'

Andrew sat back in his chair trying to gather his wits. How long had Ratsakis being setting this confrontation up? It was pointless trying to resist at this stage, or contemplate a counter-attack. He really needed time to think it through. 'You really are an evil bastard Ratsakis. I thought you said you owed me a favour from years ago.'

'Yes, I admit I did say that and it still holds, but I've since discovered you cost me millions so this is a different matter. As for our first encounter, I gave you my word I owe you a big favour I won't renege on. On the second matter, give me my money back and we'll be on a level playing field. If you don't, I can assure you things are going to get very unpleasant.'

Andrew could see Ratsakis was not making an idle threat.

'It's business Hanna. All business people are evil to some degree. We all think of playing the advantage rule when we've got the opportunity and it suits us. And don't be a hypocrite, as you've played the game superbly until now. It's just that I want you to play the game for me now.'

'And where do I fit into your thinking?'

'You tell me your tender price for Rangemoor and Lucy Plains and I'll beat it. It's as simple as that. I think that's exceedingly generous in the circumstances. You don't have anything to counter my offer?'

'Excuse the pun, but I smell a rat. You then intend to offer the properties to Chloe Boyce for a couple of million more?'

Ratsakis laughed. 'You're starting to get the drift Hanna. I recover all the money I lost. Then again I mightn't. I just might get into the cattle business again.'

'What about Geddes? He's Chloe's principal banker. All legitimate and above board. Are you going to attempt to blackmail him to finance the purchase of the properties?'

'No, I could never trust the guy. From what I can see he's too close to you and Boyce. I've no doubt my business dealings would soon be quickly trickling down the phone line. I've already tapped another bank for a good portion of the funds and the remainder will come from Asian interests desperate to acquire cattle properties, but are all too aware of local resistance to foreign ownership. They will provide any shortfall in funding, while I assume control of an entity that rings all the right bells and escapes scrutiny. However, what I lack is someone with your apparent skills, someone who can identify the right assets to acquire and handle the negotiations.'

'Ronnie, I'm not your man and don't want to be involved. However, I will put a proposition to you. I will give you our tender price for the two properties so that you and your friends can beat it. You then lease the properties back to us and we'll manage them for you, or you can sell them to us if the price is right. You don't know the cattle business as I don't know yours, or the identity of your Asian bankers. We'll work the terms out later, but they will be to your advantage. Chloe Boyce will have first right of refusal if you or your backers ever decide to on-sell the properties. On the other hand if you just want to recover the money you lost through Ike, I'll give you an option to sell them back at a twenty percent premium to your purchase price. The offer will remain open for six months. That will recover the bulk of your losses. My suggestion is you arrange some short-term facility to finance the whole deal yourself, give the Asians the flick, and cash in. You wouldn't know the front from the back-end of a cow, so why get involved. I'm offering you one hell of a deal.'

Ratsakis stroked his chin while he contemplated the offer. 'Twenty percent of what? What are you going to bid for the properties?'

'Twenty million will buy them as they're being offered in a single lot. You walk away with four mill in your hand if you accept my offer. That should cover any losses you've suffered.' Andrew could read the greed in the man's expression. He knew what was coming next.

'So if my bid's successful, I can flick them onto you the next day. Correct?'

'No, you can't exercise the option within six months. And just so there are no misunderstandings, your offer must not exceed more than half a mill on top of our offer. The max you can earn is four million.'

'That's a hell of a lot of money to carry for six months.'

'I thought you said you were intent on buying the properties in partnership with the Asians, so you must have your finance lined up. Why not split the proceeds with them if you all agree to sell?'

'Yeah, I hear what you're saying about not knowing anything about the cattle industry. Neither do my Asian contacts.'

'You've done business with them before have you?'

Ratsakis laughed. 'We've been doing business together for years. They'd probably be quite happy with a quick turnover and profit. But then again I believe I can swing it without their assistance.'

It was as Andrew planned if he took the bait. Ratsakis could not help himself – *Ronnie the Rat* – was an apt description. The Asian associates were about to be cut out. It was obvious he was going to be pulling in all debts and scraping the bottom of the barrel to finance it on his own. Surely, he didn't have twenty million stashed under the floorboards?

'I don't think I can lose either way Hanna, so I'll accept your offer. Just remember though, if you set me up or screw me in anyway, you'll pay for it. And that threat will include Boyce and your son.'

Andrew leaned across and shook the man's hand. 'I hear what you're saying Ronnie. You've got yourself a deal.'

12

'You didn't tell me you knew Helen Gould?' Chloe shouted from the kitchen.

Andrew felt his blood run cold. 'Who?' He was relaxing on a sofa with a beer in his hand watching a football game on tele. He spilled the beer down his front as he swung his legs off the couch. He was fighting for his life as his mind spun out of control.

'Helen Gould. She said she met you at the beach with Charlie. Apparently Charlie and Anton her son are good buddies.'

'Oh her....Yes, I did meet her a couple of times some months back when Charlie was into surfing. She invited us to Anton's birthday party, but I haven't seen her since. Where did you meet her?'

'She introduced herself at a football match where Charlie and Anton were in opposing teams.'

'Who won?' Andrew was brushing himself off trying to regain his composure and prepare himself for a confrontation that would bring his world crashing down.

'Charlie's team of course. She's a lovely person don't you think? She invited me around to her home for dinner one night and we went out for lunch the following week. Did she tell you she's an accountant?'

'She said she was a busy mother. She never said anything about her work. Is she self-employed or does she work for some company?'

'She hasn't worked since her husband died and now Anton's older, she wants to get back to work on a part-time basis.'

'So, you offered her a job?'

'Yes I did. We need someone with her experience in the office here, don't you agree? She wants to work three days a week. Do you have any objections?'

Andrew laughed, but it was hollow without meaning or expression. It was the death rattle of guilt. 'It's your call, and yes, we could do with some additional help. It would appear you've acquired an accountant and a friend. I'm pleased for you. You should get to know a few more of those school mums. It will take your mind off cattle.'

'I'm off to Indonesia next week looking at feed-lots and arranging the sale of live cattle. Have you arranged the purchase of Rangemoor and Lucy Plains yet? We need those two if we are to fulfil our contracts.'

'I've talked to the banks, but I'm looking at cheaper sources of finance such as the greenback. Instead of nine percent from the local banks, I should be able to finance them at a lower rate from the Americans.'

'Well, get on with it,' Chloe snapped in a mock command.

Andrew was standing as she walked into the room and noticed his wet shirt front. 'Did I give you a shock or did someone just score?' she said glancing at the television.

'No, no, just me being clumsy as usual.' He turned his attention to the game again trying to hide his guilty look. He hated lying, but in this case it was imperative.

'Is there something about Helen Gould you're not telling me?' She said as she slumped down in a chair. 'You don't seem keen on giving her a job.'

'It's nothing to do with Helen as a friend, the only doubt I have is employing a friend. It's like employing relations, it invariably doesn't work out.' He was thinking hard trying to make his argument logical. 'You can't reprimand either without causing resentment. Although you may think all is forgotten over time, it's not. I would advise you not to do it.'

'Is that the only reason you don't want me to give her a job? I don't think she's the type of person to harbour a grudge. What do you think?'

He could not avoid the fixed expression of challenge. 'I don't know her well enough to form any opinion. I've only met her a couple of times with Charlie at the beach.'

Chloe nodded slowly. 'Andrew, why don't we move here permanently from Ascot Downs? What's the real reason you don't want to?'

'Darling, we've been through this before. Someone has to be hands-on up there. We simply cannot run it by remote control from down here, two thousand kilometres away from the heartbeat of the operation. Problems always start slowly and appear insignificant, but before you know it they're like a runaway grass fire.'

'I would find it impossible if anything happened to you Andrew. You're my rock. I want to be with you permanently, unlike the present hello-goodbye as we greet each other at the doorway.'

Andrew leaned down and kissed her cheek. 'Chloe, you mightn't be aware of it, but you are one tough and very competent lady. If anyone thinks you're a soft touch, they're in for a shock.'

'That's only because you've been at my side guiding me all the way. I couldn't survive without you.'

'When are you going to stop and smell the roses for awhile my dear? I've been thinking about Rangemoor and Lucy Plains. You're starting to lose count of the number of cattle properties you own, or have interests in. I know it's me who's been pushing the idea of acquiring them, but now believe you should consolidate what you have and stop expanding.'

'That's rich coming from you. It was your idea to acquire them. Why the sudden change of mind? But before you answer that just remember whatever belongs to me, also belongs to you. As for Ironstone and Baracool, I don't want to do anything about the iron-ore. It's a beautiful untouched wilderness and should remain that way. I don't want to see it scarred by mining.'

'You'll lose it then. The government won't let hundred of millions in royalties and taxes lay unrealised while you worry about some ancient cave art and exotic plant, animal and bird species being threatened. You've got plenty of time to run on the permit, but as you've seen, the sharks are already circling. You won't be able to resist the force of big money and government wanting to rip it out of your grasp.'

'I'll fight them all the way. You will help me, won't you?'

'Of course I will, but let's forget about business for now. There's an important game on I don't want to miss.'

She laughed and smacked him on the shoulder as she got up and walked out. 'I don't know why I put up with you. I want serious advice and all you want to do is watch a bloody game. Stay there, I'll get you another beer.'

Andrew was walking towards his office building when he felt the tap on his shoulder. 'Hi there stranger. You're in a hurry I see?'

He froze. What he dreaded had happened. Chloe had not taken his advice. He turned and glared at her. 'What the hell are you up to Helen?'

She adopted an air of offence. 'What you mean by that? What have I done that warrants your attitude?'

'You know very well what I'm referring to. You cannot possibly be seriously thinking of accepting the position?'

'But I already have and I'm on my way for the first day in the Boyce organisation as a part-time accountant.'

'We need to talk Helen,' he said as he steered her into a coffee bar and sat down. 'What would it take for you not to turn up and phone Chloe with your apologies?'

She gave a mocking laugh. 'Are you trying to bribe me Andrew? Because if you are you're wasting your time. I'm going to be looking at you every time you walk in.'

'But why? I don't understand what your game is. Okay, we had a brief fling which was a lot of fun and we really enjoyed each other's company, at least I thought we did. I could never understand why you suddenly broke it off without warning.' He looked into her cold pitiless smirk of success.

'For someone so bright you didn't notice it was indeed a game. You're just like any male; grab them by the brain in their pants and they're yours.'

Andrew sat back stunned. 'You set me up? I don't believe it. What did you hope to gain? Who the hell are you? Is it money you're after? You're a scheming bitch, that's for sure.'

She slowly shook her head. 'You're getting desperate Andrew. You screwed up and now you're frightened of paying the price. However, I can assure you I'm not going to break up the wonderful partnership you have with Chloe. I don't want to lose her as a friend. You just called me a bitch. Normally, that would bring instant retaliation from any female, but not from me. I would advise you to go have a look in a mirror before you start tossing around insults.'

'You haven't answered my question – what are you after?'

'Oh, I think I'll keep that to myself for now.' She glanced at her watch and stood. 'I don't want to be late on my first day, so I'll be off. A word of warning Andrew, you stay out of my way and you're safe. I take it you're not going to accompany me and introduce me to the staff?'

Andrew sat shocked as she walked out. He could not believe his stupidity in not recognising it was a carefully orchestrated game and he was the patsy. When would she blow the final whistle signifying she had won, because there was no doubt in his mind he was going to hear it. He had been suspicious of her intentions when she first approached him at the beach, but he had fallen into the trap after the second meeting when she phoned him to come around for dinner. Her approach had been smooth and seamless, a casual encounter he thought neither of them could resist. How wrong he was. As practised in the world of spies - *the complete honey trap seduction* - only this one didn't have to be caught on camera to finish him – the whisper of a rumour would accomplish that.

'Hello, I'm Helen Gould.'

'Welcome Helen, Chloe told me to expect you. Let me introduce you to some of the staff.' Maria Palacci was clearly the manager, a short middle-aged woman with an air of authority and organisation. The introductions to a dozen staff glued to computer screens were acknowledged with a nod and smile before the head turned back to the screen. 'They trade grain futures throughout Asian and Pacific markets as well as a number of other commodities we are involved with. We also trade currencies to hedge our exports.'

'That's not handled through Ascot Downs? I was under the impression Ascot is head office?'

'It was, but computer links are not always reliable and they have dropouts. It would be much better to move the whole operation down here.'

Helen was taking in the atmosphere of the intense activity. There was an overtone of conversations and the constant ringing of phones. She shrugged and turned to Maria with a look of surprise. 'I agree with you, so why hasn't it happened? Surely, Chloe must realise that?'

'She does, but Andrew is resisting it. He doesn't want to move away from Ascot Downs, so Chloe just goes along with it.'

'Don't you find that a strange setup?'

Maria ignored the question as she walked away. 'I'll introduce you to Max Schubert our accountant. You'll be part of his department, but there's no hierarchy in this office, so he's not your boss. I expect everyone to work as a team with no rivalries and no back-biting.'

Schubert was about her age, tall with short fair hair and glasses. She immediately determined he would not be the life of any party. The smile was brief and the handshake weak. He was not comfortable with women. It would take time, but she was in no hurry.

'I'll leave you two together then. Max, would you introduce Helen to the rest of your group please?'

Helen went through the ritual induction while trying to remember some of the names. 'You're the only accountant, I take it?' She pulled up a chair and sat down beside Max.

'Yes, we're totally computerised with the latest systems. The girls are very proficient and well trained. My job is not difficult, but I'm sure glad you've joined. You'll certainly relieve some of the work load.' He started to explain the systems and show her examples. Helen nodded and asked the occasional question to show she was following the procedure and regimen. In fact, she was well ahead of him and completely familiar with the system he was using. She quickly identified efficiencies and improvements that could be made and the glaring deficiencies, but determined she was not there to instruct and made no comment. She had her preconceived game-plan and had no intention of deviating. It was going to be easier than she first thought. The time factor was the only question. Schubert was engrossed as he eagerly ran through the structure of the various operating divisions, a look of pleasure on his face as he could see she understood and could follow his every comment and direction.

'I'm sure pleased you've joined us Helen. You'll certainly relieve some of the pressure, which can get stressful at times.'

She patted him on the knee. 'We'll get along just fine Max, I'm certain of that. It may take a little time before I become completely familiar, but I can follow everything so far.' He flinched as though to move his knee in surprise, but then relaxed as she smiled at him.

It took her a couple of weeks before she had become familiar and on first name terms with all the staff and felt comfortable in asking any supposedly innocuous questions as she probed for weaknesses. Too many questions too soon would raise eyebrows. It had to be taken slowly. She was continually surprised at the scale and escalating profitability of the conglomerate. She was slowly taken into Chloe's confidence and she made every effort to encourage that contact on a professional level. There was also the more social friendship of talking about Charlie and Anton's sporting activities and common women's interests.

Her plan was working. Rarely did Andrew come into the office when it was his bi-weekly turn in Perth. She chuckled at the memory of one encounter when she had exited the lift just as he was about to enter. He nodded, but his look was that of a frightened animal caught in the headlights. He was nervous and she knew it. He had no choice but to comply with what she had in store for him. She could imagine the torment he must be going through.

13

They were riding down in the elevator when she turned to him. 'Do you feel like a drink?'

The reaction was one of relief and delight. 'Helen, I've been trying to pluck up the courage to ask you the same question.'

She laughed. 'Well, that's settled then.' They found a quiet little bar and settled into a corner table. She waited for him to open the conversation as she twirled the ice cube in her scotch and he sipped on his beer.

'Are you going to sit there in silence? What are you scared of?'

Max looked up and grinned sheepishly. 'I suppose it's just that I'm very reserved and I know you're married because I've heard you talking with Chloe about your son. And you're also better qualified than me.'

Helen reached over and covered his hand. 'It's true I have a son and have been married, but my husband is dead. Now tell me about yourself. Do you have a girlfriend?'

'I was engaged, but it didn't work out. I live alone because I like to be by myself. I'm certainly not gay, if that's what you're thinking.'

'No, I didn't pick you as gay. But tell me, what are your interests?'

'Photography is my passion, landscape, portraiture, the human form, nature, in fact anything to do with photography.

I would love to travel. I've been to the usual places such as Bali and Phuket, but I would really love to spend time in Europe. I imagine myself living in a villa in Italy, but I can't see myself achieving that goal.'

'You're selling yourself short Max. If you want something, go for it.'

'What are your interests? Do you have a goal?'

'I most certainly do, but I won't tell you what it is right now. I'm still working on it, but I've got a feeling everything is going to fall into place.'

'So you won't to tell me what it is?'

Helen laughed. 'No, not at the moment, but if it looks like coming to fruition, you will know about it.' She looked at her watch. 'There's a nice little bistro around the corner. Do you feel like an early supper?'

Over a pizza and a bottle of wine they both became more relaxed in each other's company. Gone were the restraints of the office environment as Helen encouraged Schubert to talk about himself. She feigned strong interest in photography.

'I would like to see some of your work Max. I can see you have a real artistic streak from what you've told me. Why did you become an accountant?'

'My father insisted I get a real job, as he put it, when I graduated. He didn't really discourage my interest in photography, but he said there was no money or future in it. So I became the dutiful son who went to university and then took up the dead-boring job of counting beans.'

'You hate it that much?'

'Hate is not too strong a word. I absolutely detest it, but I have to live and pay the bills so this is where I'm stuck. It's too late to establish my name and make an income from photography. Don't tell me you love what you do?'

'My case is different to yours Max. I have a son whose needs and wants are never ending. He's high maintenance as they say. I don't really need to work, but I can't stand hanging around the house all day and I'm not into gardening or golf or playing ladies at morning teas. This job suits me fine. It was originally for three days a week, but I'm already up to five and enjoying it.'

'Yes, I was certainly relieved when you agreed to the extra days and I know Chloe was also. We would have had to take on another full-time accountant if you'd declined and that would have probably meant your termination. I told Chloe and Andrew you were just too valuable to lose and I meant it. I doubt whether we would have been able to find someone with your experience and knowledge and work ethic.'

'That's very sweet of you Max. Initially I was going to decline the offer, but then I got to thinking about it and realised I really enjoyed the people and the work. I really like working with you. I think we're a very good team.'

Schubert beamed at the compliment and the sincerity of her smile which did not betray her true feelings. She detested the work and was not attracted to the incompetent person opposite her. If she was in control in a normal situation she would have fired him. He was leaning on her experience and expertise to mask his shortcomings of indifference and incompetence she could not expose, not yet anyway. She was forced to carry him.

'I'm a pretty fair cook. Would you like to come for dinner some evening?'

'I'd like that Max, but on the condition you don't go to any trouble. Plain and simple is how I like it.'

'Plain and simple it is then with a nice bottle of wine.'

He was incredulous at how simple it had been. He'd expected some resistance or a complete rejection of his invitation. He wasn't that bad looking after all and surely must have some personality and charm no one else could see, but had now been identified. He felt the bloom of acceptance and self-confidence rising in his chest. And to think he'd been fighting the demons of rejection since the moment she walked into the premises. What shocked him most was that she'd made the first move. It had never happened to him before.

'I really must be going Max. However, before I do I want to make it clear our friendship must not be visible in the office. I don't know where this is going, but I'm very fond of you. The last thing I want is office gossip. If that happens I will definitely resign.'

Schubert beamed with a look of acceptance. 'I couldn't agree more Helen. I don't want any office chatter either. Can I get you a taxi?'

'No, my car is in the car park around the corner from the office.'

'I'll walk with you. My car is also there.'

She fixed him with a steely glare. 'That's exactly what I'm referring to. I don't want us to be seen together out of office hours. Give me five minutes start.'

He ordered another drink to contemplate his good fortune. She was one good looking woman any man would be proud to be seen with. He couldn't believe his luck at someone apparently so compatible walking into his life. And it was she who propositioned him. He just couldn't believe it. Max Schubert could feel himself being totally captivated.

Helen wandered along lost in thought. It had been easy, but would it be successful? What were his weak points and where was his Achilles heel? There had to be one and she was determined to find it. He wasn't particularly good looking, but neither was he someone you would avoid. He was the standard male who didn't stand out in a crowd, but was acceptable at any party or function. However, there was something about him that both attracted and subliminally rejected. He said he'd been engaged, but didn't have a current girlfriend and hadn't had one for some time, from what she could ascertain.

She found her car, remotely unlocked it, tossed her bag on the passenger seat and drove out. She grinned wryly to herself – it was going to be an interesting exercise.

It was the following week when he leaned over her as she was engrossed in a list she had brought up on her screen, a common occurrence that didn't attract attention, just two accountants scrutinising figures.

'How about dinner at my place Wednesday night at around eight? Here's my address.' He attached the yellow post-it note to her keyboard. She gave an imperceptible nod as she folded it and put it into her blouse pocket.

It was a neat little single-storey colonial worker's cottage in trendy Subiaco. The front door security light switched on as she pushed open the wrought-iron gate, lighting the small neat garden and potted jardiniere's on either side of the doorway. She noticed the tiny camera above as it went active with a momentary pin-point flash of blue light. Was he that insecure, or was it because he had valuables he wished to protect? She dismissed it. Everyone was security conscious these days. The door opened as she was about to reach for the antique knocker.

'Hi Helen. Come right on in. I've just cracked a nice bottle of cab-sav and I've got one of my special pasta's on the menu. You're really going to like it.'

She pecked him on the cheek as she stepped past and walked down the narrow hall into the lounge and through to the adjoining kitchen. He poured her a glass of red.

'Cheers.'

'I'll drink to that,' Helen replied as she took a sip and shrugged off her jacket 'You look very happy tonight. Not the usual Max I see in the office.'

'You told me to keep our association quiet and that's what I do. I can't be bothered with that gossipy lot.'

'And you hate your job?'

Max gave her a wry look and nodded. 'With a passion.'

'Yes, it's obvious to me, but then I work with you all day. The remainder of the staff just look on you as the stuffy accountant and that's how they also view me probably.'

'Oh, you're more outgoing Helen. You know more about every aspect of the business because you talk to everyone. In the past six months you've made significant changes to the way we operate. I could go on about the efficiencies you've instigated. I got a compliment from both Chloe and Andrew the other day. I told them it was entirely due to your efforts. Have they mentioned anything to you?'

Helen smiled as she sat down. 'They both brought it up, but I said it was through you raising doubts about certain things that triggered my suggested improvements. I wasn't going to take all the credit. I told them you were worth more money.'

'That's nice of you Helen, I could certainly do with it.'

'Still dreaming of travelling and living in a far away place are you?'

Max nodded. 'I can't wait for the day, but I certainly don't have the money to realise that dream.'

'Have you been anywhere overseas other than Bali and Phuket? There are beautiful women there, were you attracted?'

'Certainly, but there are other beautiful things that attract me about those Asian countries.'

'Such as?'

'The scenery, the people, the whole spectrum of life and their simplicity of approach. You can buy anything.' He trailed off as though lost in a guilt thought.

The microwave timer sounded. He turned to retrieve a container of pasta, drained off the water and tossed it into a large bowl along with a basil dressing. A minute in the microwave to heat the cooked prawns and he stirred the whole mixture together before ladling it out into two large bowls.

'Simple and easy.' He leaned across and cut up a baguette and placed two pieces on her place mat. He pushed across the butter dish. 'Now let's forget about talking shop and tell me about yourself?'

'What would you like to know, other than I'm a widow and have a small son? I'm comfortable financially, have a nice house and car and enjoy working for Chloe Boyce? What more is there to tell you?'

'I don't know Helen. I just can't put my finger on it, but I feel you have more than a passing interest in the company. You ask a lot of questions. I would even go far as to say if Chloe or Andrew died tomorrow you could step in and run the whole organisation.'

Helen laughed to hide her discomfort at the comments. She would have to be careful, but where was his weak point? He had to have one.

'You're way off the mark on that one Max. I would not want to step into anyone's shoes or manage anything. I just like what I'm doing and I'm a naturally organised individual. Anyway, you said we wouldn't be talking shop. Tell me about yourself.'

'Lousy childhood, dominating father combined with an equally unappealing mother. Did okay at school, but not interested in sport, scraped through university to become an accountant and you know the rest. Nothing but laughs and excitement all the way through as you can tell, that was until you walked onto the scene. You really give me a buzz every time I see you.'

They both laughed together as they engaged in idle chatter while they finished dinner and the bottle of wine. Max got up, opened another and indicated the large sofa.

'Let's make ourselves more comfortable. The dishes can wait.'

'You don't have a housekeeper?'

'No, I can handle it easily. Besides housekeepers are never reliable. They're okay for a start, but then it reduces to a quick dust and vacuum and a request for more money after a month or two. They invariably can't help themselves and start going through your things. I learnt very quickly never to leave personal papers around or filing cabinets unlocked.'

If he was aiming for seduction, he did not handle the second bottle well as he became gregarious and started to slur his speech. Helen was able to resist his insistence on topping up her glass by placing her hand over the top and shaking her head.

'I think I've had too much to drink.'

'Here, don't waste the rest of this excellent bottle,' Helen said as she poured the remainder into his glass.

He took the glass and quickly downed the contents before laying back on the couch and closing his eyes. Within minutes he was asleep. She got up gently so as not to create a sudden movement that might alert and wake him. She went into the kitchen and retrieved her bag and coat and walked back into the lounge. He was exactly as she had left him, except for the fact he was in a gentle snoring mode. He was out to it. Some lover, she murmured to herself as she made to leave. She was almost at the front door when she changed her mind and quietly opened the door to the room which she could tell looked out onto the front verandah. It was as she suspected, the main bedroom. She looked around, but there was nothing out of the ordinary except for a queen size bed, a chest of drawers and large free-standing wardrobe. She moved over to the drawers and opened one. It was full of magazines which she thought at odds with what Max would read. She picked one up and began to flick through it. It was the shock of the contents as a loose photo dropped to the floor. Everyone had their innermost secrets, but this was a total revelation. She quickly picked it up, inserted it back into the magazine and shoved it back into the drawer. Her mind was racing as she quietly retraced her steps down the hallway. Max was still in the same position with his mouth wide-open in full-strength sleep.

What was behind the second door in the hallway? She opened it, entered and quickly closed it behind her. She turned on the light, which was unnecessary because of the glow from an array of computer screens. All looked benign enough with the changing patterns of screen savers and scenes. She sat down and brought the computer to life. Nothing of real interest in any of the files she quickly scanned, but she could see there were encrypted files, denying her entry. She was onto something. A thrill went through her as she finally cracked the first file after half an hour of trying. Max was no expert at encryption. It turned out to be a simple reversal of the letters and numerals of his Christian, surname and date of birth, all of which she knew.

'Bingo,' she muttered softly. Her assumptions were correct as she rummaged in a drawer for a USB stick, slid it into a port and quickly downloaded the contents of the file. She had everything she needed.

She shut down the computer and went to check on Max. He was still in the same position, oblivious to the world. She quietly let herself out of the house, got into her car and drove home. She could not believe how easy it had been. No need for seduction and some sweaty sessions in bed with a person who now repulsed her. She had all she needed to ensure he complied with her intentions. All it had taken was two bottles of red wine and a photo dropping out of a magazine. It had been all too easy. However, the time taken in unlocking his security code had been frustrating and dangerous. What if he'd awoken and staggered into the room? She was tempted at one stage to just shutdown the computer and go back and take the photo. It was evidence, but not very strong evidence and it was far too premature to contemplate such a move. And if Max had discovered the photo missing it would not have taken him long to deduce what had happened and who was responsible. From here on Max Schubert would be a straight work colleague until she decided to spring the trap. Boyce and Hanna were going to pay the price.

14

Geddes picked up the phone. It was his private line only accessible to his best accounts - accounts with assets, strong cash-flow and excellent financial positions.

'Geddes.'

'Arthur, it's Andrew Hanna.'

'Andrew, it's a pleasure to hear from you. How can I be of assistance?'

'It's to do with our bid for Rangemoor and Lucy Plains. I think we should discuss it over a coffee.'

'But that's all taken care of. The bank has lowered the interest rate substantially to accommodate the deal. We want your business. Is there a problem, because I'm sure we can fix it?'

'Are you free for a coffee at our usual place?'

Geddes caught the note of urgency. Andrew wanted to discuss something, but not on the bank's premises and not where it was mandatory to record a diary note of every client meeting.

'Of course.' Geddes glanced at his watch. 'I'll meet you there in an hour.' Normally, he would never countenance such a peremptory summons. He was the most senior executive of the bank and soon to become chairman. It was accepted all chief executives could assume the top job was theirs on retirement of the incumbent. Life couldn't be better. Hanna had kept his word all those years ago. He could have wiped him out and put him in jail, but he kept his promise never to disclose his involvement in a major crime. It had started when he was a small town bank manager with a meagre income and few prospects for advancement. He needed money, the same as everybody and it looked a simple one-off arrangement he could easily terminate at will without any repercussions. All he had to do was grant an overdraft to a near-bankrupt cattle station owner so he could run-off a few head of clean-skin cattle from an adjoining property, brand them and market them as his. Very simple and he'd been assured it was only for a six month period until the overdraft was covered. It was good business for the bank. The instruction from head office had been to clean up the errant accounts, by calling in the overdrafts and selling up the clients who couldn't comply. There had been three years of drought and the bank wanted its money and ignored the social or mental ramifications of its actions. The faceless bank hiding behind its head-office brass plaque was deaf to the desperate people it had lent money to. By doing what he did, he'd removed the need to call the mortgage and arrange for the auction of the property. Little did he realise he was trapped by the astute manipulation of a financier with huge property interests and influence in the region and the cattle-man he'd helped. He could not extricate himself from the criminal activity which continued despite his pleas to be released from his obligation to participate. He also could not resist the cash-flow of his silent ten percent interest in the crime. It grew to a sizeable constant income in return for no effort on his part. He lived in fear his involvement would be uncovered with the consequent horrendous result.

And it was discovered by Andrew Hanna. He can vividly remember when Hanna approached him in his driveway, the game was up although he endeavoured to bluff it out and deny his involvement. His world came crashing down in an instant. He clutched the door of his car for support as he watched Hanna walk away down his driveway. The young lawyer was playing a dangerous game, but he held all the high cards. He knew Geddes had to fold. If he didn't it was he, the young lawyer, who would likely be charged with blackmail and extortion.

It turned out Hanna only wanted information, compliance and ongoing support for his client, the new owner of Venus Downs, the cattle station which had been central to the original crime. In return Geddes' involvement would be terminated and buried. His position with the bank and in society, would be safe. Hanna had kept his word. However, that dangerous relationship had turned into very lucrative and legitimate business for the bank Geddes was determined to maintain.

'Good afternoon Andrew,' he said as he sat down opposite. 'I think it's my turn to buy the coffees.' He turned to signal for a waitress. 'Now what's this meeting all about that I have to meet you here.'

'I like coming here Arthur. After all, this is where our business relationship started.'

Geddes gave a hollow laugh. 'I prefer to forget that particular day, but let's cut to the chase. What are you after?'

'It concerns Rangemoor and Lucy Plains.'

'I thought that was all done and dusted. The bank's not pulling out of the financing, if that's what you're concerned about? The bank's comfortable with the security it holds – you can bid higher if you like.'

'It's we who may have to pull out of the purchase Arthur.'

'I don't understand? For what reason? Don't tell me there's trouble on the horizon the bank should know about?'

Andrew ignored the question. 'Is Ron Ratsakis a client of the bank?'

Geddes thought for a moment before shaking his head. 'No, he's not someone I'm aware of, but there are thousands of clients and I only deal with those of major importance. He may be one of the smaller clients dealt with at a level further down the management chain. I can easily check though. What's this Ratsakis to you?'

'He's a criminal with an operation based on drugs and extortion. He formerly operated back east, but now it looks as though he's moved over here to the west.'

'So, where does he fit into the picture with you?'

'Obviously you were never aware he was laundering money through Ike Shulman and in effect was a silent partner in his operations?'

Geddes looked thunderstruck. He mumbled thanks to the waitress as she put the coffees on the table. 'Does he know of my involvement?'

Andrew nodded slowly. 'Yes, I believe he does. But he didn't get it from me.'

'I take it you're on first name terms with Ratsakis?'

'It goes back a number of years. I was a young lawyer desperate for an income, and I assisted him in avoiding a drugs charge. It would have put him away for at least five years. Let's just say I got the charges dropped.'

'Andrew, why do I suspect something sinister here? You're not trying to blackmail me again, are you?'

'Calm down Arthur. No, I'm not trying to blackmail you. We settled that years ago. I do have a bit of baggage in regard to Ratsakis and he's applying some pressure, which with your help I may be able to alleviate somewhat.'

Geddes picked up his cup, but put it down when he realised his hand was shaking. 'Wh… what type of help are you talking about. There's no way I'll take Ratsakis on as a client, if that's your intent?'

'Ronnie has told me he wants to buy Rangemoor and Lucy. He's aware they're vital to expanding our business, both local and live export.'

'So, what's the problem? If he outbids you there's not a lot you can do about it. You're not thinking of trying to outbid him I hope?'

'Nothing like that Arthur. He just wants us to disclose our bid price so that he can top it by half a million. He'll then give us an option to buy them back to cover some of the money he lost through Ike. He's got Asian backing, no doubt intent on money laundering to hide their illegal operations and I've no doubt it involves the proceeds of drugs and the like. Ratsakis has to come up with part of the purchase price which he will be sourcing through some local banks or financiers.'

'How the hell did you get involved with Ratsakis? It's obvious he has some hold over you which you want to keep quiet?'

'Arthur he has, but to settle any concerns you may have, it has nothing to do with money – it's from the past - a skeleton I want to keep in the closet.' He had no intention of telling Geddes he was hiding from a killer by the name of Maggot Evans.

'What is it you want me to do?'

'I want you to find out which bank or banks are financing Ratsakis and drop a word in their ear they're dealing with a major drug lord. A real criminal who's into money laundering and a host of other illegal practices. No bank or financial institution wants to be named in such an investigation, or face the likelihood of stiff penalties.'

'How do you know he's into money laundering?'

'How do you think Ike Shulman got his start? Did you ever attempt to enquire about his money trail when you were in league with him?'

Geddes shook his head in despair. 'No, I didn't. Oh Christ, I thought that nightmare was behind me. I was only a lowly branch manager at the time and any business was good business. I simply don't believe it. Did you know at the time?'

'Of course not. In fact it wasn't until recently when I had dealings with Ratsakis he boasted about it. However, it really wasn't a boast, but more an off-hand comment Shulman cost him a fortune when he walked in front of that cop's shotgun.'

Geddes gave a rye smile. 'You've gone the full circle haven't you?'

'What do you mean by that?'

'You've gone from blackmailer to now being blackmailed. How does it feel?'

Andrew smiled at the remark. 'I think you know the answer to that. However, in your case I did you a big favour. Where do you think you'd be if Ike was still alive? With the likes of Ratsakis standing behind him, you're future was on very thin ice. Truth be known, I believe you would have been taken for a one-way ride into the wilderness. You would have proved to be too much of a risk which Ike could not have allowed to continue once he got title to the Boyce properties.'

'Ratsakis is still a threat if what you say is true?'

'He could make noises and threats, but he doesn't have any real proof. He's a very astute and intelligent criminal. He's totally unscrupulous. In fact he knows from some source, and it wasn't Ike who told him, that you were somehow involved. And as you know Arthur, wherever there's music there's sure to be a band in the background.'

'It's not very ethical what you're asking me to do. I just can't cold-call my contacts or people and start spreading rumours. I've got my reputation to consider.'

'Arthur, you're on first name terms with your opposite numbers in the major banks in town. I'll guarantee one of them is participating in the financing of Ratsakis' purchase, or more likely acting as a conduit for Asian money.'

'Okay, I don't have too many concerns with that, but I can't guarantee anything. You do understand, don't you?'

'I know you'll try your best Arthur and that's all I can ask. If you fail, you fail and there will be no repercussions on my part. You're a vital and important part of Chloe's ongoing operations and I'd never jeopardise that.'

'So, if I'm successful you'll buy the two stations?'

'Yes.'

'You're a devious and cunning individual Andrew. You keep your agreement with Ratsakis to disclose your tender price which he then trumps. However, you're running the risk he does come up with his share, or the Asians bankroll him into it. What happens then?'

'You do your part in getting his local financing pulled and I believe the Asians will also pull the plug. They're only using Ratsakis as the front man to make it all look legitimate.'

'By getting the local bank to show Ratsakis the door, you can claim ignorance of any involvement and Ratsakis takes the heat off you. Is that it?'

'You're assumption is correct Arthur.' Andrew nodded with a broad smile. 'You can see why I couldn't discuss this with you at the bank.'

'And I haven't heard a thing in the past half hour. However, whatever it is Ratsakis has got on you, it must be more than a threat of embarrassment. From what I know and what you've just told me about him, you're playing with fire. I don't want to attend your funeral.'

'I can look after myself Arthur. You play your part, that's all I'm asking.' Andrew got up and walked off, leaving the banker staring after him. He was sure Geddes would use his influence to upset Ratsakis' plans.

'Hanna, it's Ronnie.'

Andrew had been dreading the inevitable phone call. The sharp tone and use of his surname signified the caller was far from happy.

'What can I do for you Ronnie?'

'I've had my financing pulled. It was all set up and then at the last minute the bank dropped out. Fucking bank wouldn't give a reason. It's cost me a hundred thou in valuation, investigating accountants, lawyers and bank fees, plus there are still more bills to come out of the woodwork.'

'Don't bleat to me Ronnie. I had nothing to do with it. I don't know who your bankers are, but you obviously aren't an important account.'

Ratsakis ignored the sarcasm. It must have been a shock when the bank gave him the bad news. Andrew would have loved to have been within earshot of the phone call.

'You didn't buy the properties did you Hanna?'

'Ronnie, did you lodge the tender?'

'Of course I bloody did. My part of the finance was arranged and now the bank refuses to meet me to even discuss it. When I phoned my Asian contact this morning, he told me the deal was off. His group wasn't interested and wouldn't lend me my share. I'm stuffed.'

'You realise the tender is binding and can't be withdrawn. The vendor will come after you personally. How much did you bid?'

'Half a million on each above yours as agreed.'

Andrew gave a low whistle. 'By the way you were indicating the other day, I got the impression you didn't need the bank's money, you could have swung the whole deal through your own financing sources. You didn't need the Asians either.'

'I was dreaming Hanna. I tried a few of my wealthy motorcycle contacts, but they weren't interested in financing cow shit. If it was something the public could shoot-up, swallow or smoke, they would have been in it. What the hell do I do now?' The despair in his voice was palpable. 'However, I suppose they'll accept your bid now and I'll be off the hook.'

'No chance of that Ronnie. They'll come after you, clean you out for what they can get and then re-list the properties again.'

'Jesus man, why did I ever think I could outwit you. Why do I get the feeling you've got something to do with this?'

'Ronnie, you witnessed me signing the tender bid and you even witnessed me posting it. As I've already told you, a bid cannot be withdrawn. It's total commitment. The only saving grace is that there's a bid that topped yours. You'll know in a day or so.'

'You saved my arse once Hanna...'

'For which you still owe me a favour,' Andrew broke in.

'Yeah, I haven't forgotten. But you've got to help me with this one.'

'Ronnie, I don't believe I can, but I'll try. What I can't understand is why you made a bid when you didn't have your financing set firm.'

'It was to keep you honest you bastard. I was going to exercise my option to sell to you and make a killing. I couldn't lose.'

'Well, my hands are clean Ronnie, but if the sharks do come after you for payment, let me know.' Andrew laughed out loud as he closed the call.

15

Chloe flew slowly along the deep gorge that separated two magnificent cliffs bleeding the vivid ochre of the weathering iron-ore formations. The serenity of her surroundings was over-ridden by the noise of the chopper's motor at her back and the gyrating blades overhead. She was heading for her favourite clearing to just sit for half an hour to take in the timeless scenery. The machine threw up clouds of red dust as she landed softly and shut down. She took off her flying helmet, retrieved a small back pack containing a water bottle and food from underneath the opposite seat and stepped out. She jammed a wide-brimmed hat on her exposed head and started to walk slowly up an incline to a lookout from which she could not see the limits of the vast expanse of Baracool. No intruder, other than the noble savage of her forebears, had ever set foot on the ground she was now walking over. Finally reaching the highest point, the magnificence of the vista spread in every direction. The petroglyphs beneath her feet were carved into the solid haematite by an ancient hand, their meaning or significance lost in time and only known to the artist who had laboured at his task millenniums ago. She stepped down and sat under the shade of an overhang with a clear view to the east and south. Tossing her hat to one side she took a swig of water and opened a sandwich pack. Andrew objected to her taking off by herself without company, but she had laughed it off.

'I like getting away by myself. I need some space of my own to sit under a rock and be alone away from the pressure of business.'

'Anything can go wrong out there. There's no need for you to take risks.'

'Andrew I've got my satellite phone and the chopper has an emergency beacon. I don't need anybody holding my hand. I know exactly what I'm doing.'

He knew it was no use arguing. She was right. She was perfectly capable of handling any situation. 'Why don't you at least take Charlie with you for company when he's here?'

Chloe laughed. 'He's precisely one of the reasons I like to get away by myself. When he's home, the moment he hears a chopper, he's out like a shot. He'll be flying solo as soon as his feet can touch the pedals. He can already handle the cyclic and collective when I let him, which is every time I take him up. He knows the check-list off by heart and can start the engine and do the run-up without my instruction. I like just once in a while to get away by myself and I've made that very clear to him. He doesn't like it, but he understands.'

'I don't like it either. I worry about you.'

'But you fly by yourself, so what's the difference?'

'It's just that.......'

'It's just that I'm a woman and you don't think I'm capable of being careful. I would remind you Andrew, I've got more flying hours than you. And who was it who set his Robinson down in a patch of dried grass, contrary to all warnings of the hazards of doing so and started a fire when the exhaust touched it. If I hadn't noticed, we'd have both been fried.'

Andrew had looked sheepish. 'Yes darling, that was almost a fatal mistake. If you hadn't pulled on the power and taken control, the consequences would have been as you say. I just wasn't thinking.'

Chloe chuckled to herself as she thought back to the incident and their more recent discussion. He hated to be reminded of it. She was looking out over the sparse tree-studded plains when she caught sight of a flash of light as it disappeared and then reappeared as it emerged into a clear patch of ground. She realised it was the reflection from the windshield of a vehicle. The location was too remote to have attracted a tourist. Maybe it was some government ranger making a casual inspection as often happened, or a group of university students studying geology or archaeology – the unique formations offering a magnificent canvas to study. But they always phoned or called in at the homestead to announce their intentions. Maybe someone at the home-stead had failed to pass on the message. However, that would have been out of the ordinary as everyone was concerned about everyone's welfare and presence on the property, if they did not report back in the time-frame indicated. A day late would be noted with concern, but when it rolled into the second day, a search was always mounted. She had the feeling she was looking at an intruder, but for what purpose? She kept watching as the vehicle disappeared into a patch of trees she knew surrounded a large spring-fed waterhole. She waited, straining her eyes for some movement for half an hour, but the vehicle did not reappear. It was time to check it out before heading home.

The rotor blades gathered speed and spun into the lift-off zone of the tacho. Chloe gently pushed forward on the cyclic, lifting the Robinson into the transition phase as it gathered speed and height. Within minutes she was circling the waterhole and what she saw surprised her. There was no sign of life, but she could see a vehicle almost obscured under the trees and the outline of some structure which appeared to be covered with camouflage netting. She found a suitable landing site about three hundred metres distant and set the chopper down and switched off. She waited for someone to appear above the bank of the waterhole depression and identify themselves. Minutes ticked by before she stepped out and began walking towards the trees and down the gentle slope towards the vehicle. She could see the camouflaged netting covered an expanding camper trailer and by the look of the utensils and gear lying around, it had been there for some time. She noted neatly laid out rows of rocks and a table with more samples and a large microscope. This was not a casual visitor. The whole setup had the look of some permanence about it. The tray of the Toyota was covered with calico bagged samples identified with black ink numbering.

'Can I help you?'

Chloe spun around in fright. She had not heard the approaching footsteps. The stranger was a wiry looking individual, bearded with a crooked assumed smile. The khaki shirt and shorts were well worn, the footwear simply old sneakers. The tattered baseball cap looked as though it was a permanent fixture covering his greying hair. Despite the shabby appearance Chloe could see the strong physique of the man's legs and arms which were deeply tanned from exposure to the sun. She could not see his eyes behind the dark sunglasses.

'What do you mean by sneaking up on me like that? Who the hell are you anyway and what are you doing out here?'

The crooked smile reappeared. 'I could ask you the same questions.'

Chloe could feel the fear arising, as she attempted to dominate the exchange. 'You are trespassing on Baracool station which I own. Who gave you permission to be here?'

'I didn't think I needed any. I'm just an amateur interested in the outdoors and nature.'

'Don't hand me that. You're a geologist aren't you?' Chloe demanded as she pointed to the bags of samples. 'By the look of it you've been very busy accumulating that lot. And by the look of your campsite you've been here for a number of weeks. What's your name and more to the point, who do you work for?'

The crooked smile remained fixed. 'The name's Hunter, Bill Hunter and I work for myself.'

'Well, I suggest Mr Hunter you pack up your goods, minus all the samples you've gathered and get off my property. I'll be out tomorrow to make sure you've gone.'

Chloe took a note pad out of her work-shirt pocket and moved around to the front of Hunter's vehicle and then around to the back. 'This vehicle has no licence plates. Why is that?'

'Rough roads and tracks. They must have fallen off.' It was a plausible explanation.

'In that case Mr Hunter would you show me your driver's licence? I want some form of identification so I can report your presence to the authorities. You know entry to private land is restricted to the permission of the owner and in the case of taking geological samples, it is an offence under the Mining Act without the permission of the owner of the minerals rights, which happens to be me.'

The smile disappeared as Hunter nodded. 'Lady I don't have identification with me, so you've lucked out there. But I will be packed up and off your property by first light in the morning.'

'Good, and make sure you leave those samples here. In the meantime, I'll just take a photo of you and the evidence of your trespass for my records.' She had hardly got the small camera out of her pocket before it was knocked out of her hand. She stepped back in shock as Hunter picked it up, quickly removed the chip and tossed the camera back at her feet.

'Get out of my hair lady, before you get into trouble. You're out here alone and you're one good looking woman. Your husband, if you have one, is a very lucky man.'

The message was clear as Chloe picked up the camera, swung around and attempted to stride away without showing any signs of panic. Inwardly, she was trembling with fear. She had put herself in a dangerous and vulnerable situation without thinking of the possible consequences. The chopper would have been eventually found, but there would be no trace of Chloe Boyce. She did not look back as she climbed the bank on legs of jelly and stumbled towards the chopper. She climbed in and broke down in tears at the thought of what might have happened. Memories came flooding back of an incident in London those years ago. It took her some minutes before she snapped out of it to regain control of her emotions and trembling of her hands as she fired the machine into life. How could she have been so stupid to confront a complete stranger, knowing full well he was trespassing? She should have just noted his position and returned tomorrow with Ray Massie, the manager of Baracool. As she gained height and swung around and over Hunter in a lazy arc she could see he was hastily throwing the sample bags into the tray of his ute. The camper trailer tent had already been collapsed back and the trailer hooked up to the tow-bar of the vehicle. Hunter was in a hurry to depart the scene. Whatever was in those sample bags was of vital importance to him. He had no intention of complying with Chloe's demand to leave them. She decided to fly to the south following the rough mustering track Hunter had used to gain entry. It was the only way in and stopped at the stockyards a further kilometre to the north of the waterhole. Ten minutes later she was over the point where the track joined with a minor road which ran both north and south. Hunter could go in either direction, but she guessed he would go south to be clear of the Baracool boundaries. She was planning to set down and wait, but a glance at her watch and fuel gauge jolted her into the realisation she would barely make it back to the homestead before last light. She had also become oblivious to the fuel-burn and limited range of the Robinson – pure pilot error and a common fatal mistake for the unwary. She swung around and headed back up the track. Minutes later she saw the advancing dust cloud thrown up by Hunter's rig. He was in a hurry. She lowered the chopper to pass just to one side and could clearly see his sneer and contemptuous hand gesture as he glanced up.

Half an hour later she put down at Baracool homestead in the afterglow of the disappearing day. Ray Massie was standing by the hangar with a concerned look on his face. She shut down and pretended not to notice as she waited for the rotor to stop turning before stepping out.

'Where have you been Chloe? You should have been back hours ago.'

'I'm sorry Ray. I should have been more aware of the time. I just found a beautiful spot and time ran away with me. Give me a hand to fuel up and put it away.'

Massie nodded as he put the trolley wheels under the skids and ran out the fuel hose. 'You look a bit rattled Chloe. Did something happen out there I should know about?'

'Yes, I did run into a situation I'll discuss when we get inside.'

Massie filled the main and auxiliary tanks before shaking his head. 'You're damned lucky you made it back. You were flying on fumes when you landed. You know better than that. In future don't be such a bloody fool.' It was a shout of frustration rather than a restrained employee to employer rebuke.

'There's no need to raise your voice with me Ray.'

'I'm not going to apologise. You were due back two hours ago. What the hell do you think was going through my mind?'

Chloe put her hand on his muscled forearm. 'Ray, I can understand your concern. I admit I stuffed up. Let's go in and I'll explain what happened.'

Tina Massie gave a worried smile as they entered the room. She'd heard her husband shout at their employer and understood why. She clearly heard what he'd said from a hundred metres away. For the past hour he had been outside pacing around listening and waiting for the sound of a returning chopper.

Chloe caught the concerned look. 'Don't worry Tina. It was my fault and Ray had every right to bawl me out.' She sat down at the kitchen table as Massie tossed his hat on a couch and sat opposite.

'Now tell me what happened?'

'Have you ever heard of someone by the name of Bill Hunter? Has he ever checked in here or phoned to ask permission to be on the station?'

Ray shook his head. 'Never heard of him. Why don't you start at the beginning. Would you like a drink because I'm going to have one?'

'Just a small straight brandy please.' Chloe sipped at her drink as she related the incident. 'What do you think he was doing there Ray? He was nowhere near the iron-ore bluffs, and the samples I saw looked to be of a different rock type.'

'Are you sure the vehicle had no registration plates?'

'I checked both front and back. There were no plates.'

'You really did put yourself in a dangerous situation. You know now you should have come back here and picked me up first.'

'I'm well aware now Ray, but at the time I thought he might have been an innocuous tourist, or some government ranger, or university type just out looking at something of scientific interest.'

'I can accept the tourist, but the other two you mentioned don't fit because they would have checked in prior. As for someone taking rock samples over land on which you hold the mineral rights, that's very suspect. And from what you describe, he wasn't a tourist interested in the scenery. He knew what he was looking for, but I don't know enough about rocks or geology to answer that one. We'll fly out tomorrow and see whether he's left any of the evidence.'

It was first light when Chloe with Massie sitting beside her, lifted off and headed for the water hole of the previous day's encounter. Chloe flew around the site a couple of times to ensure there was no sign of a vehicle before putting down close to Hunter's camp.

'He sure took off in a hurry by the look of the rubbish he's left behind,' Massie observed as he scanned the abandoned cooking utensils, part of a lean-to awning, a pile of empty food cans and empty beer bottles near a hole intended for their burial.

'I saw lines of small calico bags and rocks lying around. They're all gone now. What was he up to Ray?'

Massie didn't answer as he began to study various loose rock chips which he could see had recently been broken off some larger mass. He picked up a piece the size of his hand and handed it to Chloe.

'I'll bet that's the reason he was here.'

Chloe took it and rolled it around to get the sun to reveal its various surfaces. She recognised the green copper staining of malachite, the result of weathering of a copper ore-body.

'What's so interesting about that? I've seen dozens of those occurrences, but none have amounted to much as a mining prospect.'

'Don't be too sure about that Chloe. There could easily be a very large copper deposit somewhere on this property. It has never been explored properly because the companies are only looking at the big picture and that's iron-ore. That's where the big money is,' Ray replied as he swept his arm towards the giant iron formations in the distance. 'Look closer and you'll see another colour.'

'You mean that pink staining?'

Ray nodded. 'Unless I miss my guess, that's cobalt and I'm sure that's what your man Hunter was really looking for.'

'Cobalt? What's so important about that?'

'I'm not trying to be smart Chloe, but don't you read the papers?'

'I run cattle Ray. What the hell is cobalt and why is it so important?'

'It's worth thousands of dollars per ton. It's one of the most sought-after minerals today because of its application in electric car batteries along with lithium, the other vital element. The whole mineral world is looking for cobalt and lithium because we're all going to be driving electric vehicles in the next twenty years according to the experts.'

'And Hunter has found it on Baracool?'

Massie ignored her as he continued to walk slowly along a line depressed in the soft red earth. 'This is where he had his sample bags laid out and if you look closely you can see the pink dust mixed with the malachite everywhere.'

'I knew there was copper and gold on the property because of the numerous pits and workings the old-timers must have dug. But they never found anything large enough to turn into a mine.'

'Well, Hunter certainly found something and my guess he got very excited by it and wasn't going to share the knowledge with you. He certainly wasn't going to stick around to be subjected to interrogation. You may have looked dumb, but he wasn't going to take the risk of you realising what he was particularly interested in.'

'So, whatever he found must be somewhere in this vicinity. I can get one of the local homestead boys to easily follow his wheel tracks.'

Massie nodded lost in thought. 'That's a possibility, but I don't think Hunter was operating within half an hour of here and anywhere within that radius there are miles of old vehicle and animal tracks that get covered in hoof prints everyday as the cattle return to the nearest water. My guess is Hunter only used this as a base because of the water hole and coverage of the trees that would obscure his position from the air.'

'So that's the end of it. We've seen the last of Mr Hunter?'

'My guess is Chloe, you've only just seen the beginning. If Hunter has found something of real significance you're going to get approached by an exploration company in the near future. They won't be able to resist it when he shows them the samples and assays and spins them a convincing story.'

'They'll have to approach me first and you know the answer to that.'

'Don't wipe them off so quickly Chloe. My guess is whatever Hunter found, the locality won't be anywhere near your beloved iron-ore ranges. And don't for a moment think they'll knock at your door and ask for permission to have a look at what Hunter is trying to sell them. They'll chopper in for a few days and be gone before you know it. Tell me what did this fellow look like?'

'Unshaven, stocky build, about my height, in his late forties early fifties, by the look of the greying hair hanging out the sides of his baseball cap. It was very hard to tell his age. He could have been younger than that because he was lean and looked very fit. He was wearing a khaki shirt and shorts which looked as though they'd never been washed. No boots, just battered old sneakers. One thing I did notice was he had an accent I couldn't pick.'

'Would you know him again if you saw him?'

'Of course. I could pick him out in a crowd if he was in the same gear.'

'No one I know,' Massie replied as he dredged his memory for images Chloe described. 'Not a local for sure. I suggest we just wait and see if someone turns up at the homestead, as they surely will if he believes he's made a significant discovery.'

16

Jack Gibbs picked up the rock and turned it over studying the colouration. 'What the hell is it?'

'High grade copper and cobalt with a gold credit.'

'And you reckon this is big?'

Johan Petreus nodded as he studied the blatant example of avarice and power before him. 'I've been in this game on and off for fifteen years Jack. This is a big one.'

'Where's it located?'

'On Baracool Station in the Pilbara.' He was quite comfortable in disclosing the area, but there was no way he going to disclose the exact location of his discovery, especially not at this point.

Gibbs snorted and threw himself back in his high-backed chair. 'You're talking about one of Chloe Boyce's properties. What hasn't that bloody woman got locked away?'

'Do you know her?'

'Yes and no. Did you meet her to get permission to prospect on her land?'

'No, I'd been warned not to bother as the answer would be negative.'

'You're right on that point. She's got a fortune in iron-ore locked away for another two years, unless I can find away to take it off her, and now this.'

'She's not interested in money then?'

'She already has interests in more cattle stations in the Pilbara and Kimberley than I can count. And those along with the mountains of untouched iron-ore make her potentially the wealthiest person in the country. No, she doesn't appear to be interested in cashing in on what would surely make her mega wealthy. That doesn't appear to impress her.'

'Surely, with your power as Minister of Mines you can do something about that?'

'My hands are tied. She inherited her wealth from her father, although she was wealthy by the time he cashed in his chips and departed to the dream-time. Her iron-ore permits come to an end in two years if she doesn't do something about putting them into production. On the other hand, if she does, I've got no real control who she gets into bed with. It would have to be a major company as it costs billions to put an iron-ore mine into production.'

'And, so no one with that sort of money has approached her?'

'I could introduce her to a partner tomorrow. I've got the Chinese and Koreans hammering at my door every day.'

'You keep referring to her in the singular. I take it she's not married?'

'She has a partner and they have a child between them, but no she's not married.'

'She's an aboriginal is she?'

'You've met her then?'

'Yes. She caught me in my camp which I thought was well hidden. She said it was her property and told me to leave which I did.'

'And?'

'And what?'

'You seemed hesitant in the answer to my last question. What happened?'

'I could have stepped out of line a bit. I didn't believe her when she said it was her property. I got a bit aggressive. I took the chip out of her camera and trashed it when she tried to photograph me. I must say she's one good looking woman - a real stunner and feisty with it.'

'You bloody fool Petreus. This isn't South Africa. Just because a person is coloured and a woman, you can't go around insulting them and destroying their equipment. You're going to be in trouble if she complains to the cops.'

'Surely you can handle that?'

'Not on your Nelly. It's your bloody problem. How could you be such a bloody idiot?'

'But she doesn't have a clue who I am.'

'Well, I suggest you make yourself scarce. Go interstate for awhile and just pray she doesn't make a complaint. Anyone in the Pilbara would have known you weren't a local with that accent of yours. And I suggest you get out now, but keep in touch. If I hear nothing in the next month or so, I'll give you the all-clear to return.'

'Are you going to pay me for my time?'

'I shouldn't, but I will.'

Petreus nodded. 'You'd be wise to do so, because no one except me knows the exact location of my discovery. Are you sure you can't take the ground off her? My discovery is worth hundreds of millions if my estimates are correct.'

'If only I could. If only you'd used a bit more tact you may have been able to do a deal with her, if as you say, the deposit is miles from her beloved iron formations.'

Petreus stood up to leave. 'I'm not leaving the State. I'll go south for awhile.'

Gibbs threw up his hands. 'Okay, but if the cops catch up with you and start asking questions, don't use my name as a reference. I've never laid eyes on you will be my answer. Just don't go near the Pilbara again, but keep in touch so that if I hear anything about Boyce making a complaint I can tip you off to disappear.'

It was some moments before Gibbs realised Petreus had not moved. He looked up from the distracting paperwork scattered around his desk.

'Well, what are you waiting for?'

'It's called money Jack. I don't send invoices or extend credit.'

Gibbs reached into a drawer, pulled out an envelope and flicked it across his desk.

'And put the bloody thing in your jacket. I don't want the staff to see you leaving with that.'

'What's my next assignment?'

'Let the dust settle for a month or so until I see what problems you've created and then it's back to the Pilbara. There are huge inaccessible unexplored areas other than Boyce's which you can chopper into and cattle station own-ers who will welcome you with open arms as long as they can get a part of the action. You could even find another orebody.'

'It would have to be spectacular to even come close to what I've just found,' Petreus replied. 'I've seen some great ore deposits in my travels throughout Africa, but here's one just sticking out of the ground barking out loud. It doesn't need a sign-post on it.'

'You're not going to give me the map or **GPS** co-ordinates are you?'

'No Jack, not until I've got an agreement with Boyce and all the loose ends tied up. You don't take me for a complete mug do you?' Petreus sat down again dond lowered his voice. 'What would happen if this Boyce woman was to meet with an accident? I'm talking about a fortune sitting out there and

I don't want to wait another two years to get my hands on part of it.'

Gibbs looked thunderstruck as he pushed back in his chair. 'You're bloody insane Petreus. I would never be party to what I believe you're suggesting.'

'I wasn't suggesting anything. I was just making a hypothetical observation.'

'Like hell you were. Now get out of here.'

Petreus smiled as he picked up the envelope and stuffed it inside his jacket. 'Don't forget Jack, you hired me on an exclusive basis and I know it's not as a government employee, so I expect to be paid even while I'm on leave. Who's backing you Jack? They must have deep pockets.'

Gibbs waved him away. 'See you later Johan. And please don't come into this office again. We'll meet in more discrete surroundings in future.'

Gibbs looked up when the door closed and then swung around to look out at the city below. Bloody woman was a real thorn in his side. Now she was sitting on three fortunes, iron-ore, copper and the fortune every desirable female sat on.

17

Petreus found a barber and sat back to enjoy a shave and haircut that dispensed with his long flowing locks and moustache.

'Do you want your eyebrows clipped sport? They're far too long with the haircut I've just given you.' Petreus was lost in thought, but jolted back to the present as the barber repeated the question.

'Yes please.' He looked at himself in the mirror as the barber completed the action and brushed off the excessive clippings from around his forehead, neck and collar before removing the familiar barber's shroud with a deft flick of the practised hand.

'You're not the same person who came in sport. I doubt whether your wife would recognise you now.'

Petreus nodded as he handed over cash without comment and walked out. A plan had been fast-tracking in his mind. It could be an invitation to disaster or he just might pull it off. He felt awkward in the casual clothes he had bought the previous day. He would go unnoticed in this city, but he was uncomfortable out of his usual khaki working clothes. It was a short walk to the familiar bar.

The barman eyed him with suspicion. Here was someone he didn't recognise. He was immediately on guard. 'You sure you've got the right address mate?'

Petreus grinned in satisfaction. 'Yeah Mickey, it's me Johan.'

'Christ, what a transformation. I can't believe it's you. What have you done to yourself?'

'Cut the crap Mickey and give me a beer.' Petreus glanced around looking into the gloom and darkness of the far corner tables. 'Is the man in?'

'Yeah, he's in his office. I better let him know it's you who's coming through, otherwise he might pull a gun and blow you away if you barge in without warning.'

'You do that,' Petreus tossed ten dollars on the bar and picked up the bottle. Mickey punched in the correct amount on the register and put the change into his pocket. Petreus was always generous that way. He'd drifted in about two years before, disappeared for months at a time, never discussed what he did or where, but he always had money. Probably running from a wife or shady dealing in South Africa, or the law. Perth was full of Afrikaners, a close-mouthed bunch who didn't integrate, but were immediately identifiable the moment they spoke. Mickey didn't ask questions.

Petreus knocked on the door and heard the lock release. He did not have to look up to see the camera in the black ceiling trained on the doorway and him. If Mickey had not announced his arrival there was no way that heavy door would have opened.

The figure sitting behind the desk eyed him with an evil grin. The tattooed arms and hands were clenched on the heavy desk. The head was completely shaven, but the short peppery stubble on his chin and chops gave some idea of his age. He wore a tight black skivvy which stretched over the huge biceps and torso. Here was a man who was not to be messed with and a man who didn't trust anyone. The look in his eyes broadcast danger.

'What can I do for you Petreus. I thought you'd left town for good and gone back to that shit-house country you came from.'

Petreus ignored the insult. It was par for the course when meeting Maggot Evans. He knew he could kill Evans before he'd taken two steps. He had studied the man the first time they met and immediately picked his weaknesses and strengths. His weakness was his belief his size and strength were overbearing and could not be challenged. It was obvious he was a killer, but Petreus had killed far more in his time with the Selous Scouts, the ruthless bunch of mercenaries who killed countless terrorists during the Rhodesian conflict which supposedly ended in 1980. However, a gathering of disaffected misfits, psychopaths, sociopaths and remnant dregs of macho-humanity had adopted the Scouts name and sold their services to the highest despot who wanted to keep his corrupt regime in power. The motto *pamwe chete,* which in Shona translated to "all together" was the glue holding the remains in close contact and attracted a steady stream of new recruits. All were killers, hired by other African despots to take *care* of dissident challenges to their power and control. Robert Mugabe, the president of Zimbabwe had hired Petreus and a dozen of his fellow Scouts on numerous occasions to permanently remove any threat. The threats were all close members of his inner circle of senior police, army, judiciary and public servants who professed fealty to their benefactor. Now Mugabe was gone, removed by the army who put the next despot in power to continue the endemic corruption, intimidation and exploitation of the masses. Despite the changing of the guard the inner circle were still economically trapped – their existence reliant on a continuing stream of pillaged wealth. Also they could not flee for a better life – tribalism dictated their boundaries, their status and the level of intimidation they could expect outside their homeland. And they realised the secret police followed their every movement. They also knew if they managed to get away their family and relatives would pay the ultimate price. There was no escape.

Under Mugabe and his goons, Petreus' assignments were easy as he and his accomplices quickly and quietly went to work. No one was spared in the targeted families, woman and children included. It was a money-up-front commission paid into an offshore bank account in Uncle Sam dollars. However, Petreus well realised they were living on borrowed time if they stuck around after the latest assignment by his successor – it entailed killing a senior Colonel and his entire family. The game had not changed – the Colonel was a Mugabe stalwart and perceived future liability. He was to be removed by a group of well-known foreign murderers with no connection to the regime. Petreus knew his Scouts would be signing their own death warrants on its completion. They would be dealt with immediately so their crime and corpses could be displayed in public – the killers of a loyal soldier and supporter of the new order had been brought to justice – threat removed – case closed. They would never be permitted to leave the country and tell the world what they knew – the new regime had changed nothing.

The final target was stationed at an army base on the South African border. The idea was they would kill the Colonel and return to Harare for a final bonus pay-off. It was to be a lavish affair with everything laid on, including of the pick of Zimbabwean "beauties." However, to ensure there was no pay-off, a Major and a detachment of army thugs was assigned to accompany the Scouts to ensure they carried through on their contract and to be their executioners when the job was complete. A few miles from their destination Petreus stopped on the pretext he had to relieve himself. The thugs were relaxed in the knowledge the Scouts were unaware of what was coming as some of them joined their charges on the side of the road. It was a fatal mistake on their part. They were still pissing and laughing when Petreus took a step back, pulled out a pistol and shot three of them dead. Two remaining stood petrified, reduced to quivering wrecks as they realised their deception had been recognised. They threw up their hands and started pleading for mercy – they were following orders and had wives and families. He shot them as they collapsed on their knees knowing their pleadings were in vain. The escorting Major was left sitting motionless and stunned by what he had just witnessed.

One of Scouts drew level with Petreus. 'What about the remainder?'

'Shoot them.'

Petreus walked slowly around to the passenger seat of the lead vehicle as he heard the burst of gunfire behind him. He pushed the pistol into the Major's ear. 'What about you. You were going to kill us the moment we terminated our target weren't you?'

The Major pulled a wry smile and turned to his executioner. 'Those were the orders, but I know what's coming, so just get on with it. If you don't do it I will be shot if I return having failed.'

'Major, do you have any family?'

'No. I did have a wife, but she died and I have no children. Any relatives fled to South Africa years ago. I have no one.'

'I'm pleased to hear that. Would you like to get out of Zimbabwe?'

'It would be a dream fulfilled, but I know it's not going to happen.'

'Do you know Colonel Mboya, the man we are supposed to kill.'

The Colonel shuddered. 'I know him very well, not as a friend, but someone to keep well clear of. He was a trusted Mugabe stooge, but it's obvious there must have been a falling out with the new president. You have no hope of getting across the border and over the bridge into South Africa. You cannot possibly swim the Limpopo river. You are also as good as dead my friend.'

'Don't be so pessimistic Major. You are going to introduce us to the Colonel and explain to him our presence and purpose.'

'I can do that. I have my written authority right here.' The Major pulled several documents from the inside of his jacket.

'Good, none of us including you has anything to lose. We are going to call on the Colonel and then we're going to cross the border.'

The Major shook his head in resignation. 'You won't succeed, but anywhere is a good place to die I suppose.'

The vehicle drove up to the gates of the border compound. It was well guarded. The Major handed the papers to a smiling Captain who studied them, saluted and waved them through. He then picked up a phone on the side of the boom gate.

Mboya was standing on the verandah of his command post. The Major got out and greeted his superior whose face turned to stone when he saw Petreus and one of his Scouts also alight and join them.

'Who is this? What's he doing here?' was the barked command to the Major.

'Colonel, I'm here at the specific request of the President as my orders show. This man is accompanying me along with some of his friends in another vehicle parked outside the compound. We are on a special mission. Can we go inside and talk.'

Mboya had recognised Petreus for what he was. There were no secrets amongst the despots and murderers running this country. He turned and walked inside indicating for them to follow. He indicated a suite of chairs and a large sofa. The place was no ordinary army barracks. It was a sumptuous setup of ill-gotten gains. Patreus chose a large chair facing the doorway and with a clear view of another leading out of the room to one side. He was not going to be taken by surprise. Any surprises and the Mboya would be the first to go down.

'Okay Major, what's this all about?' There was a distinct note of weakness in the demand. The authority of rank had disappeared, he knew what was about to happen.

'The President wants you dead and this man is here to carry out that order.'

Mboya was about to shout for assistance, but hesitated when the Major held a finger to his lips. 'Don't do that Colonel, you may still have hope.'

'Tell me more.'

'You recognised this man immediately. I saw the look of fear on your face.'

Mboya nodded. 'Yes, I know what he is, but I don't know his name.' He unfolded the stamped and sealed orders the Major had given him. He slowly read, but there was not much to read. The instructions were clear.

'You have family here Colonel?'

'My wife and two children. Surely this does not include them?'

'You know the drill Colonel. There are to be no survivors.'

'But you'll never get out of this compound if I call the guards.'

'No we won't Colonel, but you'll be dead seconds later along with your family. You're as good as dead now. If this man doesn't kill you, another team will be sent to finish the job.'

'What are you suggesting?'

'Gather up your family and take them out the back to your command vehicle. Don't let them take anything with them. You then come back here and take us back out to our vehicle. Give the instructions the boom gate is to be opened as you intend to escort us to inspect the border crossing.'

'And then?'

'Do I have to paint a picture for you Colonel. You're dead and I'm dead if we stay. This man and his team only have ice in their veins. They murdered my whole crew before my eyes ten miles back up the road. My orders were to make sure they killed you and then I would have them shot.'

Mboya got up without a word and disappeared through the side door. Petreus nodded for the Scout to follow him. Minutes later they returned. Mboya quickly opened a bottle of scotch and poured three stiff shots. He handed one to the Major, but Petreus shook his head. Mboya downed both glasses before strapping on a sidearm and donning his gold-braided cap. 'I'll have to take one of my guards with me. He's my appointed driver - he wouldn't hesitate to shoot me if I try anything out of the ordinary at the crossing. He's your problem to deal with.'

'He will be taken care of. I'll sit in the back seat Colonel. Where is your family?'

'In the back under a tarp Major.'

'Good, I will make the conversation on the way so the driver doesn't get suspicious. I suggest we start swapping army stories with a bit of laughter to keep him distracted on the way.'

Mboya picked up a phone and gave orders for the boom gate to be lifted as he was going on an inspection tour with the Major.

Petreus had followed them out and got into the rear of the Colonel's armoured vehicle. The Scouts trucks followed at a safe distance, prepared for trouble. Mboya was playing it cool. No rush, just a surprise inspection of the border guard - all very casual.

As they approached, Petreus could see a lone soldier with an AK47 slung over his shoulder leaning up against the boom. He saw the man open his mouth and shout something back into a large guardroom when he recognised Mboya's vehicle. Moments later two more individuals stumbled out attempting to adjust their uniforms and bring themselves to attention. As their vehicle pulled up, Petreus shot the driver in the back of the head. There was a burst of gunfire from the vehicle behind and the armed boom guard was also dead. His two accomplices quickly raised their arms in surrender.

The Major got out and pulled the dead driver from his seat. He turned towards the guardhouse. 'Do you two want to die here, come with us over the border, or do you want to go back to your villages and family.'

One of them stammered. 'We go home Major.'

'Well, open the boom and go.'

18

'Do you want anymore shit delivered up north? I'm heading up that way in a week or so.'

Maggot Evans smiled. 'Sure, I'm always looking for reliable couriers I can trust. I lost one last month, or rather he tried to run off with the proceeds. Not a wise move.' It was a veiled warning.

'You don't have to give me that Carl. I make the delivery, take my cut and you get your money. I'm taking the risk I won't get pulled over by the cops, or won't be mugged by someone trying take the goods without paying.'

'You're a cocky bastard Petreus. I don't know what your real background is, or how much time you've served, but you're a cold calculating arsehole I wouldn't like to get on the wrong side of, that much I can tell.'

'I've never served time. I would not have got into this country if I had a record in South Africa.'

'You must tell me your life's story sometime.'

'Why don't you start now by telling me yours. Give me the complete history.'

Evans leaned back and burst out laughing. 'It's too long to relate, but I think you can guess I've served time for murder, violence, armed robbery, right down to the minor crime of wife bashing. You name it, I'm guilty of it.'

'Get pleasure out of hitting women do you Carl?'

'I don't give a shit who I hit. If it's a woman and she steps out of line, I'll beat the crap out of her.'

'Must make you feel like a real man does it? But if that's what gets your rocks off, who am I to pass judgement.'

It took Evans a few moments to analyse the thrust of the comment. 'Fuck off Petreus before I give you a taste of what I'm capable of. I don't like your bloody attitude. Come and see me this time next week and I'll have the details of a delivery for you.'

He watched as Petreus shrugged, got up and departed. Evans knew there would have to be a day of reckoning coming for the yapie prick. However, he would have to be careful because this was no *farm boy* as inferred by the Afrikan insult. All his couriers had their use-by date and Petreus was no exception. The cops had their contacts and snouts and it would not be too long before he got pulled over and charged with possession and dealing. Once he came to their attention he was no longer of any use.

Petreus likewise, was well aware this would probably be his last delivery. Drug running had financed his activities to date, but now he had a clear objective. He had found what he'd been looking for. Those years since he got out of Zimbabwe and worked as a geologist's assistant in South Africa had paid off. He had taken notice of their comments as they studied the rocks and minerals. At first he thought it a boring occupation, but the more he became involved and listened and read scientific papers on geology, the more he became engrossed in the science. Then came the day the geologist said the company was moving onto exploration in other African nations and naturally, Petreus was expected to follow. He did for a short time, but knew his luck would not hold. It happened in Zambia where he was recognised for his former occupation. The geologist was in bed when the panga wielding crazy crashed into the room screaming revenge. Petreus understood what he was saying from the next room – the Scouts had slaughtered his whole family. The geologist struggled to get to his feet, but he was too late as the blade cleaved his skull in two. The assailant then turned his attention to the closed door. He had been watching from the outside and knew Petreus was present in one of the two rooms of the portable accommodation block. Petreus was waiting – the blasts from the pump-action shotgun completely eviscerating the killer as he opened it. Within a minute he had packed a few of his belongings and fled to the vehicle still carrying the gun. Already he could hear raised voices and see the tribesmen appearing out of nowhere running towards him – he could expect no mercy from them or the authorities.

'Hi there. The name's Johan Petreus.'

Andrew shook the outstretched hand. 'Andrew Hanna. Won't you come in?' One look at the nondescript individual dressed in immaculate khaki clothing indicated he was dealing with a person representing the profession Chloe detested.

'You're a geologist are you Johan?' Andrew indicated a seat on the verandah He was about to call out when Alice appeared with a pitcher of cold lime juice and two glasses. She had heard the vehicle pull up and the introduction.

'Would you like something to eat sir?'

'No, I'm fine thank you. The juice will be sufficient.'

Alice smiled and went back inside.

'To answer your question Andrew, no I'm not a geologist, but I must confess I have enough experience to be one. I'm a prospector looking for likely mineral deposits such as copper, gold, cobalt or lithium, to name a few.'

'You're South African are you?'

'Was, but now I'm an Australian citizen. The climate and people suit me just fine.'

'And the purpose of your visit is?'

'I'm not interested in iron-ore, so you can put your mind at ease there. But I am interested in looking for other minerals on Baracool Station.'

Andrew stopped him before he could continue. 'You're wasting your time Johan. Chloe knocks back constant requests from mining companies and there would be no point in even raising the subject with her.'

'Is she here? Can I talk to her?'

'No, she's in Perth until next week. I'm here with our son Charlie until his new school term resumes. And then it's back to Perth for me and Chloe will be up here at Ascot Downs. We take turns to alternate two weeks on two weeks off.'

'Andrew there could be a fortune in valuable mineral deposits on Baracool. Are you just going to let it sit there? After all Baracool is a vast holding. Surely, a few thousand acres exciscd as a mine, and nowhere near the iron-ore, would be of interest?'

'You sound as though you know something we don't?'

'I've studied the geological records and all previous data available. The whole of the Pilbara presents real opportunities for first-class discoveries.'

Andrew smiled and shook his head. 'I've no doubt you're probably correct, but Chloe's answer will be to tell you to go look elsewhere in the Pilbara. There should be plenty of open exploration ground available outside her properties.'

'That maybe so, but I've pinpointed Baracool as having very similar rocks and mineralisation to ground I've walked over in Africa. I'm sure there's something of real significance somewhere on Baracool. I'm aware Chloe has a blanket ban on exploration, but surely the thought of having another huge cash-flow to add to her present holdings in the cattle industry must be of interest. After all, you are her partner from what I understand. I would emphasise I'm not interested in the iron-ore deposits. Can you tell me why she is so opposed to mining?'

'She has her reasons, but I won't go into them, other than to say she wants to protect the beautiful natural resources with ancient significance to the aboriginal people.'

'I can understand that, but someday they are going to be mined for what they contain. However, I won't take up anymore of your time. Maybe Chloe will change her mind at some point.'

Andrew was surprised at the abrupt termination as Petreus got up and opened the screen door. He followed him out to his Toyota ute. 'You are quite sure there are significant mineral deposits to be found that wouldn't impact on the Baracool iron ranges?'

'Quite sure, and I don't think it would take me longer than six months to prove that theory.' Petreus could see Andrew was interested. How much influence did he have over his partner? He held out his hand and applied a momentary iron grip Andrew could not match.

'Can I contact you when you're in Perth in a month or so? Maybe you can convince Chloe about letting me have a look around?'

'You can do that, but I don't think her position will have changed.'

Just then a horse and rider galloped towards them and pulled up in a cloud of dust. A boy jumped from the saddle, his smiling face lost under the wide brim of a bush hat.

'High there, I'm Charlie.' He held out his hand introducing himself to Petreus.

'Charlie, how many times have you been told not to gallop your horse anywhere near the homestead. Alice and the girls have enough to do without you creating dust storms that find their way inside.'

'Sorry Dad. I didn't want to miss meeting your visitor. What's your name sir?'

Petreus laughed. 'Johan Petreus.'

'Oh a yapie. We have a lot of them at my school. Real tough lads, but okay when you get to know them.'

Petreus' facial expression hardened for a second. 'Do you call them yapie's to their face.'

'No, that's asking for trouble.' Charlie looked sheepish for a second. 'I apologise for calling you a yapie. It just slipped out.'

'No offence taken Charlie, but beware of other people's sensitivities.' Petreus could see the boy was genuinely repentant as he swung up into the cab and with a wave of his hand drove off.

'What did he want Dad?'

'Another geologist looking for exploration rights on Baracool.'

'Fat chance Mum will agree to that. You should erect big signs at the entrance to every station stating geologists will be shot on sight.'

Andrew laughed as he took off his son's hat and ruffled his hair. 'You unsaddle that horse and let him go, them come in and cleanup and tell me what you've been up to.'

'No, I'm going for another ride. Be back soon.' Andrew made to shout, but it was pointless. The boy was in the saddle and raising a cloud of dust as he spurred the horse into a gallop. Andrew shook his head in despair – kids just don't think.

Charlie wandered into Andrew's office an hour later and put a slip of paper in front of him.

'What's this?'

'It's the number plates of Johan's wagon and the other guy he met up with down the track.'

'Where were you?'

'Up on an escarpment about fifty metres away. If they'd looked up they would have seen me. I was about to ride down when a shouting match broke out between them.'

'Could you hear what they were saying?'

'Something to do with something Johan was carrying. The other guy pulled a pistol, but the next moment he was flat on his back in the dust. I saw Johan pick up the gun and drive off. I watched, but it was a good five minutes before the other fellow got back on his feet. He sure looked groggy when he got into his wagon and drove off. He wasn't in a hurry to catch up with Johan, that's for sure. Are you going to report it to the police?'

'None of our business son. No crime has been committed and I don't want you mixed up in something you think you may have witnessed.'

'I saw it Dad,' Charlie protested. 'I saw the guy pull out the pistol and I saw Johan deck him with a single blow. And I saw Johan pick up the gun and drive off. I saw it all.'

'Well, let's forget about it for now. And please don't tell your mother. Promise me.'

'Okay Dad. I won't say a word. It's just between you and me. I'm off to get something to eat.'

Andrew folded the notepaper with the scrawled registration numbers and put it in a drawer of his desk. What was Petreus mixed up in? And was he the same person who Chloe accosted and destroyed her camera chip?

'Chloe, that fellow you had a run-in with and destroyed your camera card, can you describe him to me?'

'A real hobo look with long hair and beard. I would say he was in his late forties, early fifties. I can't describe his clothes and footwear, they were beyond description.'

'Did he have an accent?'

'Yes, it took me awhile to pick up on it, that was until I was listening to a couple of South African mothers picking up their kids from Charlie's school one day. He sounded very much like them. Why do you ask?'

'I had a South African call on me at Ascot Downs. I think he really wanted to see you. He said from his research there was probably a fortune in minerals, other than iron-ore to be discovered on Baracool. And I got the distinct impression he knew more than he was letting on.'

'So what did you tell him?'

'Baracool was out of bounds and he was wasting his time. However, I'm sure he's going to try and pay you a visit.'

Chloe snorted softly and shrugged her shoulders. 'I'll soon put him in his place. He'll learn we're a team and whatever you say, is how it is.' She had a sudden thought. 'Did he give a name?'

'Johan Petreus. His appearance was very presentable, probably in his late forties, no beard and certainly no flowing hair as you described the fellow who gave you a fright. Fresh work khakis and geologist's boots, pens in top pocket along with notebook, you know, the usual gear geologist's get around in. And he was driving a near-new Toyota. I think he was a geologist although he denied it.'

'Let's assume then there have been two South African geo's on Baracool, one with a violent intent and the other of professional appearance and manner. I would assume they are working for unknown exploration companies, although the one I encountered was too rough looking to fit into that category. More likely he was a prospector trying his luck.

It could be they're one and the same. There are plenty of prospectors here in the north looking for diamonds, gold or copper.'

'Perhaps we should rethink our policy then?' Andrew continued anticipating the swift rebuttal. 'The pressure is only going to mount and we've only got two years left on the exploration permits. My guess is that those shiny-arse politicians in Perth will simply refuse to renew them. The exploration companies are big donors to any party in power they believe they can manipulate. Money has no smell and politicians of all persuasions are easy targets if they believe it will enhance their position to remain in power. Why not let someone in to look for the other metal deposits Petreus was alluding to?'

Chloe did not answer immediately with her usual burst of indignation and denial. Andrew could see he had finally struck a note of doubt in her mind. He pressed on. 'We'd be foolish not to listen to the murmurings becoming louder from the mining companies and politicians and their persistent rhetoric, the north needs development. Stand in the way of a relentless build-up of pressure and we'll eventually be run-over. We'll have no say Chloe. You've got to understand that.'

'So you've saying we should give ground and let the exploration companies in?'

'It's your call, but you can see what I'm thinking.'

'It's not my call alone,' she flared. 'We're a team Andrew. Without you I wouldn't be where we are today. Anyway, let's drop the subject. I'll give it some thought overnight.'

It was early morning - Andrew was sitting on the verandah with a coffee looking out over the Swan River when Chloe emerged carrying a small overnight bag. 'I've made up my mind Andrew and it hasn't changed my attitude - exploration companies will not be allowed on Baracool or Ironstone Park.'

He nodded in resignation. She was one stubborn lady who couldn't be shifted. He resigned himself to it.

'I've decided we are going to start our own exploration company.'

He turned in shock as the statement registered. 'Are you serious?'

'You heard what I just said, didn't you?'

He stood and kissed her on the cheek. 'A very wise decision Chloe Boyce.'

'Do you want to set it up and hire the appropriate people?'

Andrew beamed and laughed at the same time. 'You bet I will. I've got a feeling we'll locate the mineral prospects your aggressor and Johan Petreus were referring to.'

'Okay, I've got to be off, so I'll leave you to sort it out. See you in two weeks.'

19

'That's the last run I do for you Carl.' Petreus dropped the shopping bag on Maggot's desk. 'I've already taken my ten percent.'

Evans took a cursory look inside the bag. It was all there in cash, the only currency he was interested in. 'Why the sudden cold feet?'

'It's getting too dangerous. Someone's onto me. I was nearly on the missing-in-action list when someone tried a stick-up in the boondocks of the Pilbara.

'What happened?' Evans expressed surprise.

'Some goon waved me down when I was leaving Ascot Downs Station. You naturally stop for anyone who appears to be in distress in that country. I didn't suspect a thing until he pulled a gun on me.'

'What were you doing out there? That wasn't on your drop-off list.'

'I do work for myself Carl. You're not exclusive,' Petreus shot back. 'My contract with you has been a sideline occupation and a very hazardous one at that. Next time, I might not be so lucky, so I'm handing in my runner's badge today.'

'Why did you go out to the Ascot place?'

'I wanted to see the owner about prospecting on one of her properties. She wasn't there so I had a word with her partner and it was while driving out I got pulled over.'

'You're here, my money's safe, so obviously you took care of the situation. That doesn't explain why you're suddenly pulling the pin.'

'Because I smelt cop the moment the arsehole started to pull the gun. I decked him and took his piece. I got out of there as fast as I could and I'm not going back delivering any more shit for you. That cop was working for himself- he wasn't out to arrest me.'

Evans nodded. 'I can understand that. I wonder how he latched onto you as a courier. I must have a weak link somewhere. Someone must have tipped him off.'

'I'd have thought that was bloody obvious Carl and that's the reason I'm out. The next time he'll have another bent copper with him and I'll meet a very messy end. Up in that country no one would find a missing person. You would of course have assumed I'd bolted for greener pastures with your money.'

'Yeah, I lost a courier last year. He phoned in from his final drop and that was the last contact I had with him. Cost me a hundred grand. If he took the dough he would have to be living in Bali, but even there I've got very good contacts. And I know none of my contacts here have seen him pop up from one coast to the other in that time. If he had, he'd have been dead meat by now.'

'All I can say Carl is one of your trustworthy associates has tipped off a free-lancing cop and as we both know there are plenty of those bent bastards in every force.'

'So you're going back to prospecting?'

'There's no money in it until you find something worthwhile, but it's a hell of a lot safer.'

Maggot shook his head. 'I can't understand you fucking around breaking rocks all day getting fly-blown for no return. Surely, a cop with a gun is not going to scare you off the dough you make with me? I didn't take you for such a bloody chicken.'

Patreus eyed his accuser. 'You know nothing of my background. I would advise you to shut your mouth before you go too far.'

Maggot's face flushed with anger as he began to rise. Something stopped him. Petreus hadn't moved. He was not cowered by the threatening enormity or danger of the man. He gave a dismissive wave as he sat back down. 'Okay, so you're a tough bastard Petreus. Why do I think someday I'm going to test just how tough you are?'

'I'm not looking forward to that Carl. There's no call for threats of violence. I've seen too much of it and don't want to go through the experience again.'

'So you really are pulling the pin. No one just resigns on me. It's always the other way around and the termination is permanent in both senses.'

'I'd advise you not to come after me Carl. You would only have one crack at it before your door opened and I'd be standing there.'

'Okay, okay I get the message. My immediate problem is to recruit another courier I can trust. Plenty of guys around here, but they'd be spotted immediately in one of those outback towns, no matter how they tried to conceal their tattoos and jail-time written all over their faces.'

'Your problem, not mine, but I'd be bloody careful if I were you. They got onto me quicker than I thought and I took all the precautions. You've got a traitor in the ranks or competition wanting to see you out of the game. That is a very lucrative run someone wants a part of.'

'Ronnie the Rat,' Maggot muttered under his breath.

'Ronnie who?'

'Oh, no one you know Petreus. Now changing the subject, I accept your resignation, so tell me a bit more about your prospecting and what you're looking for? You'll need money for that and I may be able to help for part of the action.'

Maggot was the last person he needed as a partner and it wasn't a partner nor finance he was looking for at this stage. 'It's not a matter of money Carl. It's getting around a stubborn bloody kaffir who won't let me onto her property.'

'Kaffir? What's a kaffir?'

Petreus laughed. 'It's what we used to call the blacks of South Africa to their faces. You wouldn't dare to it today with all the racial equality bullshit. The country is screwed up because of them. In my opinion they're still a bunch of corrupt bloody kaffir's who will eventually drive the country into bankruptcy.'

'So, who's this kaffir you're referring to?'

'Chloe Boyce - she controls vast cattle properties in the Kimberley and Pilbara. She also has huge deposits of iron-ore, as well as the minerals I've been searching for.'

'Married? Surely she hasn't achieved all that without help?'

'No, she's not married from what I can ascertain. But she and her boyfriend have a kid between them. So I guess he could put his hand up for a share if anything was to happen to her.'

'You say you met the partner. What's his name?'

'Hanna, Andrew Hanna.' He noticed the stunned look on Maggot's face. 'Do you know him?'

Maggot grinned menacingly. 'I sure as hell do. I was wondering when that scum-bag would turn up again and here he's been right under my nose the whole time.'

'What's between you two?'

Maggot ignored the question. 'Hanna is hiding on this Ascot property is he?'

'He's not hiding. Apparently he and Boyce alternate between there and another home they have here in Perth. The boy is in school down here somewhere and they take it in turns to spend a couple of weeks in each location. The nerve centre of her operation is here, while the cattle export, killing and trucking empire are situated in the north.'

'How good is this mineral project you've located on one of her stations?'

'Top class. It's a copper-gold-cobalt ore-body, just sticking right up out of the ground inviting someone to discover it, which I've done.'

'So Boyce and Hanna are standing in your way?'

Petreus nodded. 'That's correct.'

'What if I got their approval? What's in it for me?'

'Depends on how much money you'll pony-up to get a share. The deposit is worth in the hundreds of millions.'

'Okay, I'll finance you to the tune of a million for half.'

'Knock it off Carl. I don't need a mill. All I need is the okay from them to farm-into their exploration permit and I'll be able to raise all the money I need within a few weeks. I can approach any number of mining companies that would give multiples of that to get involved.'

'You've got my offer. Take it or leave it.'

'What makes you so sure you can strike a deal with Boyce? She's the one who holds title. There's no mention of Hanna being involved.'

'You leave that to me boyo. I guarantee my charm will win her over. Well, what's it to be?'

'Let me think about it. Fifty per cent is just too high for what I'm bringing to the table.'

Maggot shrugged and leaned back in his chair. 'Don't piss me off Petreus. I've made you a good offer, which you can't refuse. You have no alternative is the way I see it. What's to stop me cutting you out altogether and doing a deal with Boyce? From what you've told me she knows exactly where you were camped on her property. I've got no doubt a team of geologists would find your ore-body very quickly. The only reason it hasn't been discovered to date is that no one has been allowed on the permit area. Now fuck-off and come back tomorrow and tell me we've got a deal, otherwise I'll go my own way.'

Petreus sat stunned. There was no moral consideration or a modicum of ethics. This over-inflated shit would walk right over him without a second thought. He'd made the right move in handing in his resignation as a drug runner. It was far too dangerous an occupation. Maggot could easily have him disappear permanently. The money he made was good, but the brush with the gunman told him his card was marked. Was it this *Ronnie the Rat* Maggot had mentioned, or was it Maggot himself who'd decided he was dispensable? And now this. He cursed himself for not keeping his mouth shut. What knowledge or hold did Evans have that would make Chloe Boyce suddenly cave-in and accept exploration over her permit areas?

'I'll see you tomorrow.' Petreus got up and started to walk out followed by a derisive belly-laugh from behind. 'Don't bother to come if you're not going to accept my terms. They're non-negotiable. I only ever make one offer.'

Was it a bluff, or did the bikie thug have that much influence with Boyce? He appeared to be absolutely sure of himself. Petreus was confused. Why would Boyce even take the risk of being associated with Evans, let alone agree to a deal with him? It didn't make sense. He had no alternative. It looked as though he would be on Maggot's payroll for awhile yet. However, he realised his days would be numbered if he thought Maggot was going to honour his side of any deal. The prize was too big - Maggot would not be able to resist taking him out of the picture permanently.

20

ndrew was sitting in his favourite café when an empty chair opposite was pulled out and the hulk sat down. The huge hands were clasped in front of him so as to display the array of tattoos covering his forearms. This was not a place he would frequent, but he had someone to see. And someone to deliver a message to.

'Hello Hanna. It's taken a long time to catch up with you, but I knew someday my luck would hold.'

Andrew froze. He could not mask his shock as it hit his brain and blood pressure. He felt sick and faint. It was all he could do to put down his cup without dropping it.

'Yes, it's mc Carl Evans.'

'Maggot.' The name barely came out as a whisper.

'You seem surprised to see me Hanna. Are you going to buy me a coffee or are you having trouble in your pants at the moment and can't stand up?'

'What do you want?'

'I would like something with a sprinkling of chocolate coloured topping, just like your woman, but not now. As to what I really want, we won't discuss that here. I'll be at your place sometime late this evening, so wait up for me.' With that Evans pushed his bulk up out of the chair and ambled away closely followed by an equally thuggish look-ing character observing from a distance. A minute later he heard two motorcycle engines roar into life. Maggot and his accomplice rode past without a sideways glance - the sudden rip of power and the dull thud of the powerful Harley's delivering the desired effect.

Andrew could not think straight. If it was money Maggot was after, he could probably accommodate him, but he had a feeling it was more than that.

He was staring at the blank tele screen, the empty bottle of red on the coffee table beside him. He looked at his watch. It was late and he decided Evans wasn't going to front so he may as well go to bed. He was about to climb the stairs when he heard the soft melody of the front gate chime - his visitor knew how to play mind games. Let the target stew for hours while the tension and anxiety of the meeting slowly ate away at him. Andrew had been tempted to open another bottle of red to calm his nerves, but knew it would only dull his mind during the confrontation.

He slowly walked to the front door, looked into the security camera to see his tormentor's ugly face staring straight back at him and pushed the gate release. The car slid into the driveway as he composed himself and opened the front door.

'What no Harley tonight?'

Maggot laughed. 'Didn't want to wake the neighbours Hanna. The Harley would immediately identify your killer. With the car I can just slit your throat and be gone without anyone noticing anything suspicious.'

Andrew stood to one side as Maggot walked straight past followed by his accomplice.

'Nice place you have here. Must have cost a fortune with this outlook over the river. Very, very classy suburb. You've come a long way since your days as a destitute lawyer.'

'I would think the same would apply to you, wouldn't it Carl?'

Evans swung on him. 'You didn't do ten years in the pen for murder. I got your mate, but I didn't get you. I can't say how thrilled I am to have finally caught up with you."

'You were convicted and jailed on the evidence which the jury considered conclusive. You murdered my friend. It was established he was a drug runner and addict, but it's filth like you responsible for his addiction. ' Andrew noticed Evan's nod of consent to the accomplice - he sensed it was coming as tried to lean out of the way, but the punch caught him on the side of the head. He was thrown sideways in concussed waves as he struggled to maintain awareness. Evans' features drifted in and out of focus before they began to stabilise.

'Your friend was the filth Hanna. He lived in filth. The bastard stole from me. I didn't force him to sample the products he was supposed to be selling. He knew the risks and he paid the price. It wasn't the first time he'd been behind in his payments. He'd already touched his old man for a couple of hundred grand, until the old boy finally disowned him. Don't feel sorry for him Hanna, he was a hopeless case who had to be made an example of.'

'You certainly did that.'

'Yeah, and now that I'm here, there's another matter I'd like to clear up and that's concerns your involvement with a certain detective Connors.'

'I was never involved with him.'

'Bullshit, you know what I'm talking about. It took me awhile to figure out the connection. Although you identified me as the guy who snuffed your friend, I sensed Connors had to be involved somewhere behind the scenes. Basili may have been your friend at some point, but you testified you hadn't been in contact for a number of years. This was because of your occupation. You couldn't afford to be associated with a hopeless junky. So why did you come forward and get involved? It just didn't make sense. It then hit me Connors had got greedy when he removed Ratsakis when I offered a bigger commission to look the other way. Obviously, a similar event had taken place and I had to be removed. Connors sold himself to whoever could pay the best. Am I making sense?'

'You'll have to ask Connors about that?'

Evans sneered. 'I did try. I went to see him in the hospice a few days before he died with cancer of the guts. He just laughed in my face, or tried to as he was so juiced up with painkillers. As I was leaving he mumbled I should speak to you.'

Andrew met the gaze of the killer. He'd tripped the concealed security cameras before he'd opened the door. At least his killer would be identified. 'I saw you coming out of Basili's apartment. I went back up and could see he was near death. I called an ambulance and his father. Unfortunately, as I was about to drive away and forget what I'd seen, Connors confronted me. It was either I testify against you or he would kill me. I had no choice. It was a matter of who would pull the trigger first. I figured I had at least ten more years of living, considering you would be locked up for that time. Whereas with Connors I would have been dead before your trial commenced – I didn't like the odds.'

'Yeah, that fucking Connors must have thought he'd won Lotto when he stumbled onto you at the scene. I always knew he would shaft me at some point, but never suspected it until I had time to think it through in a cell. However, that doesn't change your predicament. I want the half mill your friend shot into his veins and stole, plus interest for my pain and suffering in prison. Let's make it a million for starters, eh?'

'I'm not responsible for your loss Carl. The person who set you up is dead. I can't help you.'

Maggot nodded. 'Maybe you're right on that point, but I lost a shit load of money and now I want to recover it. It was you who got me put away.'

'And if I say I can't pay because I don't owe you a cent, you intend to work me over, do you?'

Maggot looked around the room. 'No point in knocking you off, or roughing you up in here Hanna. I've no doubt you've got security cameras all over this place.'

'Well, I can conclude our meeting is at an end Carl. You want a million plus, which is out of the question. And I've told you, I had nothing to do with your losses.'

'I'll settle for a million and that's the bottom line.' Maggot leaned down and leered into his face. 'Your partner is one good looking chick, beautiful in fact, according to enquiries I've made. You certainly have fucked your way into a fortune. Beautiful women do attract rapists you know. I haven't seen your son, but I've been told he's at a local school. Kids getting snatched off the street is not an unusual occurrence. You can't guard the little buggers around the clock. Fiddling with little boys is rife these days. It's not confined to the church.'

Andrew's blood went cold. The message was clear. 'You're a degenerate shit Evans. I don't regret testifying against you. Life should be life for murder, not ten years?'

'Calm down Hanna. There's no need to get offensive.'

Andrew was so rattled he got up and poured himself a scotch while the veiled threats swirled through his brain. He indicated the decanter to Maggot.

'Not for me Hanna. I'm driving and don't want to be picked up by the cops at this late hour. You go ahead though. I can see your nerves are taking a beating.'

Andrew slumped into a chair, staring vacantly at the ceiling. 'Okay, Carl what have you really got on your mind?'

'Your partner Chloe Boyce has title to exploration permits over a couple of her properties in the Pilbara.'

'There's no way Chloe will allow any exploration on those properties.' He wasn't about to tell him of her recent decision.

'Bloody meaningless in this day and age Hanna. She's standing in the way of progress and a pile of money. However, it's not the iron I'm interested in. It's the other minerals those permit areas may be covering. You're going to help me persuade her to change her mind.'

'You're not involved with a South African, Chloe chased off Baracool Station recently are you?'

Maggot gave a hollow laugh. 'It's none your business who I might be in bed with, or who I'm talking to. I want in and you're going to make sure of that.'

'And if I can't persuade her, as I'm sure I can't. What then?'

Maggot got up and made to leave. Andrew followed him out and opened the front door and entrance gate.

'The what then Hanna, is there are psychopaths and paedophiles everywhere. Women get raped and mutilated everyday of the week and kids get snatched and sold for their bums before they're murdered. I'll give you a couple of weeks to decide. And a final warning – if you go to the cops about this meeting, I'll take you out first. I reckon your missus will be easy to handle when that happens – no one says no to me.'

Andrew watched as Maggot swung the car around, grinned and waved at him as he slowly drove out. He closed the door and gate and topped up his scotch. There had to be a way of doing this without Chloe realising who she was dealing with.

One look at Maggot and the shutters would immediately be pulled down. The South African had to be involved some-where, but was it the one who accosted him at Ascot Downs or was it the one Chloe had chased off, or were they one and the same? Perhaps it was for the good. He had been at Chloe to do something about exploration on both Baracool and Ironstone Park. The time was running out. Suddenly, she had back-flipped.

21

'Carl, it's Andrew.' He had been thinking long and hard before making the call. 'I believe I might be able to put something together on the condition you're nowhere in sight.'

'I'm listening Hanna.'

'I believe you know more than you're letting on. You're mixed up with that South African aren't you?'

'What of it?'

'I want to meet you both so I can get an idea of whether he's suitable. If he's who I think he is, it's going to take all my powers of persuasion to get Chloe to go along with what I've got in mind. Don't jerk me around, is he the same guy who roughed up Chloe?'

'I won't go into it over the phone Hanna. Call into my office tomorrow around ten and we'll discuss it further.'

Maggot put down the phone and gave Petreus the thumbs up. 'Looks like I've got him on the run, but how do I explain you?'

'Simple really. I'll be here and I just tell him the truth about me giving his partner a fright. I'll apologise and explain it was an unfortunate error on my part. What's he going to say to that? The answer is very little, because you've got him by the nuts and I know the exact location of the ore-body. Even if he decided to go it alone and employ some geologists I doubt very much whether they'd find what I found in a year of looking. However, before we get into any serious discussion with Hanna, what's my share if I come up with the goods?'

'Let's just work it through first. I don't know what it will cost me and besides I've never stiffed you before, so you can be assured you're in for part of the action.'

Petreus wasn't so sure - he was dealing with one hardened criminal who would deal him out at some point. The man was utterly unscrupulous - as dangerous as a western brown snake he'd seen plenty of in the Pilbara. One strike and you had half an hour to live as the venom seized the heart muscles and lowered the blood pressure to a fatal level. No use picking an argument now though, let's hear what Hanna has to say first.

Andrew drew in a deep breath as he pushed open the door of the bar and walked in. 'Carl's expecting you. Go right through,' Mickey returned to polishing a glass. He had been given a description of the expected guest.

Maggot stood up and offered his hand which Andrew averted. He knew it would result in a knuckle-crushing signification of power. 'I believe you've met Johan?'

'Yes, I have.' He shook the outstretched hand. 'Just to clear the air, are you the same person who threatened my partner?'

'Yes, it was me and I apologise for that. It was way out of bounds. She took me by surprise and I didn't know who she was. I guess I just got angry when she came on strong and I over reacted.'

'But you knew you had no authority to be on the property doing what you were doing?'

"Guilty as charged Andrew. I thought my presence would go undetected. That station covers a huge area, but it was just my luck the owner would be out flying around on that day. I'd been camped there for more than a month.' The frank admission of guilt had the desired effect on Andrew's attitude. What more could he say?

'Now that's out of the way, can we get down to business? Johan has admitted his faults and apologised so can we start talking about money? After all, that's what this whole meeting is about.' Maggot sat back in anticipation.

'You've located an ore-body of real significance have you Patreus?'

'Please drop the formalities Andrew, just call me Johan. To answer your question, yes I've located a copper gold and cobalt formation worth hundreds of millions, possibly more.'

'What's to stop me hiring geologists to go look for it?'

'Nothing at all as far as I'm concerned, but I believe the arrangement may not be suitable to Carl.'

'And how do you expect such an agreement would work?'

'A simple farm-in agreement Andrew. Absolutely common in the mineral exploration game. A company is formed, the shareholding is agreed on and someone puts up the finance to commence exploration. The ore-body is discovered, we announce drilling results, move the company onto the Securities Exchange and cash-in or go for the ride.'

'So who's putting up the money and for what share?'

'I'll put up a million to get the ball rolling,' Maggot broke in. 'Johan reckons for that sort of money I'd be entitled to fifty percent.'

'And what's you're end Johan?'

'I hold the trump card. I've located the ore-body. I want a quarter.'

'So you're saying Chloe would only get the same?'

'That's a good offer Andrew. Normally, in these circumstances the landowner is really not entitled to anything but compensation for the use of the land. As I understand it here in Australia everything under the surface belongs to the government. If the ground was open and not covered by exploration permits I could just peg it, give you a notice of entry, wheel in a drilling rig and claim the prize for myself.'

'I can't see her going along with that proposal Johan. We can put our own geologists in there and I've no doubt they would find what you've discovered very quickly.'

Maggot snorted. 'You're not going to do that are you Hanna? It might result in events outside your control.'

Petreus was about to query the statement when he was abruptly cut off. He had no idea what Maggot was referring to.

'Don't worry about it Johan. It's just a private matter between Hanna and me. Nothing to do with these negotiations.'

Petreus was confused. It had to be something to do with the current discussions. What hold did Maggot have over Hanna?

'Carl, I can tell you now Chloe won't agree to such a split. She would want at least fifty one percent of the action, assuming she is even prepared to entertain such a deal.' Andrew was bluffing to see if Maggot's offer was an opening gambit. Was he prepared to negotiate?

'I'm putting up the money. I want half the action.'

'Chloe is putting up the ore-body which Johan has already explained is worth in the hundreds of millions, or even more. There's no problem with her putting up a million to match your contribution. You really don't have much of a bargaining point Carl.'

Maggot slammed his fist on the desktop. 'Don't screw me around Hanna. I've given you the terms. Accept them or face the consequences.'

'What the hell is going on here?' Petreus demanded. 'What are you talking about Carl.' He swung on Andrew. 'Perhaps you can enlighten me? I don't want to get mixed up in something where I'm not aware of the end game.'

Andrew shook his head. 'I'll leave it to Carl to fill you in on that score,' he said as he got up to leave. 'Carl, you're going to have to rethink the terms. I can tell you now your proposition just wouldn't fly with Chloe.' He attempted to maintain his facade of non-negotiable strength as he turned and opened the door. There was a peal of laughter behind him as he closed it.

'You look as though you could do with a stiff brandy?' Mickey was grinning from ear to ear. He had witnessed many people reduced to hopeless despair after leaving Maggot's office and here was a prime example.

Andrew ignored the remark as he walked out and drove across town to his office. He tried to compose himself as he entered and waved to those staff who recognised and returned his acknowledgement.

'I don't want to be disturbed. No calls unless its Chloe,' he muttered to Maria Palacci. He went in and quietly closed the door before sitting down to assess whether his bluff would work. He had no doubt Evans would carry out his threat. Chloe was due back in a few days. What was he to tell her? She would panic if he revealed the extent of the meeting with Evans. He would have to tell her of his past upfront, or should he let her slowly drag it out of him? She would instantly guess there had to be some connection between him and Evans. He had been stewing for a good hour, his brain lost in a complete fog of confusion when Maria knocked and opened the door.

'I know you don't want to be disturbed Andrew, but there's a person by the name of Petreus who insists you'll talk to him.'

Andrew looked up blankly and then snapped out of it. 'Yes, I will speak to him,' he said picking up the phone.

'What can I do for you Johan?'

'I'll put it straight to you Andrew. I don't know what's going on between you and Evans, but I don't like it. He has some sort of hold over you and I'm concerned I may be implicated in something that screws up what I'm after.'

'I...I really don't know what you're referring to.'

'Andrew, I've seen a lot of frightened people in my time and you're a prime example of a quivering wreck just before some goon puts a gun in your ear and pulls the trigger.'

'What do you want?'

'I want to talk to you in private. I'll be knocking on your front gate at around nine this evening.'

'We've nothing to discuss.' Andrew tried to put a hard edge to his voice, but realised it was hopeless. He was worried and it clearly came through.

'See you at nine.'

The line went dead as Andrew replaced the receiver, got up and walked out. 'Maria, I'll be at home for the rest of the day should any emergency arise.'

She nodded without comment. There were no emergencies in this place. It ran like clockwork, thanks to loyal staff and the keen interest in their welfare from both Chloe and Andrew. However, she could see Andrew was a nervous wreck. Something or someone had got right under his skin. Did this have anything to do with his last call?

22

The front gate chimed right on time. Andrew was standing in the doorway as Petreus walked down the driveway.

'Good evening Andrew. It's good of you to see me.'

'I didn't have much of a choice,' Andrew replied as he showed him in. 'Can I get you a drink?'

'A good Chivas on the rocks if you've got it.'

Andrew poured the drink and handed it to Petreus who was studying the expensive surrounds.

'So, the point of your visit is?' Andrew had decided to face this dilemma head on. What did Petreus want and had Evans sent him? He would have to be careful.

'Let's make clear the ground rules first. Whatever, is said in this room stays here. I realise you suspect I'm acting on Carl's instructions, but I can assure you I'm not. I'm here as a free agent. Evans has some hold on you, that much I have deduced, so tell me what it is and maybe I can help.'

'If that's what you've come here for Johan, you're wasting your time. Please leave now.'

'Sit down Andrew and stop spinning your wheels. I've as much regard for Evans or Maggot, or whatever you call him, as you do. I can't stand his guts, but that doesn't mean I won't do business with him. He's got the money and plenty of it, whereas I have the know-how and you have the property and appropriate exploration permits. My dilemma is how to put it all together so we all win.'

Andrew was weighing up what Petreus was saying, but could it be a trap? But why would Maggot resort to that when he knew he had him cornered. There was no way out for him. He had not alternative, but to accept his terms.

'Evans has something on you. I'm correct, aren't I?'

Andrew shook his head in denial as he slowly swirled the scotch in his glass. How much did this fellow really know?

'That denial is a lie Andrew. You're shit-scared of Evans. He's threatened your life?' Petreus let out a low whistle. 'Let me rephrase that. He's threatened your family. He's hit you right in the guts where it hurts most. Don't bother denying it, I can see it clearly now. What's the point in threatening to harm you when he can go for your weak spot?'

Andrew raised his eyes to meet Petreus' smirk and look of accusation. He nodded slowly. 'Yes, he has, but there's not much you or I can do about it.'

'Let me put a question to you. If Evans was not on the scene threatening you or your family, would you be prepared to deal with me?'

'I don't particularly like what you're inferring. I'm not prepared to get mixed up in any criminal activities.'

'I'm not suggesting anything. It's a plain enough question. Would you be prepared to deal with me if Evans dropped his threats against you and pulled out? You put up the money for exploration and drilling and I retain twenty five percent interest in the project.'

'I would have to run it past Chloe and give it some consideration. I've no authority to give you an immediate answer. I don't know what you're proposing to do about Evans and I don't want to know. I can assure you if anything happens to him and Chloe or I get pulled into it, any deal would immediately be off.'

'That's all I want to know.' Petreus drained his glass. 'Well, I'll be going. Don't look so worried Andrew, our discussion has been completely off the record. For now I would suggest you give Evans the nod and go along with his proposal. Would you mind phoning for a cab please?'

The meeting with Evans was brief, but the thug could not keep the grin of satisfaction off his face. 'Smart decision Andrew. I knew you would come around to accepting my proposition.'

'I had no option Carl, did I?'

'No you didn't and rest assured I wasn't bluffing about the consequences if you'd said no.'

'So where to we go from here? I imagine there's some paperwork involved?'

'I've already set it up with my lawyer to draw up an agreement. You've discussed this with your partner haven't you? I don't want any arguments or threats of withdrawal before we exchange contracts?'

'I haven't discussed it with Chloe yet, but she'll go along with it.'

'I want a better assurance than that Hanna. I want her signature on a contract before I put up a cent. You screw me around and her face won't look the same and your son will walk with a frame when his knee caps get smashed.'

'You'll get it, but don't push. It will take a month or so to persuade her she should permit exploration. Any attempt by me to stand over her will result in hitting a brick wall, You'll get exactly what you want if you just leave it to me.'

Evans glared at him. 'You've got two months at the outside Hanna. If a contract hasn't been exchanged by then, you'll leave me no alternative. Now fuck off, I've got work to do.'

Mickey gave him the usual sardonic grin as he walked out of the bar into the fresh air, his brain trying to work through the dilemma. He was trapped by events that happened years previous. In hindsight he should never have bent to Connors' threats. He should have just got out of town, but it was too late now for regrets. He had no doubt Evans would carry out his threat if he didn't deliver. He had two months at the outside, but knew it was an impossible timetable.

23

'What progress on Baracool and exploration?' Chloe had arrived back from Ascot Downs a few hours earlier and they were sitting relaxing with a glass of wine.

'You sound very enthusiastic for someone always opposed to mining.'

'I've given it a lot of thought Andrew and have really changed my mind. I also think we should look at the iron-ore on Ironstone as well.'

'What about your beloved area within Baracool? Mining would totally destroy all you've held dear.'

'Not necessarily - I believe it would be possible to excise an area which protects the sites I'm particularly interested in preserving.'

'By the way, I found the South African who you confronted.'

Chloe slowly put her glass down on the coffee table. She was nervous. 'Where did you come across him?'

'When I put feelers out for a geologist to commence the exploration program I was introduced to him.' The lie came easily, but he could not tell her the truth.

'And?'

'He apologised for having assaulted you. He didn't know who you were.'

'That doesn't give him an excuse for being on the property without permission and his apology is not good enough.

I hope you warned him off.' Chloe raised an eyebrow as Andrew's facial expression was not convincing. 'Where exactly did you meet this fellow and for what reason?'

'He claims to have discovered a copper, gold and cobalt deposit on Baracool. That's what he got so upset about when you confronted him. He'd made the discovery, but knew he shouldn't have even been on the ground.'

'You haven't answered my question. Where did you meet him?'

'I was introduced to him by an individual who is interested in putting a million dollars into drilling the prospect and promoting it onto the Securities Exchange.'

'What individual. What's his name?'

'M...Carl Evans.' Andrew had almost blundered, he was so used to mentally referring to him as Maggot.

'Never heard of him. Mind you there are so many mining millionaires around Perth these days it's way outside my area of interest to know any of them. Are you referring to the South African, or the man with the money?'

'The fellow who ran foul of you goes by the name of Johan Petreus. Evans is on the fringes of the mining business with money to burn, or so it would seem.'

They had been together long enough for Chloe to know Andrew was not telling her the whole story. There was something sinister going on. She was not going to pursue it, as it would be revealed in the course of time.

'So, what does this individual want for his million dollars?'

'Fifty percent.'

Chloe smiled thinly and nodded. 'And Petreus?'

'Twenty five percent.'

'So we're left with a quarter. Have I heard correctly?'

'That's about the size of it Chloe.'

'And you think that's a good deal, do you?'

Andrew could sense he was going to be on the receiving end of some unwelcome advice. 'I don't know whether it's the best deal we could do, but it's the only one on the table at the moment.'

'Andrew I don't believe you're thinking straight - you're hiding something. During the past week I've had a number of long discussions with Frank Devine, one of Perth's leading stockbrokers, about how to go about realising what we might have in the ground on Baracool and Ironstone Park. I got his name from our bank manager who made the introduction and assured me any discussions would be strictly confidential.'

'No doubt you were discussing iron-ore. This fellow is not interested in that. He's looking at other minerals.'

'Like copper and cobalt. You've already told me that. But when I mentioned cobalt to Devine, his attention really picked up. His tone of voice and attitude went up in decibels of interest.' Andrew made to butt in, but she cut him off. 'I thought you were smart Andrew Hanna and I know you are, so what's this about letting some individual help himself to half of a project for a million dollars. It's potentially worth hundreds of times that figure. To hell with that. We'll spend the million and we'll decide who our partners are going to be, if any.'

Andrew was shocked by her approach and statement. Suddenly, he was being confronted with the new Chloe Boyce, forceful and absolutely sure of herself. He had not seen it coming. 'What about Petreus? You're going to need him, as he can lead us straight to his discovery.'

'I want to meet Petreus before I give you an answer to that. However, I doubt very much whether we should do business with him. In any event he won't be getting his twenty five percent.'

Andrew slumped back in his chair. He was trying to think straight. 'Okay Chloe, for the moment let's just forget about the guy with the money. I indicated to him I would consider the deal, but would have to run it past you for approval. As for Petreus, we can't do without him.'

'No one's indispensable Andrew. I'm not and neither are you. If either of us fell under a bus tomorrow, the other is perfectly capable of running this organisation. You can tell your financier we're not interested. I'll leave that to you to give him the bad news. As for Petreus, I'll make up my mind after I've met him.'

'Haven't we got enough on our plates without venturing into the mining industry. It's a highly risky business where you can get burnt very easily.'

'Andrew, why the sudden about face? What could be more risky than the cattle industry? Droughts, floods, low prices and fickle Asian countries we deal with suddenly pulling the pin on orders with some opaque excuse our cattle are carrying some sort of disease. Those people don't need to be honest and upfront, it's in their very nature to try and screw us around. Why don't you come clean and tell me what's really on your mind? What are you worried about?'

Andrew held up his hands in resignation. 'I hear what you're saying Chloe and it makes sense we should go it alone. It's just that we're getting into uncharted waters.'

Chloe finished her wine and stood up. 'I'm going to bed. It's been a tiring two weeks.'

'I'll be up in awhile. There's a program on tele I want to watch.'

Chloe turned at the base of the stairs. 'Andrew, arrange a meeting with Petreus for tomorrow in the city. They won't miss you in the north if you stay a few more days down

here. And no, I don't want to meet the other person involved.
I don't like what's being offered.'

Andrew showed Petreus into the boardroom. 'A cold drink
or coffee?'

'No thanks Andrew.'

Chloe swept into the room in complete control. 'So we
meet again Mr Patreus. You've cleaned yourself up since we
last met. I trust you've paid similar attention to your attitude,
because if you haven't this meeting is over before it starts.'

Andrew was stunned. He had never heard Chloe take such
a dominant role before. It was as though the latent bud had
suddenly burst into full bloom.

'Chloe, I must apologise for my behaviour.' Petreus
attempted a disarming smile which she did not acknowledge.
'Yes, I have cleaned myself up and once again I apologise for
my actions that day. It was just that I'd made an incredible
discovery and unfortunately took the attitude I didn't have
to share its existence with anybody. I was just so excited.
I didn't know who you were as I'd seen no one in the month
I'd been there. When you flew over, it just gave me one hell
of a shock. And when I heard you land and shut down I was
trying to cover all my samples. I thought you may have been
another geologist who would have recognised what they
were and the minerals contained.'

'Mr Petreus.'

'Please call me Johan. You didn't mind when I addressed
you as Chloe, so I can we do away with the titles?'

'Okay Johan. Now tell me what you're proposing?'

'I assume Andrew has filled you in, but I believe I've found
a major deposit of copper, gold and cobalt on your property.
In return for showing you where it is, I want twenty five percent of the action.'

'And you expect this company to assume all exploration and development costs?'

'No, I don't know what Andrew has told you, but there is a company prepared to put up a million for half the project.'

Chloe began to laugh. 'So we're left with the remaining twenty five, is that it? Before you answer, perhaps I should enquire as to the name of this company? Is it a significant mining or exploration outfit, or is it some shell with no money?'

Petreus looked uncomfortable. 'I don't know the name Chloe. I've only met one of the directors.'

'What's his name?'

'Carl Evans.'

'Johan, I think this meeting is over. First you have the temerity to venture onto one of our properties without permission and now you are expecting us to swallow some story about a company which you cannot name. You are wasting your time. I was prepared to accept your apology, but on the second count you clearly are not prepared to disclose the name of the company standing behind this Evans fellow? You've just lost my trust.'

'Okay Chloe, I was bound by the investor not to disclose his identity until such times as I had some sort of verbal agreement from you. You can understand can't you?' Petreus could see his world slipping away as Chloe closed her notepad and began to rise. 'I admit the million for fifty percent is probably only an ambit claim, but would you consider taking on the project yourself? You certainly have the means to do so from what I understand of your extensive spread of business interests. If you agreed I would be prepared to negotiate on what I'm asking. It's just that you cannot lose this opportunity to realise the value of what I've discovered.'

'You are telling me you have no firm arrangements with this unnamed company or individual?'

'No I don't. I'm committed to no one.'

Andrew tried to suppress surprise. Maggot was not going to like this for one moment. Chloe and Charlie were in grave danger. His brain was in a fog as he tried to think it through.

'In that case I'll discuss it further with Andrew and we'll let you know. I admit it does sound a very interesting project, but the terms are unacceptable. Andrew will get back to you within the month and if our answer is positive, we'll then sit down and discuss terms. Has Andrew told you we're starting a minerals division to look at our iron-ore deposits? Your project would be handed to that group in the event of a deal being finalised. You will of course, have to give some thought to your interest, as what you're asking for is too high.'

'I beg to disagree Chloe. I've made the discovery. I should be entitled to a significant percentage of what I've found.'

'The problem with that Johan is you have no title to what you've found, I do. When our team of geologists is established I don't think it would take them long to locate your discovery and in that event you would wind up with absolutely nothing.'

Petreus made to answer, his desperation apparent as all appearance of the confident negotiator evaporated.

'Johan, let's leave it at that for now. I will make you a promise however and that is we won't cut you out. You are entitled to something, but we haven't established exactly what that will be at this point. I would advise you to accept my advice now and leave.'

They watched him walk out. Andrew was still in a state of confusion at Chloe's attitude. What had brought about this transformation? He remained silent waiting for her to say something. He slowly turned his head to see her eyes boring into him.

'What are you up to Andrew? One thing I've learned from you over the years is how to negotiate from both a position of strength and weakness. I have the distinct feeling you would accept any terms and that denotes weakness. Why I would agree to those terms just doesn't make sense. I think you'd better come clean with me.'

'It passed the smell test with me. I thought it was a good deal as it wouldn't cost us a cent.'

'Andrew, don't try that on me. You taught me the game, but even before any real negotiations have started you're ready to throw in the towel. I can see you're stressed to hell. When I came down this morning you were non compos on the couch with an empty bottle of scotch beside you. I'm not suggesting you drank the lot, but you must have given it a good nudge.'

Andrew put his head in his hands. 'Yeah, I'm really feeling the effects of it.'

'So what's worrying you?'

He did not move or look up at her. 'There are problems I can't tell you about at the moment. I need time to sort them out.'

Chloe was worried. 'We've never had secrets. What have you got yourself into? What are the problems you're referring to? You must tell me.'

'I can't. I just can't. Please understand.'

Chloe sat back looking at the crushed form before her. Where had all his strength gone? Two weeks ago she had left the usual fully confident Andrew Hanna, but now she was looking at a prime case of major depression.

'It has something to do with Petreus, doesn't it? If it's not him, then it must be the person offering to pitch in a million dollars.' She slammed her open hand on the table. 'For god's sake tell me what's going on.'

He sat up with a jerk. He had never heard such an angry tone of frustration. 'Chloe I can't tell you what it is at this moment. I'm heading north again in the morning, so give me the two weeks to think it through. I promise I'll give you the full story by the time I get back.'

'I think you need help and by that I mean mental counsel. I've never seen you like this before. You are worrying the hell out of me. Can't you see that?'

Andrew reached out and covered her hand. 'I know, but let's just leave it there for now. Give me the two weeks I'm asking for.'

Chloe pulled her hand away and stood. 'Okay, but I don't think you should go north. I think the problem is right here in town and you should stay and sort it out.' She left him sitting at the boardroom table as she went out to mingle with the staff as though nothing had happened. He could hear her laughing as she made her rounds, stopping at everyone's desk or work station.

He was sitting in his car in the basement car park when his phone rang. He glanced at the number and was about to let it go to message bank when he changed his mind. No use trying to dodge the inevitable.

'Hello Carl. What can I do for you?'

'I take it the proposition didn't go down well with your other half?'

'You don't have to ask me that. Obviously Johan has brought you up to date. You'll just have to give me time to work on it. I'm away for the next two weeks. You'll get what you want, just don't push it.'

There was a peel of mocking laughter. 'I'm going to push it hard as I can Hanna. If I haven't got the answer I'm looking for when you get back, you know what to expect and I'm not bluffing.'

'I hear you loud and clear Carl. I'll speak to you in two weeks.' He didn't wait for an answer as he pushed the disconnect. Petreus must have high-tailed it back to report in as soon as he left the meeting. He put the car in gear and slowly drove out of the building. There was no way out of the problem. He would simply have to tell Chloe what was happening when he got back. The police would become involved, but how long could he hide from Evans, or protect Chloe and Charlie? The thug was vicious and would no doubt eventually seek him out for revenge.

Chloe drove him out to the airport in the morning. She was bright and cheerful, but he could see it was a shallow attempt. They had been together too long not to know each other's moods and thought processes.

She leaned over and reached out to pull his head towards her. 'Don't worry yourself sick darling. I need you, we're a team.' She kissed him gently on the cheek, before he turned and they embraced. She patted him on the back and gently pushed him towards the door. He stepped out and retrieved his bag off the back seat. 'And keep off the booze while you're up there. It won't solve anything.' He had no time to answer as she accelerated away.

Andrew slowly shook his head as he headed for the waiting jet. For Chloe to say something, the stress must be very visible.

24

Chloe was idly watching the meter on the pump racking up the dollars when she became aware of a motor bike swerving around her and pulling up at the pump directly in front. She watched as the heavily tattooed character wearing a leather jerkin over a sleeveless denim shirt, faded jeans and motorcycle boots alighted and took off his helmet. The expression was fixed – the face hard and devoid of feeling. He stood for a moment just glaring at her before a thin smile appeared for an instant.

Charlie wandered up to the bikie as he unhooked the pump. 'Mind if I look at your bike mister?'

'Help yourself kid. Too big for you to ride though.'

'Might be now, but I would be able to handle it before too long.'

'Ride bikes already do you?'

'Yeah, we've got a lot of mustering bikes at the station. I'm down here at boarding school, but I go rounding up cattle and just messing around on them when I'm at home.'

'Where's home?'

'Ascot Downs in the Kimberley.'

'That your Mum eh?' The bikie nodded towards Chloe who had just walked off to pay for the fuel.

'Yep, that's her.'

'You want to come for a ride on my bike?'

'I'd love to, but I can't right now. Anyhow I don't think Mum would let me.'

The bikie took a spare helmet out of the saddlebag and put it on Charlie's head. 'You've got a phone I see. Hop up on the pillion and I'll take a selfie.' The bikie swung into his seat and pulled on his helmet. 'Lean to one side. You can tell your mates you met a real bikie when you get back to school.' He handed the phone back.

Charlie was grinning from ear to ear below the oversized helmet when he felt the bike fire into life. The surge of power threw him onto the backrest as it leapt forward. He grabbed at the thick waist of the rider to hold on.

'Hey stop mister. I want to get off.' Charlie was looking around desperately for the help of his mother who had burst through the swing doors and was running towards them.

'I'm taking him home lady. Just follow me,' the bikie yelled.

Chloe was in her car in an instant and quickly fell in behind the bike which accelerated away in bursts she could not hope to match, before dropping back within the speed limit for her to catch up. The bikie looked around and laughed as he teased her by constantly repeating the action. Charlie turned and waved as the bikie made all the right turns. Within five minutes they had pulled up in front of the house.

'Did you enjoy that kid?'

"Sure did, but my Mum's going to be mad at both of us. You'd better go if you want to live.'

The bikie laughed. 'She's that bad is she?'

'You're going to find out mister,' Charlie replied handing back the helmet and taking off through the opening front gate which Chloe had triggered.

She swung the car across the footpath into the driveway and pulled up with a heavy foot on the brakes. The door flew open as she emerged in blind fury.

'What the hell do you think you're playing at? You kidnapped my son.'

'Calm down Chloe, I only took him for a ride. He really
enjoyed it and I've delivered him safely home without breaking any bones.'

Chloe was stunned and pulled up short. 'How do you know
my name?'

'I feel I'm going to get to know you very well Chloe Boyce,
or is it Hanna? And I'm sure Charlie loved the ride. He's a
really nice kid with nice manners which is rare these days.'
The grin delivered the desired message as he opened the
throttle and took off in a reverberating roar of power from
the straight-through exhausts.

She turned to her son who was trying to make himself
very inconspicuous just inside the gateway. 'Did you tell him
my name?'

Charlie knew when his mother was angry, but she was
beyond that stage now. He had never seen her like this
before. She was breaking down in tears. 'No, I didn't Mum.
I couldn't get off the bike. He just took off.'

'Why did you get on the bloody thing? Why did you tell
him your name?'

'I didn't tell him my name and he didn't ask. He just took
my phone and told me to get on and he would take a selfie.
I thought he was just being friendly. I didn't know what he
intended. But what's the big deal, I'm home aren't I?'

'You stupid, stupid boy. Come here.'

Charlie hesitantly moved from the shelter of the gateway
post expecting the worst. She had never hit him before, but
he could feel it coming now, she was just so angry. He closed
his eyes and waited for the blow. Instead he felt himself
being crushed in her arms as the tears developed into sobs of
shock and relief. She held him until they subsided and then

pushed him away holding him by the shoulders and looking into his eyes.

'Promise me you'll never do anything like that again? Say it,' she demanded as she shook him.

'I promise Mum. I'm sorry, I really am.' He threw his arms around her neck and buried his face into her shoulder. She grabbed him around the torso and hugged him with all her strength.

'Hey Mum, you can let me go. You're killing me.'

'I will kill you if you ever repeat what you've just put me through.' She kissed him on the cheek as she released her grip. 'Now go inside.'

Charlie had poured himself a cold drink and was making a sandwich after she put the car away and walked in. 'You okay now Mum?'

'I'm okay Charlie, but I'll never get over it.'

'I can't wait to tell Dad when he gets back. And my mates at school will be impressed.' He began to scroll through the phone looking for the selfie. 'I bet none of them have ever been taken for a ride by one vicious looking dude like this fellow.'

'That's because none of them would be stupid enough to get on the bike in the first place,' Chloe snapped. 'And you're not to say a word to your father either. It's strictly between you and I. Have you got that?'

Charlie nodded. 'I'll delete the selfie then. I won't show it to anyone.'

'No, no, send it to me now.'

She saw Charlie's thumb move. 'There you go, you've got it. But why don't you want me to show it to Dad?'

'Because I said you're not to. You're father has been under a lot of stress lately, he's been so busy. You just saw what effect this event has had on me. Your father would immediately want to take this matter further, most probably to the police. But I don't want that and I don't want you subjected to any investigation.'

'Yeah, I thought he was a little touchy when I saw him last. He wasn't the usual ball of fun to be around. It took me all my time to get him to take me to the surf club. What do you think is wrong?'

'Why don't you stop asking questions and go for a swim? Make yourself scarce for awhile and get out of my hair.'

Chloe slumped into a chair as she watched Charlie finish making the sandwich and amble outside with it in hand. He would be in the pool in a second, all clothes discarded. What was Andrew hiding? The bikie was no casual incident. It was fully rehearsed with a clear message, but to who and what, was something she could not figure out. It just didn't make sense. Andrew would have to come clean. It was clear now he was carrying too much of a burden he couldn't handle.

She picked up her phone, but put it down again. It would have to be a face to face confrontation where she would be able to tell immediately if Andrew was continuing to lie, which she was sure he would. There just wasn't enough personal contact in a phone call. He would be able to make some excuse everything was fine and would explain it when he got back. That would give him too much time to think of appropriate answers. In any event, if she told him of what had just happened he would immediately return. Better to let him relax for a couple of weeks and see whether it had relieved any of the apparent stress. Charlie was not going to be out of her sight during that time.

The strain on his face was obvious as he walked in the door trying to act his normal cheerful self. Chloe did not return the greeting.

'What's the long face about?'

Chloe opened her phone and began to scroll down. 'Do you know this person?'

Andrew shook his head, but could not hide the shock of who he was staring at. The face had to be something to do with Evans. 'No I don't. Who is he and what's Charlie doing on the pillion?'

'Are you sure you've never seen him before?'

'Quite sure.'

'Don't lie to me Andrew. You know very well who he is.'

He lifted his eyes to meet hers. 'No I don't, but I can guess his occupation. He doesn't have film star looks, does he? How did Charlie get onto his bike?'

'I stopped at a gas station and was inside paying when I saw this fellow talking to Charlie. I didn't think much of it until I glanced around moments later and saw Charlie sitting on the bike with the helmet on. Before I could get to them, the bike was already moving. I followed them and they wound up right outside our front gate. He knew our names Andrew. Charlie says he didn't tell him, so it has to be something you know about.'

'So that accounts for the car and person sitting in our driveway?'

'I'll give you points for astute deduction,' Chloe replied sarcastically. 'Yes, I hired around the clock security, but I doubt whether it would deter your thuggish looking friend. We are in danger Andrew and I've no doubt that includes you. You've got to tell me what's going on. I demand to know now.'

His shoulders slumped as he let out a sigh of resignation. 'Come and sit down, I'll explain everything. It's not a long story, but I need a scotch to keep me together.' Chloe said nothing as she followed him through. He turned. 'Will you join me in a drink?'

'Not at this time of day. By the look of it though you've been hitting it hard. Now, for God's sake tell me what this is all about.'

Andrew leaned back in the lounge chair and related his historical involvement with Evans and the threats being made. 'So there you have it.'

'What are you going to do about it?'

'I don't believe we have any choice. We let Evans and his buddy Petreus have what they want. We'll wind up with a minority interest, but at least the threats will be removed.'

'You know it's not going to stop there Andrew. The threats will always be there. This Evans has got you on the run and he's demonstrated how easy it would be to put his threats into reality. We're all in danger, but I'm not going to allow Charlie to be exposed. Do you realise the hell you've put me through in the past couple of weeks. I can't sleep. I wake at any strange sound during the night. We can't have security parked in our driveway permanently. If Evans is going to do anything he can quite easily do it when I'm shopping with Charlie. When I turned around and saw him on that motorbike I nearly collapsed. I was trying to scream, but couldn't.' She slammed her palm on the arm of her chair. 'Do you hear me Andrew? Look at me instead of staring at the floor.'

'Do you think I haven't thought about it every moment I've been away. I never thought for a moment Evans would resort to the stunt he's pulled.'

'That wasn't a stunt,' Chloe exploded. 'He's pure evil. What would it cost to pay him off? We have the money.'

'A million plus interest he maintains I cost him would only be a down payment. We could handle that easily, but he wants more. He wants revenge for me sending him to jail. He wants the lion's share of the riches Petreus has discovered.'

'So you are resigned to giving it to him?'

'I don't know what to think, but I'm inclined to say yes. We've got plenty of money and mining is not our business. Now I've told you everything, do you have any ideas?'

'Let me think about it for awhile. One thing's for sure, I'm not going to let the likes of your friend Maggot Evans take advantage of me. I'm going to tackle him head on. I want to meet him.'

Andrew shook his head in disbelief. 'You can't do that. You run too much of a risk.'

'Just set up a meeting Andrew, or better still let's just walk in and you can introduce me. What's the name of his bar?'

He could tell by the defiant look there was no point in arguing. 'Okay, we'll do that in the morning. You can't go alone - I'm coming with you.'

25

Mickey was too late in pressing the warning buzzer. He was kneeling down filling the bar fridge when he saw two forms walk past and push open Maggot's door which was ajar.

'What the hell...?' Maggot was taken completely by surprise as he quickly terminated the phone call and stood up.

'So you're Maggot Evans?' Chloe demanded with an icy tone while trying to hide the tremors of fright.

The shock of surprise quickly turned into a broad grin. 'And you must be Chloe Boyce. Please sit down and tell me what this visit is all about.'

'This will only take a second Mr Maggot. You maintain Andrew owes you a million. You want the lion's share of a mineral project I'm not prepared to give you. You have also made threats against the welfare of me and my son. In reply I'm going to put a two million bounty on your head today. I don't think the thug you sent to intimidate me, or some other bikie animal, will be able to resist that.'

Maggot gave a shallow laugh of derision. However, Andrew could see Chloe's remarks had hit home. 'Chloe you don't know my people. They've all pledged loyalty to the chapter. All are patched members.'

Chloe pulled her phone out of her bag and opened it. She flicked through it until she found the selfie and held it in front of him, not so close as he could grab it, but close enough for him to see it. 'They may all be blood brothers Mr Maggot, but I've no doubt there are rival gangs in this town who would be glad to pick up a couple of million and see you disappear. And I wouldn't put too much trust in the loyalty of your brothers when it comes to that much money. You can also tell this patched idiot he'd better make himself scarce as I intend to lay a charge with the police. I'm sure they've already got him in their data base for past crimes.'

Chloe did not wait for the reply as she spun around and walked out. Andrew was stunned as he watched the smile fade from Maggot's face.

She was in the car, motor running and pulling away from the kerb when he flung open the passenger door and hurriedly slid in beside her. 'You certainly know how to win friends and influence people.'

Chloe glared at him before breaking into laughter. 'Do you really think I pulled it off?'

'He certainly wasn't expecting that, but it's no guarantee he won't retaliate. You're playing a dangerous game Chloe Boyce.'

She did not answer as she gripped the wheel. He could see the blood rising in her cheeks.

'Slow down Chloe. You're going way too fast.'

She swung on him. 'I did something you should have done if you had the cajones. He made the mistake of threatening Charlie and as you may or may not be aware, if you threaten the offspring of any animal species you are likely to be torn to pieces by the mother. And the same applies to humans.'

'You would really do it wouldn't you? You offer that bounty and you'll wind up in jail. Tell me you're not going to do it.'

She shook her head defiantly. 'If one of his thugs comes near me or Charlie again, I will do it. That's no idle threat.'

The security guard was asleep in his car as Chloe pulled in beside him, got out and tapped on his window. 'You can go. I'll phone your company and tell them you're no longer needed.'

'I..I must have dropped off,' he stammered as the window came down. 'I apologise for that. It won't happen again.'

'No, it's nothing you've done. It's just that I won't be requiring security any longer. I'll phone your company to let them know.'

It was with a nod of relief the guard started the engine, swung around in the driveway and drove out the gate.

'Aren't you being a bit premature?'

'No Andrew, I'm not. It was costing a thousand a day which you've just observed wasn't worth the service being provided. Anyone could have walked past him into the house. Charlie could have been snatched before we were aware he'd gone. And I believe the bounty I just put on Maggot's fat carcass will provide all the security we need.'

She turned to walk into the house and stumbled. Andrew quickly caught her as she broke into wrenching sobs as the enormity of what she had done caught up with her.

'Come on Chloe. I'm really proud of you. I think you need a stiff brandy.' The front door opened and Charlie came bounding out.

'What's wrong Mum. Why are you crying?'

She went down on one knee and wrapped her arms around the boy. 'Nothing's wrong. I'm just happy to see you.'

Charlie glanced at Andrew who gave him a shake of his head with an admonishing look not to pursue the subject.

'Something's wrong. It was only an hour or so ago I saw you last. You didn't look happy then and you're crying now. I really don't understand adults,' he said with a shrug as he walked off.

Andrew took her arm and guided her into the house. He sat her down and proceeded to pour her a drink.

He raised his glass. 'That was quite a performance you turned on. I couldn't have done it, or rather I couldn't have pulled it off with the authority you did.'

Chloe dried her eyes and nodded. 'I couldn't believe it myself. What a ghastly looking creature. He intimidated me the moment we walked in. I was inwardly shaking like a leaf.'

'I didn't notice and neither did he. Your voice was powerful. He sure got the message.' However, Andrew wasn't so sure that would be the last they would hear from Maggot Evans. He would be trawling through all his options. Threats against his life were an everyday hazard in his criminal occupation. Rival gangs vying to take over his lucrative drug turf were a constant he had to deal with. A woman storming into his office, threatening to put a price on his head had confused him, but not for long. He would be thinking how to remove that threat and still gain what he was after. Chloe didn't realise the vermin she had threatened would loom even larger and the next time it would be more serious and dangerous. In the meantime Andrew would let her assume she had removed the threat while he worked out how to counter its effect.

'You don't look happy Carl. I take it things didn't pan out with Hanna?'

'It's not him, it's her,' was the brusque reply. 'She stormed in here the other day and put a two million buck bounty on my head?'

Petreus burst out laughing. 'And you took it seriously?'

'I didn't take it as some kind of joke, if that's what you mean. I sent Lennie out to deliver a message and give her a scare, but it backfired. The idiot took off with her kid on the pillion seat. Christ, if she'd called the cops, Lennie would have been up on a charge of kidnapping. He's as thick as a brick that guy. I'll have to get rid of him, he's just too much of a liability.'

'I wouldn't do that Carl. Just give him jobs his mentality can handle. Anyway, what's this about her? I thought we were working towards an agreement with Hanna?'

Evans shook his head. 'No, Chloe Boyce is firmly in control. Hanna just followed her in here like a beaten lap dog and said nothing. She laid it on the line that if I came near her or her son she would put it around my arse is worth two mill.'

Petreus whistled softly. 'For two mill I'd better give her a call. I wouldn't want anyone beating me to that kind of money.'

The joke fell flat as Evans gave him a withering stare. To him it wasn't a joke to be ignored. He knew little of Petreus' background, but he could sense the underlying danger emitted by the cold blue eyes combined with the humourless permanent expression. He might look a no-match, but the iron-fist handshake and biceps straining the short- sleeved shirt suggested otherwise. He was an unknown quantity who had that look of being constantly aware of possible danger around him. Evans had noted one day when Mickey had barged in without knocking, Petreus had sprung to his feet and turned in an instant to face the danger. Maggot was uncomfortable with him, but he held the key to a fortune. He felt the time would come when Johan Petreus would be too much of a threat and no longer useful. He didn't look like a killer, not like any of his bunch who would kill without a second thought if their illicit existence or income was threatened. Evans ruled by fear, cross him and you died or wound up permanently crippled. Rival bikie gangs were a constant threat, but in recent times Evans had arranged a truce whereby they divided up the territory so each mob got a share they were comfortable with. However, that could disintegrate at any point when someone got greedy or felt they could horn-in on the fringes of a neighbouring fiefdom.

'Ever killed anyone Petreus?'

'I've had my share of danger Carl.'

'That wasn't the question.'

'I know, but you'll have to be satisfied with that. I don't care to go into history. I'm only interested in the future and what I can gain from it.'

Evans nodded in agreement. 'My sentiments exactly. We're going to get along fine. Now let's get down to business. What are we going to do about our present problem?'

'The way I read it, Hanna doesn't present as a problem. He will not stand in our way because of the threat to his missus and the kid. He doesn't want to see them come to any harm, but doesn't know what to do. The problem is his missus or partner or whatever you call her. She's the one that must be cracked if we are to reach an agreement granting us access to her permits. And by the look of it neither of us has made a very good start in that direction.'

'I could arrange for an accident.'

'I didn't hear you say that Carl, but that's one way of handling it. However, leave me out of that solution.'

'What ideas have you got then? You're not going to let a fortune slide through your fingers are you?'

'We have no other course than to work on Hanna in the hope he will be able to persuade his partner to come good. We don't have any other option at the moment.'

'That Chloe Boyce is one firey bitch. I thought she was going to come over the desk at me, she was so steamed up. She's got a bit of chocolate in her which probably accounts for the fire. I've seen the gins in the camps up north going at each other with sticks and clubs. They're worse than the fellas when it comes to fighting. I'll give her one thing though, she one good looking broad. In fact she's bloody beautiful. Apparently she was an international model who chucked it all in and swapped the glamour for the stink of cow shit. I would love to give her a roll in the hay. That Hanna is one lucky guy.'

'I can vouch for her stunning looks and I've also been on the receiving end of her aggression. Where did she get her money from? I didn't think the abo's had the brains to run any operation, they're so fucked up with alcohol.'

'Rumour has it her father was a white gin-jockey who ran a cattle duffing operation from his property in the Kimberley. He turned up his toes and she got the lot. But from what I can gather it was Hanna who has been the brains behind her acquiring a whole string of grazing properties, a major abattoir as well as the biggest trucking operation in the north. Her whole operation is vertically integrated due to him.'

'And she's got vast iron-ore deposits in the Pilbara which remain untouched, as well as the copper deposit I've discovered, which alone is worth a fortune. She could buy and sell us out of her petty cash tin.'

'What concerns me is the statement she could, or is intending to set up an exploration subsidiary. I've checked and she's only got less than two years left on her exploration permits, then all the ground becomes open to new applications.'

'That maybe so Carl, but if she starts work she'll be able to show she is complying with the terms of licences and can renew them. I don't know if she's got any political clout, but it's possible she could just keep rolling them over.'

'So, if we don't move now, we're liable to miss the opportunity. Leave it with me Petreus. I need time to think it through. Give me a week or so to figure it out.'

Petreus nodded to Mickey as he walked through and out into the overcast day. He grinned to himself. He could read Evans' mind, but whether he had the guts to put it into operation was another matter. He would give him a week to come up with a solution, then he would put his own plan into operation. He was not going to play around if the fat useless bag of lard failed.

Evans made sure Petreus had left the premises before picking up his mobile and hitting speed dial.

'Lennie, I want to speak to you stat. Be here in half an hour. And don't park out the bloody front.' He did not wait for an answer as he put the phone down again, leaned back in chair and swung his studded motorcycle boots up onto his desk. He waited for the throaty sound of a Harley as it pulled into the large garage in the rear or the building. A minute later Lennie tapped on his door, waited for a second for the guttural entry call and pushed it open. Evans signalled for him to come in and sit down.

'What's this all about boss?'

'You really screwed up you lame-brain. I should tear your head off for frightening the shit out of that Boyce broad.'

Lennie adopted a pained expression as he threw his arms wide. 'But you told me to give her the message and that's exactly what I did.'

'You kidnapped her son. If she lays charges you're going to be back in the can serving eighteen months or more.'

Lennie grinned like the retard he was. The motorcycle accident that nearly killed him had left him with brain damage. For all that though, he was rat-cunning. 'She doesn't know who I am, so I'm not worried about that.'

'Lennie, you took a selfie with the kid. The fact you had your helmet on won't save you. One look at that and the cops will be tapping on your door and I'll be forced to disown you. I'm not going down with you. Understood?'

Lennie sat back stunned. 'I'd better get out of town then. I'll pack my things and head east first thing in the morning.'

'You're not going east numb-nuts, I'm sending you north. I've got a job for you.'

'What kind of job? I thought you said you didn't want me as part of your courier team?'

'That hasn't changed. You're so bloody stupid you'd be selling shit to any undercover cop riding a Harley. Anyway, it's not my area any longer. I've sold the franchise to a new mob.'

'You're paying for my trip are you?'

'All expenses paid Lennie. You are not to use a credit card. In fact I want you to leave your phone behind so you cannot be connected with what I have in mind. I'll get you a replacement so you can report in. You're not to use your bike. I'll get you a vehicle and some camping gear. You're not to stay in motels or go near hotels. Have a shave, get rid of that long hair and all your bikie clothing for this assignment. Wear a hat at all times and dress like you're a local and not the criminal beacon which will flash every time you roll into some outback town.'

'Just a minute. Who the hell do you think you're talking to?'

'I'm talking to some dumb shit who could be arrested at any moment. Don't you understand I'm trying to save your arse?'

'What the hell am I supposed to do for money?'

'I'll give you all the cash you need. You only deal in cash, is that clear? When you get back I want you to head east out of my sight and out of sight of the cops.'

Lennie nodded in resignation. 'Okay, tell me what am I supposed to be doing up north?'

26

He was walking into the hangar which housed the helicopters and other small aircraft belonging to the company.

'Hi there Andrew, you planning to go somewhere?' The engineer had the cowl up on one side of the Squirrel.

'Yes Jerry, I want to go up to the freight division and discuss something with management. I'll be away until early this afternoon.'

'Give me an hour and I'll have this one prepared for you. I've just finished a maintenance check, but I've got to fill out the paperwork and gas it up.' Jerry saw him glance across at the R44. 'No, you can't take that as I'm about to look for a fault in the fuel gauges. One of them is out of whack. It may take me a minute or an hour to rectify. Hey, what are you doing here anyway? I thought this was Chloe's two week stint? That's why I'm doing the maintenance.'

'No, she couldn't make it. She wanted to attend one of Charlie's sports days. Would you put this machine out on the apron when you're finished. I'll be back in an hour.'

'Sure, but I'll put the R44 out as well if it's airworthy – just take your pick.'

There was no sign of Jerry when he returned. Both machines were sitting on the apron. He circled the Squirrel and then changed his mind – the R44 was a lively alternative he had not flown for some months. It would have been thoroughly inspected by the engineer, but he followed strict procedure as he dipped the oil and checked the fuel. He pulled out the log book to make sure Jerry had signed off on it. A minute later after strapping himself in and going through his cockpit checks, he flicked the master on and engaged the starter. The machine rocked as the two blades started to turn slowly before reaching lift-off revs. After a final check of the instruments he gently pulled the collective up to increase power and put the cyclic just forward of neutral to control the attitude. It gave him a thrill as he reached transition and the chopper was in full flight. He headed out over open country following the entry road to the station. Out of the corner of his eye he saw someone running from the direction of the hangars towards a vehicle parked out of sight beyond a clump of dense bush. He thought it curious, and turned the chopper to follow. Suddenly his mind went blank as his hand dropped from the cyclic. The machine began to spin out of control. In a brief flash of consciousness he managed to lower the collective and point the nose down in a futile effort to retain inertial speed of the blades to prevent the inevitable stall. His brain and sight switched off and on like a semaphore lamp. One moment he was fighting for control and the next everything was opaque. He saw the trees coming towards him.

Chloe picked up the phone and gave a cheery hello as she recognised the voice. The colour drained from her face as she slowly sank back into the chair, her world an absolute mirror of despair.

'Is....is he dead?' There was a pause as she drew in her breath. She could feel her heart starting to race. 'How badly is he injured?'

There was another long pause as she listened. The news was all bad as far as she could gather - broken legs and an arm as well as serious head injuries. The possibility of spinal injuries was high on the list. She fought to keep her composure and the tone of panic out of her voice.

'Have you called the Flying Doctor? Four hours before they can get there? That's too long to wait. Jerry's rated to fly the Falcon. Just do it immediately and get Andrew down here. Yes, yes I understand he might have serious spinal injuries, but I've got to take that risk. He can be here in Perth before the Flying Doctor reaches you. I'll have an ambulance waiting at the airport. Now please Ray, get off the bloody phone.' She did not wait for a reply as she switched off.

Chloe new she could depend on Ray Massie, the overall manager of her vast holdings. Although a man with a tough exterior she had seen his compassionate side and devotion to both Andrew and herself. From being involved in cattle duffing and on the verge of being charged with the offence, Andrew had seen the merit in maintaining the man and promoting him, something that Massie had never forgotten. He would look after Andrew.

The twin engines of the jet were still spooling down when the stairway dropped and the over-size doors were swung open. The two paramedics hurried aboard with medical equipment. Chloe was immediately behind them looking for any signs of life from the form on the stretcher. His head was bound. His protruding legs were strapped in splints while the bandaging on the broken arm was oozing blood from a compound fracture. The medics quickly checked his blood pressure and lifted his eyes lids to reveal the deep concussion. One medic took a syringe out of his kit, filled it from an ampule and pushed it into the exposed arm, the only limb not damaged.

'How is he?' Chloe asked quietly, afraid of the answer.

The medic looked at her without answering. He did not have to. She clearly understood the telepathy as they prepared to move him. She glanced at Massie, but did not have to ask the same question, it was clearly visible.

'Do you know what happened Jerry?' She was standing on the tarmac watching as they manoeuvred the stretcher down the stairway and into the back of the ambulance.

'I don't know Chloe. I'd just serviced the machine and signed off on it. I wasn't expecting Andrew this week.'

'You didn't see it crash?'

'Yes, it was a good half a kilometre away when I walked out of the hangar and saw it heading for the ground out of control. I knew it was going to be a bad scene. Luckily Ray was just driving up so he took off to phone you and the Flying Doctor.'

'Was Andrew conscious when you got to him?'

'Yes and no. He just drifted in and out muttering, but really making no sense. It took us some time to get him out of the wreckage, bandage him up and stabilise him as best we could. Luckily the fuel tanks didn't rupture otherwise there would have been no hope. We gave him a couple of shots of morphine while he was in the wreckage. I was petrified he'd suffered a spinal injury which you know is quite common when these machines go down. I just pray I haven't caused any real damage by moving him. It's the probably the last thing I should have done.'

Chloe put her hand on his shoulder. 'Jerry, it was my decision to fly him down. You had no option but to get him out and patch him up as best you could. I understand all about the odds of him winding up a paraplegic if he has serious spinal damage. But it was my decision, I don't hold you responsible.'

'I just hope I've not missed anything when doing the service - it would kill me if I've stuffed up.'

'I've no doubt Civil Aviation inspectors will determine that when they do a thorough inspection of the wreck. But I know you well enough to assure me you've not missed a thing.'

'Thank you for that vote of confidence Chloe. I daresay it will take a couple of months before CA hands out their findings. What would you like me to do now?'

'You're in no condition mentally to fly back today, so you and Ray take the car and let yourselves into my house and get some rest. Help yourself to whatever you want. I'm going in the ambulance.'

Chloe was well aware Jerry's main concern was Andrew's condition and prognosis. He also had the combined stress of the time it would take for the CA report. If he had overlooked something his licence as an engineer would be subject to cancellation or at best a restriction of what types of aircraft he could work on.

She kept looking at the unconscious figure lying on the stretcher with the medic constantly checking his vital signs while the other drove with sirens and lights clearing the way at maximum speed. It seemed like only minutes later Andrew was being unloaded and rushed through to emergency admissions as she followed closely behind. The senior medic described the injuries to a doctor who took immediate control, assessed the situation and gave urgent commands. Chloe was ignored as Andrew disappeared. A nurse took her by the arm and directed her towards a waiting room.

'You can wait in here. Can I get you a tea or coffee?'

'No, I'm fine thank you. How long will it be before I know anything?'

'I really can't tell you, but I'm sure one of the doctors will come and talk to you in due course. You may be in for a long wait. Would you prefer to go home? I'll have you phoned as soon as we have any news.'

Chloe shook her head and sat down. The nurse quietly walked away. She was used to witnessing utter distress and from what she had observed the prognosis did not look good for this patient. She had seen the imperceptible shake of the trauma surgeon's head as he gently lifted the eyelids and shone a penlight into the dilated pupils.

Other people came and went from the waiting room. Every time Chloe saw a white coat appear in the corridor outside her heart took a leap, but the coat never stopped as medical staff hurried past in both directions. It was a blur of gurney's and people, some sobbing while others just appeared to be in a state of catatonic shock. As the night progressed there were the shouts and obscene language from a steady stream of drunks and drug addicts and the demands of individuals trying to get priority for their minor ailment. Then there were the mutes who just stared silently at the doorway waiting patiently for someone to give them attention. The world outside was oblivious to the suffering within, no one cared nor understood until something happened to them, or a relative or friend.

Chloe became one of the mutes, just sitting there trying to comprehend what had happened and contemplating the worst. She could not put it out of her mind as she kept glancing at her watch and then at the corridor. A nurse appeared in the doorway and beckoned her to follow. They seemed to walk forever in silence until finally the nurse pushed open a door to a small office. The tired looking doctor she had seen on admission was writing some notes. He glanced up and indicated a seat before putting down his pen.

'I'm sorry, but I don't have very good news for you. I take it he is your husband?'

Chloe nodded. What was the point of correcting the assumption. She had prepared herself for it, but the shock of the initial statement suddenly came in a finite wave of despair.

'Is he dying?'

The doctor hesitated before slowly nodding. 'I don't think he will see it through the next few hours. His condition is beyond critical, it's terminal. He has suffered a massive stroke.'

'Was that a result of the accident?'

'No, I don't think so. Our scans show he has suffered a pre-existing brain trauma. Do you know anything about that?'

Chloe started to shake her head and then the scene flashed back. 'Yes, someone attacked him some years ago. I'd forgotten about it.'

'He should not have been flying anything. He should never have held a licence, not even a licence to drive a car. He must have been aware of this, but chose to ignore the consequences. From what I've been told he was alone, so that's some consolation. These types of crashes in small helicopters invariably result in death.'

Chloe was shocked by the blunt comments. They were completely clinical with very little expressed compassion. 'So the crash was the result of the stroke?'

'Undoubtedly, in my opinion. I must be frank with you, he was living on a time-bomb which finally exploded. It could have happened at anytime and it wouldn't have made any difference if he'd been seated at the kitchen table, or in bed - the result would have been the same, but without the present injuries.'

Although abrupt, the tone was as gentle as he could make it. He had been through this situation countless times as the messenger of terminal news. It was never easy, but there was no point in prolonging it or holding out false hope. Some fainted, some burst into hysteria and tears, some screamed for him to do more, some nodded in submission, some thanked him, while others just got up and walked out. He waited for a reaction until a slow smile appeared.

'Thank you doctor. We had some wonderful years together. I should be thankful I've still got something of him, our son.'

'Can I bring up another delicate subject. It's...'

Chloe held up her hand to stop him. 'I know what you're going to ask and the answer is yes, you may. I know that's what Andrew would want.'

The doctor pushed across the form he had been filling in. 'Would you authorise this then for me please.' He handed her a pen and pointed to the signature line. 'Are you sure you don't want to read it? Do you want to discuss this with any members of his family.'

Chloe shook her head. 'That won't be necessary. His son and I are his family. There's no one else.'

'I would like to thank you most sincerely for the gift of life your husband will give to someone else.'

Chloe did not bother to correct the lie she had just perpetrated. She was his wife. Why was a piece of paper the sole arbiter of a union? She could never understand why they had not married, that was until recently. Initially she had been angry and determined to confront him with the truth, but calmed down as she sifted through the facts. He had never lied to her, he had simply stalled a commitment which would have required a signature and admission. But the thought lingered – what else had he hidden?

'Could I see him now?'

The doctor stood and put his hand behind her back as he gently guided her out. She clamped a hand to her mouth and let out a guttural cry of grief when she saw him. He was beyond recognition with a heavily bandaged head and bruised swollen face. One splinted arm was lying on top of the sheet. Sensors stuck to his chest and head - machines with glowing lights blinked in patterns. One screen just had a flat red line running through it. She kissed him on the forehead and lips as she tried to restrain the sobs of grief.

'He's dead isn't he?'

The doctor nodded. 'He has no brain function whatsoever.'

'You have my permission to turn the life support off then. I don't want our son to see him like this.'

A nurse hurried up and passed the doctor a note which he opened and read. 'Oh, I can't do that immediately Ms Boyce. A close relative has just contacted the registrar requesting no action be taken until he arrives tomorrow morning. There may be an objection to your consent.'

'Did that person give his name?'

'He did, but I'm not at liberty to disclose it.'

'I see. I believe I know his identity, but I have no objections. I'm sympathetic to his request.'

'Why don't you go home and rest and come in again around eight in the morning. I believe he will be here by then.'

Jerry was watching tele when she walked in and tossed her coat and bag onto a chair. 'Be a good chap and poor me a stiff cognac would you. Where's Ray?'

'He's in a bedroom out back. Do you want me to get him, he's not in a good state?'

'No, leave him be.'

'How's Andrew?'

'He's brain dead Jerry. I'm going back in the morning to turn off the life support. I would have done it tonight, but a relative is flying in first thing.'

'Who's that? I've never heard Andrew talk about relatives and I've never met any. Do you know who it is?'

'I believe I do, but I'll know for sure in the morning.' She sat back as Jerry handed her the drink. 'Did Andrew happen to say anything when you got to the crash site?'

'Not really. He was quite lucid for about thirty seconds and then he just collapsed.'

'What did he say?'

'He muttered something about seeing someone running towards a vehicle parked out of sight amongst trees.'

'And that's all?'

'That's about it, but I knew it wasn't anyone from the property he'd seen. It had to be an intruder. I wondered if the chopper had been sabotaged so I phoned the homestead to get one of the boys to look at the tail rotor to see if it had been tampered with. That could have been the reason the machine suddenly went into a spiral dive. However, the rotor blades appeared to be intact, although damaged. I guess we'll just have to wait and see what Civil Aviation inspectors arrive at in their report which will take six months at least to filter through.'

27

Chloe was impervious to the hurrying orderlies and patients wandering around as she walked along the seemingly endless corridor. She pushed open one of a pair of wide doors to enter an area of stillness and quiet. One or the two nurses glanced up from behind a desk and smiled in recognition.

'He has a visitor, but you're free to go in.'

Chloe nodded as she walked towards the end of someone's life, a life she was devastated, but resigned to lose. She slowly opened the door. The person had his back to her, oblivious to her entry until she put her hand on his shoulder and gently squeezed it.

'Hello Alexander Hammond, or should I say Alexander Hanna? I'm pleased you could make it.'

He looked at her in surprise as she took a seat on the other side of the bed. His eyes were bloodshot, there was no hiding the effect of the tears.

'You know who I am then?'

Chloe smiled as she gave a shallow laugh. 'Alex, the moment I first set eyes on you, I knew who your father was. Andrew tried to hide you away by burying you in our trucking and freight operations. If I recall, that was close to a year ago.'

'Yes, Dad gave me the job when I graduated from university. He wanted me to start at the bottom and work up. I hated it at first, but I can now understand his reasons. He told me to keep my head down and out of sight if you should visit, which he said was very rare. But I guess my profile was not low enough.'

'I blew in one day without warning. Someone pointed you out as the IT guru working wonders in coordinating the whole freight business. You didn't see me, but there was no mistaking the likeness. I declined to be introduced to you as I didn't want to intrude on your father's secret. I've been following your progress and I hope you're going to stay with us? I must apologise to your boss when I next visit. He probably thought I didn't want to meet a lowly junior staff member, so I can now tell him the truth. What of your mother?'

'Mum died two years ago. She never married again after Dad walked out. I was born six months after he left so she gave me her maiden name. As I was growing up I used to ask who my father was, but she would never give me a straight answer. I learned to forget about him. It was when I was clearing out her things I came across a letter from Dad which mentioned me. It was clear he was replying to a letter from her. It took me a long time to track him down. The hard part was in approaching him. I just didn't know what his reaction would be, or more to the point, whether I really wanted to know him.'

'I feel for you. I could not understand why Andrew never told me he was married, although I suspected it at times. You have a brother now, named Charlie? When he was a toddler Andrew often called him Alexander by mistake when they were playing, so I gathered there was something I wasn't being made aware of.'

'Did you and Dad marry?'

Chloe shook her head slowly. 'No, we didn't and it wasn't because of me not pressuring him. He just always brushed it aside with the excuse we didn't need to be. You realise he was my whole being. The road has been long and littered with obstacles, but he overcame every one of them.'

'He loved you, I can tell you that.'

Chloe turned as the door pushed open. The doctor was standing there trying to maintain a passionate expression.

'C'mon Alex. Say your goodbyes.' She moved around the bed and took his arm. 'One life is over and another is waiting to be saved. I loved your father dearly and I can see you did as well, but it is time to move on.' She nodded to the doctor as she guided Alex out the door, down the corridors and out into the sunlight.

'I'll see you at your home later Chloe. I know the address. I just want to walk for awhile.'

She squeezed his hand and was walking through the car park when someone called out to her. 'Hi, Chloe.'

She ignored the voice until she heard footsteps hurrying up behind her. 'Chloe, hang on a moment. You probably don't remember me, Oliver Gibbs?'

Chloe turned as the person drew level. Yes, she remembered him, but not fondly. It was years before when she had walked out of his parents house after overhearing a racist and sexually offensive remark about her.

'I remember you Oliver. I remember the day and occasion very well.'

'Chloe, I just want to apologise. I was young and stupid and I've never forgotten the pain I caused you. You heard what I was saying to my father and I realised at the time that's why you walked out. I did try to phone and apologise, but your aunt said you were not taking my calls. I hung around your favourite coffee bar in the city, but you never did appear again. I followed your career in Europe and when you came back I didn't have the guts to make contact to apologise, that was until I saw you moments ago.'

'Oliver, I accept your apology. What happened had long faded from my memory until I heard your voice just now.'

He nodded and smiled. Gone was the dress and attitude of a university student. The flaxen hair had lost the casual unkempt styling to be replaced by a carefully maintained professional look which matched his suit and appearance. 'Can I ask what you're doing at the hospital? Have you been visiting a patient?'

'The patient has just died. He was my partner.'

The smile disappeared. 'Oh, I'm sorry to hear that. Can I ask whether it was the result of an accident?'

'No, it was a stroke, the result of a brain injury suffered some years ago when someone tried to murder him.'

She was still as beautiful as ever. It had to be near twenty years since he'd seen her last in person. However, he realised it would never have worked. Both were dedicated to their chosen paths, but he could see her attitude towards him had softened in the past few moments. Her voice had become softer to match the smile creeping from the upturned lips. However, it was the expression in the large brown eyes that acted as a mirror to her soul.

'If I'd known, I may have been able to assist.'

'And how would you have done that Oliver? What are you? You look like an accountant?' The remark was out before she realised what she was saying. She put her hand to her mouth. 'I didn't mean that Oliver.' She was on the verge of tears.

'I deserved that Chloe. I didn't mean to sound patronising. I can understand the grief you're going through. I'm actually a professor of forensic medicine at this hospital.'

'It's my turn to apologise Oliver. The remark was uncalled for.'

'Forget it Chloe. Can I ask whether you have any family?'

'A son Charlie. And you?'

'My wife Melissa, who I met and married in England, but no children. Say, I would love to catch up with you sometime and introduce you to Melissa.' He took a card out of his pocket and handed it to her. 'If I can ever do anything for you, please give me a call. I'm sorry for what's just happened to you.'

Chloe nodded and walked away quickly to hide the tears.

Alex was reading the morning paper when Chloe glanced over his shoulder at the photo. 'I know that person. What's it say about him?'

'Killed in a smash with a road train loaded with fuel. He's been identified as a member of a bikie gang. Has served time for drugs, assault and manslaughter so I can't see too many people mourning his passing. He was seen in an outback roadhouse and died about an hour later on the road to Broome trying to outrun the police. Look at this photo of the vehicle. There isn't much of it left. How do you know him?'

'Oh, paths cross in life Alex. He abducted Archie on his motorbike, brought him here and then threatened me.'

'That must have been scary. Did you report it to the cops?'

'I was still thinking about it until I saw that photo, so there's no point now.'

Chloe was lost in thought about the person Andrew had seen running before he crashed. She had no doubt now it was Maggot's associate and he could have sabotaged the chopper. Ray Massie had checked when he got back to the homestead, but reported the blades appeared to be intact with all the retaining bolts wired in place. Jerry had reported he saw it go into a spin which would suggest the tail rotor had come apart. She shuddered at the thought of all the times she had flown with Andrew as pilot and what might have happened to her or Charlie or any of the staff. It was entirely irresponsible on his part, but maybe he wasn't aware of the danger. It was pure negligence on the part of the medical examiner who had recently signed off on his flying licence renewal – not that it would have made any difference from what she now knew.

28

Maggot shook his head in despair as he threw the newspaper aside. He was pleased he no longer had to suffer the brain-damaged Lennie, who had been identified as the bikie threatening that bloody Boyce woman and her kid. Would she blame him for Hanna's crash and trigger the bounty she had threatened? Could the cops link Lennie to the crash? He sat back and recalled the phone call

'What is it Lennie?'

'Mission accomplished Carl – you owe me twenty grand.'

'Which one did you get – Boyce or Hanna?'

'Hanna. There's no way he could have survived that crash.'

'Well that's where your wrong. He's down here in hospital so he must be alive. If he dies you'll get your money, but if he doesn't you are out of luck – I only pay for results. By the way how did you do it?'

'It wasn't easy. I cased the place for a day just to get the layout. There was always someone around so I had to be careful. The mechanic almost caught me hiding in the back of the hangar when Hanna rolled up and distracted him. There were two choppers and I wasn't sure if I would have the time to nobble them both. However, the mechanic told Hanna he could take either machine if they were both out on the apron, but Hanna said he preferred the Squirrel. That gave me enough time to take a hacksaw to the tail rotors – I sawed them halfway through right up near the hub so they wouldn't easily be noticed. I was about to do the same to the smaller machine when I saw Hanna returning – I hot-footed it out of there.'

'And you witnessed the crash did you?'

'Yep, but I think he spotted me as he turned in my direction before he suddenly went down.'

'And other than him, no one saw you?'

'Not a soul. I'm on my way back to collect my money.'

'You'll collect if he's dead. I'll know by the time you get back. And keep off the drugs and booze.' Maggot disconnected the call. For once in his life Lennie had proved useful.

What Lennie had not told him was he thought he was in trouble when he saw the police Toyota approaching at speed as he pulled out of his concealment onto the solitary track leading out of the station. He had intended to wait until nightfall before breaking cover. No ambulance had appeared and he heard a jet take off so he assumed it was carrying a corpse or injured patient. He cursed his luck and impatience – he had been waiting for hours and in another five minutes they would not have crossed paths. The Toyota did not slow down as it sped past and neither did he as he put his foot down. He was puzzled as to what had happened – it was the smaller machine that had crashed. He had not had time to do anything to it when he saw Hanna returning. He shrugged – what the hell, he'd picked up twenty grand if Hanna died – he had to be as good as dead as no one could have survived a crash at the speed it hit the ground. And he knew it was Hanna because he had seen him get in and startup.

'Holy shit.' The constable was looking at what was left of the chopper. 'You mean he survived this mess?'

The station hand shook his head – grief written all over his face. 'He was alive when we pulled him out and put him on the jet to Perth, but I don't give much for his chances.'

'You witnessed it did you?'

'No, I didn't - Jerry, the person who witnessed it is flying the jet.'

'Any idea how it happened?'

'Not a clue. I was just leaving the homestead with Ray Massie when I heard it hit the ground less than half a kilometre away. Jerry was first on the scene and apparently Andrew did mutter something before he passed out. It was something about seeing someone running from the direction of the hangar towards a vehicle parked in bush, which I assume is that heavy patch over there.'

The sergeant looked to where he was pointing. 'We'll take a look at that. Have any vehicles entered or left the station since the accident?'

'You're the only vehicle.'

The sergeant pulled out his notebook and flipped it open. 'What's your name son?'

'Luke Massie, the manager's son and Jerry's offsider.'

'Do you recognise this number plate?'

Luke looked at the pad, 'No, it's not one of ours. Where did you see that?'

'Just past that bush you've indicated. It was pulling out as we approached. I had a feeling at the time we should have pulled it over.'

'So you're thinking this may not have been an accident. I did check the wreck over as I help Jerry service it, but it's impossible to determine why it crashed. However, the government investigators will be out here in the next day or so.'

'I'm not making any assumptions. I've been too long in this business to venture down that path. However, I do think it's odd we saw a vehicle driving away and Hanna mumbled about seeing someone running. As you know, no one runs out here except from the law. The sergeant turned as climbed into the cab. 'Luke, it might be a good idea to have a thorough look over your other chopper before anyone starts it up. If someone was intent on sabotage, they could have got at both machines. In the meantime, no one is to go near this wreck, and I mean no one, until the inspectors arrive. Constable, let's go and have a look at that patch of bush.'

The wheel tracks were clear where a vehicle had driven onto the road. 'Pull in and let's see if he left any evidence.' They weaved their way through sparse trees and around a sandstone overhang until they saw a small clearing hidden from the road. 'Over there near those beer stubbies,' the sergeant pointed.

He got out and picked up a bong by his fingertips and smelt it. 'Our man's been puffing on this sometime today. And bag a couple of those stubbies – there's sure to be fingerprints on them. This fellow has got some questions to answer.'

He reached into the cab and switched on his satellite phone. He relayed the description and number of the Toyota. 'Yeah, I want this fellow apprehended for questioning in regard to a possible murder. Also make a thorough search of his vehicle for drugs. Also check whether the vehicle has been stolen. Treat him as dangerous.'

Lennie drove all night – he wanted to put Ascot Downs as far behind him as possible. He was worried about the cops, but it was the payoff from Maggot that overrode his concerns as he kept driving. He saw the parked semi-trailers and pulled into an isolated road-house for breakfast. The truckies were all talking loudly as he picked up his stacked plate of bacon, eggs, hash and a coffee. He looked around for a table where he could observe the car-park and cafe entrance – he felt trapped. He quickly finished his meal, gulped down the remainder of his coffee and picked up the remaining slice of toast as he made for the door. He did not notice a pair of eyes following him. As soon as the screen door closed the person picked up the phone on the wall behind her.

Lennie rolled himself a toke and inhaled it deep into his lungs. Reaching down he snapped the top off a stubbie and took a swig as he put the vehicle into gear. Ten minutes later he pulled another toke out of his top pocket and lit it with the dash lighter. He felt good, but nervous. If those bloody cops had got his rego number he was in danger – he would have to steal another vehicle. He had to steal another make as the cops would be on the lookout for any Toyota Landcruiser no matter what rego plates it was carrying – they would stop and check it. He was doing everything Maggot had told him not to do, but it was no use worrying now. Broome would be an ideal town to find another vehicle – it was full of tourists at this time of the year. He would be able to scout around at night and find a couple of matching targets. It was a simple matter of swapping their plates – one driver would report his car stolen while the other would be ignorant of the swap until pulled over by the cops days later. Who looked at their rego plates every time they went to start their car? Lennie grinned at the thought of how many cars he had stolen over the years and never been caught. No need to buy a car – he had his choice from the nearest parking lot. It drove the cops mad. It was time to drop this one.

They passed on a long sweeping corner. He kept his eyes straight ahead, well aware of the unmistakable RayBan's looking sideways at him. He saw the brake lights come on as it slowed, pulled off and began to make the turn. It fish-tailed as it straightened up with the blue and red lights flashing.

Lennie opened his mouth in a silent scream as he glanced up and tried to correct his drift into the oncoming lane. The blast of the air-horn and the bull-bar of forty tons of immovable force were the last thing he heard and saw as they met head on.

'Oh fuck,' the cop yelled to his partner. 'Get onto base for full backup. We need a fire truck and ambulance immediately.' He pulled off the road and jumped out just as the flames began to rise from the front of the smashed Toyota. One look told him the driver was dead, the whole firewall and steering column crushed into his body. Blinded by blood from his smashed face, the tanker driver was trying to extract himself from the distorted cab as the burly cop grabbed him, dragged him clear and swung him into a fireman's lift. It was a good hundred metres down the road when he first felt the heat and then the blast as the tanker erupted.

29

'What do you mean, you're cutting me out of the deal?'

'Chloe Boyce doesn't want you anywhere near it Carl. She doesn't want your money and is not concerned about your threats. It wasn't one of your goons who sabotaged her partner's chopper was it?'

Maggot snarled at him across his desk. 'That had nothing to do with me Petreus. Did she say it did?'

'No, she didn't, but I just thought it strange that your Lennie, who I've seen hanging around here, suddenly winds up dead not far from Boyce's homestead a couple of thousand kilometres north of here.'

Maggot ignored the remark. 'You're the one who's going to wind up dead if you attempt to cut me out of something I'm entitled to. After all I funded you.'

Petreus did not react to the threat. His cold merciless eyes were partly concealed beneath a furrowed brow. His expression was deadpan. 'Carl, you paid me to run drugs. The minerals I found on the Boyce property were entirely at my expense. You didn't contribute a cent. I've finished with your activities and am now a free agent to pursue my own interests.'

Maggot launched himself to his feet, his massive fists resting on the desk as he leaned forward. 'I'll say it just once Petreus, you're a dead man if you cut me out.' The sheer bulk of the man and menace were meant to petrify anyone opposing him. Petreus had not moved during the outburst. He knew he could kill him with a single blow or permanently blind him if he moved around the desk to carry out his threat.

'Sit down Carl. And don't ever threaten me unless you're prepared to carry it out. If any of your thugs come near me, I'll send you their heads. And then I'll come looking for you.'

Petreus got up out of his seat as Maggot slumped back into his. He turned as he opened the door. 'And don't even think about going after Boyce or the kid. She's my meal ticket now.'

He had got a surprise when Chloe phoned asking him to meet at her office. He was not kept waiting and quickly shown into the boardroom.

Chloe entered, seated herself opposite with a pad and pen and smiled warmly. 'Well, Mr Petreus I've asked you here to see if we can't arrive at terms for the development of the copper discovery you claim to have made. Shall we cut to the chase?'

Petreus had expected to be dealing with a confused mental wreck asking for help, still trying to get over the death of her partner. Either it was a thin veil of denial she was hiding behind, or he was dealing with a woman who was clearly in control. He decided to play his high cards.

'I want a quarter of the action, carried, so I don't have to put up another cent. And please call me Johan.'

'You and I both know that's a ridiculous request. I'm funding it, so I want ninety percent. You can have ten percent free carried through to the development stage when we list it as an **IPO** on the securities exchange. I'll have to dilute along with you, but you can cash-out if you want to at that stage. If the prospect is as good as you say it is, you'll be a very wealthy individual.'

'But, I found it. Surely, that makes my claim valid?'

Chloe nodded. 'It does, but the problem is I own the permit area and I'm putting up all the money. I will of course put you on a substantial retainer in the capacity of an adviser. You don't have the technical nor engineering qualifications to take this through to the mining and production stage, but that doesn't mean you will be locked out of any involvement. You are also free to go and look for other likely projects on the permits with the present agreement extending to any new discoveries you may come up with.'

'So I've got carte blanche to prospect all over Baracool?'

'That's correct, but iron-ore is out. I want to see part of Baracool turned into a nature reserve.'

'You're thumbing your nose at a mountain of money Chloe, but I can see what you're aiming at. By allowing me to develop my project you can then renew your exploration permits. Everyone expects you to forfeit the area when the government rules you have not carried out any exploration or development. I believe you're going to wrong-foot a lot of hungry people waiting on the sidelines for a tilt at the iron-ore.'

Chloe smiled. 'You've done your homework Johan. That's precisely what I'm aiming at. Your discovery will satisfy all the government conditions.'

'What about your other property?

'You mean Ironstone Park. It's not as important to me so I may have to sacrifice that one to iron-ore mining to save Baracool. I'm setting up an exploration division to attract major companies and international interest. It will cost billions to develop, which is way beyond my means. Anyway, back to the point of this meeting. Do we have an agreement in principle?'

Petreus thrust out his hand. 'We do. Are you going to put that in writing?'

Chloe started to write on her pad. It was five minutes of silence while she put down the points of agreement before signing it, tearing off the page and handing it across. 'That's a letter of intent covering the main points we've just discussed. Sign it and I'll have it drawn up into a full legal document.'

Petreus read it slowly before countersigning it.

'What are you going to do about Evans? I would warn you, it's not an idle threat he made against you and your boy.'

'I would imagine he's also threatened you. What are you going to do about him?'

'I can look after myself Chloe. However, you're very vulnerable.'

'Read carefully what you've just signed Johan. This is a personal agreement between you and I. There is no company involved. If anything happens to me or Charlie you wind up with zero. Also, if you do get a whisper he's about to do something, you can let it be known I've put a two million dollar bounty on his hide.'

Petreus burst out laughing. 'And I thought I was dealing with someone who stood in the shadow of her partner. I must hand it to you, you know how to lock someone into a commitment and buy solid insurance.'

'I had a very good teacher. Andrew was my pillar of strength, and I learnt from him. What are you going to do about Evans, or have you come to some agreement'

'No agreement, just an understanding. But in view of our agreement you can forget about his involvement.'

Chloe nodded, but she was not sure the threats could be averted. Evans would go for the soft targets first, before getting to Petreus.

'I wish I could, but I'm not so sure.'

30

'Helen what's the problem. You seem to be very distant lately. Have I done something wrong?' Max Schubert thought it strange she had moved into another office and appeared to be keeping her distance.

'I'm sorry Max. It's just that I've been so busy with the increased work load and now Chloe is adding a new business. As you're aware we're going into mining which she has asked me to get the finance side rolling and controls in place. On top of that I've been busy with Anton and all his school activities. I get home at night and just want to crash.'

'Would you like to come around for dinner again? I promise I won't get drunk and fall asleep.'

She laughed, but there was no humour or sincerity in it. She was about to decline and vent her feelings when a sudden thought occurred to her. 'Yes, I would like that. Why not next week, let's say Tuesday.'

Schubert beamed. 'That's settled then. I thought I must have offended you in some way.'

'Well, I admit you did when you fell asleep and I had to let myself out. But I soon got over that, so there are no hard feelings. Next Tuesday it is then.'

His eyes followed her out of his office. There was something wrong in their working relationship, but what was it?

He decided it could not be much otherwise she would not have accepted his invitation.

Helen drew a deep breath as she pushed open the gate and walked the few steps to the front door which was already opening.

'Hi there,' Max beamed as he held the door open and showed her in.

She immediately felt uncomfortable. Why had she accepted his invitation when she could quite easily have taken him out for a drink after work and then hit him with her demands. It would have been safe in those surrounds, but now she had ventured into dangerous territory where she had no guarantee of the outcome. How would he react?

Max was the complete opposite to his usual reclusive existence at work, removed from the staff and their ephemeral office camaraderie. He was a loner and she knew why. He was oblivious to her mood and chatted incessantly as he served dinner along with an excellent bottle of pinot noir.

Finally she gathered the courage to broach the subject, the reason for her acceptance of the invitation. 'Max, you've always wanted to travel and live in another country, haven't you?'

He laughed. 'Of course Helen, but I can't see myself living anywhere overseas. I would never be able to afford it.'

'I believe you can. Now listen to me carefully.'

From an attitude of humour, his face turned ashen as she laid out the scenario of what she had planned.

'Are you mad Helen? We'd never get away with it. I suggest you leave now and I'll forget this dinner or conversation ever took place. In fact, I should report you to Chloe first thing in the morning.'

She showed no emotion, fully anticipating the outburst. 'Max, you don't surprise me. I guessed what your reaction would be, but you're going to change your mind. You're not going to be reporting anything to anyone. You're going to do exactly as I say, otherwise you are going to be serving time for a very nasty offence.'

'W.....what offence are you referring to? You're bluffing.'

'I'm not bluffing Max. You're nothing but an abhorrent paedophile, the lowest of the low.'

He rose to his feet in anger and came around the table. 'What the hell are you talking about?'

Inwardly she was shaking with fear as she maintained an iron-hard exterior. 'You know very well what I'm referring to Max, so sit down.'

He stopped short when the reason for her change of mood suddenly became apparent. 'How the hell did you get at my computer?'

'You were drunk remember. You went to sleep on the couch there, so I helped myself.'

'I could very easily kill you now, you bitch.'

'Max, you don't think I'd be stupid enough to come here tonight and tell you what's going to happen from now on without thinking it through? Anything happens to me and a certain USB stick, along with your name, will wind up in police sex crime hands. It didn't take me long to unravel your password and get around your encryption. Really, you should have been more careful.'

'And I thought you were a friend? That accounts for your change of attitude at work.'

'I was your friend Max, that was until I unloaded some of the foul images on your computer. You forget I'm a mother with a young son. You don't think I wasn't repulsed at what I saw?'

'Helen, it was personal. I didn't share it with anyone. The whole world is bent when it comes to sexuality. Take the ancient Greeks or the Spartans as prime examples. They...'

'That was more than two thousand years ago Max. I know nothing has really changed since and never will, but we're dealing with the present and the penalties regarding breaches of perceived morality are severe. I'll give it to you straight - if you refuse what I'm planning, you're going to jail. I will remain anonymous when I mail the contents of your hard drive to the police. I'll deny all knowledge if you try to point the finger at me as blackmailing you. Get it into you head Max, you can no longer hide what's in that room down the hall. You can get rid of the drive, but the police will have the evidence, including the passwords to your dark servers from where you derive your sick obsession. You're on your own, so what's it to be?'

'I can't do it Helen, I just can't.'

She got up and picked up her jacket. 'You can and you will. And stop worrying about it. They won't have a clue what you're up to. I'll make sure of that. And then you can go for the big hit. They may guess who did it, but they won't be able to prove it.'

'You believe you can set up offshore accounts and make the money disappear?'

'Yes, I can. The money will go through various accounts in the Caribbean before winding up in Israel where the trail ends and your privacy is protected by law. I also have another way of moving the funds into an untraceable destination.'

'And what do you get out of this?'

'Absolutely nothing in the way of money. It's all yours to live a life in Europe at your leisure. You won't be able to come back here, but I don't think you'd be too concerned about that. You don't have any close relatives from what you've told me.'

Max shook his head lost in thought. 'No, I don't. But when do you plan to put this into action.'

Helen smiled thinly. It had been easier than expected. 'I've already thought it through. We've got the annual accounts being prepared at the moment. We can drain off a couple of million without raising any eyebrows with the bank. It's normal for such large sums to come and go through the accounts depending on sales and receipts of cattle alone. We then go for the big lick a day or so before the auditors arrive by draining the bank overdraft and standby facility as well as the cash balance in every account. As you're aware that could be anything between twenty and thirty million.'

Max was wringing his hands and shaking with fear. 'We won't get away with it, we won't. You can't move that much money in one hit. It's too easily traced, no matter where you intend to put it.'

'You just keep your nerve and we will. I've laid the groundwork already and it's foolproof. You step out of line by going to Boyce or the police and you know the consequences. Your alternative is to go to the police now, lose your comfortable position and wind up in jail where you'll find out what a bunch of hardened crims think of paedophiles. You wouldn't last five minutes before they rearranged your looks or attacked you with a broom handle in the shower. And I can assure you they wouldn't be hitting you over the head with it.'

Schubert broke down into wrenching sobs of distress. 'What do you have against Chloe Boyce? Why are you doing this? She has treated us both with the utmost respect and decency. Are you not telling me something? This is some sort of vendetta isn't it?'

'It's none of your business Max. Don't concern yourself with my reasons. Just do as I say and you'll soon be retiring in Italy or the south of France. I can also recommend Greece.'

'But they will point the finger at you, so you won't be in the clear.'

'No I won't, but that's for me to worry about. Now I want to go home, so what's your answer?'

'Can I give it to you in the morning?'

'No, I want it now.'

Schubert looked at her blankly in total submission. 'What choice do I have? Yes, I'll go along with it.'

Helen showed no emotion as she got up and left. Inwardly she knew she was playing with fire. Would he go through with it, or would he break under the pressure? She had no alternative but to trust him.

31

Chloe picked up her phone and glanced at the caller. It was a number she did not recognise and it was no one on her contacts list. She was inclined to ignore it and let it go to message bank to vet the identity first.

'Hello, Chloe Boyce speaking.'

'Ms Boyce, my name is Christine Morley. I'm calling on behalf of the Mines Minister, Mr Jack Gibbs.'

Chloe was surprised. How did he get her mobile number and what did he want. 'How can I be of assistance?'

'Mr Gibbs is hosting a small social gathering of leading mining company executives at parliament house next week. It's informal with drinks and canapés and he would like you to attend. Would you be free?'

This was a complete surprise. All she had heard were rumours Gibbs was hell bent on confiscating her mining permits. She had taken legal advice Gibbs had no power to do so. What was he up to, or was he just being sociable?

'It depends what day. I'm due to fly north Friday.'

'Wednesday at six pm. Would that be convenient?'

'Yes, you can tell Mr Gibbs I will accept his invitation.'

Her cab pulled up in front of parliament house half an hour late. She did not want to be the first to arrive to face an immediate inquisition by Gibbs.

'Hello there, you must be Chloe Boyce, I'm Christine Morley.'

The room full of men went quiet as they turned towards her. She felt she was back on the runway, the centre of attention which she had abandoned to a distant memory.

'Come, let me introduce you to Mr Gibbs.'

Chloe recognised him immediately as she walked into the room. He now had his back to her pretending not to have noticed and in animated discussion with a group of men. Another dozen or more men and a couple of woman were also present.

'I feel like a trophy on display,' Chloe murmured quietly as Christine took her by the arm.

'Don't worry about him, he's full of his own importance. He was desperate you wouldn't attend only moments ago.'

Gibbs turned as if on cue, unable to control his patronising tone. 'Ah, Ms Chloe Boyce. I'm so pleased you could come. Gentlemen this is the lady who controls the new copper cobalt discovery in the Pilbara. It's a major project which will result in employment and wealth to the north as well as much needed royalties to the government. Chloe also controls as yet unexploited iron-ore deposits in addition to her large cattle grazing operations in the Kimberley and Pilbara. Gentlemen, as you probably know, Chloe was once an international model who gave it all away to run cattle.'

A waiter held a tray of drinks out to her. Chloe took an orange juice although she would have preferred something stronger to calm her nerves. She did not understand why she was nervous. She was used to crowds and men trying to develop a more intimate contact. She had learnt to handle the attention and fawning admiration that had only one real purpose, seduction. However, tonight she would have to be on her guard. Gibbs made her skin crawl, the previous meeting all those years ago was still vivid in her memory.

The men within the small group he was talking to slowly detached and introduced themselves. All seemed genuinely interested in her mining and business interests and did not mention her past. She noted the conversation invariably drifted back to the topic of iron-ore.

'It's no use getting too excited about the iron,' Gibbs broke in as he noticed a couple of high-power mining company executives trying to button-hole her. 'Chloe's permits have got a few years to run. But, if she doesn't start work soon, you can then come and see me, gentlemen.'

'I've already started an exploration and mining division. The conditions of the permits will be complied with Mr Gibbs. The government will not be confiscating them.' It was a short sharp retaliation for Gibbs' overbearing attempt to establish his authority. Chloe saw one of the group nod and give a wry smile as if to say *"good on you girl, he had it coming."*

Gibbs was flustered by the response. He was not used to someone challenging him and in particular not some female from the never-never with dubious lineage who had inherited everything by default. It could be safely assumed she did not have a brain in her head. It was her partner, who had recently died, who was responsible for her success and ever increasing wealth.

'I meant no offence Ms Boyce. I was purely talking from the government's standpoint and it was not meant as a personal remark. The State government wants the iron-ore mined – that's where revenue and royalties will derive from and not from some isolated copper project – there's no comparison.'

'Your concerns are being addressed Mr Gibbs.'

He was about to reply when she felt someone take her elbow. 'Chloe, I'm so pleased to meet you. I've been following your activities for some years.'

Gibbs could not hide his flash of anger when he saw Chloe's attention being diverted as she turned away from him.

The woman was tall but plump with a beaming smile that immediately disarmed any suspicion of intrigue. 'I'm Clare Bartel. Come over and I'll introduce you to a few people you should know.'

Chloe recognised Clare from photos and articles in newspapers, television interviews, political comments, charitable bequests and unrelenting drive to attract investment and business to the State. She held royalty income from well established iron-ore mines as well as holding controlling interests in others. She was a person who politicians treated with the utmost respect. Her cattle properties exceeded Chloe's in area and number of head, but then again she'd had a considerable start Chloe was not aspiring to match.

'Likewise Clare, you're someone I cannot hope to match in size.'

Clare Bartel burst out laughing as Chloe realised her blunder. 'I....I did not mean it to come out like that Clare. I was referring to your business interests.'

'I know what you meant Chloe. My father used to tell me I only opened my mouth to change feet. It would appear you have the same affliction. I admire that trait. Now let's get down to business before I introduce you to a couple of people. Beware of Gibbs, he's a real sleaze and rumoured to be on the take. I have it on very good authority he's after your Pilbara iron deposits. I know you have clear title and have commenced work, but he's up to something. Can I ask you what your intentions are in regard to the iron-ore?'

'We've started exploration on Ironstone Park, but the project is far too big for my resources. I need an international partner with deep pockets.'

'I can put you in touch with two companies who have the money and would be keen to get involved with large projects. See how you go with them and get back to me so we can compare notes and give you advice regarding any negotiations. I would emphasise I'm not a competitor, I just want to see you succeed. My advice is don't go near anyone Gibbs suggests you do business with.'

Clare made the introductions and then moved on to circulate within the room. She noticed without direct eye contact, that Gibbs was closely following her various discussions and people she was talking to. One executive had engaged her for too long as Gibbs detached himself and wandered over.

'You two appear to be really hitting if off Mr Fujimori?'

The Japanese executive smiled and gave a polite nod. 'We are Mr Gibbs. My company would be most interested in becoming involved with Ms Boyce's iron-ore deposits. She tells me she has already started outlining a major iron-ore deposit on Ironstone Park. And my company would be very interested in taking a part of her recent exciting copper discovery.'

Gibbs drew in his breath and turned on his heel. 'Yes, she may as well enjoy it while she can I suppose.'

Fujimori looked at the departing figure in surprise and then back at Chloe for an explanation.

'I don't know what he was referring to Mr Fujimori. I'm as surprised as you are.'

The executive gave a slight bow as he handed her his card. 'Can I arrange a meeting convenient to you to discuss our possible involvement?'

'I will look forward that.'

She was left standing alone until Clare Bartel rescued her. 'I saw that and caught part of what Gibbs said to make you both look as though you'd been given a backhander. What did Gibbs actually say? Fujimori is one powerful individual who commands a lot of respect. I hope Gibbs didn't insult him. As you can see he's already had too much to drink.'

'Oh, it was nothing really Clare. Just some comment I should enjoy it while I can. I haven't a clue what he was referring to.'

'I think I may, but I won't elaborate on that now other than to say I've heard mutterings he's about to attempt to change the mining legislation in regard to permits. He may be able to do it for future grants, but he can't make it retrospective. He'd be signing his own death warrant as a minister if he tried. There is simply too much in the way of billions of dollars of foreign investment already committed. Any move to expropriate assets would quickly see that investment dry up. He wouldn't be able to withstand the backlash - he would be a victim of his own hubris. I'll keep my ear open and let you know if anything is about to happen.'

'Thank you for that Clare. It's been a pleasure meeting you.'

'Why don't we make it a regular occurrence. Let's say we get together over lunch every month? It's about time you joined the mainstream of political influence in this State. I don't think you realise just how powerful a voice you have if you were prepared to come out of your shell.'

Chloe laughed. 'I don't like the spotlight. I had years of that exposure and prefer the way I am, low-key and inconspicuous. I cannot claim I've created what I have solely from my own efforts. It was largely due my partner.'

'Yes, I read about his tragic death and feel for you. However, I read it was the result of a stroke and not pilot error or sabotage. How's your son handling it?'

'Oh, he misses Andrew terribly, but like any child they quickly learn to adjust. Their memory span is very short, unlike an adult where we can trawl back over years of instances and occasions. I have my moments where everything just floods back and I drift into melancholy.'

Clare Bartel nodded. 'I think you are a very lonely person Chloe. I don't want to appear pretentious, but in addition to the cattle and mining industry, you have got to get around and meet more people in politics and business. They're the people who drive this State and are wholly responsible for its prosperity. I'm not suggesting you be outspoken, but you should make your presence and opinions felt. I started in the shadow of my brother who inherited the family cattle stations and associated interests. It was he who took us into the iron-ore business twenty five years ago. When he died I bloodied a few noses on the way, but no one takes me for granted these days. And that's exactly the attitude I want you to adopt. Don't take crap from anyone.' Clare looked around the room. 'I think the meeting's over, so I'll head off. Now remember, let's make it a regular meeting every month so we can compare notes. Here's my direct phone number and don't hesitate to call if you have something to discuss?'

'Hello there Clare, aren't you going to introduce me?'

'I didn't see you come in - Cleve McCormick meet Chloe Boyce.'

Chloe smiled and shook the outstretched hand. She was attracted to him with his disarming smile and dancing green eyes – colour she had never seen so intense.

'What are you doing here Cleve? I thought you were strictly cattle and had no interest in iron-ore or minerals?'

'Clare, there are no iron-ore deposits on my property, but as you know it's very prospective for other metals such as copper or gold or the new hot topic of lithium and cobalt. I heard this meeting was on so I just phoned up and invited myself. Are you two staying around?'

'No, we're just on the way out.'

'Can't you stick around? Chloe, I would love to hear about your recent copper discovery and how you went about financing it. I've just got to catch up with Jack Gibbs for a minute or two and I'd like you both to join me for a coffee.'

'Cleve, why don't you give me a call in the morning and come around for lunch. You know where I live.'

'What about you Chloe? I won't be long with Gibbs.'

'Okay, I'll be down in the foyer.'

'Handsome fellow isn't he?' Clare remarked as they walked down the sweeping stairs to the forecourt.'

'I suppose he is, but I'm not really looking at the moment Clare.'

'He was a bit of a wild-child, but since his father died last year he seems to have quietened down. He's been married, but there weren't any children. He could be on the lookout for a replacement. He inherited a very large holding, but there have been rumours of problems.'

'I hear what you're saying Clare, but I'm not interested.'

Clare patted her on the arm. 'I'll leave you here then. I wouldn't wait around too long.'

'I'm not going to, Clare.'

'I can give you a lift? I've got to drop someone else off and it won't be any problem.'

'No, I'm fine. I'll catch a cab, if he leaves me standing around.'

She was standing on the kerb waiting for a cab when the black limo pulled up beside her. The driver in a cap got out and quickly walked around and opened the rear passenger door.

'Get in Chloe,' Gibbs beckoned. 'I'll drop you home. You'll be perfectly safe.'

She hesitated as she looked around for a cab to save the situation - a constant stream of traffic, but no unoccupied taxis. Before she realised it, the driver had taken her arm and gently guided her into the car.

'That was a good meeting, don't you think?' Before she could answer Gibbs carried on. 'A lot of very important mining people and I could see you made some worthwhile contacts.'

'It was interesting, but I was out of my depth discussing mining with any of them. Cattle are more my topic.'

'Mining is where the money is Chloe. It's a pity you've taken so long to understand that, or will have the time to cash-in.'

There it was again, the blunt warning about what? 'Mr Gibbs, why don't you explain yourself? This is the second time in an hour you've made some obscure reference to my mineral interests. What are you trying to tell me?'

Gibbs resented the direct approach. There was no deference to his position as Minister. He could see she was not intimidated by his authority. 'I didn't mean anything by it other than to point out time is running out on your permits. If you don't perform I'll take them off you, and I'm in particular referring to Baracool. You should really learn to work with me. It would be in your interest to do so.'

'And time is running out for your government. You've got an election coming up and you may lose from what I see and read in the media every day.' Chloe delivered the stinging rebuttal in a quiet voice. She could sense the comment found its mark.

Gibbs snorted. 'We won't lose, I can assure you of that my dear. Now let's enjoy the rest of the evening. Where would you like to go for dinner?'

Chloe had already realised the driver was heading towards the social night-life centre of the city rather than in her direction.

'I'm not going to any dinner with you. Now would you take me home please.'

The driver hesitated as he looked into his rear vision mirror for instructions.

'There's no need to take that attitude Chloe. I simply asked you out for drinks and dinner. Do you find me that offensive?' He reached over and clasped his hand over her knee.

She struck it away. 'You're more than offensive, you're repulsive and you've had too much to drink.'

Gibbs swore as he reached over and put his arm around her shoulder. She could smell the stench of alcohol as he pushed his face into her cheek. 'Now listen you upstart, I'm going to take you down a peg or two.'

The car weaved as the driver shouted. 'Hey boss, knock it off. I don't want to be called as a witness to an assault.'

Gibbs pulled away. 'Okay, let's take her home.'

Fifteen minutes later the car pulled up in front of her house. Gibbs had been sitting quietly contemplating his folly. He had been stupid. If she laid a complaint his career as a Minister would be finished along with his fat salary and allowances.

Chloe picked up the phone. It was Clare Bartel. 'Hi there Chloe, how did you get on with Gibbs last night. Did he take you home or out to dinner?'

'How did you know about that?'

'I drove past when you were standing on the pavement waiting for a taxi. I got delayed in the car-park talking to a couple of those at the meeting. By the time I turned around to pick you up it was too late. I saw you getting into his car.'

'It wasn't a very pleasant experience.'

'Tried to maul you did he? You should lay a complaint with Angus McDonald. I could see he was ogling you all evening, but he wasn't the only one. None of them could take their eyes off you.'

'I really can't be bothered doing that Clare. I don't want to be dragged into anything that could reflect on me. Knowing him as I do now, he'll twist the facts and throw mud, some of which will stick.'

'Yes, I suppose you're right. Mind you he's never tried anything with me, I'm too bloody ugly.' Chloe held the phone away at the peel of self-deprecatory laughter. 'I overheard the comment about enjoy it while you can. What did he mean by that?'

'I think he was playing mind games. He made several negative comments regarding my tenure in front of people. I believe he was giving a clear message to anyone thinking of approaching me that my titles were in doubt – he was the person to talk to, not me.'

'Hmm..I'd take that threat seriously if I were you. He would have real problems in confiscating your concessions at this stage, but he can disrupt any discussions you may have with interested partners. He has the power to frustrate and delay any negotiations so that you would be forced to deal with a partner of his choosing. That's his real strength. Make no mistake, he's dangerous.'

'Well Clare, I'll have to face that situation when and if it arises.'

'Don't hesitate to call on me. I've been through the grinder with bureaucrats, politicians and big business and know how they think and act. I can see from the reception you got last night you're going to need a good lawyer to guide you through the process, which brings me to the real reason for my call. What are you doing for lunch today?'

'Nothing planned.'

'Good, I'll have you picked up at twelve thirty. I'm lunching with someone you may find very interesting. He represents one of the large Korean Chaebols with interests in steel and just about anything you can think of. I've done business with him and found him to be straight up and down. He either likes you or he doesn't. If he doesn't, you only get one meeting and you'll never hear from him again. His name is Minjum Lee, but I just call him Min.'

32

Chloe had invited Alex to spend the weekend with her at Ascot Downs. She was impressed with his work ethic and dedication, but she wanted to determine whether he would stay, or it was just a transitory phase in his life. Surely, he did not want to be isolated and away from the social life of a city forever? They had just finished lunch and were sitting outside in the enclosed verandah when she decided to raise the subject.

'You appear to be enjoying the work Alex, but how long do you think you'll be able to put up with living away from the attractions of a big city? There's no social stimulation out here, no people your age of either sex. Don't you miss that?'

'To be truthful, I really can't answer that. I'm on a learning curve at the moment and enjoying it. You have a dynamic operation I can see growing every day and to be part of that is all the education and experience I really need at the moment. I suppose there will be a time when I decide to stay or move on, but I promise I'll give you plenty of notice.'

'Does Rick Giles know about your connection to Andrew?'

'Not that I'm aware of. However, I don't know whether Dad told him and told him to keep quiet so there could be no appearance of nepotism.'

'What do you think of Rick?'

'He's a good manager, totally committed to the company. Why do you ask?'

'No reason in particular.'

'C'mon Chloe, you and I both know that's not true. Where's this leading?'

'Rick is what Andrew called, a rough diamond. We employed him when we bought our first road- train and from there we've established the largest cattle hauling operation in the north.'

'So?'

'Just prior to his death Andrew decided to run a background check on Rick which highlighted a few possible grey areas of suspicion. For one, he has accrued far more wealth and possessions than is possible taking into account his salary and bonuses. This indicated he has an additional source of income, but the question is, what is its source?'

'Well, if you're asking me, I haven't noticed anything out of the ordinary. He drives a nice company vehicle and lives in a nice company house. He told me he has a house in Darwin where his wife and kids live. Other than that, I know nothing about him.'

'Have you ever seen him in the company of a South African by the name of Johan Petreus, or with bikies?'

'He introduced me to Petreus when he called into the office some time ago, but he hasn't been around for ages. As for the motorbike boys, I've seen him talking to them in the pub on the rare occasions I've ventured into town. He seemed to be pretty friendly with them. In fact I recognised one of them as a bikie who was killed in an accident recently.'

'I think you're referring to the bikie who threatened Charlie and I.'

Alex looked at her in surprise. 'What was that all about?'

'The bikie known as Lennie was an associate of Carl Evans, a notorious gang leader heavily into drugs and everything else those gangs get into. Evans was pressuring me to get involved financially to develop the copper discovery on Baracool. In return for his money he wanted a controlling interest. There was no way I was going to entertain any such proposition. Andrew heard a whisper Petreus was into drug running for Evans while he was working on the side prospecting for copper and other metals on Baracool.'

'But aren't you in bed with Petreus? I...I'm sorry, I didn't mean it that way.'

Chloe snorted and laughed. 'Yes, metaphorically I am in bed with Petreus in that I've given him a share in the project. It was simpler to reward the man for his discovery, although his actions were somewhat illegal, rather than have my exploration team spend valuable time searching for it over such a vast area.'

'Andrew suspected Giles and Petreus have a tie-up with the bikies running drugs, is that it? It has to be, as there's nothing else the bikies could make money out of in this neck of the woods.'

'That's correct. And from what Andrew told me he believed they may be responsible for running drugs further north and right through the Northern Territory. It was the only explanation he had for Giles assets. He went so far as to have him checked out in Darwin. Lo and behold he's a Harley enthusiast, with not one but two very expensive bikes, and likewise an expensive forty-five foot fishing boat completely rigged with all the latest technology, along with jet skis for the kids and an upmarket house in an exclusive suburb.'

'And you're suggesting it's not possible on what you pay him?'

'What do you think?'

'There could be a number of explanations. How do you know his wife's not loaded or a great-aunt popped her clogs and left him a fortune. I think you could be jumping to conclusions.'

'You haven't noticed anything suspicious then?'

Alex looked thoughtful before shaking his head. 'No I haven't, but then again I haven't been looking for anything. Rick Giles and I get along very well, but we only ever discuss the business. He never talks about his outside interests.'

'Andrew was concerned he may be using our drivers to distribute drugs. And you say you've not seen Petreus for some time?'

'Yes and no. As I said, he only came into the office once, but I've heard Giles talking to him on the phone, although not recently. He took one call and had it too loud on speaker. There was no mistaking the accent and identity of the caller. As you're aware I sit right next to his office which is hardly sound-proof. He told Petreus to hold while he walked out into the yard.'

'And you think it was Petreus?'

'Well, it certainly wasn't Rick's wife. In that case the greeting is always the usual grunts and acknowledgement of kids and domestic concerns while trying to appear interested, but intent on shaking her off.'

Chloe leaned back with a laugh. 'I often wonder if that's what Andrew thought about me?'

'No, he was head over heals about you. I realise now he was always trying to hide the guilt of leading a double life. He should have come clean he was married when you first met. He undoubtedly knew I existed - he could have been more honest.'

'You're being too hard on him Alex. I can forgive him.'

'Getting back onto the subject of business Chloe, I have limited access to all the group's activities. I'm more or less constrained to the transport division. I would like to be able to pull up any division and look into it. I could easily hack into them now, but would not do so without your permission.'

Chloe was studying the face for any sign of deceit. None was apparent, but she could sense the cunning intelligence that lay beneath the genial expression. 'You've already done that, haven't you?'

Alex nodded with a grin. 'Yes I have. But I really haven't pursued it because I didn't want to tread on anyone's toes if it became common knowledge. I didn't want to get the boot.'

'You know, you're just like your father, always probing looking for weak spots and always aware of the business and what could go wrong. I'm more of a broad-brush person while he was always interested in the smallest detail. That's you isn't it?'

'Chloe, you're getting to such a size now you cannot possibly keep your finger on everything. You've got to delegate the responsibility and I believe I can contribute. Give me free-rein and I'll soon find out where Giles' wealth is being generated from. I can easily check into any division of the business. Your business is no different to any other diversified conglomerate which eventually declines due to lack of governance, unless strictly monitored.'

'How are you going to check on where Giles gets his money from? That's a bit of a wild statement isn't it?'

'On the contrary, Giles has a laptop with wireless access locked in his desk. I know he must be using wireless as the laptop's not connected to the company server which raises my suspicions – what's he hiding? I happened to walk into his office one day when he wasn't expecting me – he logged off and and closed the lid too quickly. It was an unmistakable guilty movement. He let me know in no uncertain terms

I should knock first. From then I made it my business to watch closely whenever the laptop appeared. I only caught him once when I returned early from an outside appointment. I immediately booted up my laptop and hacked in, but I was a minute too late. However, what I did get a glimpse of before he logged off was the balance in a bank account and I'm sure it was not an accumulation of salary deposits. I was too late to the get the account number or any other details. I think he makes sure no one's around when he opens that computer.'

'What are you proposing?'

'I've got to get access to that laptop.'

Chloe shook her head. 'I couldn't condone that Alex. I've no doubt it's illegal.'

'If I can get access to his computer it should only take me half an hour to crack the passwords to any bank accounts. From then on he won't have a clue I'm watching. I can also monitor all his emails.'

'I still don't like it.'

'Chloe, you've got to use every means to protect yourself and the business. The world is full of crooks looking for a loophole to take advantage. I'm not suggesting Giles is crooked, but don't get too comfortable with the assumption he's beyond reproach. You've already said the guy appears to be living at a level higher than his salary would prudently allow, so I would suggest you follow up on Andrew's concerns and let me see what I can find. I can assure you, if he or anyone else discovers my activities I will take the complete fall. Your name will not be mentioned and I'll deny this conversation ever took place.'

Chloe knew Alex was right, but she still felt very uncomfortable. 'Okay, you have my permission, but let's see what you turn up in the next month. If it's negative, then you cease.'

'Fair enough. Now what about giving me permission to look at the rest of your organisation. No one will be any the wiser.'

'Why have I got the feeling you know more than you're telling me? Has something already raised your interest?'

Alex shrugged and gave a wry grin. 'Yes, but I won't expand on that, it's early days yet.'

Chloe could see she was not going to get any further. He was just like his father, analytical rather than alarmist, the suspect innocent until proven guilty.

33

Petreus sensed danger as he pushed open the door and walked into the bar – the danger was the three thugs confronting him. Their intent became clear he was the target. There was no sign of Mickey or customers at that time of night – the bar had long closed. Maggot had told him he wanted an urgent meeting. He had faced such situations many times in the past and there were no surprises in what he faced now – Maggot had not made an idle threat. With a scream of rage he charged, an action which took them by surprise. Before they could recover he had taken the first one down with a clenched fist smashing his nose. The thug stumbled back trying to stem the blood streaming from the pulped mess while attempting to regain vision through his tear-strained eyes. His only thought was self-preservation while trying to anticipate and avoid the next blow. Petreus turned like a cat, but could not dodge the swinging fist which caught him on the side of the head. He began to fall backwards, but was arrested by an arm locking around his neck in an unbreakable grip. He tried to bite the arm as he threw himself backwards in an attempt to break the hold, but his move had been anticipated. There was a bellow of laughter as he was lifted off his feet and was swung around to face the third assailant. He tried with all his strength to avoid the studded boot aimed at his groin. He twisted sufficiently for it to miss the intended target and smash into his thigh. He let out an uncontrollable cry of pain as he drew up the wounded leg. It was all over as the fists smashed into his stomach and then worked on his head and face. His surroundings started to disappear in waves of nausea and pain.

'You don't look so good Johan.'

Petreus identified the voice, but could not see the face because his eyes would not focus through the swollen lids. He turned on his side and vomited on the concrete floor. A boot smashed into his back barely overriding the pain which wracked his body.

'Leave the bastard there for now. Lock the door and take it in turns to watch he doesn't try to leave.'

'He's not going anywhere Carl. He's out for the count. Why don't we take him for a ride now and dump his body?'

'No, I want to have a word with this shit before you do that. Leave him for now, he's not going anywhere.'

Petreus groaned in pain as he rolled on his back. He had no idea of how long he had been unconscious. The concrete floor was cold and he was chilled by the blasts of air coming from under the roller-door of the garage. There were four gleaming Harley's parked under covers to one side. At least he knew how many bikies he was dealing with. Too many for him to handle. He slowly rose on one elbow and looked around, fully expecting another boot from some thug hovering in the shadows. He was alone. It took him minutes to slowly regain his feet and stagger towards the bikes for support. He reached out to the wall for support and slowly walked towards the roller-door. He could see a street light through the narrow gap in the side, but otherwise it was complete darkness. Escape was imperative. He had to get out now otherwise he was as good as dead, but he knew his exit back through the bar was not an option as Maggot's goons were sure to be there. He glanced up at the roller-door lifting mechanism and laughed softly to himself. He had a chance, but could he pull it off? He was almost back to the bikes when he heard voices approaching the interior door. He limped back to where he had been lying and dropped to the concrete as it swung open.

'The yapie's still out cold.'

'He could be dead, check his pulse.' Maggot was present.

Petreus felt the rough hand as it felt for a pulse in his neck. 'No, the prick hasn't snuffed it – the blood's still pumping.'

'Get him to his feet and bring him into my office. Give Mick a hand you two.'

The thugs hauled him to his feet and dragged him out of the cold surroundings before dumping him onto a leather couch. Petreus opened his eyes to the glare of light and the mist that shrouded his vision. His lips were swollen and raw as he made to swallow.

'You lot can piss off now. I want a private word with this character. Go and pour yourselves a drink,' Maggot dismissed the trio. 'Don't worry about this jerk, I can handle him.' He waited for them to leave before turning to Petreus.

'You double-crossed me Petreus.' The accusation was low and menacing. 'You know what that means, don't you?'

Petreus did not answer. He was intent on keeping his swollen mouth shut and just listening as he shook his head in recognition and resignation.

'Not only have you cut me out of your copper discovery with Boyce, but I hear you're running errands for Ronnie Ratsakis. Suddenly all the contacts I trusted you with have dropped off my radar and they're now dealing with the Rat. I can't let you do that Johan. Nod your head if you understand otherwise I'll rearrange your teeth with my boot.'

Petreus' mind raced as he slowly nodded. He only had one chance and that was to play for time. 'I...I..did...didn't cross you,' he mumbled through swollen lips. 'Boyce wouldn't deal with you and I know nothing about the Rat.'

Maggot gave a mocking laugh. 'Like hell you don't. You tell me you're not working for me any longer and a minute later the Rat is muscling in on my turf. That's just too much of a co-incidence in my opinion.'

'Co....co-incidence it is because I had nothing to do with it. And as for Boyce, your mate Lennie screwed that up. You send some lame-brain like that to scare hell out of her and then expect her to do business with you? You've got to be soft in the head.'

Maggot bellowed at the door. Within seconds the three reappeared. 'Chuck him back in the garage.' He glanced at the most mute of the trio. 'Marko you go steal a van so we can dispose of the body. And make sure it's inconspicuous without any sign-writing. You can torch it as soon as you've found a quiet spot out in the bush.' Maggot chuckled to himself. 'I wonder what barbecued yapie smells like? And make sure you tie his hands and feet before he leaves here. I don't want him suddenly recovering and causing an accident you'll find hard to explain. Rizzo, you and Mick follow and make sure the van is well alight and the screams have stopped before returning. I want confirmation the bastard has suffered."

Petreus was able to stagger as they dragged him out and dumped in a heap. He waited for the sound of the door being closed before slowly getting to his feet and rolling back the cover off the Harley's. He found what he was looking for sitting on the tank. *"Strength in numbers but weak in the brain,"* he muttered to himself as he strained every tortured muscle and tried to mask his grunts as he slowly pushed the big machine to block the door into Maggot's office. It would only slow them down, but that's was all he needed. He pushed another machine until it touched the garage door. He would only have seconds before the alarm was raised. He mounted the bike and triggered the door opener before tossing it on the floor as he pressed the engine starter. The motor leapt to life with a throaty roar as he put it into gear. He swore as the door slowly began to open. It was barely at head-height when he heard the door open behind him, followed by a bellow of rage and cursing as someone tried to get around the bike blocking their path. No time to look around as he slowly slipped the clutch and eased the Harley forward. He could sense someone closing in as the door retracted sufficiently. With a twist of the throttle the machine roared into life and he was out into a narrow lane-way. He lowered his foot as he sharply corrected his direction. The machine began to slide, but suddenly bit into the roadway and he was clear. He throttled back as he rode out of the lane-way onto a busy road and accelerated. He knew he was only seconds in front of his pursuers as he weaved in and out of the traffic. The police car travelling towards him flashed its lights as it engaged its siren and made to turn to pursue him. Riding without a helmet, combined with the dangerous riding and speeding carried a heavy fine and loss of licence. It was the least of his concerns. Petreus grimaced as he increased speed to outrun the law. Two other Harley's flashed in front of the police vehicle as it made to turn. They quickly peeled off at the next exit and separated as the police decided which one of them was an easier target to catch. Petreus glanced behind him as he throttled back. The flashing lights had disappeared. It was time to deal with Maggot as he turned off and made his way back. The two thugs would be leading the cops on a wide ride well away from Maggot's lair. They would be gone for hours. Petreus slowly turned off and rode back until he was only a couple of streets away before dumping the bike behind an abandoned building where it would be quickly vandalised for parts. He was sure it was Maggot's machine, it was so heavily adorned with Harley accessories.

To his surprise the garage door was still open and the place empty. He picked up a heavy flat tire-lever off the work bench. Normally he would have considered such support unnecessary, but he was still suffering and weakened from the beating. He picked up the automatic opener from where he'd dropped it, pressed it to shut and quickly walked towards the inner door. He slowly opened it. Maggot's office door was open. Surely he would hear the garage door closing, but Petreus could not hear any movement. At that precise moment a door opposite marked *Toilet* swung open and Maggot emerged fastening the heavy metal studded belt of his pants. He realised his predicament, glancing at his assailant while trying to find the fastening eyelet, but he was too late. He let go the belt in an attempt to defend himself as Petreus sprang at him, thrusting his fingers into his eyes. Petreus ignored the screams of pain as he thrust deeper, permanently blinding him. Maggot turned in circles and lurched into walls in his futile attempt to avoid the anticipated killer blow. The screams grew louder as if to ward off the moment. It came quickly as his executioner stepped forward and smashed the tire-lever into the exposed neck. Maggot's knees buckled under him as his hands clutched at his throat in a futile attempt to get air into his heaving lungs. Petreus watched with satisfaction as the hands dropped, the convulsions peaked and then slowly subsided as Maggot toppled forward before rolling on his side, the blood from the sightless bloodied eyes trickling down into his bearded jowls.

Why get into a fist-fight when the exposed throat or eyes were the most fragile of human anatomy? Petreus could not recall the number of African terrorists he had killed with the larynx-smashing punch or the number he had blinded and then dispatched as they cried out in confusion, realising that death was only moments away. He invariably finished them off with a quick merciless knife-thrust to the throat. He took no pleasure in it, it was simply a matter of survival. If the tables had been reversed he could have expected a slow lingering death such was his reputation and the reputation of other mercenaries. The English used to specialise in hanging, drawing and quartering whereby the helpless victim was dragged naked to the place of execution by horse and hung until near death on a triangle, before being emasculated and the genitals thrown to starving dogs. Then a knife was thrust into the anus and quickly ripped upwards to spill out the entrails which the dogs fought over. This was followed by the severing of the head which was mounted on a spike and the cadaver chopped into quarters. Petreus had observed African terrorists inflicted similar brutal punishment on their captives. He had seen the bloody evidence of some of his mercenary associates hacked to death. No point in burying them, the hyenas would tidy up the remains that night. The most horrifying scene he had encountered was when a white farmer, his wife and daughter were stopped and pulled from their car. The wife and daughter had been stripped and gang raped before being subjected to obscene disfigurement. They were still alive, but beyond help, when his group reached them. None of his three man party showed any emotion as Petreus shot the two women. The father was already dead.

Petreus showed no emotion as he felt for Maggot's extinct pulse before retrieving the tire-lever and walking back through the garage. He picked up and pressed the garage door opener and wiped it clean before crunching it under his boot as he walked away. He wiped the tire-lever before tossing it into a pile of rubbish in a vacant lot. There were no witnesses and the three thugs would disappear quickly when they returned and viewed the scene. The last thing they wanted was to be implicated and grilled by the police. It would be up to Mickey the barman to report Maggot's death in the morning. He had no doubt Mickey would profess complete ignorance as to the identity of any of Maggot's visitors or friends. In fact, he doubted whether Mickey would stick around once he walked in and discovered the corpse.

34

Chloe was sitting out in the morning sun with a coffee when the phone rang. She did not recognise the caller as she swiped the symbol, but a premonition told her who it was.

'Hey, you didn't wait for me last night. I thought we had a date.'

Chloe caught the rebuke in his tone. 'Cleve, I wasn't going to hang around while you talked business with Gibbs. I thought half an hour was enough.' She waited for him challenge her as she had not even waited five minutes.

'Oh, I'm sorry about that. Yes, I did go up to his office and waited, but he didn't show. I should have got your mobile number when Clare introduced us. I phoned her this morning for it. Can I make it up to you? How about lunch today?'

'Not today Cleve. I've got a couple of appointments and I'm off to the Kimberley tomorrow for a week. We'll have to make it some other time.'

'I'm flying back there tomorrow. My property is about one hundred kilometres north east of Ascot. Why don't you come up and visit?'

Chloe laughed. 'I don't have time for that, but thanks for the invitation.'

'You expecting someone boss?' Luke Massie was shading his eyes as he looked up at the sound of the approaching aircraft. 'Oh, oh, by the look of this clown he's going to buzz the homestead. I hope he sees the aerial wire.'

They both followed the plane's approach as it came in low at speed. The reverberation shook the homestead as it passed within metres of the roof. 'Crazy bastard,' Luke yelled as the plane pulled up to circle and line up for the runway. 'Its a miracle he didn't hit that wire.'

'Luke go down and tell whoever it is to leave immediately. Make it very clear they're not welcome.'

Chloe saw the the ute returning about fifteen minutes later. Luke had not followed her instructions – there was someone sitting beside him and she could see them talking and laughing.

'Hi there Chloe. You wouldn't come and see me, so I thought I'd drop in on you.'

She was furious. 'Cleve, I don't care if you kill yourself, just don't do it on my property.'

'Luke told me about the wire, but I'd seen the tower on the hill and realised their must be a direct line across to the homestead. I'm not that bloody stupid. However, I do apologise if I scared you. Are you going to invite me in or do I leave?'

'You didn't scare me, I just didn't want to pick up the pieces. You may as well come in and have a cold drink although I wouldn't be surprised if Alice doesn't put strychnine in it. Every dish and jar would have moved in her pantry.'

He laughed it off. 'Yeah, I've also got one of those old bats running the household – the slightest infringement and I get bawled out. But I've got to put up with it, although she's no relation. She's been on my case since I was a kid.'

'Probably with good reason. You don't appear to have learnt too much.'

He glanced at her for some mirth in her comment, but was met with a blank stare of censure.

'I'm not getting off to a very good start, am I? Can I rewind and apologise for the stunt? I should have known better in the light of your recent tragic accident. However, I understand your partner's death was not due to pilot error.'

'It was pilot error – he should never have held a licence. And neither should you judging by what I just witnessed.'

Cleve ignored the drink Helen had placed in front of him and stood. 'I think I should leave Chloe. I've made a real mess of things.'

'You're here now, so sit down and relax.'

He picked up his drink and sat down again. 'I came in and had a look at this place just when it was being finished by the English owner. It's one helluva homestead and it's a magnificent property. No one can understand how you came to own it.'

Chloe laughed. 'Yes, I believe it has been the subject of some speculation.'

'Dad wanted to buy it when he heard the rumour it was about to be put up for sale. He was going to buy it in partnership with Ike Shulman. It was a real shock when you beat them to the punch and the rest is history. Would you tell me how you did it?'

The question never failed to be asked – people could not help themselves. 'I was on the spot with money to spend at the right time. It's as simple as that.'

'From what I heard on the rumour mill some years ago, it was financed by Henry Boyce duffing cattle off this property and selling them through Venus Downs.'

'Yes, I am aware of that, but I was not involved.'

'But, you must have been aware....'

Chloe's face hardened. 'I was aware of nothing my father was alleged to have done. And my purchasing this property had nothing to do with his alleged activities.'

'I...I'm sorry, I did not mean to be intrusive, but...........'

'But you're wondering how I not only acquired Ascot Downs, but how I've bought a string of cattle stations since that time? I admit, I did have some help.'

'And you think you can retain control of the operation?'

'Cleve, why don't you change the subject? Instead of me, why don't we talk about you?'

'For instance, what would you like to know?'

'What is the real reason you've come here? Your property joins Ascot to the north and other than our meeting at that Gibbs function, I've never seen you although I was aware of your family's holding.'

'I'd heard so much about you, I figured it was time we met. Dad died last year and I took over the property which has bccn in thc family for four generations. Dad could never understand how you managed to acquire so many cattle stations and in particular how you acquired this one.'

'It all relates back to my father duffing cattle off this station, branding them and selling them through Venus Downs.'

McCormick looked surprised. 'You admit to that?'

'Of course, what's the point in denying a fact everyone is aware of. I've even openly admitted it in a court of law, but I was not aware of what was happening until he died.'

'Are you aware Ascot Downs was originally owned by my father. He got into financial difficulty when he bought a string of stations during a drought period. He thought he could service the debt, but he miscalculated. The bank moved in and took this one, which was the prime holding and sold it off to the English mob.'

'That's the way of the world Cleve, one man's loss is another man's gain. So what do you want now?'

'I would like to buy it back.'

'It's not for sale. It's my home and my son will inherit it one day.'

McCormick laughed. 'I can understand that, but there's nothing lost in asking. I might have caught you at a weak moment? Turning to another subject, I've had a Johan Petreus approach me about prospecting for minerals on my property. He said he was responsible for your copper discovery on Baracool. Is that true?'

Chloe nodded. 'Yes, it was his discovery although he had no authority to prospect on my land at the time.'

'And you let him get away with it? And now he has a share of it? You could have just shut him out and claimed the lot.'

'I could have Cleve, but it didn't suit me. Despite the fact he was trespassing, he made a significant discovery that would have probably gone unnoticed for years. Its development can only assist the State and I felt he deserved some reward. What would you have done?'

McCormick was about to express his true feelings when he caught the thrust of her question. 'My first reaction would have been to tell him to clear off and then go look for what he'd found.'

'And probably spent years of frustration looking for it. Petreus took a risk whether he knew it or not, but I was prepared to let him share in his find. The risk paid off. And now you're asking me whether I have any objection to him looking over your land, and the answer to that is no.'

'What if he finds another copper deposit on Baracool, does the same arrangement apply?'

Chloe pulled a wry face. 'Cleve, I would welcome him finding another twenty such deposits. And that applies to anyone's cattle stations in the Pilbara. He's got a big score on the board and I've no doubt he will capitalise on it if he can.'

'Yeah, well I don't take the same attitude. I've got my lawyers drawing up an agreement and dividing my station up into sections so he doesn't have rights to the whole area. If he finds something it will then attract bidders for the open ground adjacent to the discovery. I'll have the opportunity to dictate terms and cash-in on every deal.'

'That's your decision Cleve. I don't really want to know about it.'

'No, I suppose you're in the position you don't have to. One of the largest station owners combined with trucking interests, and now a major copper discovery, not to mention your iron-ore holdings on Baracool and Ironstone Park. Combined it makes you one of the wealthiest people in the land. Maybe my old man should have started duffing cattle?' He could not constrain the blatant tone of sarcastic envy.

'The truth is my father left me in a very precarious position financially. It was my partner Andrew Hanna who saved me from ruin and it was he who is largely responsible for my success.'

'Yes, I did hear rumours about him. A very astute guy by the sound of it. And to think Ike Shulman thought he had you cornered. The properties you inherited were about to fall into his hands before he was murdered.'

'What do you mean murdered? The coroner found it was death by misadventure. The policeman who pulled the trigger was cleared of any charges.'

'It was straight out murder. The cop was up to his neck in the duffing, taking a sling on the side. A certain bank manager was also in on it, as was your father and Ike.'

'You sound very bitter Cleve. Where did you fit into this?'

'Although Dad and Ike were planning to buy this place in partnership, Dad had the option to purchase Ike's share anytime within five years. Looking back now, I would say people had the wrong impression of Ike, he was not a black as people painted him. What do you think?'

'I really can't comment on that Cleve, other than to say it sounds something similar to an agreement my father had with him. If Andrew hadn't stepped I would have lost everything to Ike.'

'Yeah, Dad could never figure out how you pulled it off, managed to finance it and send Ike to the wall. He was still bitter about it weeks before he died.'

'And that's the basis of your bitterness?'

Cleve McCormick sighed and shook his head. 'Just a little, but it's all water under the bridge now. I really did just come over to say hello and I'm sorry if I let my feelings get the better of me.'

'I didn't take any offence to your comments Cleve.'

'There's one more subject I would like to raise with you.'

'I'm listening.' Chloe sensed what was coming. She had noted vehicle tracks of intrusion on a boundary flight the previous year when she overflew the solitude and grandeur of Gramps' grave and the concealed sacred site – the home of the Rainbow Serpent. One was on a hilltop never to be disturbed, the other well hidden from any aerial observation. Over the current dry season she had seen the wheel tracks become more definite and widespread. They were not cattle tracks or casual vehicle tracks of government employees in a National Park, they were the wheel tracks and paths of regular use. The park bordered Ascot and Venus Downs to the east and the tracks led directly back to Sapphire Springs, the McCormick property.

'I read some years ago about your possession of a red diamond. You were aware of the exact location from where that diamond originated, but would not disclose it?'

'That's correct and it's pointless asking me about it. In any event, it's now enclosed in a National Park and out of bounds to any exploration.'

'I realise that, but don't you realise you could be throwing away a fortune?'

'Why don't we leave it at that Cleve.' She had confirmed her suspicions. 'I'm not interested in fortunes I may be forgoing. Would you like to stay for lunch?'

'Thanks for the invite Chloe, but I've got to be on my way. Can I call in again?'

'Anytime, you're most welcome. I'll get Luke to drop you back at the airstrip.'

Luke was already back at the homestead by the time she heard the Cessna engine revving and the plane takeoff.

'I know it's none of my business, but can I ask whether that was a social or business call Chloe?'

'Masked as social, but strictly business Luke. Why do you ask?'

'He's not very well regarded by his staff. He has a reputation for getting what he wants and doesn't care who's standing in his way. He's not very complimentary about you either. He's got a nickname for you.'

Chloe ignored the invitation to ask. She could see the lad was trying to protect her by telling her all he knew. He made to leave and then hesitated.

'C'mon Luke, out with it. You know something don't you?'

'You'll probably give me the bullet for saying this, but I don't want to see you hurt in view of what you and Andrew did for my Dad and Mum.'

'Luke, I'm not going to fire you, just tell me what's on your mind.'

'I went through his plane while he was talking to you. He'd locked it, but that was no obstacle. I read the entire contents of his briefcase. He's got a meeting with Jack Gibbs next week to remove the no mining or exploration clauses in the gazetted National Park east of here. The proposal is the area will be open for exploration for a period of five years. If anything of significance is found in that time the National Park will be annulled. McCormick is to be granted a five year exclusive exploration licence and sole title for a further ten if he should find what he's looking for. The letter even mentioned diamonds and your reluctance to tell anyone the source of the red diamonds. I realise your attachment to that area and its significance and thought it might be of help if you are planning to get involved with him.'

Chloe nodded. 'I can't say I condone what you've done, but I certainly appreciate you telling me.' She sat back as she watched him walk off. It confirmed her suspicions McCormick's was no social visit. If Gibbs was in league with him, there was nothing she could do about it.

35

t was just after midnight when Alex let himself in and within the required thirty seconds had immobilised the alarms. The interior was dimly lit by the outside security floodlights. He knew he had an hour before the guard conducted the next security sweep. He moved quickly into Giles' office and sat down at his desk. There was only one lock and it was on the bottom drawer. It presented no barrier, it was all too easy. As he was about to pick it with the opener he had fashioned, he hesitated. Something told him to beware, Giles would not be that careless as to leave a computer with personal data in a locked drawer, without taking precautions? He knelt down and shone the torch around the underside of the desktop, but there was nothing out of the ordinary. He was about to pull back and straighten when his blood ran cold as he caught sight of a tiny wire taped to the underside. It ran across to the opposite leg of the desk and down before disappearing under the carpet. The desk was alarmed, but was it hooked into the central system which would sound the moment he opened the drawer, or was it silent which he would be unaware of until he saw the lights come on and his intrusion confronted? If hooked to the central system he had already disarmed it, so it had to be a silent monitor. But where was the switch to turn it off? Giles had either a remote electronic connection or was the answer more mundane? Alex looked under the desk top again for a concealed switch, but could see nothing. He searched all around the desk for any clue, but all that was evident was the wire disappearing under the carpet. He shone his torch on his watch and sat back in defeat. It wasn't so much the frustration at not being able to open the drawer, but the shock of what he'd almost triggered. What sixth sense had warned him Giles maybe not as naïve as he appeared? He was staring at the outline of the bank of drawers in the darkness when he grinned and chuckled to himself. The answer was in one of the remaining drawers. He gently pulled out the top drawer and felt for the underside of the desktop. His hand stopped when he felt the concealed button. He hesitated and then pressed it. He heard the click as the bottom drawer lock released. He could feel the sweat breaking out on his forehead as he slowly pulled the drawer out to reveal the computer. If he had triggered a silent alarm he had five minutes at the most before Giles leapt out of bed and drove a couple of kilometres, trapping him in the fully fenced administration compound. He opened the computer and waited an age for the screen to light up. Password, password, flashed through his panicking mind as he tapped the keys. Giles was not too concerned about security. His security relied on the constant patrols of the compound, the central building alarm and finally the concealed system on his desk drawer. Even if a thief had got through the first two obstacles the third would surely trap the unwary, as it almost had.

Alex quickly pulled up bank statements on four accounts in four different banks. To his surprise he discovered a fifth in an offshore account situated in the Isle of Man. He was staggered by the balance. He had read, if you want to hide money, deposit it right under the nose of the tax man. It was an analogy he would be disinclined to try, but obviously someone had given Giles the advice. He inserted the memory stick and downloaded the contents before quickly shutting down the computer and carefully putting it back in the drawer. As he stood he saw the glow of headlights shining on the office wall. He glanced at his watch. Security was early or it was Giles? He quickly ran over to the entrance and reset the alarm before crouching down behind a desk in a vain attempt at concealment. If it was security they would look for the constant blue light on the panel just outside the door and leave without checking further. However, if they'd been alerted or it was Giles driving in, then the game was up. He huddled down as he heard a vehicle door open and footsteps approach. He counted them as they mounted the three steps to the landing and then there was silence. He could not move from his crouched position as the slightest noise would be heard or movement activate the alarm. Was, who ever it was, waiting for backup or were they going to open the damned door? He saw a subdued glow from underneath. The person had lit a cigarette and was just sitting on the wooden bench outside on the landing. It was a good ten minutes before he heard the footsteps retreating, the engine start and the vehicle drive off. He slowly rose from his position, every muscle in his legs and back protesting as he regained his posture. He immobilised the alarm, quickly let himself out and then reset it again. He stayed in the shadows as he walked around the perimeter and exited through a side-gate situated in the far southern corner of the compound behind a storage and maintenance shed. It had been overlooked by security as it had no CCTV camera. He had discovered it when he happened to open a door in the back of the storage facility months earlier. Sure enough there was a key for the gate hanging just inside the backdoor of the shed. So much for security? The narrow passageway between the hedge and the fence was completely overgrown, concealing it. He had been meaning to bring it to Giles' attention, but was now glad he hadn't. The main gate was covered by a camera. Although he had a key and could have shut the camera off, the entry would have been immediately noted by security. He would never attempted tonight's incursion unless he'd discovered the hidden entry point. He walked back to his comfortable company-provided accommodation a kilometre away at a casual pace just in case he was being observed by someone sitting on a verandah of any of the identical houses scattered around a large semi-circular compound. He paused and casually looked around as he unlocked the door and let himself in. He had seen no one, but that didn't mean he'd not been seen and someone would innocently reveal his late night sojourn if questions were asked, or someone made an off-hand comment. He told himself he was being paranoid as he sat down at the table and began to think through his next move. It was all very well he had complete readouts of Giles' bank statements, but what could he do with them? He had absolutely no proof as to the source of the balances or transactions in each account. He could not show them to anyone as they would be immediately complicit in the felony he had just committed. How was he going to match the various deposits with illicit actions on Giles' part, if indeed they were illicit? Giles had already given him the message to stop investigating areas he had no involvement with. He was going to have to be very careful in accessing information from the company mainframe for clues and who he talked to without Giles becoming aware. He felt totally frustrated. He could identify the possible proceeds of the crime , but he hadn't a clue how the crime had been committed or where. It was going to take time, but he was positive he would come up with the answers.

Slowly over the next month, a pattern started to emerge as he continued to access Giles' accounts. The deposits followed within a week of the company's creditor invoices being paid out on the standard thirty-day cycle. He had noted this was a busy time for Giles on his private laptop. Alex was almost caught completely unawares one day when he inadvertently left his own laptop open on his desk when distracted by another staff member. He turned back to find Giles standing over it and about to tap the space bar to bring the screen alive.

'What's this here for, and more to the point, what are you doing with it? I hope you're not uploading company data?'

Alex shook his head. 'No Rick, I was just replying to a couple of personal emails. Nothing to do with the company.' The lie was smooth and without hesitation.

'Fair enough, but could you do that in your own time. It makes me nervous when I see people working away on pc's instead of what we pay them for.'

'I can understand that Rick, it also makes me nervous.'

Giles turned to walk off, then checked as his brain absorbed the riposte. The hesitation was momentary. Alex pretended not to notice as he flipped his laptop shut. It was a lucky escape. Another moment and Giles would have tapped the space bar and seen one of his bank accounts come alive on screen. Alex cursed his recklessness. It had only taken a moment for the staffer to distract his attention, but it was almost fatal. His final remark to Giles was stupid, but which his brain was unable to suppress in the millisecond of transmission. Giles was not that ignorant he would not have been left wondering at the thrust of the comment.

It was half an hour later when he saw Giles walk out through the main gate and over towards the central haulage yard where the road-trains and prime-movers were contained in a separate high security compound. Alex was staring idly out through the window when a sudden thought struck him. It should have been apparent well before this. Why were the transport yards so well guarded, including security fences, dogs, alarms and automatic high-power flood-lighting, while the nerve centre of the whole operation was contained in this central block with limited security which he'd already taken advantage of. There was no way anyone could enter the transport premises day or night without being recorded or unnoticed. The dozens of rigs, accompanying spares, tires and fuel ran into tens of millions of dollars, any part of it liable to theft and be turned into quick cash. In contrast the administration block had limited security, the assumption being all information was generated and received on computers and replicated in off-site memory storage. Other than an act of pointless vandalism, a fire would have limited effect before operations were quickly restored at some other location. Alex unconsciously nodded. He was convinced he was looking directly at the source of the balances in Giles' accounts. But how was he doing it? Every spanner, spare part, tire or litre of diesel was strictly accounted for. It would be impossible to falsify records without him, or one of the other staff picking up on it. As he returned to his desk and sat down, a light flashed in his brain. It wasn't what was delivered and in the yard - the crime occurred prior. It was then the pattern fell into place along with the impenetrable wall impossible to surmount. He had found it, but couldn't prove it. There was only one way to progress his suspicions and that was through a direct approach. He would have to go right over Giles' head and take the consequences if he was wrong. Chloe had the power, but did she have the fortitude to authorise an investigation? Giles was an integral trusted employee who had been with the company for years and ran the transport operation with absolute professionalism and apparent integrity, whereas he was an expendable nepotic blow-in. Alex discounted his chances of retaining his job if he did not have conclusive evidence on which to base his case.

Rick Giles had some questions to answer, but who was going to ask them? Since his meeting with Chloe, Alex had paid particular attention to the financials of the live cattle export, slaughtering and meat packing side of the group, but he concluded there was really no room for Giles to be acquiring ill-gotten wealth from that source. It was too well controlled. He had looked closely at the cattle freighting and contracting operations, but could find no obvious anomalies. Maybe he hadn't looked close enough? It had to be from somewhere within the group operations, but where? He noted in addition to the random deposits there was a large single deposit received during the week after the close of every month and it was never less than around ten thousand. Giles was on the take, but from who? The light of recognition began to form in his consciousness. It would be a slow process, but he was determined to identify the source of the illicit income. It was the following week when Giles called him into his office, which was unusual because he always approached a person at their desk if he wanted to discuss something. He could tell the manager was not in his usual jovial mood where everyone was his friend, a mood which he engendered within his staff.

'Something on your mind Rick?'

Giles gave a strained smile and indicated a seat. 'It's come to my notice you've been checking through records of our transport division. Why's that?'

'I'm trying to learn and understand the business from top to bottom. I want to look at everything.'

'And have you found anything of particular interest?'

'No, but I'm not looking for anything in particular. I just want to get an understanding of how the business ticks.' He could see Giles was not buying his explanation, despite his look of feigned disinterest.

'Okay, I can understand that, but I would like you to stick to your allotted responsibilities. Making random enquiries of various section managers suggests they have something to hide. They resent the intrusion.'

Alex nodded in acceptance. 'Your comments are noted Rick, I'll stick to my knitting. However, I've had full co-operation from everyone I've approached so far. I haven't had a murmur about any intrusion.'

'They might not express it to your face, but I get feedback you're not aware of. Keep your nose out of other divisions unless I authorise you to do so. Good staff are hard to come by. I don't want any of them feeling they should start looking elsewhere for employment or bitching to their wives I don't trust them.'

'I understand. You've given me the message and I respect that.'

Giles gave a wide smile as he reached out with his hand which Alex shook. 'I'm pleased that's sorted. The last thing I want is dissension in the ranks. That's the way Andrew ran things and I'm sure Chloe is of the same mind.'

He idly tapped a pen on his desk as he watched Alex leave. Was he on a learning curve as he proclaimed, or did he know something and was pursuing his suspicions? He was too dangerous to have around if he did. There was too much money involved. He picked up his mobile phone as it began to ring and went over to close his office door. 'Yes, Ronnie. When can I expect the next lot?'

Alex had heard the name and the question as the door was firmly closed.

36

'Alex, there's a rodeo on in Kununurra this weekend. Are you a starter? I'm going stir crazy in this place. I need a few beers and some women to chat to.'

'I'll be in that,' Alex replied.

They were both in a jovial mood of release as they drove along the endless highway. Alex was waiting for the conversation to turn to the subject of work. He had a clear motive in mind, but was reluctant to bring it up. He didn't have to, his companion was intent on doing exactly the same.

'What do you think of Rick?'

Alex restrained his surprise. It was exactly the question he was going to ask. 'Good manager with plenty of experience. A real asset to the business I would say.'

Ben Ridgeway took his eyes off the road and glanced over at him. 'You really think so? I believe he may be running his own race on the side. Dipping in the petty-cash tin somehow.'

'What makes you think that?'

'Let's just say I've got my suspicions. The guy's overbearing and shifty. I've been to his house in Darwin and boy, has he got all the toys. A couple of the latest Toyota Cruisers, his and her Harley's, plus a boat, jet-skis and that house must have set him back north side of a million. How does he afford all that on his salary?'

Alex was immediately on guard. He had the feeling he was being suckered. 'I don't know anything about his house or what he owns and I'm not interested. However, I don't believe the guy has held up any banks, so he's worked for what he has. Good luck to him.'

'I saw him paying you a bit of attention recently. What was that all about?'

'Nothing really. I was just sending and replying to a couple of emails in company time. I don't think he appreciated it, but he didn't say too much.'

'So you think the guy's on the level? No suspicions about where he gets his money from?'

'Look Ben, I do my job and get paid well for it. I'm not interested in what Rick Giles may or may not be up to.'

Ridgeway laughed. 'Don't bullshit me. I know you've been ferreting around asking questions and Rick has pulled you up on it. C'mon, you can tell me what you're doing? Who the hell are you anyway? What is your background? I've asked Rick and he's none the wiser except you were introduced by Chloe's stud, Andrew Hanna. I've got to hand it to that guy, he knew how to screw his way into a fortune. Mind you, it didn't do him any good now that he's only an urn-full of ash.' Ridgeway noticed the sudden tensing of the person beside him. 'Hey, what was he to you? How did you get to know him?'

'He was introduced to me by a mutual friend,' Alex lied without hesitation. 'I was just out of uni and needed a job. I thought I'd try it for a year or so and then move on. I don't really like being out here isolated in the boonies.'

'Rick thinks there's a closer connection. He knows you spent a weekend with the boss at Ascot Downs homestead. He's never received such an invite. Boy, what a conquest that would be. She's old enough to be your mother, but I wouldn't pass up the chance of giving her a roll in the hay. I'd roll her in chocolate and lick her all over, she's one gorgeous looking woman. Did you get a leg over? '

Alex was aware Ridgeway was baiting him, but did not react. 'Yes, she's one stunning woman. I don't know why she invited me, but I really enjoyed her company. Charlie, her son was home from school. That kid's one interesting character.'

'Yeah, I suppose he would have cramped your style?'

Ridgeway was becoming obnoxious with his insinuations. 'Ben, why don't you just concentrate on driving and leave personalities out of this.'

Ridgeway's annoyance at not being able to get a ribald remark from his passenger was showing. 'Okay, okay, I was only trying to make conversation. You don't have to be an arsehole about it, I was only making a joke.'

'A joke in very poor taste.'

Ridgeway drove in silence as the hours ticked by. Finally he slowed down as they approached the township and he pulled into a motel. 'I'm staying here. I was going to let you bunk in with me as the whole town is booked out, but you can find your own accommodation sport and good luck to that. You really are a boring bastard.'

Alex had no time to answer as Ridgeway gave a dismissive laugh and walked off. Alex was pleased to be rid of his companion. It was obvious he was under surveillance and suspicion. He didn't bother to check whether the motel was fully booked as he picked up his small backpack and walked into town. The first hotel was booked out as Ridgeway had predicted, but a second had a spare room in a detached accommodation block. He lay down on the single bed and drifted off. It had been a long day mesmerised by an endless strip of sealed road with its shimmering mirages morphing in and out, accompanied by the stench of rotting cattle and kangaroos killed by forty tons of unstoppable road-trains.

It was late afternoon when he awoke. He was hungry. He splashed his face from the rudimentary sink which had the smell of urine about it, combed his hair and went through to the hotel bar. It was packed with station hands all dressed in the identical kit of riding boots, jeans, checked shirts and wide-brimmed Akubras. They all knew one another, or immediately bonded with a stranger who fell into their category of a hard-living, hard-working, and now hard-drinking, loud-mouthed individual looking for the relief of a few days before returning to the atrophying monotony of looking at cattle until this time next year.

Alex bought a beer and went outside into the beer garden in the front of the hotel. He found an isolated table in a corner from where he could observe without being conspicuous. His was the only chair at the table, as the others having been commandeered by surrounding tables where groups attracted individuals jostling to join friends. He was sitting up against a wall with a line of leafy planters to one side, shielding him from a further extension of the beer garden towards the roadside. He was beginning to feel he should have stayed at home. He didn't know anyone, it was not his scene and he was disinclined to join in.

The clash of styles was instantly noted, but did not raise any comment as two Harley's pulled up in front of the hotel. Long hair pulled back and tied into pony tails, tattoos on both arms, leather gear and jackets, but no patches or colours. The pair strode through into the bar. A few minutes and they were back out with beers and sat at a table where they could observe their bikes. Alex lost interest in them until he saw Giles with Ridgeway in tow, walk out of the bar and join them. This was not a casual meeting as they shook hands and sat down. After a couple of banal exchanges they all leaned in towards the centre of the table careful they could not be overheard as the conversation became more intense. None of them was here for a good time, it was strictly business for the next half hour. The conversation finally ended, the bikies stood and with a handshake returned to their bikes before briefly talking to a cop who had pulled his ute up alongside. The acknowledgement was friendly with an ensuing brief discussion before the cop slowly drove away. The bikies then rode off without the usual roar of powerful engines denoting their parting arrogance. Giles had some interesting friends Alex mused, but he could not see a connection and it was none of his business. He turned his attention back to the crowd in front of him.

He finished his beer and was about to go through to the dining room when he glanced through the greenery and across at Giles and Ridgeway. It only took him a moment to recognise the person dressed in standard dark green work clothes. He did not have to guess the identity of his employment, the name clearly emblazoned on his chest pocket. The logo on the vehicle parked in front also confirmed his matching occupation and employer. Alex pulled back as he watched Giles dispatch Ridgeway to the bar. A few minutes later he emerged clutching three glasses which he spilled as he caught sight of Alex. He set each glass down and leaned over to whisper something to Giles.

Alex had seen enough as he rose and walked out. The pieces had finally fallen into place. The bikies he could not account for, but they no doubt had something to do with Giles' bank accounts. As for the other person, he now knew exactly how Giles acquired at least one income stream. The problem was, how could he prove it without getting full access to all company records? It could only be instigated from the top, but would Chloe go along with such an audit? He believed he could make a convincing case and he was going to try as soon as he got back.

The steak was tough and overdone instead of rare, the chips were soft instead of crisp and the salad limp, it had been sitting out on the counter for so long. What was supposed to be a pepper sauce was a thick re-heated gravy which swamped the plate. At least the garlic bread was up to scratch and the wine relaxed him. He pulled a wry grin as he finished, pushed the plate aside and wiped his mouth with a paper napkin. He waited for a few minutes for the gravy taste to subside before leaning back and savouring the remainder of the wine. The dining room began to fill with increasing levels of beer-induced sound as the station-hands wandered in.

'Do you mind if we sit here mate?'

Alex looked up at the gruff request. He was about to nod his assent when three chairs were suddenly produced and the fourth person looked around the crowded tables in the hopeless quest for a spare.

'Here, have mine, I'm just leaving.' Alex's gesture was not acknowledged as the individual plonked his glass down and stumbled as he brushed past.

Alex walked back to his room and lay down, his mind racing as he contemplated what he had just witnessed in the last hour. How could Giles be such a bloody fool as to meet in full view like he just had? But then again what did he have to fear? He was not under investigation. Giles was an employee who had gained the total trust of both Andrew and Chloe and it was through that establishment of trust he had managed to perpetrate and prolong the crime. But how long had it been going on for? Alex had suspected the auditors were to blame. The accounts were audited, but a long and continuing association with the contented client, meant the auditors may not have bothered to dredge further back than matching invoices with payments. The two cancelled each other out, no one was inserting false invoices, nor were there any phony creditors, so all was in order. He let out a sigh of exasperation and relief. The auditors appeared to be in the clear. He would have made a complete fool of himself if he had pushed Chloe into launching a full investigation with the object of trying to identify fraudulent invoicing and joining the auditors to a negligence action for damages. Someone above was looking over him, or was it Ridgeway's harmless invitation to a rodeo that revealed the truth? He knew he must disregard caution and really take a firm approach with Chloe. To hell with her sensitivities about upsetting Giles. She either agreed to his demands or he would immediately resign and leave.

He awoke to a gentle tapping on the door. Without thinking he rolled off the bed and still half asleep, opened it. The last thing he remembered was the huge fist crashing into his jaw, that was until he came to in the back of a moving Toyota LandCruiser.

'What are we supposed to do with him?'

'Take him for a ride and finish him off. There's five grand in it for you.'

The psychopathic laugh made him freeze. He closed his eyes as the person turned to look at him. "Easy money. Just pull up anywhere and I'll take him for a walk in the scrub.'

As the Toyota began to slow Alex gripped the door handle and gently tried to open it, but the driver had taken no chances, it was locked. The vehicle came to stop and he felt the lock release as the passenger got out.

'And don't mess around,' the driver shouted. 'I'll keep the motor running in case someone appears on the horizon. I don't want someone stopping to offer help, or noting the registration.'

The laugh peeled even louder as the figure stepped out and made to open the rear passenger door. 'Don't worry about that, it will only take me half a min....' He had not finished the sentence as Alex threw open the door with such force it knocked the assassin to the ground, the shotgun flying out of his hand. He did not look back as he ran for his life dodging amongst the trees and scrub.

'Ah, a moving target, I like giving someone a sporting chance,' The maniacal peel of laughter followed him. He tripped and fell forward as the first of two shots rang out. He felt the pellets from the twelve gauge hit him in the back instantly exploding into a mass of shredded shirt and bloodied flesh. He could feel no pain as he struggled to his feet and staggered on before collapsing. He propped himself against a tree and waited for the end.

'There are headlights approaching. Get your arse back here Spook, or I'm leaving without you,' was the panicked command from the Toyota.

The killer was only about twenty metres away pushing cartridges into the gun when he heard the yell. He glanced back at the vehicle and then at his target, contemplating which action was more urgent. Alex curled up on the ground and covered his head as he saw the gun come up. Spook stumbled as he turned to run. Alex heard both barrels discharge, but felt nothing - the gunman had panicked and missed. He raised his head to see the killer climbing into the moving cab as the vehicle pulled away in a cloud of thick dust.

'Did you get the bastard?'

'Sure did. He took both barrels full in the back.'

'Yeah, I think you're full of shit, Spook. He was still running after you hit him from what I could see.'

'I gave him two more barrels after that. He's dead meat. Now, don't fuck with me mate, I got him and I want my money.'

The driver nodded his head as he glanced across at the gunman. This was not the time nor place to argue.

On the long country road, headlights of the approaching vehicle could be seen for minutes before the sound of the engine became audible. The headlights were approaching from the rear of the accelerating Toyota. Alex could hear the reverberating diesel motor of a heavy transport as it approached. He pulled himself to his feet and stumbled towards the roadway as the bouts of pain and shock began to overtake him. He could feel the blood flooding from dozens of wounds running down his legs. His shirt was a shredded blood-soaked rag as he reached the road and collapsed, the multiple sets of tires inches from crushing his head as the truck roared past.

37

He was propped up in a bed when he slowly opened his eyes and cast them around the tiny curtained cubicle. He could feel the tape holding a thick pad on his back and another on the back of his head, his left arm also heavily bandaged.

'What's your name son?' The khaki uniform with three stripes signified police.

'Alex, Alex Hammond.'

'Do you know who shot you?'

Alex slowly twisted his head. 'All I know is someone knocked me out and I found myself in the back of a Toyota being driven along a dirt haul-road. It stopped, so I made a run for it and here I am.'

'You mean there was only one person?'

'No, there were two. One was the guy who knocked me out and the other was a psycho who did the shooting.'

'Did you catch any names?'

'Only the psycho, the driver called him Spook.'

'You didn't have any ID on you when they brought you in. Whoever it was, took your wallet.'

'How did I get in here?'

'A truckie came within inches of turning you into road-kill. All he saw was a figure falling in front of his rig. If he hadn't stopped, you would have bled to death.'

'I certainly owe him one when I get out of here. Can you give me his name?'

The cop ignored the question. 'You're not into running drugs are you, or involved in some other illegal activity? I've already run your prints.'

'No, I work for Chloe Boyce. I was in town for the rodeo.'

The cop was still asking questions when Alex drifted off as the dominant painkiller enveloped his senses and relieved the pain.

'You won't get much more out of him today sergeant. He's very lucky he was found in time, otherwise I would have been writing out a death certificate.' The doctor had stood back from where he had been silently observing the interrogation.

'He'll pull through okay, will he?'

'When he was admitted yesterday I didn't give him much chance because of the blood loss. It took hours to dig all those pellets out of his back and arm. Luckily, only a few of the slugs grazed his head so he must have been falling forward at the time. He's got nasty lacerations, but if he'd been upright the full blast of shot would have put a very big hole in him. That would have been the end. Because he's now awake means he's pulling through the critical stage. He's young and fit and should be out of here in a few days.'

The cop nodded as he began to walk out. 'If he says anything interesting would you let me know? I know every crim and feral within five hundred kilometers of here, but I've never heard of a Spook. The culprit could be some blow-in for the rodeo, but I'm beginning to believe this was a targeted hit. I don't think this lad is as innocent as he makes out.'

'I know Chloe Boyce well sergeant. If he's involved in something unlawful he can look forward to receiving a red card. She'll sack him immediately.'

It was the following afternoon when he awoke to find Chloe standing beside him holding his hand. 'What happened Alex? I know you've been shot, but do you know why? Did you get involved in a fight?'

Alex smiled and squeezed her hand. 'It's good to see you Chloe. No, I didn't get into a fight and I don't know why I was targeted.'

'Ben Ridgeway said you were intending to go to the rodeo with him, but took off on your own. You just disappeared. He offered to share his room with you because the town was booked out, but you declined.'

'That's partly true, but there's more to it than that.'

'I'm listening Alex. Come on, out with it.'

He clasped her hand firmer. 'It's all pure speculation at the moment. I don't have any hard facts to go on, so why don't we leave it until I have?'

'Okay, you're going to be in here for a couple of days and then you'll need time off to fully convalesce. Why not spend a week or two with me at Ascot Downs before you get back to work?'

'I'm not going back Chloe, I'm resigning.'

'You,...you, can't do that, I won't let you. You can't just walk out on me like that.' She had grasped his wounded arm in an involuntary action, but quickly released it when she saw the look of pain flash across his face. 'Oh, I'm sorry Alex, but please tell me you're not serious?'

'I'm very serious. I was lucky this time, but that doesn't mean whoever it was won't try again. I just don't want to be offering myself up again as a clay target.'

Chloe was sitting in the screened verandah when Alex walked out. 'Hello, how are you feeling today?'

'Fine thanks Chloe. It's almost time to move on.'

'You're serious about leaving me then?'

'I certainly can't return under Giles' management. I believe I would still be a target for some no-good with a shotgun. Tell me, do you still trust Giles?'

'I've got to trust him. He's the backbone of the haulage operations, which under his direction run very smoothly. Why, have you found something to confirm Andrew's suspicions?'

'Yes, I certainly have. I believe Giles has got a connection with several of your local suppliers as well as some contact with a bikie gang, who have only one reason to be this far north and that's to run drugs. Giles met a couple of bikies in Kununurra and I saw those same bikies talking to a cop who rolled up just as they were leaving the pub I was staying at. I'm convinced Giles is taking kickbacks as well as pushing drugs. I can't prove the drugs, but I've pulled up all his bank accounts and the balances both here and offshore leave no other credible explanation.'

'So you're suggesting if I don't allow you to have access to the trucking operations with full authority you are going to walk away?'

'Precisely.'

Chloe sat back in thought. 'How long would it to take you to prove to me Giles is guilty of what you suggest?'

'A hope within the month.'

'I don't know about that Alex. You're asking me to risk losing him if you're wrong.'

'Chloe, I know I'm right. I'll show you his bank statements. Would you like to see them?'

'No, they've been obtained illegally, so I can't admit to having seen them or authorised you to obtain them.. And don't confirm to me you have. Breach of privacy is not something I want to be accused of. You must understand my position.'

'I do,' Alex snorted as he turned turned to look out at a swirling patch of dust. 'Chloe wake up to what's going on. Take your head out of the sand. How do I know my own father was not mixed up in this. If he was as smart as you say, he should have nailed Giles long ago. I know it's a ludicrous suggestion, but I just don't know what to think. That's why I want out of here and out of the company. I just don't want to be around if you won't listen. In fact, you're flying to Perth in the morning, so I'll hitch a ride.'

She was stunned by the attack and its determination, but she was resolved not to lose him. 'Okay, you can come with me tomorrow, but you can't resign. I want you to work out of Perth and report directly to me. In the meantime I want you to think about it overnight and give me a complete plan of how you wish to proceed. I don't want to know what you suspect, I want to know what you can prove or how close you are to proving it. I want to know how he's doing it and how you think it escaped Andrew's attention. Will you accept that?'

'Only if you give me a free hand.'

'I will, but you'd better be right, otherwise I will accept your resignation.'

Alex nodded in acceptance. 'That's okay with me, but I will prove it.'

Alex tapped on the glass panel of Chloe's open door. 'Can I have a few minutes of your time boss?'

She smiled and nodded for him to come in and take a seat. 'You're ready to reveal all are you?'

'I am now, but I was wrong in my initial assumptions as to how Giles is ripping you off. I thought he had to be generating invoices from dummy companies. It's an old trick. However, I believe I've nailed him and it will be a simple loop-hole to close. I want you to give me the authority to call for new contracts for the supply of fuel, tires, new prime-movers and trailers. In fact, anything Giles has the authority to sign off on."

Chloe made to ask a question, but Alex cut her off. 'I know what you're about to ask, but hear me out. Giles is taking a kick-back on everything. The fuel supplier is an independent who gives Giles a backhander to ensure he keeps the contract. And so it goes on through every phase including insurance where the agent receives a trailing commission on all new business and the renewal of that business. I haven't checked to see what insurance costs you a year, but it would have to be in excess of a million bucks. The commission on that alone would add up to a nice little earner for Giles. You name it and he has his hand out. It's taken him a few years to perfect, but obviously something must have roused Andrew's suspicions. Do you know how many million litres of diesel you purchase a year, or how many new rigs you buy? A kickback of say twenty grand on a new million dollar rig and trailers would go unnoticed – it would fly right under the radar. I'm talking about big dollars Chloe and that's where Giles is taking you to the cleaners.'

'You're quite certain of this?'

'I am. Give me the nod and I guarantee you'll notice the difference almost immediately.'

'You mentioned drugs.'

'You have more than a hundred rigs on the road and rapidly expanding. You lost five rigs last year. Total write-offs with another ten almost totalled, but able to be rebuilt. The result is your insurance premiums have taken a twenty percent hike.'

'We lose a few rigs every year for various reasons. It's a difficult business to retain good drivers.'

'You've put your finger on the problem. The five rigs you lost included the deaths of five drivers. Forty tons of rig and cattle overturning at speed on some outback dirt road is pure driver error. I've discovered, by looking at police records, all five drivers had drugs in their systems.'

'And you think it all points to Giles?'

'The drivers are picking up cattle from distant stations close to aboriginal settlements where there is endemic alcohol and drug abuse. I've no doubt certain of your drivers are Giles' handpicked couriers. Unfortunately, the ones that died last year and probably those in previous years, all had drugs in their systems, so they were either not giving the natives what they paid for, or were being supplied direct by Giles.'

'So the bikie gang is supplying Giles and a cop is in on it?'

'Where there's smoke there's usually something burning. However, I believe by removing Giles the problem will resolve itself. There's no need to pick a fight with the bikies or the cops as their involvement will disappear overnight.'

'So how do you want to proceed?'

'Chloe, I'm not going north again to confront Giles. I want you to summon him down here where I can confront him with what I have.'

Chloe drew in a deep breath and laughed. 'Andrew was smart and very clever - I think you're cut from the same cloth.'

'One person alone is not the sole reason for success Chloe. You look behind the scenes and success is spread across a whole spectrum of people who remain in the background. At first I thought my father could have been complicit in what's been going on, but now I'm about to clear his name.'

Giles was in an aggressive mood as he walked into Chloe's office and saw Alex sitting there. 'Why have you called me down here when you could have handled it over the phone Chloe?'

'It's because of these Rick,' Alex replied flipping over copies of Giles' most recent bank statements. 'How do you explain these?'

'What the hell is going on? This is theft and a gross breach of privacy. I'm going to bring this police in on this.'

'Be our guest Rick.' Alex indicated the phone. 'You can explain to us how these various balances have been derived, or you can explain it to the cops. It's obvious this theft has been going on for a number of years, so I think the balance in these accounts rightly belongs to your employer.'

'That's my money and I can prove it. How the hell did you get hold of my bank records anyway?'

Alex ignored the increasing belligerence. 'We'll look forward to you explaining in court just before you go down for theft. You've been siphoning off backhanders from every source possible, but it has just stopped this morning. You're also into distributing drugs which won't be too hard to prove. The lawyers will apply to have caveats slapped on your accounts until a judge decides just who the money belongs to.'

'You haven't answered my question. How did you gain access to those accounts?'

'Let's just say they came into my possession through your carelessness. You were also very careless in botching the attempt on my life.'

Giles ignored the accusation. 'So you're going to bring the law in on this?'

'That's up to Chloe, but my advice to her is to set you as an example to anyone contemplating proceeding down a similar path. I would say you'll get five years for taking secret commissions and at least another five for peddling drugs.

I would add, at this precise moment every driver entering or leaving the yard is being tested for drugs. And don't think for a moment the guilty ones won't point a finger at you as will all those trade suppliers who've been giving you backhanders. You will be nailed as the prime instigator.'

Giles looked at Chloe for clemency, but there was no facial acknowledgement of compassion. 'Rick, I'm very disappointed in you. However, I'm willing to draw a line under this with your resignation and the transfer of the funds in those various accounts back to my transport group. You may retain the funds in your salary account.'

'B.....but that will clean me out. I'm not going to agree to that blackmail.'

'Call it blackmail Rick, but you've got no choice. You either hand back money which you've indirectly pilfered from the company, or you serve time. It's your decision. You walk out of here without a job, but still have a healthy balance in your personal account.' Chloe picked up a bank statement. 'I would say fifty thousand should keep you going until you find another position. It's that or you get convicted and lose everything.'

Giles slowly nodded and sat back defeated. 'I don't suppose I have any choice. I'll move my personal things out as soon as I get back. You've got a good man in Ben Ridgeway when you promote him to manager.'

'Your belongings have already been removed from the premises Rick and Ridgeway was terminated this morning. He's already been escorted off the premises by security. It was decided to remove the next lingering threat of a cancer.' Alex could not keep the tone of satisfaction out of his voice. They watched as Giles got up and walked out of the office.

'That could have blown up in our faces Alex. How were you going to explain how you got hold of those bank statements if he'd called your bluff? What you did and I condoned by looking in the other direction, was illegal. You had no concrete proof as to how or when, or from who he was taking backhanders, only a very confident suspicion. With good legal advice he could have drawn me into a dispute I would have been forced to settle just to keep my name out of the media. It would have cost me more than he's stolen. I just pray he goes quietly.'

'He will. There won't be any repercussions. I know it was a calculated gamble Chloe, but it worked, so you can forget about Rick Giles. I'll follow up to make sure he refunds those monies.'

'Alex, I've got a mess on my hands which only you can fix. You know the transport business and you're the only candidate to address the problems in that division.'

'I should have guessed that was coming, but I'll only stay for three months to appoint a new manager and call for new tenders to straighten out the complete supply chain. After that I'm out of here.'

Chloe did not reply as she watched him get up and walk out. *'I've got plans for you Alex Hammond, or should I say Hanna,'* she murmured to herself with a smile.

38

Chloe had taken an earlier call from a secretary with an overbearing attitude. It had the tone of imperious command, rather than polite enquiry. She was told the call was confidential and not to be discussed or conveyed to the media. The caller was to be addressed as Mr Premier rather than Mr McDonald.

'Ms Boyce, I believe my secretary has given you an outline of the purpose of this call?'

'Yes, she has Mr McDonald.' There was a brief silence. She was not complying with protocol as laid down, or his secretary had not made it clear enough.

'I've been closely following your activities for some time now. It has come to my attention you are preparing an application to have part of your iron-ore holdings on Baracool station declared a nature reserve. That action would deprive the government of royalty revenue to which it is entitled and as Premier of this State I must oppose it. However, I would like us to get together and discuss it further to get a proper understanding of what you wish to protect. Could you find time to meet me?'

Chloe was surprised. There was no command, but she was well aware by reputation the request was not to be denied. Angus McDonald had been in office for twelve years and didn't hold that position by being soft or malleable.

It was the following week when she was shown into his sumptuous suite. He rose from his desk and moved across the room. 'Take a seat over here Ms Boyce, I'm so pleased you've come.'

Chloe was inclined to believe the size of her contribution to his incumbent political party funds was one of the reasons for his gracious manner. He would be no doubt aware she also likewise contributed to his opposition. There was no point in getting her offside. She was an influential personality who did not pick sides and was to be treated accordingly. However, he knew she played the game to win, a game he was a master of.

'Let's get down to business Ms Boyce.'

'It's Chloe, Mr Premier.' He was exactly as she had seen him in the media, a strong person in his late sixties, a white salt-and-pepper mane pulled back over his collar in one continuous flow with no parting. The face was rugged and strong with a fixed smile brought on by incessant campaigning and kissing odorous babies. The back was ram-rod straight. There was complete absence of overweight indulgence and she could tell the mind was totally alert.

McDonald was caught off guard, but quickly regained his composure, ever the consummate politician. The protocols would be overlooked in this private meeting. 'In that case please call me Angus. As indicated, I want to talk to you about Baracool and the iron-ore. Why are you opposing it's development?'

'I'm not opposing the development of the entire licence area. I just want part of it to be annexed into a nature reserve. Angus, once you've seen what I'm wanting to protect, I believe you'll agree with me.'

'My Mines Minister, Jack Gibbs believes there's nothing to protect and I should refuse your request. Of course I could over-rule him, but that's not the way we do it in my government.'

'Angus, if I could show you the natural beauty of its surrounds, along with the animals and unique bird life you would begin to move in my direction. However, there's a more compelling force than that, a force that has growing political pressure to recognise. The part of Baracool I want to protect is one that encompasses ancient aboriginal ceremonial sites. I can show you dozens of bora rings, rock carvings and paintings which have been there for tens of thousands of years. Civilisations through history have virtually removed all traces of previous occupants. Just look at what has happened in Iraq and Syria in recent times. I would like your support to ensure it doesn't happen on a unique location in the Pilbara.'

'But you've already submitted plans for the development of a part of Baracool. You are very close to starting a copper mining operation and you've established an exploration division. I'm aware you're negotiating with various companies for the iron-ore deposits on your other property, Ironstone Park. Your request to annex part of Baracool while intending to mine on the remainder as well as your other property, I find somewhat incongruous '

'Angus, why don't I take you on a tour of what I'm trying to protect which is just over a quarter of the permit area. I'll fly you up there and you can stay at my homestead on Ascot Downs. I can then fly you around in a helicopter to show what I'm trying to insulate from mining. I realise you no doubt have a full appointment book, but parliament is in recess for the next few weeks so I'm asking for a few days of your time.'

McDonald sat back as he considered the request. 'I would have to take Jack Gibbs with me. Against his opposition you need to convince me your area of interest needs to be retained rather than the whole area be opened for mining. Gibbs has been in my ear for some time now pressing me to invoke special powers to terminate your exploration permits.'

'I'm quite aware of Jack Gibbs' intentions, but I've complied with all the conditions of the licence, albeit somewhat belatedly. Work is progressing at a fast clip now.'

McDonald got up, walked back to his desk, picked up a phone and keyed in an extension. 'Jack, Angus here. I've got Ms Chloe Boyce with me, she's going to show me the area she wants to protect on Baracool. I can fit it in next week and as Minister responsible I think you should accompany me.'

Chloe could hear the muffled response of objection from across the room. It was clear Gibbs was not in agreement.

'Well, cancel your engagements for a few days, this is important.' There was another outburst which McDonald just nodded to without emotion. He wasn't going to allow any sub-ordinate dictate to him. 'Look Jack, I've made the commitment. I'll leave it to you to tag along or not. We leave Monday.' McDonald replaced the hand-piece to cut off any further protests as he turned to Chloe. 'I trust that fits in with your plans. I really don't have time to be messed around with other people's schedules. I wasn't referring to yours, of course.' McDonald did not sit down, signifying the meeting was over. 'Monday it is then. I'll get my secretary to confirm everything with you.'

Chloe walked out with a feeling of elation and trepidation. She had got the number one citizen in the State to listen, but she realised she had made a sworn enemy of the man who would continue to oppose her. And she was uncertain as to whether McDonald would finally support her views.

McDonald's car pulled up beside the jet. He smiled and shook Chloe's hand before introducing her to his wife, Sophie. Chloe had seen many media photos of her, but she always seemed to be one step behind her husband and out of focus. She was surprised by the warm acknowledgement and handshake. Sophie was about her husband's age with the same vitality of life.

'Chloe, I'm so pleased to meet you. I'm looking forward to a couple of days in the outback.' When her husband was out of earshot being guided to the stairway by the pilot, Sophie turned to Chloe. 'All I get taken to is boring parliamentary functions where everyone is trying to impress everyone else. At least on this trip I'll only have to put up with that lech, Gibbs. Why Angus doesn't give him the boot I can't understand. It's all party politics of course, but that's another story.'

Chloe took an instant liking to her. She had been expecting someone with superior dismissive airs, but the exact opposite was apparent. Would she revert to type, the wife of an important person who demanded as much attention as her spouse?

McDonald hesitated as he was about to board and looked around. 'No sign of Gibbs I see. Well, if he's not here in ten minutes we leave without him.'

The luggage had been loaded and the door closed when Chloe tapped on the pilot's shoulder and pointed towards a car driving through the gates. 'Here's the missing passenger.'

Chloe was relieved as she went back to lower the steps. She had delayed the flight as long as she could by prolonging the cockpit checklist. She realised the game Gibbs was playing, as did McDonald.

'Good morning Mr Gibbs. We were just about to leave.'

'Leave without me at your peril.' Gibbs replied in a muffled but audible tone. It was clear he resented McDonald pulling rank on him in deciding the date and time. Chloe could see she had probably made a serious mistake by accepting McDonald's meeting invitation without making Gibbs aware. Gibbs would no doubt double his efforts to frustrate her ambitions. However, it was too late to offer an apology.

'I'm Christine Morley, Mr Gibbs secretary, but everyone calls me Chris. Can I call you Chloe?'

Gibbs had not introduced them as he turned and headed towards the stairs unable to hide the mood so obvious on his expression.

Chloe held out her hand with a warm smile. 'Of course you can Chris. But let's get you on board so we can get out of here. We'll have plenty of time to talk.'

The cabin was in silence as Chloe raised the stairway and checked everyone had their seat-belts fastened. She had noted Sophie give her a big smile and roll her eyes as Gibbs moved past with a brief nod of acknowledgement to McDonald as he slipped into a seat two rows behind. He was not accustomed to being delegated to the back of the bus - after all, he was the appropriate Minister. He immediately put his head against the window and closed his eyes silently cursing his driver for being late. Fifteen minutes earlier and he would have claimed the front row so McDonald would have had to move to the rear.

It was early afternoon when they touched down at Ascot Downs, but Gibbs' mood remained unchanged as he alighted and climbed into the LandCruiser.

Alice, Violet and Rosebud stood to one side with shy smiles as the guests were ushered inside the homestead and into the expansive lounge.

'I just love your taste Chloe, this place is beautiful.'

'I'm not responsible for the construction or the interior design Sophie. I inherited it when I bought the station. Now, please come through to the dining room as lunch has been prepared.'

Gibbs remained withdrawn and reclusive from the animated conversation over lunch. McDonald tried to include him, but was rebuffed with grunts of indifference. Chloe had made an enemy. There was no point in her telling him she had not requested the meeting with McDonald. During the course of lunch she had seen Gibbs furtively casting glances around, enviously taking in the surrounding wealth.

'I might take an afternoon nap. Could show me to my room?' Gibbs said as he finished and stood.

'You are in one of the guest suites Mr Gibbs,' Chloe said with all the civility she could muster. 'Your bag is already there. Violet will show you the way. Dinner is early at seven here in the dining room. Breakfast at six in the morning as it will be a long day and I want to get away early.'

'Can I have dinner in my room please?'

Chloe was taken aback, but recovered in an instant. 'Of course Mr Gibbs. Violet will drop over the menu later this afternoon.'

Gibbs was already in one of the two front seats of the Squirrel when Chloe appeared with the rest of the party. Gibbs had finished breakfast quickly with the excuse he wanted to go over some notes.

'That's Jack, always wants to be in the driver's seat,' McDonald murmured to his wife as Chloe helped them into the rear seats, strapped each of them in, showed them how to adjust the headsets and closed the door.

Gibbs looked concerned as Chloe climbed into the pilot's seat and began her checks. 'Are you qualified to fly this thing?'

'The the last time I looked, my licence was still current. Calm down and sit back Mr Gibbs, you'll enjoy the scenery I'm sure.' The polite slap-down had the desired effect. She had established who was in control. Gibbs made no reply.

Minutes later they were airborne and passing over the grasslands and rugged escarpments as they headed towards the Pilbara. She could see Gibbs gradually relax as she pointed out various features of the landscape. It was half an hour later when she pointed to a range of cliffs. 'Okay Mr McDonald we are now over the area which I'm most concerned about. I'll take you through a couple of these deep gorges so you can get an idea of their scale and beauty and why I believe they should be protected.' She could sense Gibbs tensing beside her. Should she have addressed him first, or was it caused by the fear written all over his face as the chopper appeared to come within a metre of the red cliffs of haematite? It was as though they could reach out and touch the rock wallabies as they took fright and leapt from one precarious foothold to another. She landed on a clear patch atop the highest escarpment and shut the machine down.

'No European has ever set foot in the gorges I just flew you through, yet man has walked through them for tens of thousands of years and left their indelible presence. Let me show you the evidence of that.' The three of them followed her towards a vivid red outcrop. 'Can you see anything?'

'Can't see a damned thing. What am I supposed to be looking at?'

'Perhaps you need glasses Jack?' Sophie McDonald replied with a laugh. 'I can see a snake and what looks to be a human figure carved into the surface. Is that right Chloe?'

'That's correct Sophie. I'm not an expert, but an anthropologist I brought out here said they marked an aboriginal boundary. He thought the carvings were in the region of four to five thousand years old. They represent history that can be wiped out with a single explosive charge.

'Is this all you're talking about? If it is, I believe that could be cut out and removed to another location for protection.'

'No, they're not the only example Mr Gibbs. I could show you dozens of them if you spend a week out here. Also there are the cave paintings which date back a thousand years and the ceremonial bora rings where the warriors carried out their secret ceremonies no woman could witness on pain of death.'

Gibbs was using his towel hat to sweep away the swarms of tiny flies attracted to the sweat on his face and neck. They were a thick mat on the back of his shirt. 'Bloody flies, don't they ever have an off-season? I've seen enough of this.'

'I just think it's beautiful,' Sophie McDonald remarked as she scanned the horizon. 'You're concerned about a few flies and yet you are Minister of Mines. Perhaps Angus should have appointed someone more suited to the portfolio if you don't like being bothered by a few flies.'

It was a stinging rejoinder that hit home. Gibbs swung on his antagonist who had her back turned, pretending to be engrossed with her surrounds. 'I don't believe in obstructing the inevitable. The blacks abandoned their tribal lands long ago. Their only concerns now are receiving sit-down money from the government every fortnight and the location of the nearest grog shop.'

Chloe tried to keep the anger out of her voice. 'And who do you think is responsible for that degradation Mr Gibbs?'

'Knock it off Gibbs, you've gone too far.' Angus McDonald's face was creased in anger. 'You might be my deputy against my better judgement, but you will refer to these people with respect while I'm Premier.'

Chloe stepped in to defuse the situation as she could see Gibbs was going to retaliate. 'Let's all get back in and I'll show you some more of this area before we set down for lunch. After that we'll head further west which is not as significant or spectacular, but has high-grade iron deposits which will take a dozen lifetimes to mine out.'

Chloe put the chopper down near a spring-fed lagoon surrounded by ancient eucalypts. She laid out rugs and a simple cold lunch. Gibbs was sullen and withdrawn as he declined the food, snapped the top off a water bottle and walked away as though lost in thought.

'I don't know why you put up with that bloody racist, Angus?' McDonald shot a reproachful glance at his wife. 'Oh, don't give me that look. I'm sure Chloe is discrete. Nothing said here will be repeated.'

Chloe nodded. 'I know exactly what Gibbs thinks of me, but it doesn't bother me. Anything said on this visit will never be repeated by me. Now, why don't I pack this up and we'll finish the grand tour?' Chloe called to Gibbs who turned and began to walk back slowly, intent on taking his time.

'My sentiments exactly Chloe. Now take it easy Angus and don't let Gibbs bait you. I thought you were about to blow a valve a moment ago, your face was so red. You should really get out of politics before you have another heart attack.'

'Yes, I know love, but I don't want that ignoramus replacing me. The State would go backwards under his leadership. You hop in the front again Jack. You love driving,' he said to the approaching figure. Gibbs did not react to McDonald's sarcasm as he climbed in without comment.

They flew directly west as they passed over formation after formation of iron-ore escarpments. 'You can get an idea of the extent of the deposits Mr McDonald,' Chloe spoke into the intercom. 'Billions of tonnes of iron. This is the area I believe can be opened for mining. You can see it's a considerable distance from the area I want protected.'

Gibbs suddenly broke his petulant silence. 'That's all very well, but the whole of your permit should be opened to mining, just not an area that suits you. The more mines, the more royalties and the more the population can benefit. The deposits belong to the State and it should not be dictated to by a solitary voice.'

They were back in Perth the following day standing on the tarmac when McDonald turned to Chloe. 'I totally agree with your proposal Ms Boyce. I will have my people draw up the boundaries for a perpetual nature reserve to annex the area of interest. It may take a few months to progress, but I can assure you it will happen.' He glanced at Gibbs as he guided Sophie into his ministerial car.

Gibbs snorted in defiance as he turned to his car. 'It isn't going to happen on my watch.'

Chloe cringed. McDonald could not have failed to hear the remark. She had certainly made a confirmed enemy.

39

'How long has Helen Gould been with the company?'

'Coming up for a year now, why do you ask?' Chloe did not look up from the document she was reading.

'And Max Schubert?'

'I would say about five years. He's very quiet and keeps to himself, but he delivers what he's paid for. I've no problems with him. Are these just idle questions or are they leading somewhere?'

'Just curious.'

'You're never just curious Alex,'

'Yes, I know Chloe. I thought they might have been an item, but I've noticed they hardly talk to one another. Who is the boss of those two?'

'Max is the longest serving, but Helen has more experience. They compliment one another. And to answer your question, neither is the boss.'

'You and Helen get along well, I can see that.'

'We do. We socialise a bit. She comes around to my place for dinner and likewise, reciprocates. The real contact is that Charlie and her son Anton are good friends. They met down at the beach, they're both into surfing and members of the nipper's life saving club.'

'Just a casual meeting was it?'

'It was Andrew who first met her. She just wandered up when he was watching Charlie surf and struck up a friendship.'

'Is that all it was, a friendship?'

Suddenly he had her full attention. 'What are you implying? If you're suggesting they had an affair I think you're way off the mark.'

'I'm not suggesting any such thing. Did Andrew give her the job here, or was it you?'

'It was me and she's proved to be a very valuable employee. Any more questions? I didn't realise you'd been appointed to run human relations in this company?'

'Okay, okay Chloe.' Alex held up his hand in resignation. 'Please ignore the fact I brought the subject up.'

'I don't buy that excuse Alex. You're like a bloodhound and I can tell you're following a scent somewhere. Please tell me what it is.'

Alex shook his head. 'Now's not the time Chloe. Let's just say at this point you are correct. I am following something, but until something other than a notion eventuates, I'll keep it to myself.'

'So it's Helen you're looking at?'

'Not particularly - Max is also of interest.'

'Alex I want you to stop now. I'm starting to get very irritated that you come in here and start asking questions that relate to the loyalty or integrity of the staff. If you've got grounds for what you're up to, spit it out, if not clear out and get back to work.'

Alex nodded and stood to leave. 'Just one last question.'

Chloe laughed. 'Why don't you join the bloody police force. They're always looking for good detectives. Okay, let's have it.'

'Have you ever done a background check on Helen or Max?'

'No, I've always trusted my own judgement and I believe I caught the habit from your father. He was very good at sizing up people and judging their character.'

'It might be time to re-think that policy. There's something about Max which doesn't add up.'

'In what way?'

'Single, well into his late forties, lives alone, quiet and reclusive. You don't find that a little odd? I've asked around and it would appear he was very friendly with Helen when she first joined. They shared an office and out of the blue she asked for an office of her own. Why do you think she did that?'

'Familiarity breeds contempt, is the old saying Alex. Maybe she didn't like the scent of his deodorant. I don't know. Now buzz off, I'm busy.' As he turned to leave she caught the smirk on his face. He had achieved what he set out to do, raise doubts in her mind. He had already exposed a huge fraud, something Andrew had suspected, but Alex had detected and fixed. He had introduced mandatory drug tests for drivers and haulage staff signing on and off for each shift, a procedure which had resulted in the zero deaths, loss of broken rigs, gear and injuries. Fuel, tire and insurance providers had all been replaced, with a clear message all would have to re-quote annually. Although the perpetrators of his intended murder had not been caught, it was clear their money-tree had been cut down. His pinpointing of Giles had shaken the whole transport division back into full compliance. Now he was on the trail of Helen and Max, or was he tossing out a red-herring chasing shadows? Her mind began to mull over. He was quite right, what did she know about her two accountants? Maybe she should start delving deeper? After all she had shown total misguided trust in Giles, so could Helen and Max be any different? It was then the tiny bell rang in her brain. She realised it was a warning there must be something about Helen and Max that raised his interest.

She recalled Andrew's rejection when she announced she was hiring Helen. He could not give a straight answer for his negative attitude. 'She's becoming a close friend Chloe. I urge you to keep her as a friend and hire someone else. There's something about her that doesn't ring true.'

'And what is that? Why don't we discuss your concerns with her present. Maybe she can remove any doubts you have?'

'No...no, that would create an untenable situation for me. In her eyes I would be made to look the enemy. The situation would be impossible.'

'You're hiding something Andrew. I saw the look of shock on your face when I first suggested I was going to hire her.'

'I'm not hiding anything Chloe,' he snapped. 'It's just that I've got a very mixed vibes about her. It stems from when I saw a photo of Helen as a child, sitting on her father's knee. Charlie and I were around at her home attending Anton's birthday party. She quickly shoved the photo in a drawer with some lame excuse she was embarrassed by the braces on her teeth. There was something about her father I recognised. I have an image in my mind, but the image is vague. It drifts in and out and won't adopt a final form. I can only put it down to the brain injury I sustained. My recall is far from being total as you are well aware. Okay, if you're intent on employing her, it's your call. However, I've no real need to be in the office when it's my turn down here with Charlie, so I won't raise the subject again.'

She was startled by the abruptness of his objection and swift retreat. It was out of character and she could see he was searching for an excuse as he began to regain his composure. They had been together long enough that they could

read each others thought patterns, the telepathy well established. She had put any suspicions out of her mind at the
time. But now she'd just heard his son making some vague
insinuations.

Chloe got up from her desk and closed her office door
before picking up the phone. Ten minutes later she had
relayed the assignment. She had been caught out putting her
trust in Giles, she didn't want the failing repeated.

40

Max Schubert was worried and it showed as he slumped into a chair on the other side of her desk. 'Where does Alex come from? Do you know anything about him?'

Helen Gould shook her head. 'I don't know much about him other than he's got Chloe's ear. Is he bothering you?'

'He's asking too many questions which don't relate to his brief. I thought he was involved solely with our currency exchange dealings, hedging currency variations in our exports and forward transactions. I got in very early the other morning and saw him walking out of my office. He didn't see me, but I could see he'd been going through paperwork on my desk.'

'And what do you think he was looking for?'

'I suspect it was my password. I change it every day when I leave. There's no way he could break it in a couple of hours.'

Helen was about to challenge him on that point. How easy it had been to get into his personal computer in his home? 'Has he asked for access?'

'Not recently, but he did try stand-over tactics when he first arrived before Chloe gave him his current assignment.'

'What are you worried about? He's also asked me once, and once only. My reply soon put him in his place. I went straight to Chloe and told her it was a very retrograde step in allowing any staff access to another department – particularly accounts. I told her I would not be held responsible.'

'That may be so, but I've got a feeling he's going to be authorised to take a close look at us. If that happens our game will be up.'

Helen could see Max was visibly trembling. 'Pull yourself together man. It will be all over the moment he gets authorisation to come snooping on our patch. I will immediately remove any trace of what you've done, or how it was done.'

'What the hell do you mean? It was not my doing - I had no choice in the face of your blackmail. You've really have set me up to take the fall, haven't you?'

She could see she was dealing with a weak individual who she now utterly despised. Her voice took a hard edge. It had been a slip of the tongue. 'You'll do exactly as I tell you and don't accuse me of setting you up as you're suggesting – we're in this together.'

'But any forensic investigation will lead back to me as the culprit. It won't take them long to trace the money and where it's gone.'

'Max, when I crash this system it will stay crashed, the complete accounting records will simply disappear for good and Chloe Boyce will be out of business. At first the banks and creditors will get nervous, but it will quickly degenerate into total panic mode when the full extent of the problem emerges. Of course, we're going to be subjected to some tough questions when the law gets involved, but we can just profess total ignorance. Super viruses are being developed every day of the week. Hackers are not a problem that can be dealt with easily. They are a universal scourge out to pillage any business that hasn't taken precautions. Even then, nothing is safe from their intrusions. Boyce will be hit. She's going to have to eventually take the blame and financial repercussions of not spending a lot more money on protection of the systems.'

'You seem very sure of yourself?'

'I am and as long as you don't crack, it will work. Look what we've got away with already. Your share is enough to buy you a very comfortable retirement.'

Schubert pulled a grim expression. 'I can't sleep at night. That bloody Alex is getting too close. He must suspect something.'

'Calm down, he's got nothing to be suspicious about. If he had, he would have already gone straight to Chloe. He just can't walk in her door and make unfounded accusations and be handed the authority to look over our shoulders. Knowing her, she wouldn't take the risk of us resigning if nothing came of his fishing expedition. You can't hope to keep staff if you run a business where someone can query their integrity and probity and not escape a backlash if nothing comes of it.'

'But, but we've got to finalise the accounts next week to hand over for auditing. The game will be up then,'

Helen gave a laugh of reassurance. 'The game will most certainly be up for Boyce. We're going to lift twenty million in a single hit and more. She won't recover.'

Schubert looked at her stunned. 'Impossible. Have you gone nuts?'

'Far from it. If you're going to steal Max, don't mess around with petty cash. Go for the big withdrawal. It doesn't matter if you fail in either case because you're going to serve time, give or take a few years, so you may as well aim for as much as you can. You're right, the auditors will very quickly find things are amiss if I let them, but they're never going to be given that opportunity. The money will simply disappear offshore. Chloe's company collapses and as long as you don't buckle, all we have to do is sit tight until the heat subsides.'

'But we never have twenty in the combined accounts at any one time?'

'I'm perfectly aware of that, but we do have a floating facility of twenty million from the bank. Remember, that's automatic which doesn't require the bank's authorisation to draw down. It's fixed against Boyce's assets. Can you imagine the blood-bath when that hits the fan? In addition to that we'll drain the company of its working capital, which is in the region of another ten million, probably more. Not a bad day's work wouldn't you agree?'

'I'm not going along with it Helen. It's crazy.' Schubert was beyond the shaking stage, he was petrified with fear. He would not stand up to even the slightest scrutiny, but she'd already arranged for that problem to be solved.

'Can't you get it through your head we're not responsible. Someone hacked into the system and committed the crime. Boyce will be busted and shell-shocked when everyone deserts her after the bank shakes her down for her last cent. No one will want to know her and I couldn't wish it on a nicer person.'

'But you're wrong, she's got huge assets. She won't go bust.'

Helen laughed. 'She won't survive when the bank puts in the receivers to secure its debt. Those licensed thieves will gouge out huge upfront fees and make sure they also put first dibs on any money flowing through. From there it's just a fire sale as everything is tossed to the highest bidder with no reserve. The bank just wants to write off the mess and bury the experience along with the adverse publicity. I know, because I've seen it happen to someone I knew.'

'Wh.....what have you got against her? Whatever has she done to you, but treat you with kindness and respect?'

Helen ignored the question. She had said too much. 'Just shut up Max, you don't have a choice. You either serve ten years for possessing that vile stuff you have on your computer or you serve ten years for stealing thirty plus million if you open your mouth. You have no options.'

'Okay, so do we disappear prior to the crime or stay around for the heat of the investigation?' A sudden thought came into his mind. 'And where is this money going to land up? How do I get my share?'

'We stay and see it through. To run would be a big mistake – it would immediately set the alarm bells ringing. I've set it all up with a series of offshore accounts. Your share will be in an account I'll give you the details of the day we lift the funds. From then you're on your own.'

'When do you intend to do this?'

'The accounts will be full of cash next Friday. I'll action the plan on Sunday so the panic will set in Monday morning when the bank takes down the shutters.'

Schubert leaned forward with his face in his hands. 'Oh God, how am I going to get through this? You're totally corrupt Helen. You set me up the moment you walked into this place didn't you? In fact I can see the whole picture now. This is all about revenge for something that happened between you and Chloe in the past. That doesn't make sense because she didn't know you, but there has to be some connection. What is it?'

Helen Gould laughed. 'Yes, there is something, but I won't go into that. It's a long story which doesn't concern you. All you've got to do for the next week is remain calm and don't show any signs of nerves, otherwise you're likely to come under the spotlight very quickly. I'm counting on you Max, so don't buckle or you'll be serving time.'

Chloe was still trying to digest the implications of what she'd just heard when he strode into her office.

'I know who she is.' Alex sat down with a broad grin of satisfaction. 'After I joined the company, Dad briefed me on the background of his involvement with you, so I now know where her father fits into the picture. I think you've let a fox into the hen house and my advice is to get rid of her now.'

'Alex, I found out about half an hour ago her maiden name was Shulman. Her father was Ike Shulman who was killed when he made the mistake of standing in front of a police sergeant holding a shotgun. Ike and my father had a cosy arrangement where Dad would duff clean-skin cattle, brand them as his and sell them through Ike as agent. The cop was involved along with a certain bank manager who cleared Dad's overdraft in exchange for a cut of the proceeds. The cattle were being runoff Ascot Downs, the station I now own, by a complicit manager who confessed his crime to your father when he discovered he had terminal cancer.'

'Why didn't you tell me this before?'

'How could I, I didn't know Helen's background until my private enquiry agent phoned me only minutes ago. And I couldn't see the point in acquainting you with past history as to my father's activities and your father's involvement in me retaining my cattle stations. Andrew's contribution to where I am today has been priceless. Just when I thought all was lost to Shulman, he came up with the brilliant strategy of me buying Ascot Downs, covering up my father's crime and selling off part of the vast herd on Ascot to settle the purchase.' Chloe trailed off lost in memories. 'I think about him every moment of the day.'

'The aviation authorities concluded the cause of the chopper crash was a stroke brought on as a result of a previous injury. There was no evidence of any sabotage. What do you know about that?'

'The short answer he was knifed in the lung in a fit of psychotic rage, by my then husband Marcel Faroud. He fell backwards and smashed his skull on the hardwood floor. It was a refugee Afghani doctor, who operated and saved his life. However, he'd been warned he'd suffered a brain trauma which may manifest itself and kill him at any moment. Andrew was living on borrowed time. I begged him not to fly alone, but to no avail. I don't know how he passed the medicals. I should have reported him and had his licenses cancelled, but he would have known I'd done it, so I let it go. It 's a guilt I live with. My only consolation is he was alone when he crashed.'

'Don't blame yourself Chloe. He knew the risks and I can see now why he told me he wouldn't let me fly with him when he was pilot. Did that also apply to you?'

'I always did the flying when he was with me although he did fly station hands out to remote mustering locations when we were busy. On reflection it was completely irresponsible on my part.'

'So what are you going to do about Helen?'

'I'm wondering that myself. She's proved herself a valuable asset and backup to Max who just can't match her skills or drive. He's good at what he does, but doesn't show any real initiative.'

'It hasn't occurred to you Helen might be running an agenda you're not aware of? You busted her father and he was shot by a cop who obviously wanted to shut him up. The cop is probably dead or as what happens with all internal police investigations, was cleared of any charges and retired on full pension. End of story. So who's the next person to blame for her father's untimely demise. That would be Dad and seeing he's not around you're going to be carrying the can in her eyes. My advice is to pay her off today and get her out of here immediately. Then haul Max in here and apply the pressure in the hope he will reveal something of her intentions.'

'No Alex, I just can't fire her without a good reason. She might be Shulman's daughter, but that doesn't mean she's out to get me. How can she?'

'I probably know a little more than you do. She's a fully qualified accountant, but she also holds degrees in computer science. Helen Gould is a very clever woman who doesn't need to work the hours for the peanuts you pay her. She doesn't need you or the job. Why would she work for you when she could earn twice the money elsewhere?'

'What else do you know?'

'That's as far as I've got at the moment, but what I do fear is that you're asking for trouble. Helen Gould is no dedicated employee, of that I'm certain.'

41

lex was sitting in a Macca's, having finished a limp burger and warm fries when the person pulled out a chair opposite and sat down. He thought nothing of it, the place was crowded.

'You're Alex aren't you?'

He looked at the heavy-set individual with hair pulled back in a pony-tail and open smiling face. He was wearing a black open-neck shirt and tailored sports jacket. The gold chain around his neck and the numerous rings on his fingers denoted some other occupation than office work. He held out a large hand. 'My name's Ron Ratsakis, I knew your father.'

Alex shook the outstretched hand warily. 'What's this about Ron?'

'Your father acted for me years ago and managed to keep me out of prison. Perhaps I should rephrase that. Your father never acted for me, but assisted me in avoiding a prison sentence, a favour which I've never forgotten.'

'And?'

'I think I'm in a position to repay the debt. I know Andrew died recently. I always intended to catch up with him, but finally decided against it. He and Chloe had become very high profile and didn't need the likes of me damaging their image.'

'What do you do for a living Ron? Just looking at you I would say you're still a criminal underneath that smart clothing. Why don't you take a hike.'

Ratsakis grinned and gave a shallow laugh. 'You can't insult me Alex, if that's what you're aiming at. Now pin back your ears and listen, because I'm not going to repeat myself. There is a contract out on the life of one of Chloe's employees, a certain Max Schubert and the word is the contract has been generated internally.'

Alex was stunned and was about to pursue the information when Ratsakis stood and patted him on the shoulder. 'I'm not taking questions. You've got the tip-off and I believe I've repaid my debt to your father. You won't be hearing from me again and this meeting never took place. And if I hear it did, you might put yourself in grave danger.'

Who the hell was Ron Ratsakis and how had he been able to recognise him? He was about to get up and follow him when he noticed another figure rise from a nearby table and shake his head to discourage such a move. Alex remained seated in disbelief at what he'd just heard. Someone had put out a contract for the murder of one of Chloe's employees was too far-fetched to be believable. He dismissed the idea of Schubert being mixed up in drugs or some other criminal activity. It was laughable. The guy was a bean-counter and nothing more. But Ratsakis had gone out of his way to deliver a clear message, a warning he could not ignore. He sat there for ten minutes mulling over his options of whether to tell Chloe, go to the police with some vague threat he could not substantiate, or quietly pursue it further. Ratsakis openly introduced himself so he wasn't concerned about the rumour of an obscure hit being reported to and dismissed as hearsay by the police. They would only start investigating if the hit happened. He would then have to decide whether to disclose the source of the information.

He pulled up a few metres from the front of the house and sat considering his approach before getting out and opening the iron gate common to workers cottages of a bygone era. The light came on the moment he approached the low-set verandah. He was about to use the brass knocker when the door opened a couple of inches. Max Schubert had a startled look on his face.

'What do you want Alex?'

'I'd like to have a word with you Max. Can I come in, it's important?'

'It's not convenient, I'm busy. What's so important that we can't discuss it in the office in the morning?' The door began to close.

Alex shoved his hand out to stop it. 'Because you might be dead by then and cadavers are in no position to discuss any-thing - you'll be laid out on a very cold slab. Someone wants to see your mouth permanently closed.'

The shock was evident as resistance on the door released. 'What did you say?'

Alex pushed the door open further. 'You heard me. Now, do you want to hear what I have to say before it's too late?' He was closing the door behind him as Schubert yielded without further objection and turned to walk down the hall. He slammed a door shut just as Alex was drawing level, but not before he saw the glowing aura of computer screens.

'Are you so busy with those, you don't want to hear what I have to say?'

'None of your business.' The rebuff was blunt. 'Come on down to the lounge. Would you like a drink? I'm going to have one.'

'Yeah, make it a single measure of scotch with a little water.' He watched with barely concealed amusement as Schubert fumbled with glasses and the bottle as he tried to control his nerves. He handed a glass to Alex and sat down opposite.

'Wh.....what's this about me being murdered. Is this a joke?'

Alex raised his glass. 'Cheers. No, this is not a joke Max. I've got it on very good authority someone has put out a contract on your life. I'm merely conveying the message. Are you mixed up in something to do with the company, or is it some other activity someone would rather see permanently erased?'

Schubert spilt his drink down his front as he attempted to take a sip, his hand was shaking so badly. He attempted to regain his composure as he set the glass down on a low coffee table. 'This is a joke, isn't it? You're just trying to scare me? What the hell are you playing at knocking on my door this time of night?'

Alex could see he had struck a chord of confusion and decided pursue the advantage. 'I wasn't just driving by in the hope you would have your lights on. My sole purpose is to warn you of the danger you're now in. It's no joke, it's real. Although I've never laid eyes on him before, the person who tipped me off, is from my brief observation, a member of the underworld of this city. Now how about telling me what this is all about? Why would anyone want to knock you off?

Schubert made to pick up his glass, but realised his shaking hand would not hold it. 'I..I haven't a clue. I don't have any enemies.'

Alex snorted and sipped his scotch. 'We both know that's bullshit. You're into one of three things. It either has to do with your work, or you're into drugs, or perhaps pornography.'

Schubert's face drained of colour as he rose on unsteady feet and faced his accuser. 'I've heard enough Alex, now get out of my house.'

Alex ignored the urgency as he finished his scotch and stood. 'There's an old proverb Max, don't kill the messenger. I hope I'm not called to identify the stiff in the morgue drawer.' He brushed past and walked on up the hall. Before Max could stop him he opened the door from the hall Schubert had closed. 'Nice setup you have. Must be an interesting hobby to keep you amused this late?'

The front door was slammed behind him as he unlatched the front gate and walked to his car. He sat for a few minutes contemplating the confrontation and its effect. He had no doubt he'd rattled Schubert's cage, but what was he involved in that initiated a threat with ultimate prejudice? Was Ratsakis being straight with him? What did he have to gain by approaching a stranger with a warning? The answer was nothing, so the message was real. He pressed the starter and put the car into gear. With a brief glance in the mirror he pulled out into the road and drove off, his brain clouded by questions.

Schubert's office was empty when he walked in. 'Max not in yet Helen?'

'He's not coming in today Alex. He phoned to say he's not well and is staying in bed. Not like him, as you know he's always first in and last to leave.'

Alex nodded. He could quite understand why Schubert was taking a sickie. It was a case of shot nerves and bilious stomach. 'Are you busy Helen?'

'Always busy, that's what I'm paid for.' She laughed as she signified a chair. 'Something on your mind?'

'It's Max. Have you noticed anything odd about him lately?'

'I'm not into psychology Alex, but the answer is no. Why, what's concerning you in particular? I didn't know you'd been appointed to run health and safety in this company? It's not your department is it?' The reprimand was loud and clear. He'd struck a nerve, or rather stood on a very sensitive toe.

'No it's not and I'm being presumptuous in asking,' he said as he got up and walked out.

Helen Gould scowled as her eyes followed him. What was his sudden interest in Max? Alex had obviously caught the odour of something, but he couldn't possibly be aware of what she had planned. That was unless he had got at Max? She dismissed it - this time next week the Boyce organisation would be in the hands of the bank. By then her associate would have disappeared without trace, but with all the blame. She would make sure his paedophile preference would be made public to add further weight to his appearance of guilt. All she had to do was sit tight and endure the questions, an inquisition Schubert would not be able to withstand for more than thirty seconds. The price was higher than expected, but she had no choice but to accept the verbal guarantee no trace would ever be found of him. She watched as Alex headed for Chloe's office.

'Chloe, I've got to talk to you now. It concerns Helen and Max and it's serious.'

'This is getting tedious. Close the door please, I don't want any of the staff to overhear what you're going to tell me.' She attempted to remain impassive as he related the details, but cracks in her disbelief at what he was saying started to widen. 'Frankly, I find it rather fanciful. It's just too far-fetched that an unknown person walks up to you and says someone within this organisation has put out a contract on the life of one of my employees. What are you suggesting I should do?'

'I'm convinced Helen is behind it. I went to see Schubert last night to tell him what I knew. I know it really shook him up.'

'Alex, what do you want me to do? Are you suggesting I sack them both on the spot? I'm running a business here, or at least trying to, not an investigation agency.'

Alex could see the impatience mounting. He had over-stepped the mark, but pressed the frontal attack. He would be walking out the front door in a few minutes, or he would succeed. 'Chloe,' he hissed as he leaned forward. 'I believe your whole image and organisation is in jeopardy if you don't act now. Someone has taken out a contract on Schubert and the rumour is the contract originated from somewhere internal. You're going to be in an indefensible position if anything happens to him, now I've made you aware of the threat. Can't you see, if the information I was given is true, someone within this company wants to cover up something you're unaware of at this time. Ask yourself why is Max the target? My answer to that is because he's the weak link. With him out of the way, whoever is planning the murder stands to gain financially. It's got to be money, there's no other explanation. I would start by putting the spotlight on Helen. After all it was her father you and Dad sent to the wall and revenge is a strong motive. It could be you she wants dead, but that won't give her the complete satisfaction she seeks – she's out to destroy you financially, just as you destroyed her father. And I believe that's where Schubert comes into the picture. They've cooked up some-thing together and Helen is about to remove him before the crime is revealed. Something is about to happen, of that I'm certain.'

'You're suggesting Helen is responsible? Impossible from what I know of the woman. I realise she's probably carrying a lot of her father's baggage, but that doesn't brand her as being a revengeful criminal as you are implying. In addition to being an excellent employee, she happens to be a personal friend. Our sons are friends. They spend a lot of time together. I find your assumptions preposterous and libellous.' She reached for the phone. 'Let's settle this now. You can make your accusations to her face, then you can get out of here for good.'

Alex reached over and held her hand down. 'Don't bother Chloe, you won't listen, so I'm out of here now. You wouldn't listen when I raised concerns about Giles and now this. You're too bloody ignorant and blinded by your friendship with the woman. It's a well established fact the ignorant will always defend their ignorance and in this case that applies to you. I don't think it will be too long before the implosion takes place and your whole operation collapses around your ears. For Christ sake, Ike Shulman was Helen's father, can't you see the red light flashing? It's flashing revenge. Ah, what's the bloody use.'

Chloe was too stunned by the outburst as Alex stormed out, her brain in total confusion. He had been right about Giles, but was he right about Helen?

'I couldn't help overhearing parts of that Chloe.' It took her moments to realise Helen Gould had walked in and sat down. 'I can't believe what I just heard. You don't believe I'm involved with what he was saying do you? I heard him mention my father's name which really concerns me. I was estranged from him when he divorced my mother and although we had no contact, he was still my father. If he was involved in crime, then so was your father from what I've been told. You would expect me to protect my father's memory as you would yours. Questions could be asked of you as to how you really acquired my father's cattle stations and financed Ascot Downs? Everyone has questions to answer in business.'

'Of course I don't believe you're involved in anything Helen. I'm just so shocked Alex would make the accusation and walk out like that.'

'He was a misfit here. I believe you're lucky to be rid of him.' Chloe did not notice her get up and leave, closing the door quietly behind her.

She sat lost in thought. Was Alex on the right track? If Helen was so estranged from her father, why did she mention both their fathers were involved in crime, or the acquisition of Ike's cattle stations? For someone so estranged, she obviously was more concerned with her father's affairs and how he had lost his huge land holdings, than she admitted. She recalled Andrew had told her about the birthday party when Helen had flipped a photo over and shoved it into a drawer explaining it was a photo of her father and her as a child. The tiny seeds of doubt and suspicion began to arise in her mind. But if Alex was correct, where was the revenge? It couldn't be anything to do with the accounts department as the books would be closed off in the next week and the auditors would walk in the door. Any irregularities would be quickly picked up, something Helen would be well aware of. The doubts began to recede as she searched for any other vulnerable areas open to theft or abuse. Following his investigation and termination of Giles, Alex had been given clandestine authority to look at every division within the group. He had found nothing until his current suspicions were aroused and now he had aroused hers. She determined to let him cool down for a few days and see if she couldn't mend the fences.

42

He was slowly stirring the sugar crystals into a long black when his mobile vibrated. He looked at the identity of the caller and raised his eyebrows in surprise. 'Hi Max, I didn't think I was on your speed dial list any longer? You weren't at work today. Are you recovering?'

'I....I would like to see you. I want to tell you something. It's urgent.'

'Shoot. I'm all ears.'

'N...No, not over the phone. This evening at eight.' The line went dead. It wasn't the phone call of a sick man, it was the phonc call of an individual in mental meltdown.

The front door opened a crack just as he put his hand on the gate. Schubert almost pulled him through the doorway as he glanced around him to see if anyone else was present. He could feel Schubert's hand pushing his shoulder with urgency as he was ushered down the hall. He noticed the doorway to the computer room was open, the screens and room in darkness. Schubert pointed to the couch as he poured them both a scotch. By the look of his dishevelled and agitated state, he'd already got through most of the bottle.

'Th....thanks for coming,' he said as he sat down opposite and peered into his glass, lost in another world.

'What's bugging you Max, you said this was urgent. You're worried about what I told you last night?'

'You're not trying to frighten me are you?'

'I can see you're already beyond that threshold. However, I do believe the person who told me you're as good as dead was not indulging in idle gossip. He was very sure someone within the company had already paid for it to happen. Do you know who that might be, not that I can't guess already?'

'Jesus Christ, it's that two-timing bitch,' Schubert screamed as he rose and threw his glass into the defunct fireplace. Alex threw his arm across his face to protect himself from the flying glass as Schubert turned, grabbed the bottle and opened a cupboard for another glass.

'What two-timing bitch are you referring to?'

'Gould, Helen Gould you klutz,' he spat. 'I thought you were smart. I thought with all the questions you've been asking, you must have worked that out.'

'What did you two have planned? What hold does she have over you?'

'She plans to clean out Boyce without trace and destroy her whole company.'

'So why haven't you reported this to Chloe and cleared yourself of any involvement?'

'Because Helen's blackmailing me. She came on strong when she first joined and me being lonely, sucked it up. I've never had a real girlfriend and she's about my age with no money worries, so I thought she was genuine. I invited her around for dinner one night and I had too much to drink. While I was sleeping it off she got into my computer and downloaded some personal files.'

'Let me guess Max, you're a paedophile heavily into porn and that's what she's got on you?'

Schubert hung his head and nodded. 'You're not a klutz after all, but how did you guess?'

Alex looked at the broken man without satisfaction of his accusation. 'It's your lifestyle. You're in your forties, live by yourself, reclusive, and no girl friend. I'll bet Helen also woke up to that very quickly. She picked your weakness and went to work on it. You said she intends to take Chloe to the cleaners. Correct me if I'm wrong, but you two have been fiddling the books already and you've been lining Chloe up for the big cash withdrawal. Is that it?'

'I had no alternative. She got into my computer when I invited her around for dinner. I finished almost two bottles of red and passed out. I either went along with it or she would drop a copy of my private files into the appropriate authorities, or I could take my chances with her. Of course she promised me a fifty-fifty split so I could live in retirement in some far-off locality.'

'So you've been siphoning off funds, but the main game has yet to play out. You're both going to be serving time together. You haven't a hope in hell of getting away with it.'

'That's what I thought and believed until you showed up last night. I realised I was the fall-guy in that Helen knew I would not be able to resist concerted interrogation, so I had to be removed from the scene. Hence the hit you referred to. I will tell you now Helen Gould is one tough bitch who won't crack, no matter how much pressure she's put under. The entire bank facility of twenty million and whatever is in the divisional cash accounts, which I think will be in the region of another ten, will simply disappear in one hit. Boyce will be instantly crippled.'

'Impossible. Any transfer can be tracked. It will lead straight back to her.'

Schubert smiled thinly. 'You are a klutz after all. Haven't you heard of Bitcoin?'

'But her fingers will be all over the transfer button?'

'Wrong again. The mainframe computer will be hacked by an expert and she is an expert. She's already set it up to get access via some overseas server, most probably Russian, Iranian, or some other obscure non-English speaking jurisdiction. The funds will disappear immediately into untraceable Bitcoin, or into a series of offshore accounts in tax havens. There you have it, the perfect crime.'

Alex could feel the blood draining from his face. 'When's this supposed to happen?'

'Over the weekend, so the shit will hit the proverbial Monday morning. The timing is perfect as the auditors are due then and our activities up until now will be discovered very quickly. She's moved about two million already with my compliance, so that's gone forever as is my retirement nest egg. You can see I'm as good as dead now.' He trailed off as they heard the bell on the front door.

'Expecting someone?'

'Yes, my lawyer, but he's a bit early.' He glanced at his watch as he set down his glass. 'I'm going to make a full statement. I invited you here so you can immediately alert Chloe and the cops. This has got to be stopped now.'

Alex sat back as he rolled the scotch around in his glass. He suddenly became alarmed, sprang to his feet and yelled. 'Max, don't open that door.'

He was moments too late as he heard two shots from a small calibre weapon. Schubert fell backwards, the blood already gushing from a wound in his neck while blood oozed through his white shirt from another in his chest. The masked killer saw Alex and fired wildly before turning and disappearing into the night. Alex slowly walked up the hall and looked down at the dying man. He could see there was nothing he could do. Death was only moments away as the surge from the severed carotid artery in his neck quickly drained life from his brain and shut down his heart. He turned off the hall light and waited for any sign of neighbours investigating the gunshots, but there was no sound. He turned and walked back down the hallway, washed his glass and looked around for any other evidence of his presence, before quickly making an exit. He stepped around the corpse and minutes later was on a main road in traffic. He had committed a serious offence by leaving the scene, but it would take hours of questions followed by waiting for a time-consuming witness statement to be prepared and signed, before he could get clear of police. It was a delay he could not afford. If the killer had already reported the hit had been successful, Gould may be tempted to immediately initiate the theft.

Chloe was reading when she heard the chime of the front gate. It became more persistent as she got up and peered into the video screen at the front door.

'What do you want at this time of night Alex?'

'Chloe, it's urgent. Let me in now.'

'Can't your apology wait until the morning?'

'Chloe I'm serious, this affects your very existence. For Christ sake open the bloody gate.'

She triggered the gate and waited at the door as Alex sprinted towards her and up the steps. He pushed her inside and slammed the door.

'What are you doing Alex? Have you gone completely insane? I want you out of here now.'

Alex ignored her as he flung himself breathless into a lounge chair. 'Max is dead - pour me a double brandy and I suggest you pour yourself one. You're going to need it. I was right about Helen Gould. Are you going to listen, or do I leave and watch you go broke on Monday morning?'

'What do you mean Max is dead – how did it happen?'

'First the brandy.'

Chloe sat stunned as he related the story. 'How do I stop her?'

'You've got to move immediately by shutting down your server and pray she hasn't already initiated the crime.'

'I can't possibly do that, it will bring every division within the company to a standstill.'

'Can't you see you will be at a standstill the moment she gains access anyway. You've got no option - let me do it.'

'So what will that achieve? Surely, all she has to do is wait for another day and another time?'

Alex shook his head. 'She can't wait. The auditors are due on Monday and her game will be up. They will quickly point to missing funds she's already transferred with Max's compliance. She's got to do it this weekend. She's going to panic when she sees your main-frame is down. Bearing in mind she's a highly qualified specialist in the computer field, my guess is she will access the premises to find the problem and re-boot it.'

'And we're going to be there when she does it? Is that what you're proposing?'

'I'll go in now and check the account balances and bank facility are still intact.' He noticed Chloe raise her eyebrows and laughed. 'Yes, I know I've been asking for access, but I was lying. I've already had complete access and was only looking for your tick of approval in case Helen discovered my activity and complained of my intrusion. Don't say I didn't warn you she was up to something.'

'If everything's okay, what do you want me to do?'

'Knock on the door of the Fraud Squad in the morning and give them a full run-down. Schubert's murder will by then have been broadcast on the local radio and early TV. You can elude to him being connected to what Gould is intending, but make sure you leave my name out of it – I was not at the scene. If you don't, Homicide will immediately come looking for me and I'll be hauled in for a grilling. If they subsequently find out I witnessed the murder, I'll admit to it and take the flak, but in the meantime I want to be there when Helen turns on the lights.'

Alex parked his car a street away, walked back towards the building and let himself in. He took the stairs and punched in the security code which immediately turned on the hidden overhead camera to the office entrance. The internal lights lit up the whole interior as he went into Chloe's office and booted the desktop computer. Two minutes later he had entered the codes and accessed the various bank accounts. He heaved a sigh of relief before logging off and heading to the rear of the suites of offices. The lights on the banks of server modules were blinking in uncoordinated patterns with a steady humming tone as he walked their length and began to shut them down. It was now a waiting game. Would Helen act as he predicted?

He walked back to the staff room and turned on the espresso machine, made himself a sandwich from the contents of the well-stocked fridge before switching off the internal lighting. The place was almost in total darkness except for the reflected light from an adjoining office block. He went into Chloe's office and opened the door to her private room with its suite of furniture and bed. He grinned at the thought of telling Chloe he had been bold enough to use her private facilities. He picked up a magazine, kicked off his shoes and sprawled in a chair.

He awoke to someone kicking his foot. 'Hey, some watchman you turned out to be. Do you know what time it is?'

'Oh, hi Chloe. I must have dozed off.' Alex sprang to his feet, glancing at his watch.

'This is Detective Miller. I've given him the background and also what you intend to do if and when Helen fronts.'

Miller nodded. 'I've no intention of waiting around for Gould to appear. Here's my direct number. If she does show I want you to call me immediately. I'm only five minutes away and if I'm unavailable the number will divert to a colleague. You'll have our full co-operation.'

'Pleasant sort of a character isn't he - full of charm?' Alex commented out of earshot of the departing detective.

'I've just spent an hour with him and two other detectives. I can understand why he just can't hang around waiting for her to appear. However, he's taking this very seriously. You will get immediate help when she arrives. By the way, use my shower and facilities if you want to freshen up. I'll bring you some meals.'

'No, don't do that Chloe. She may come in at anytime and I don't want her alerted if she spots you. I'll be okay, there appears to be enough food in the fridge before I get down to the snack foods. Now get out of here.'

She leaned forward and pecked him on the cheek. 'You're a real brick Alex. First your father and now you.' She turned and was gone before he could think of a smart reply. The remainder of the day was boring. He didn't keep track of the number of laps of the entire floor of the office space he completed. He found an office looking out over the river and put his feet up on the desk to watch as day turned into dusk. He dozed off and was awoken by the lights suddenly coming on. It was dark outside. He slowly put his feet down to suppress any sound as he rose and looked around. He was in a far corner of the offices, well away from the entrance as he slowly walked forward and across towards the central corridor leading to the computer servers. He froze and listened and then breathed out as he heard her fast moving walk on the tiled floor. She was scared and in a hurry.

He slowly moved around a screened office on the corner of the corridor and caught a glimpse of her throwing open the door to the server control room. He thumbed in the number which was immediately answered. Miller was on his way. Alex watched as Helen strode out, picked a random desk and took a laptop and small notebook out of her bag. She had her back to him as she waited for the mainframe to boot up before keying in her laptop password. She was totally unaware as he quietly walked up and stood partially inside an office to observe. He waited until she keyed in codes from the notebook which started a long series of meaningless lines of code appearing and disappearing at blinding speed. She grunted in satisfaction as she finally linked into some untraceable foreign server. With a panic of fast moving fingers she keyed in more code and tapped her fingers on the desk as she waited impatiently. He recognised Chloe's central bank account come up on the screen.

'Putting in a bit of overtime, are you Helen?' Before she could react he grabbed the collar of her coat and pulled her back into the seat. He leaned over and pushed the laptop out of her reach, the evidence clearly visible.

She turned trying to break free and screamed at him. 'This is assault. Take your hands off me.'

'I'm not the only one who wants to put his hands on you Helen. In fact he's just arrived. You know, if you hadn't put that contract out on Max, you'd have got away with it.'

43

Chloe had turned on the tele and was sitting back not really concentrating when the news-reader opened with the solemnity required for such an event. 'The Premier, Mr Angus McDonald collapsed in his office earlier this afternoon. He was rushed to hospital, but died soon after admission.'

Politics quickly overtook the solemn voice of condolence as a brief history of McDonald's rise to power was followed by the tone of the voice changing to the urgency of a horse-race caller. 'The question is who will fill McDonald's shoes. There are a number of candidates, including Jack Gibbs the most senior member of the Party.'

Chloe turned it off and dropped the remote on the coffee table. Politics never changed, the king is dead, long live the king. The party-room politics would be in full swing with phones running hot as factions lined up behind their choice of candidate. If Gibbs was the chosen successor her idea of a nature reserve on Baracool had just disappeared with the death of her sponsor. She had come close. McDonald was due to sign off on it within the next two weeks, Sophie McDonald had told her in a confidential phone call. She picked up her phone and was about to dial Sophie's private number when she put it down again. She would do it in the morning. Sophie had enough on her mind at the moment. All she wanted now was a strong coffee. It had been a particularly trying three days, the first being briefed by her barrister as to what to expect from the defence during the course of the trial, and the final two being harassed and attacked by the barrister for the defence. Helen Gould had hired the best. He was like a Rottweiler lying docile giving the appearance of complete indifference. He gently led her through the background of his client's so-called crime. She had been warned to be on her guard which only increased her nervousness as she waited for the attack - it finally came. The nerves disappeared in an instant as she tried to control her anger. No, her partner Andrew Hanna was not complicit in any crime – he was the prime reason for her wealth and no, he was not the mastermind behind the plan to drain the bank and her company of millions and hide it in untraceable cryptocurrency or in tax havens. He had no reason to steal. No, she did not believe her partner was in a criminal association with Max Schubert who was now confirmed as having moved two million into offshore accounts. And no, she was not the instigator of the whole criminal scheme. The incessant questions were twisted and turned to be asked repeatedly, but always with the same intent of getting her to admit inconsistency in her answers. On the final day she was completely unnerved by an accusation she had not thought about. It was too long in the past.

'Ms Boyce, your father was a thief, wasn't he?' The barrister was looking at the jury as he levelled the accusation.

Chloe's barrister had sprung to his feet. 'Objection. The question is hearsay and should be struck out your honour. There is no record of Ms Boyce's father being convicted of any offence.'

'Sustained,' was the sharp reply from the bench.

The defence barrister nodded to the judge before turning to Chloe again with a look of satisfaction. He had achieved what he wanted. It was quite clear the media present would highlight the accusation in all its variations. It was the perfect fodder the media had been hoping for – scandal, the lifeblood of news ratings and audience. His intention was to cast a cloud over her background, a cloud of doubt which would not disperse.

'Were you ever made aware of rumours your father could have been involved in the theft of cattle?'

She was fighting her conscience, but she could not lie. 'I am aware of such rumours.'

'And when was that?'

'On his death and soon after I inherited the cattle stations he'd established.'

'And did you establish the rumours were in fact correct? Your father was complicit in duffing cattle, wasn't he?'

She stared at him, her mind searching for a way out of the trap which she realised was about to be sprung.

'Would you just please give the jury your answer Ms Boyce?'

'Y....Yes, I believe he was involved, but I was not aware of it at the time.' The answer came out as a stammer of admission and defeat. She picked up a glass of water and took a sip.

'And what did you do about it? Did you report it to the police?'

Chloe looked down at her barrister for subliminal support, but he was engrossed with a blank legal pad. His client had been completely blindsided. She was on her own. The Rottweiller was coming in for the kill, the smell of blood overpowering.

'So, you now admit your father was a thief and you chose to conceal the crime, which is a criminal offence in itself. By your own admission you are guilty of perverting the course of justice. And, in trying to move the blame, you are now trying to conceal your involvement with Ms Gould. She was not the mastermind, but merely followed your instructions. That is true isn't it Ms Boyce?'

'No, I knew nothing about it until it was brought to my attention by a member of staff. Why would I steal my own money?'

Chloe's barrister was on his feet again. 'Your Honour, my learned friend is attempting to mislead the Court. The witness said she believed her father was involved, but has no proof. She was only commenting on a rumour. In the case presently before the Court, theft has been established. The defendant was caught in the act of diverting tens of millions of dollars. It has also been established she had stolen large sums previously for which she has attempted to blame her fellow accountant, now deceased. Ms Boyce was in no way complicit with Helen Gould. It is a ludicrous suggestion.'

'This is yet to be determined,' the judge interjected firmly. 'I will allow the defence to proceed although I am inclined to accept the prosecution's point.' Chloe's barrister nodded and resumed his seat. He had the judge thinking his way, but it would make any impact with the jury?

'You said earlier Ms Boyce your partner Andrew Hanna was not involved in the conspiracy to defraud your company?'

'That is correct.'

'You and Hanna were not married although you had a son together. When did you first become aware Hanna was already married?'

'Just recently.'

'So despite what you may think of Hanna, he in fact hid the fact he was married for nigh on fifteen plus years. That alone would demonstrate a level of dishonesty and distrust, wouldn't it?'

'Not really. I trusted him implicitly.'

'But that was only after you found out he was married? Did he finally admit it, or how did you find out?'

'His son Alexander Hammond told me.'

'Did you ever run a check on Hanna's background?'

'No, it never entered my mind. I didn't see any need to.'

'You were not aware that Hanna was well-known to police as being an associate of motor cycle gangs and that he had been a prime witness in the murder of a drug dealing personal friend of his? Further to that he was put into a witness protection program after testifying against the murderer, a bikie gang leader. That gang leader, who served ten years for the crime, had boasted he would kill Hanna if he ever found him. It's rather co-incidental, don't you think that Carl "Maggot" Evans was found murdered right here in Perth recently? Did you or Hanna ever meet Evans?'

Chloe could feel the earth dropping out from under. 'Yes we did.'

'And did you put a bounty of two million dollars on his head?'

'It......it was only meant to frighten him. He was threatening to harm my son.'

'Just answer the question please Ms Boyce.'

'I...I did.'

She heard the scuttling feet behind her as the media rushed for the waiting news cameras outside.

The judge suddenly intervened. 'Where is the defence going to with this line of questioning? What is the relevance?'

'With your indulgence, I'm coming to that your Honour. The defence will demonstrate my client, Helen Gould, was not the perpetrator of the crime she is now on trial for.' He turned back to Chloe with a shallow attempt to conceal his excitement. 'You are aware your accountant Max Schubert was a paedophile?'

'I've only become aware of that since his death.'

'Yes, he was murdered by a person unknown – shot dead in the doorway of his home – a professional hit in the opinion of homicide detectives. The only witness to that crime was Alexander Hammond, Andrew Hanna's son and your stepson. Mr Hammond absconded from the scene, but later turned himself in. In your opinion Ms Boyce, what was his reason for running from the scene?'

Chloe's barrister was immediately on his feet, but the judge signalled for him to desist. He had seen Chloe pick up a glass of water and nodded. 'You may sit down Ms Boyce.'

'He was worried Helen Gould would immediately hack into the company computers and trigger the transfer of funds. He could not wait for the police to arrive and go through the process of an interview and a statement. He believed he had to inform me immediately of her intentions and shut down the computers. He was correct in what he did as Helen was apprehended in the act.'

'I put it to you Ms Boyce that your partner was the prime mover in this crime. Although he died prior to Schubert's murder, the wheels had already been set in motion. In association with an unknown party it was he who set out to defraud both you and the bank. He died in a helicopter crash but his associate decided to proceed. Schubert was murdered when he told the associate he was going to alert you and the authorities as to what was going on. My client's life, and that of her son, was then threatened if she did not proceed – she was the only one who had the expertise to hack into the company computers. She was under extreme duress. She is in fact innocent of this crime.'

Chloe was on her feet. 'That's absolute rubbish – you are trying to impugn Andrew Hanna's character.'

The judge looked up as the scuttling feet began to propel themselves out the door again. 'The media will remain seated,' he bellowed. 'If any of you move again I will charge you with contempt. This is not a circus.'

The defence looked down at his notes with a malicious smile of satisfaction. She was rattled and shaken, but he was about to make her day. The media would ignore the judge's warning and make a bolt for the doors in their haste to be the first to air.

'Ms Boyce, let me refer to Andrew Hanna's character. Were you aware he and the defendant were having an affair, an affair that had been going on for some time. An affair where Hanna planned to leave you and marry my client?'

Chloe gasped in shock as she gripped the rail of the witness box for support. 'That's a lie. That's not true.' But a glance across at Helen Gould told her there was some truth in it.

The barrister nodded to the judge. 'No further questions your honour.'

Chloe was exhausted as she began to walk out of the court with her lawyer. 'What happens now? I don't have to go back in there do I?'

'Not likely. Both barristers will give their closing arguments tomorrow and then its the judge's summing up with instructions to the jury. I wouldn't be too concerned about the barrage of scuttlebutt levelled at Andrew – that was pure speculation. I think the judge may have something to say to the jury about that. I don't think Gould is going to escape a jail term, but likewise you're not going to escape the interest of the media by the look of the cameras out front.'

'Hello Chloe, I take it you've heard the news?'
'Yes Alex, I have.'

'That will put paid to your hopes for a nature reserve on Baracool if Gibbs is elected to fill McDonald's shoes. What do you intend to do if he is?'

'Nothing I can do Alex, I'll just have to take what comes.'

'What about your exploration permits over Ironstone Park and Baracool? Are they at risk?'

'I've complied with all the conditions, so I believe they're out of his reach. If McDonald had died a few years back I would have had problems with Gibbs, but I can't see how he can create problems now, other than to frustrate me signing with a partner not of his choice. It's times like this I really miss your father.'

'I'm here for you Chloe. Just give me a call and I'll be right there, no matter what time day or night.'

Chloe laughed. 'I know I can count on you Alex.'

'You're still feeling the effects of the Gould trial aren't you? That barrister sure gave you a workout, but you didn't buckle.'

Chloe gave a shallow laugh. 'Buckle – I don't know what was holding me up. If the judge hadn't invited me to sit down I would have fainted. That attack on Andrew was just preposterous.'

'I must admire Gould's barrister though. He knew she didn't have much of a chance after being caught in the act, but he sure threw some mud. If Dad was still alive he would have come in for some heat. She was convicted, but you and Dad were painted as being involved by the media. Some of what they reported was clearly libellous. You should sue them for defamation.'

'And go through all that again Alex – no way. I've had enough of court's and barristers to last me a lifetime.'

'I stayed and listened to the end. Your barrister made a mess of Helen Gould. He recalled her to the stand and slowly went through her testimony. No doubt she and Dad did have a fling, but she could not back up her accusations she had been threatened by some mystery associate after he died. She could not produce phone records, nor times of meetings and more damning, describe the features of the person she allegedly met. The judge put the jury straight about taking any notice of speculation about Dad's involvement. They were told to determine the case on the facts before them, and not what might have happened. He instructed them to disregard the imputation Helen had contracted the killing of Schubert – there was no evidence to suggest so. I reckon he got it right in sending her away for five years.'

'It's a scene I never want to repeat. I didn't exactly come out of it with my reputation intact. Helen's barrister threw enough mud to make certain of that.'

'However, you must be very pleased she's no longer a threat? It was a close call, she almost got her revenge. You and Andrew destroyed her father and she was going to destroy you.'

'Yes, she would have achieved her aim if you hadn't become involved. I can't thank you enough. I'm glad it's over, but I don't get a thrill out of her being put away. I feel sorry for Anton, her son. It will have a devastating effect on him.'

'You're not thinking of taking care of him, are you?'

She laughed. 'As a matter of fact I was. I made some discreet enquiries and found out he has an aunt with a couple of kids in the same age group, so that's taken care of.'

'And what about Dad? Did you have any suspicions of the affair with Gould, or how long it had been going on for? Do you believe it?'

'I don't know Alex, but it's not relevant now, so why don't we just forget about it. I've had enough of the media camped out the front gate with their cameras hassling me when

I tried to drive out. They even climbed the fence and knocked on the front door trying to get comment. They followed me to Ascot Downs, that was until Ray Massie threatened to deal with them if they set foot on the property. Thankfully, they've now found some other scuttlebutt to feed their insatiable twenty-four-hour news cycle. I'm yesterday's news, but the damage will persist. Every time my name comes up, details of my father's crimes and Andrew's infidelity will be repeated.'

'So much for that barrister putting the boot into Dad and smearing your reputation by association. He made it look as though you were party to the crime. A person with his experience must have known it was speculation the judge would direct the jury to ignore. There was no need for that.'

Chloe laughed. 'That's called revenge. He knew he was defending the indefensible, but just wanted to take the glare of criminality off his client and support his own profile. He's in the selling game, just like any used-car salesman.'

A week later Chloe was watching the news when it was announced Jack Gibbs had been narrowly elected Premier in a party-room ballot. She knew one of his first acts would be to cancel creation of her nature reserve. It would be pure spite to show her who was in control. And she was certain more was to follow.

44

Gibbs pushed the extension to summon his secretary. He detested the man and was determined to move him out of his sight.

Michael Harrison strode into the room with his usual straight-faced efficiency, immaculate in his dress and presentation. Gibbs knew he had a partner, but was intrigued as to whether he was the husband or the wife. The man had absolutely no personality, or if he did, kept it well concealed. He didn't mix with any of the staff, but appeared to get along with everyone.

'How can I be of assistance sir?

'Take a seat Harrison, there's something I want to discuss with you.'

'Likewise the same sir.'

Gibbs raised an eyebrow. 'What's on your mind?'

'I've been your chief-of-staff and secretary for the past five years and believe I've carried out my duties to your full satisfaction. You would agree with that, wouldn't you?'

'Yes, but I would like to make a change. Now that I'm Premier, the workload is tens times what you've been used to.'

'I can handle it. I run a very efficient office and finding a couple of suitable extra staff presents no problems.'

'Damn it Harrison, can't you see I want you out?'

Harrison smiled thinly. 'I know what you want Premier, but you're not getting it without a reciprocal arrangement.'

Gibbs was barely holding his temper in check. 'You've got nothing to offer.'

'I think I have. I know about the envelopes of cash you receive from a certain Chinese contact by the name of Tony Chan, not to mention the private bar you frequent. You have a particular penchant for a certain young oriental prostitute who you know is an illegal immigrant. In fact she was entertaining you last night. Shall I go on?'

'You're trying to blackmail me Harrison, but it won't work.' Gibbs was trying to contain his rage.

'On the contrary, I believe the public should know about what you have been getting up to before you got the top job. I'm about to lose mine, so I may as well take you with me.'

'How do you know about Chan? And what's this about a prostitute?'

Harrison's expression remained dead-pan. 'You got careless once when you came back from lunch somewhat under the weather. You put an envelope full of cash in your top drawer and didn't lock it, a very careless move on your part. I took a photo of ten thousand dollars spread on top of your desk. And to confirm it is your desk there is the framed photo of Audrey and your son in the picture. And as for where, or who you got the money from, I was able to confirm you dined at Salvatore's restaurant according to the man himself. I can disclose that piece of information as Sal knows you will cut him off your favourite dining list because of your now, elevated status. By the way, Sal is a personal friend of mine. The cash exchanges and your conversations have been recorded on video during those private room trysts you've been having with Chan. As for the prostitute, every person who enters that establishment is also caught on camera, including you, members of the police vice squad, magistrates, politicians and some very notable businessmen, all the absolute pillars of society. No doubt you would have realised that. The owners naturally took the attitude they needed insurance in case someone in high places decided to shut them down. If any of this got out and in particular those videos, you'd be a very short-term Premier. Also, you are presently married and if your extra curricula activities became public I think that would result in a very costly divorce.'

Gibbs felt sick. He was completely wrong about the benign outward appearance of the person sitting opposite. This was one dangerous character who would destroy him if his terms were not agreed to. He had to play for time while he searched for answers to what Harrison had just threatened. He would immediately change the venue for Chan meetings and cease visits to the bar. A year down the track it could all be dismissed as rumours. But there was the problem of Audrey. She certainly would not dismiss the rumours. Would Harrison give him the time?

'What do you want?'

'I want a pay increase of hundred thousand a year, plus I want three extra staff.'

Gibbs exploded. 'Bloody preposterous. Who the hell do you think you are coming in here and making demands like that?'

'I thought I'd get in first Premier. However, it's not going to be a one way street. I believe I can help you cancel the exploration permits over Baracool and Ironstone Park. I'm aware you intend to cancel the permits on some spurious pretext and subject the State to a heavy compensation payout to Boyce. You will of course come under intense public scrutiny and business criticism. When that has died down you then no doubt intend to assign the permits to Chan or someone else who will pay you under the table. If you attempt such a move I will most certainly have to reveal what I know, which would be the end of you both politically and socially. Most likely you'll wind up behind bars.'

Gibbs' was shaking with rage as he rose from his desk. 'Fuck you Harrison. You've got a hide coming in here and making threats and casting aspersions on my integrity and honesty. Aren't you forgetting I'm Premier of this State.'

'I'm well aware who you are Premier, but I would advise you to sit down and listen to what I have to say. You don't need to unilaterally cancel Boyce's permits and suffer the backlash of having to compensate her to the tune of tens of millions of the State's cash. She has legal title. You simply can't take them off her without heavy financial repercussions.'

Gibbs slowly sank back into his chair. Harrison was not phased by his outburst of attempted intimidation. 'And if I give you what you want, you'll then show me how I can take Boyce's permits away? Why do I smell a rat? There's more to your demand for a wage rise and extra staff isn't there?'

Harrison nodded. 'It's quite clear we despise one another Premier. I want out of your life altogether. I have a proposition for you that will relieve you of any threat from me and you can carry on with your nefarious dealings.'

'I'm all ears.'

'The State's official representative in London is due for retirement. I want the job of Agent General along with the usual free accommodation and liberal expenses that go with the position. The term is five years and on retirement the pension, plus my pension from my current position here, will set me up for life.'

'You've got to be joking.' Gibbs burst out laughing, but he could tell from the expression on Harrison's face it was no joke. 'That's a political appointment, strictly reserved for retiring eminent members and contributors to the Party. You're certainly not in that league.'

'To hell with what a pack of rent-seekers, poseurs and party hacks think. You can appoint who you like and you're going to appoint me if you want to snatch Boyce's permits, or for that matter stay attached to that chair you're in.'

'Okay, explain it to me how I do that and I'll consider your demands.'

It was Harrison's turn to snort his derision as he shook his head. 'Not likely Premier. You will announce the appointment when the present chap hands in his resignation, which you've already given him notice of. And then I'll deliver you Baracool and Ironstone Park.'

'You're that certain of your ground? I've had the legal department look at those permits and they cannot be rescinded without attracting a huge compensation payment to Boyce. What have they missed?'

'I'm not saying anything more Premier except there will be no compensation payable, that I can promise. You will have saved the State millions and achieved exactly what you want. Your hands will be clean and reputation intact. I would call that a dream result.'

Harrison knew the moment he left the room Gibbs would be on the phone calling for the lawyers to have another look at the permits, as he had no doubt they had done so many times in the past. But he was certain they would overlook the relevant clause. Many times over the past years he thought of bringing it to Gibbs' attention, but something always made him refrain. There was no advantage in him doing so, the thought being he may be able to do so to his advantage at some future time. That time had arrived.

'You're a smug conniving fag......' Gibbs checked himself as Harrison waived his finger in admonishment.

'I wouldn't go there Premier. You were about to call me a faggot which you would have got away with once, but no longer. I would only have to level a complaint and you would be up before a tribunal trying to explain yourself. The media would lap it up. Naturally, I would accept your apology, but not before your image and reputation had been trashed.'

'You really have set me up, haven't you?'

'On the contrary, you set yourself up. I'm just taking advantage of your failings. I know what you call me behind my back, but it has no effect on me. I know what I am, but you've sold me short if you think I'm just an old queen who's too scared to negotiate a hard bargain.'

Gibbs leaned back in his chair and glared at his antagonist. The reciprocal face was unblinking, but the eyes held a mocking gleam of triumph. 'How can I trust you?'

'You can't, just as I don't trust you. However, in this case I have the upper hand in that I hold all the high cards. You will just have to take my word I will deliver. I want out of this place and the pack of grubs who pass themselves off as caring politicians, whereas they're all just like you, a scheming, lying, cheating bunch of misfits all out for their own ends and fat pensions when they quit parliament or are voted out. Following my time in London I will be retiring to the South of France or somewhere quiet in Italy. I won't be sending anyone a post card.'

'When do you want my answer to your demands and threats?'

'I'm sitting right here awaiting your reply.'

'You can have the raise and the staff, but I need time to think about Boyce.'

'Take all the time you like as regards Boyce, but remember you lose if you appoint someone other than me as Agent General.'

'Holy shit man,' Gibbs implored in a tone of defeat. 'I can't just make a decision like that. You can imagine the howls of protest that will go up if I do it without consultation. You are a servant, not a worthy politician or someone who can represent the State at all levels.'

'Rubbish. I would have no problem in bowing to the Queen or sucking up to a bunch of class-conscious poms, or squiring around any visiting freeloaders and their wives from this State. Take a look at your own party. Most of them can't pronounce the Queen's English, or know which utensil to pick up first at a formal dinner. They've all got their trotters in the trough waiting for handouts. Make up your mind now or I will do it for you. You only just fluked the top job and you'll be out in a blink if I call time-out.'

Gibbs nodded in submission. A plan was forming in his mind. 'Okay, okay you've got it. I will make the announcement without consulting my colleagues the moment the present agent formally resigns. However, at that point you must deliver regarding Boyce.'

Harrison stood and held out his hand. 'I won't let you down Premier. Your reputation will remain intact, I will be out of the scene and you will have the evidence to cancel Boyce's permits immediately.'

'And do I have your agreement if you fail, I can likewise terminate your London appointment?'

'I won't fail. I've had it up my sleeve for some time now. You'll be able to assign the permits to your mate Chan and pick up a substantial fee, I would imagine. Those areas would have to be worth a kickback of millions for the iron-ore alone. You'll retire a very wealthy man, Jack Gibbs.'

Gibbs was still staring blankly at the closed door minutes after Harrison had departed. He had called him in to give him the bad news, but in reality the roles had been reversed. He had no doubt Harrison would carry out his threat if his demands were not met. What did he know his own legal department did not? Was it a bluff about Boyce's permits being open to cancellation, or had he discovered something the lawyers had overlooked? He punched in an extension number which was immediately picked up. He was put straight through to the senior counsel.

'Gibbs here. I want you to go over the permit grant documents for two of the Boyce properties, Baracool and Ironstone Park.' He overruled the objection that quickly followed. 'Yes, I know you've reviewed them previously, but that was before I became Premier. I want you to look at them again. Get a couple of new faces on the job. Maybe they'll come up with something.' He listened impatiently as the voice protested in exasperation.

'Why the insistence you look again? It's because I've been told on very good authority the titles are liable to forfeiture. No, I can't tell you who gave me that advice, but I believe it to have some authenticity. Just get on with it now.' Gibbs put down the phone as the voice continued to protest. There was one senior counsel who would be put out to grass if Harrison proved correct. If he was any good he would have been out in private practice long ago, rather than warming a seat in an unassailable government position.

45

Chloe opened the envelope with the government letterhead imprint. She already knew the contents as Gibbs' office had phoned her the previous day.

What she held was the official notification. Her application for part of Baracool to be turned into a nature reserve had been rejected on the grounds it was of insufficient public interest and contained substantial reserves of iron-ore and other minerals central to the revenue of the State.

She folded it and tossed it on the table. Gibbs had won on that front, but she still held her exploration and mining permits, so it was a rather Pyrrhic victory. She determined the only way to fight Gibbs was with money. Political parties rely on donations to run election campaigns. She would make it known through various well-placed contacts within Gibbs' party her participation would be immediately withdrawn. Instead, the substantial figure would be directed to a wide-ranging program to make the public aware of the unique wilderness she was trying to protect. She knew she was taking on a powerful enemy, but politicians were ephemeral and Gibbs had only gained the position of Premier by the slimmest of margins. If his ratings fell to dangerous levels his party would remove him for someone more acceptable to the voting public. Politics was a cut and thrust business with no quarter given.

Chloe picked up the phone and dialled Clare Bartel's number. 'Hi there Clare. How about lunch this week, I've got something I would like to discuss? Just the two of us.'

'Tomorrow is fine with me. I'll pick you up at noon.'

They were seated in a quiet corner of the restaurant with the small-talk dispensed with when Clare raised her glass. 'Well hit me with it Chloe. What's on your mind?' She remained impassive as Chloe explained her intentions and the reasons precipitating them.

'Well, what do you think? Have you any advice or suggestions?'

Clare fixed her with a grim look of disapproval. 'You can't do that Chloe. You'll have to find another way. You cut off your funding and you're inviting the socialist free-loaders to gain power. You'll be shooting yourself in the foot. Their whole ethic is to cut down the tall poppies and both you and I fit into that category. We've got too much wealth, wealth that we created, but which they maintain should be shared with the masses through increased taxes and imposts. If you think Gibbs is a burr in your britches, it will be nothing to what you'll endure if the present government is tossed out at the coming election. I would implore you not to do it. Instead of cutting off funds you should be increasing your commitment, as I've done.'

Chloe was startled by the response. She had not thought of the implications of what Clare had outlined. 'I can see where you're coming from Clare. I'll just have to think of another way of approaching this problem.'

'I'll promote a few rumours you're very likely to withdraw your financial support. That will get the party treasurer into a lather in view of the size of your donations. However, you might not have to wait long to get what you want.'

Chloe looked at her guest in surprise. 'What do you mean by that? You obviously know something I don't?'

'I don't know anything positive, but the general feeling is Gibbs is only temporary. Too many rumours about him as regards his after-hours activities and suggestions he may be on the take. He's considered to be a liability. He has no personality or charisma, and is sure to be booted out of office at the next election. He only got the position by one vote and he's already causing a lot of friction with his party-room colleagues. You probably noticed in the media he promoted his secretary and chief-of-staff the next Agent General in London. He's stepped right out of line on that one, as the position is a jobs-for-the-boys sinecure, reserved exclusively for leading retiring members of the party. What's more he locked in a five year contract, so it doesn't matter what government gets into power, there will be an enormous payout if the contract is terminated early. And he's refusing to reverse the appointment, which makes me wonder what hold does a certain Michael Harrison have over him? Has he threatened to air some of Gibbs' dirty laundry? He's been his secretary for going on six years, so he must be aware of some very sensitive secrets. Otherwise, why he'd give some unknown public servant hack such a plum position, is inexplicable.'

46

'Now's the time to deliver Harrison. You've got the job, so that's my end of the bargain complete. You're off to London anytime within the next month.'

'I've already packed and put my apartment on the market. Lionel and I will be saying goodbye, never to return. Your personal secrets will remain buried and I wish you a long and happy stay in office. However, if you betray me, I promise I'll bury you.'

'I'll stick to my side of it. Just get on with it man. What is it my legal department has missed in regard to Boyce?'

Harrison smiled and placed the folder on Gibbs' desk. 'Contained in there is the written opinion of a prominent barrister I commissioned at my personal expense. It's a very compelling opinion based on the conditions of the grant of title of the exploration permits. It doesn't mention Boyce, as I didn't want the barrister to know who I might be referring to for obvious reasons. Read it now so I can explain anything you may not understand.'

Gibbs opened the folder and began to read. Harrison could see his facial expressions change from scepticism to gradual excitement as he flipped over the four pages. He read them again more slowly before letting them drop on his desk and turning to look out the window. He remained motionless for a brief period before swinging back with a broad grin of triumph.

'You really have earned your promotion Harrison. Why the hell this wasn't picked up years ago is beyond me. I wouldn't have believed it without this opinion. I can't wait to drop this one on Boyce. Not only have I knocked out the idea of her nature reserve, but I can now take the permits off her without compensation.'

Harrison could see the dollars written in Gibbs' expression. He had no doubt the permits would be offered to Tony Chan's associates in return for a large pay-off.

This time there was no prior warning. It came in the standard government envelope. What is it this time Chloe wondered as she slit it open and unfolded the one-page letter? It was signed by Gibbs and gave her the shattering news – she had been stripped of the mineral rights to Baracool and Ironstone Park.

The senior partner was waiting for her and showed her through into his office. He could see she was in no mood for small talk as he indicated a chair and swung in behind his desk.

'Can he do this?'

Peter Ellis picked up the scanned email Chloe had sent him of Gibbs' letter. 'It certainly appears he can. I've read the pertinent clause. Gibbs appears to have a valid reason to strip you of both permits. However, you may be able to mount a case to the contrary. I will refer this to a senior barrister, but in my opinion I don't like your chances.'

'But how can he do that? My father left them to me in his Will. I've spent millions to date on establishing an exploration division and commencing mining operations on Baracool.

'It all hinges on changes made to the grant of permits some years ago. The changes were to prevent opportunistic individuals taking up valuable iron-ore tenements and then selling them off for an enormous capital gain. The amendments were made retrospective. It goes without saying no individual has the financial capacity, or the intention of getting involved in the actual mining of the iron-ore, or any other minerals found on the tenements. They're only in it for a quick opportunistic return. The retrospective change prevented any individual from transferring a permit to a company or another individual without the express permission of the Minister. The changes were not Gibbs' making, it happened years before he came on the scene. In fact, I believe it was in force at the time your father first took out the permits. No one thought to query your entitlement until now because they had already been lodged for registration in your name and that registration has been recorded.'

'I don't understand Peter. I inherited them from my father, you confirm they have been registered in my name, so what's the problem?'

'Normally there would be none, but there is a subtle clause buried in the amendments to the grant which someone has just noticed in Gibbs' legal department and brought to his attention. And that is the title can be transferred on the death of an individual, but only to the spouse or direct issue of the holder, issue being the key word in this instance.'

Chloe was getting agitated. 'Would you please explain it in plain English? I have confirmed title and I am the daughter, therefore the direct issue of Henry Boyce.'

Ellis looked at her, uncertain how to broach the subject. 'That occurred to me also. I thought Gibbs' legal advisers had made a mistake so I phoned a contact I have in the department. They see it differently.'

'I still don't understand.' But Chloe suddenly realised the reason for the lawyer's look of apprehension. 'Oh, I see it now.

What you're suggesting is I cannot inherit the titles from my father because of my heritage, it restricts me from inheriting what is rightfully mine?'

'No Chloe, you're jumping to unwarranted conclusions. Gibbs was sure of his ground before he sent the termination letter. The problem is Henry Boyce may have acknowledged you as his natural daughter on his death, but at law it's not the case.' Ellis cut her off as Chloe was about interject. 'Did you bring what I asked?'

Chloe unfolded and handed over the slip of paper. Ellis glanced at it briefly. 'Yes, this confirms the real problem. You can see your father's name does not appear on your birth certificate. You were adopted by your grandfather Johnny Quartpot. Was Johnny Quartpot in fact your grandfather?'

Chloe slowly shook her head as the memories flooded back. 'No, he wasn't. Gramps was the dearest friend I ever had.'

'So when did you find out Henry was your father? Did he ever tell you?'

'No, it was not until the day after he died I found out the truth. Henry was married at the time I was conceived, so couldn't adopt me without disclosing his paternity. And another problem, was the fact the authorities would not have allowed him to adopt a coloured child which he had not acknowledged he'd fathered. He decided to hide the truth from his then wife and the authorities.'

'So you went to live with your Gramps on Henry's cattle station? Did Henry ever disclose to you he was your father?'

'Yes, I went to live on Venus Downs and no, Henry never told me the truth and neither did Gramps. I only found out the day after Henry died. The person who told me died on the same day, soon after he'd told me Henry was my father and also disclosed the contents of his Will.'

'Can I ask you the name of that person? May I ask how he died?'

'I....I don't know how he died.' She realised her mistake. She had always maintained Walter had simply disappeared somewhere on Venus Downs. She had never admitted she had witnessed his death or revealed the details or location. 'His name was Walter Boyce. He had a brother Carl who predeceased him. They were the adopted sons of Henry.'

'So you inherited everything?'

She was relieved the lawyer did not pursue the line of questioning about Walter. 'Yes, although I've had a lot of assistance in getting to where I am today.'

'You can now understand the problem, can't you? It's nothing to do with race as you first imagined and everything to do with establishing legally you are Henry Boyce's daughter.'

Chloe gave a wry smile. 'I understand now, but I'm going to challenge this ruling. Will you help me?'

Ellis sighed and made a pyramid of his hands as he leaned forward. 'I will, but I reiterate, I don't like your chances. From what you've told me and your father's acknowledgement in his Will, you are who you say you are, but that has no legal buoyancy. As it stands, any claim you may think you have is null and void. Prima facie you are not Henry Boyce's daughter because there is no confirmed link and therefore have no right nor title to the permits. There could be a slim chance you can plead ignorance of the legislation and produce evidence of your expenditure on the permits to date. You may able to convince the court you are not attempting to exploit the permits by on-selling them for personal gain. Unfortunately, I believe that will be an uphill battle as the court will take the view the legislation takes precedence and ignorance is no defence. In the meantime, I'll get some expert advice and phone you tomorrow. I know how important this is to you. I'll give it my highest priority.'

Chloe thanked him and walked out in a daze.

47

The black Mercedes swung into the darkened driveway with its lights dimmed. A figure emerged from the shadows as the passenger door opened and the figure got in. In one fluid movement the car had reversed and quietly accelerated away. The driver looked across at the passenger.

'It's been a good day Tony, an excellent result. Boyce was advised not to challenge the confiscation of her permits, but she did and lost. Now it's time for you and I to discuss terms.'

'But she can appeal from what I understand?'

'She can, but the advice from her legal team will be to forget it. The judge was very scathing in his written summation and during the course of the hearing itself. He said it amounted to an abuse of process in that it was a pointless action bound to fail. The legislation is very clear in that a permit cannot be transferred to a non-related individual party, end of story. That action must have cost her plenty and the judge put the boot in by awarding the government's costs against her as well. That's another hit to her purse. All told, she's had a hole smashed in her petty cash tin. No, she won't appeal.'

'So, what are you proposing Jack?'

'I can't give you both permits, but you can chose which one you want before I offer the other to someone else.'

'My group will take Baracool. It's got a major copper, gold, cobalt deposit defined and not far off actual production. Also I hear Boyce's geologists have found a top-tier lithium prospect and then there's the iron-ore. That's the most attractive project. But it really comes down to what it's going to cost us?'

'Ten mill up front before I award you the permit and a further ten within six months.'

Chan whistled softly. 'The entry fee is too high Jack. Why not make it twenty when any mine gets to the positive cash-flow stage.'

'Nothing doing Tony. A bit of clever accounting could result in my return being pushed out for years if your group decided to delay the cash-flow stage by committing more to exploration or mine start-ups. I'm awake to that one. You've got to make up your mind next week. Either you accept my terms or I start shopping the permits around. And I can tell you now, you'll have to join the queue in that event. Your group is being offered a bargain price for one mine with a drilled-out ore-body with plenty of upside for further discoveries. The high-grade iron-ore alone is worth billions in its pristine state at the moment.'

'What if Boyce does appeal? It could take months before it's listed for hearing. What if she wins? Do we get our twenty million back?'

'Not bloody likely. My only guarantee is that you'll be awarded Baracool. If Boyce should appeal and win, which is simply impossible according to my legal advice, I'll refund you ten million. Take it or leave it.'

Chan remained silent as he considered the proposition. He could approve the transaction without reference to his associates. They would accept the fee, but the non-return part was going to present problems for Gibbs if Boyce was successful. However, he was sure they would get their money back in that event. It would just take a more direct method to demonstrate to Gibbs his health and social position was more important than the money.

'Where do you want the ten paid? You can't put that under your mattress.'

'Set up an account in Hong Kong for me. You've mentioned how easy it is, so do it. I'll pull the plug as Premier and retire as soon as the other ten hits the account, which should be anytime within, six months from now.'

'Okay, I can arrange that. It certainly will be clean and easy. Now what about a little celebration? Shall we go to the club? I've arranged for your favourite to be available.'

Gibbs glanced across with a broad grin. 'Yeah, why don't we do that. I feel like celebrating.' He ignored the warning signs. He was not concerned about what he had been told about video records of his attendance. It was time to celebrate.

48

'Someone by the name of Dibley has been calling you. He wants you to call him when you've got the time.' Chloe had just walked into the office and looked at the accumulation of papers on her desk. She was in no mood to talk to anyone, particularly to a person she had never heard of.

'Did he say what he wanted Maria?'

Maria Palacci shook her head. 'No, he just said it was personal. He's phoned three times since yesterday, so I guess it's urgent. Do you want to speak to him if he calls again?'

'Probably some environmental activist wanting to give me advice and their support. I was going to hire someone to fend off these people, but I guess it won't be necessary now I'm out of the nature reserve and mining business.' She laughed as she walked out to get a coffee. 'I'll be sticking with cattle from here on. Yes, put Dibley through if he phones.'

She was walking back into her office when Maria called out. 'Pick it up Chloe. You're in luck, it's Dibley again.'

'Yes Mr Dibley, how can I help you?'

"Ms Boyce, my name is Ross Dibley, I'm the executor of Elizabeth Murdoch's estate of which you are a beneficiary. I was Elizabeth's lawyer for more than twenty five years and a personal friend. She often mentioned you with the utmost warmth and love.' It took seconds before he realised he was talking to a non-responsive listener. 'Ms Boyce, are you there?'

The shock hit her as she knocked over the cup. 'I..I...I'm sorry Mr Dibley. Just give me a moment please.' Chloe reached for a packet of tissues and began to mop up the coffee. Maria had seen what happened and hurried in with a roll of paper towels while taking the cup and motioning for her to carry on.

'When did it happen?'

'Early yesterday morning. I did try to reach you, but I understand you were involved in a court case? I know we've both been expecting it, but it's come as a shock to me losing a real friend. And I've no doubt it has a greater effect on you. I would like to discuss things with you when it's convenient.'

'I'm on the way. I'll be there in half and hour.' Chloe put down the phone, put her head in her hands and began to sob quietly.

'You've just lost another cherished mainstay in your life?' was the compassionate query from Maria as she finished cleaning away the last of the coffee.

'Yes, I have Maria.' Chloe stood and walked into her private room to wipe away the tears and regain her composure. Why did she break down like that? Elizabeth had been a vegetable with dementia living in a care home for the past three years. As the condition progressed she lost all faculties of speech and bodily function. In the first year she would visit every other day and sit and observe the accelerating decay of recognition. In the past year she had visited only once every month. It was too distressing sitting and talking to a breathing, but lifeless form on a more constant basis. It was a relief, but a deep sadness now Elizabeth had been released from her unrealised hell.

Ross Dibley showed her into his spartan office, indicating a comfortable chair. The premises were as old as him, tucked away upstairs in the decrepit row of strip-mall shops.

'I'm thrilled to meet you at long last Ms Boyce. I've heard so much about you from your aunt before she was afflicted by a horrible condition.'

'Please call me Chloe.'

Dibley smiled and gave a subdued laugh. 'In that case I'm Ross. I realise you think I'm a bit of an ancient fossil, but I've just got to do something to fill in my day. However, your aunt's Will is the last matter I will handle as I've decided to close the practice next month. Now, let's get down to business. As I've already told you, I'm the sole executor of your aunt's estate and except for a few minor endowments to charities, you are the principal beneficiary. It's a considerable sum, so let me go through it.'

Chloe was amazed at the value of the estate. It was a lovely gesture, but she did not need the money. She would have preferred Elizabeth had bequeathed its entirety to charity. Ross finally finished and looked up.

'Would you like a tea or coffee?'

'No thanks Ross. Can you tell me what arrangements have been made for the funeral and can I assist in anyway?'

'There is to be no funeral. If you agree I will arrange a memorial service as I'm sure there are a great many people Elizabeth touched who would like to attend and pay their respects.'

'No funeral? That would be aunt Liz, no fanfare or fuss.'

'No, she has donated her remains to science.'

Chloe looked perplexed. 'What do you mean?'

'I thought you may get a shock. Elizabeth has donated her body to the university for medical science, and more particularly to the faculty teaching pathology to medical students.'

'Oh my God,' she exclaimed as she put her hand to her mouth in disbelief. 'Oh my God, I don't believe it.' She felt sick at the thought Liz would be slowly dissected by groups of dispassionate individuals as the corpse was retrieved from a fridge day after day before the remnant scraps of organs, flesh and bones were finally consigned for cremation, the cadaver's identity unknown to the mutilators. The thought of Liz's remains being violated horrified her.

'I know it sounds rather macabre Chloe, but that's what Elizabeth requested. I'm as upset as you are. And yes, I will take you up on your offer to assist me with the memorial service.'

She sat in stunned silence for a few moments before looking up. 'Of course I will Ross.'

'Chloe, Peter Ellis. If you're in the city would you call in and see me. I want to discuss your grounds for appeal. No need to call me back. Just come in at any time today.'

Chloe was sitting in her office penning a eulogy when she let the call on her direct number, go through to message bank before listening to it. She sighed and put her pen down. Her mind was still confused about what she should say about Liz. What could she say? Liz had been the unfailing supporter of her success, in fact the very reason for her success.

'Maria, I'll be out for about an hour,' she said as she walked past and out of the office. Maria nodded, but made no reply. She could see Chloe was going through a rough time. The death of Andrew and now her aunt was hitting her hard.

She was shown straight through to Ellis' office. He rose and indicated a chair opposite. 'I take it you've given the appeal some thought?'

'I haven't really had much time to think about it. A person I loved dearly, died just over a week ago and I've been making arrangements for a memorial service.'

Ellis offered his perfunctory condolences, before moving quickly to the subject at hand. 'I've spoken at length to the barrister who represented you and he believes the appeal would be a lost cause and waste of money. It was very clear from the judge's original ruling you cannot prove you are Henry Boyce's natural daughter. Therefore, the legislation is clear – you have no title to the permits. I realise it's a staggering loss, but your chances of a successful appeal are nil."

Chloe smiled. 'In that case, I accept the advice. But why did I have to come here? Why didn't we just do this over the phone?'

'Because it was necessary to meet you in person. I can now formally close the file and inform the barrister of your decision. I'll walk out with you.' He rose and guided her past the myriad of offices and out to the foyer. He could sense she was not interested in talking, her thoughts lost in an unrelated world.

'I can see the loss of your friend has really affected you.' It was a lame attempt at conveying some compassion while waiting in awkward silence for the lift to arrive. He wanted to get back. He had a dozen matters to attend to and precious billing time was being lost.

'Yes, my aunt was very precious to me. I'll never forget her kindness.' Just then the lift chimed its arrival and she held back waiting for people to alight.

Ellis smiled and was about to turn and leave when he checked and put a hand of gentle restraint on her arm. 'Did you say aunt?'

'Yes, my aunt Elizabeth.'

'I don't want to sound offensive or rude, but this is a critical question. Was she a figurative aunt, or was she your natural aunt?'

Chloe smiled and gave a shallow laugh. 'I understand the question Peter. She was my natural aunt, my father's sister.'

Ellis tightened his grip and pulled her back as she was about to follow the last person into the lift. 'No, no. We've got to talk about this.'

He strode ahead as she followed him back to his office and sat down. He flipped open the file to read his notes. 'Chloe, why didn't you tell me this before?'

'Because it hadn't entered my head. No one asked me whether I had any relatives other than my father. You never asked me, the barrister never asked me and what good would it have been to mention my aunt? She was living in care for the past three years, unable to speak or communicate for the last two. How could she have possibly been able to assist me?'

Ellis shook his head. 'That's my fault Chloe and I apologise. From what I understand your father was Henry Boyce and you were brought up on his cattle station in the care of your grandfather, who was no relation. Henry was your last living relative, but it would now appear that was not the case. He had a sister, but was she...'

'Yes, she was white,' Chloe replied firmly. 'I know what you're thinking. You've accepted I'm the nondescript result of a casual liaison my father had with a coloured person - the child he was too embarrassed to recognise until his death.

Now I've mentioned an aunt and your mind has flicked into overdrive. Is she my aunt or is she another skeleton in Henry Boyce's closet? Don't apologise Peter, I've suffered the stigma my whole life. It's the lingering racism quilt this country will never surmount. But don't feel bad about it, racism is just under the skin of all nationalities, only it's disguised as patriotism.'

Ellis felt the sting, but restrained any response. 'You say your aunt died nearly two weeks ago? Was she interred or cremated?'

'Neither. She donated her remains to the medical school in the interests of pathology, and in particular to the study of the causes of alzheimers and dementia.'

'You realise where I'm going with this?'

'Yes, my whole case failed because I could not prove Henry Boyce was my father. Henry's adopted sons were both dead, so it was assumed there were no living relatives. As a result I had no title to Baracool or Ironstone.'

'And a chance comment as you were about to enter the lift has potentially won you a reprieve. I blame myself for not being more thorough when preparing your case. Give me a moment please. I've got to phone the barrister to say you will be filing an appeal.' He put the receiver down after several minutes of discussion.

'That's taken care of. However, there is a real problem in that I won't be able to prepare the grounds of appeal as I don't have the evidence to support it. However, the barrister will seek leave to file full particulars within a time limit the court may impose. The judge on the other hand, may simply dismiss any grounds for appeal on the basis we're out of time. In the meantime, let's get down to business. The only way you can prove you are Henry's daughter is by getting a DNA sample of your aunt's tissue and matching it with yours. We can then verify she was Henry's sister through birth certificates and other records. It's a good thing your aunt wasn't interred because applying for permission to disturb a grave in a civil case, versus one applied for by the police, is a long an involved process. In a civil matter the court takes the view the dead should remain buried and removed from any litigation by warring relatives, illegitimate children, mistresses or the like. And it goes without saying if she had opted for cremation this case would be closed – it still maybe.'

'So how do we go about getting a DNA sample?'

'I don't know exactly. I will have to make some enquiries. I suppose the request could be made direct to the university, but more likely the executor of her estate has to become involved. It's possible your aunt's remains have already been disposed of. To put it bluntly I don't know how long it takes for medical students to complete a dissection. I'll call you as soon as I know anything. It's a long shot, but in the meantime you might try the facility where your aunt passed away. They may have some swabs or other material they're retained for evidentiary purposes. But I would imagine they'll hang up on you with the suspicion you could be about to launch a mistreatment or negligence action.'

Two days later Chloe got the answer Ellis predicted - it was blunt and direct. No samples of any description had been taken or retained. Her aunt had been treated with the utmost respect and kindness and consideration by the staff.

Ellis' call followed soon after. 'Bad news Chloe. The university under no circumstances will allow tissue samples to be removed without the written approval of the next of kin. And as you're not the proven next of kin, that rules you out. The executor has no say in the matter, so I'm afraid we've come to the end of the line - you have no grounds for appeal. I will phone the barrister and tell him.'

A spark went off in her brain. 'Would you hold fire until tomorrow? I may have the solution.'

'Tell me more. Is this some other relation you've suddenly become aware of? Did Henry have other siblings?'

'No Peter, I believe I'm last in the line. I won't explain it now, but I will phone you tomorrow.'

Ellis put the phone down and sat back to think. Was she setting him up for a professional negligence claim? If he'd been paying full attention when preparing the action, he should have determined Henry Boyce had no living relatives other than Chloe. And he had been fool enough to apologise for his oversight, an apology that could be used against him. He had got too close to his client, too friendly and it just may cost him both a financial and reputational loss. He could not rely on the defence she had failed to disclose the existence of her aunt. It would simply not stand up to scrutiny. It was he who had made the glaring mistake of not asking the obvious question.

49

Chloe hunted through her desk for the card. Normally, she would have entered an important business contact on her computer and phone files, but it wasn't business related, so it wasn't important. She remembered his Christian name, but could not attach the hyphenated surname to the obscure face. She had always been amused by the English propensity for hyphenation, when one side of the family was lifted out of class oblivion by attaching their name to a more worthy spouse in the eyes of society. Money was seeking status or status was seeking money. She had witnessed it constantly during her years in London.

The card was not in any of the desk drawers. She must have put it in her bag and tossed it into a drawer at home as she had no interest in contacting the person again. It was too long ago and a faded memory in the past. But now she desperately needed to contact him. She was sitting at the traffic lights when it changed to green and triggered the memory cell that flashed Oliver Gibbs-Spencer, or rather Professor Oliver Gibbs-Spencer. She pulled over and punched the name into White Pages. No record, so private unlisted. At home it took her only minutes to find the card shoved into a drawer in her writing desk. She looked at the time and dialled his direct number.

'Melissa Gibbs-Spencer speaking.'

Chloe cringed at the affected vowels and modulated tone. It was obvious who had insisted on the hyphenation. Oliver had probably met her in England when studying for an advanced qualification. She had a feeling this was going to end badly. She should have waited until the morning and contacted him at the university.

'I was wondering if I could speak to Oliver please? My name is Chloe Boyce.'

'Chloe?' the voice went up several octaves in surprised recognition. 'I know who you are. I saw you in London often and bought several of the designs you modelled. I didn't believe Oliver when he told me he knew you from years ago and he'd caught up with you in the hospital car park recently. Oh, I'd love to meet you. Would you come to dinner one evening?'

Anything, if I can speak to your husband, Chloe was thinking. 'Yes, that would be nice.'

'I'll get Oliver for you.'

Chloe heard the muffled shouts as Melissa called her husband with urgent excitement.

'Hello Chloe. This is a surprise. Is this social or professional?'

'A bit of both Oliver, but I'm hoping you may be able to assist. It's something very personal and urgent. Could we meet somewhere privately tomorrow?'

'Can't you give me a hint?'

'It's something to do with your work in pathology. I can't expand on that anymore at the moment. It also has something to do with your father.' She was waiting for the curt brush-off, but there was silence as if he was trying to find the common thread that linked her to pathology and his father.

'I'm intrigued. Why don't you come up to my rooms at the hospital tomorrow morning around ten. Oh, just a moment, Melissa is signalling me.' Chloe could hear the raised voice.

Finally the line was clear again as he took the phone away from his chest. 'Melissa and I would like you to come to dinner next Tuesday. Does that suit you?'

'That's a date Oliver. In the meantime, I'll see you in the morning.' She had immediately understood the reason for the raised voices. Melissa was one pushy lady who wore the pants. Chloe smiled as she hung up. That was one dinner date she would not be keeping if Oliver declined to help, which she fully expected him to do. In that event he would understand she could not attend dinner. However, if he agreed, she would have to honour the engagement, although she could envisage the scene of Melissa exhibiting her trophy guest before half a dozen of her clique of vacuous social friends. It was the very reason Chloe protected her privacy. The social scene was compulsory in the world she frequented all those years ago. Networking, socialising, endless appearances and faux friendships were the key to selling vanity - a business she wanted to forget.

Oliver was waiting as she got out of the lift. He leaned forward and pecked her on the cheek before turning towards his rooms. 'It's great to see you and so soon.' He showed her into his large office with a plain desk and matching chairs. 'Sit over here Chloe, it's more comfortable,' he said pointing to a low table with four surrounding lounge chairs. 'As you can see, hospitals don't provide staff with comforts, not even a professor gets privileges.' He gave a nervous laugh as they sat down. 'Now, tell me, what's this all about. I'm puzzled as to what pathology has to do with my father?'

'Let me explain it to you Oliver.' She watched his facial expressions for the next fifteen minutes. He gave nothing away, not even when his father's involvement was revealed. He did not ask any questions, nor did she repeat her request. She could feel the despair rising as she finished. He remained silent as he looked at her. She imagined that was the way he dispassionately viewed a corpse - it was nothing but a tag tied to a big toe.

'Highly irregular I must say Chloe. The university would refuse point blank?'

She held out her hand as she began to stand. 'I expected that answer Oliver. I apologise for compromising you, but thank you for your time.'

'Sit down. I will do it as long as you give me your word this won't go any further. This is strictly in confidence.'

Stunned, she sat down. 'I don't want to create any trouble Oliver.'

'I will get the tissue sample provided your aunt's remains have not been disposed of already. I apologise for describing it in such clinical terms, but that's the truth of it. Sometimes, pathology dissections are limited to the study of a particular organ so they could be over very quickly. However, if your aunt is still at the university I will have the laboratory run the DNA. I will need a mouth swab from you, which I can do now. And in regard to my father, I don't have much time for him. Knowing him as I do, I believe he has an ulterior motive in confiscating your mining permits. I would never ask him and don't want to know, but I'm sure it has something to do with personal gain. He doesn't like Melissa and keeps badgering her as to when he can expect grand-kids. I've told him why, for medical reasons she can't, but he still keeps at it, particularly when he's had a skin-full of red wine. He hasn't said as much, but I know he wants me to divorce Melissa and find someone who can provide an heir to the Gibbs dynasty. My mother realises why we refuse the Sunday lunch invitations. There's just nothing between us. Anyway, we're packing up and moving back England. I've accepted a position at a large university hospital and Melissa is looking forward to being back among her family. So you see, it doesn't concern me if he loses and you regain what's yours'

'I can't thank you enough. I won't forget the kindness.'

'When's the appeal due to be lodged?'

'The barrister has already given notice and asked for an extension to file the particulars. It was my fault as I'd completely forgotten about aunt Liz until the lawyer asked a casual question whether she was my natural aunt. I felt such a fool.'

Oliver laughed. 'Now you've got to turn up for dinner next week, don't you? Don't lie to me. You were going to decline the invitation if I'd refused your request?'

'Correct. I wasn't going to compromise you. I couldn't imagine anything worse than sitting around trying to make conversation while both you and Melissa knew I was there under false pretences. It would not have been much of an evening, but I can see now I'm going to enjoy it.'

'I hope it won't be the only evening before we leave. No doubt you will find some of Melissa's friends somewhat demanding of your attention. But you've had years of practice, so I imagine you'll handle it with ease.'

50

ight rain was falling as Chloe hurried along the street against the advancing umbrellas sheltering pedestrians with the same purpose in mind – all trying to avoid one another with the same fixed expressions of frustrated indifference. She was about to turn into her office building when someone moved into her path.

'Hello Ms Boyce. Not a nice day is it?'

Chloe raised her umbrella to identify the person. She knew the face, but it was the name she had forgotten.

'Christine Morley. I was with Mr Gibbs when you took him up to the Pilbara with Mr McDonald.'

'Of course Christine. Now I remember. It's nice to see you again. I suppose you're very busy now that Mr Gibbs is Premier?' She could not think what to say, she was in a hurry, the was rain was increasing and she did not want to stand around engaging in idle pleasantries with someone close to the enemy.

'I'm no longer in the Premier's department. I haven't been fired yet, but I'm looking for a job as far away from Jack Gibbs as I can get.'

Chloe recognised the sign of a distraught woman reaching out for a sympathetic shoulder. She wanted no part of it. 'I'm sorry to hear that Christine. Look I don't want to appear rude, but I must be going.' She made to move away.

'I want to talk to you Chloe, it concerns you and your aunt. This is not a chance meeting, I've been waiting for you.'

Chloe stopped and turned. 'Me and my aunt, what are you talking about? Did you know her?'

Christine shook her head. 'No, but I believe I know something you're not aware of. Gibbs is setting a trap for you. There is no doubt you will lose the appeal based on what he has planned. He then intends to ensure the media drags up all the previous scandal regarding your father and Andrew and Helen Gould – he plans a real character assassination.'

Chloe showed no emotion. 'Look Christine, I really am very busy. I must be going.' She felt her arm being restrained.

'You don't understand, it's not what you think. I'm not running an errand for Gibbs.' The grip tightened and she could see the tears of desperation beginning to form. 'You've got to talk to me. You don't know what he's planning.'

Chloe's mind raced. What game was this woman playing, if it was indeed a game. 'Okay Christine, come on up to my office. I can spare ten minutes.' Her manner was abrupt and bordering on the rude. She was in no mood to sit through a *Dear Abby* session where the secretary had been seduced by the boss and then discarded, as was clearly the case in this instance.

Maria Palacci put the coffee and biscuits on the desk and quietly departed. She raised her eyes at Chloe as she turned and shut the door. She had been warned to interrupt the meeting if it went beyond half an hour. Chloe pushed over a box of tissues. She wanted this woman out of her office and life.

'Look Christine, I'll come straight to the point. Am I right in saying you and Gibbs were having an affair and he's now tossed you aside. If you are out for revenge, I cannot help you because I don't know of anything to be of assistance and I don't want to become involved.'

Christine Morley dabbed at her eyes with a tissue. 'I can understand your attitude towards me Chloe, but I'm about to change that. Now just sit and listen for ten minutes and then I'll leave. No need for your secretary to interrupt and remind you of an important meeting.'

Chloe smiled in admission, but over the next twenty minutes any trace of that had been eroded and replaced by a look of disbelief and shock – it was more, it was absolute horror.

'So there you have it Chloe. You can accept it as the truth, or dismiss it and suffer the consequences. I came to warn you of what he's about to put you through. You don't deserve it, the man's a pig,' she said as she got to her feet.

'I must apologise for my behaviour Christine. Please forgive me. I would like to make it up to you in some way. You say you are looking for employment? You would be welcome here if you would consider it? Maria is my office manager, but I need a personal secretary and I believe you would fit in very well.'

'I would like that, but I don't want to accept it just because you feel you owe me something. Why don't we wait until what I've just told you is confirmed. When is your appeal due to be heard?'

'I've got to file the particulars within the next two weeks and then it's just a matter of waiting until the court sets a date. However, from what you've just told me I would make an absolute fool of myself to proceed. What do you intend to do about Gibbs? And why did Michael Harrison give you all that damning information. Surely, he will also be sacked the moment Gibbs is shown the door?'

Christine laughed. 'Unlike me, Michael knows how to look after himself. He's in London now safe in the knowledge he has a five year appointment. He really screwed Gibbs down to a watertight contract – if they sack him, he gets a lump-sum payout. Michael knows that's going to happen the moment the bucket gets tipped on Gibbs, which he intends to do any day now. He's planned it that way. Of course, there are going to be howls to sack him and not pay him out, but that's not going to happen. He's done nothing wrong, he hasn't committed any crime. And Gibbs thought he was the smart one and Michael was just another pervert. I realise what I've told you is going to be of no benefit financially. You've certainly lost the two permits, but by not appealing you'll survive any embarrassment and media attention. I hope that is some consolation combined with Gibbs' downfall.'

'Can I ask how you are going to expose Harrison's information, including the tapes of the restaurant meetings with Chan, along with the cash payouts and the video clips? I would be very careful if I were you. There's big money and reputations involved.'

'Michael showed me how, but I won't implicate you by explaining it to you now. If someone starts asking questions and I believe it will be the police, you'll be able to truthfully plead ignorance. Leave that up to me, you don't want to know about the details.'

Chloe showed Christine to the lift. 'Don't forget the job offer stands no matter what.' She turned and walked back to her office and sat back completely exhausted. She had almost blindly walked into a trap. It had taught her a sharp lesson not to dismiss the messenger before first listening. She went over and over the message trying to pick holes in it. Christine Morley had no reason to lie, she had nothing to gain. She had to be telling the truth.

Finally she shoved her chair back, picked up her bag and coat and walked out. 'Tomorrow's another day Maria, I'll see you in the morning.' She had resigned herself to a force greater than she could resist – there was no point in pursuing it further. She didn't need the money nor the fight. Gibbs had won. She hoped Christine Morley would also arrive at the same conclusion and abandon her plan to destroy the man. Wasn't it Confucius who said *'if you seek revenge, dig two graves.'* She decided to phone her in the morning and tell her of her decision and advise her to do the same. Walk away before it became a nightmare of police and media attention, the strain of which would take a serious mental and physical toll.

51

The house was an unpretentious low-set bungalow in a quiet tree-lined street. Half a dozen cars were parked outside. Chloe glanced in the mirror to check her make-up and hair before stepping out and brushing down her dress. It was years since she had appeared as the main attraction, but she was about to experience it again. Could she keep up the front of being supposedly ignorant she was the centre of attention, or would she just accept it? It was only seconds after she knocked, the front door was thrown open.

'Chloe, Chloe, it's great to see you,' Oliver gushed as he bussed her on the cheek. It was all she could do to restrain her abhorrence. 'Come in and meet Melissa and our guests.'

Melissa Gibbs-Spencer was natural and charming with none of the affected airs Chloe was expecting. 'Chloe, I'm so pleased you could make it. When you called and cancelled our previous dinner invitation, I understood completely – you must be very busy.'

'Yes, I apologise for that, but I had to fly north to the Pilbara and then I spent a few days here with my lawyers preparing for a legal matter.' She pretended not to notice Oliver's sharp lift of an eyebrow and smile of satisfaction.

'I take it that was in relation to your appeal. Is it proceeding well?'

'It certainly is Oliver, with thanks to you for your invaluable help. It's been a real struggle meeting the court's timetable, but we'll make it fully prepared for the next hearing. Any news on the DNA results?'

Oliver took her arm and guided her into the lounge. 'Yes, I have them, but let's not go into that now. Come in and meet some of my colleagues and their partners.'

The guests were a blur of faces and meaningless names – some things never changed. Chloe sipped on her champagne and joined in with long-practised ease. Melissa knew how to cook – the rare roast beef fillet and Yorkshire pudding was as good as Chloe ever remembered when dining at the Savoy Grill.

'That was a superb meal Melissa,' Chloe said as she joined the departing guests two hours later. 'I really enjoyed the meal and the company, It brought back fond memories.'

'I think Oliver has something to discuss with you privately so I'll leave you to it. I must say it was a real pleasure meeting you. You must give us notice when you're going to be in London next. I have a town house there and you're welcome to use it anytime.'

Oliver began to walk her out to her car, 'I couldn't say anything in there, but I've some great news for you. Your swab sample and your aunt's tissue proved a near perfect match at ninety four percent compatibility. And that's about as good as you could hope for. I don't believe the court will have any option but to uphold your appeal. That's going to be one in the nose for my father.'

Chloe showed little emotion as she triggered the car door. 'That is good news. It looks as though I'm back in the mining game.'

'Hey what's wrong? You should be dancing and singing with excitement. I know I would be if I'd just been given that news. Look, now the guests have gone why not come and have a drink with Melissa and I to celebrate?'

'I'm just tired Oliver, it's been one hell of a strain just waiting for confirmation I do have the right to legitimately call myself Chloe Boyce. I'm not an orphan after all – you don't know what that means to me.' She kissed him on the cheek. 'You're a gem and I can't thank you enough, but I'll take a rain-check on that drink.'

'The appeal isn't going to heard for another couple of weeks. Why don't we make it for lunch out of town one day-just the two of us? I know a really good seafood restaurant an hour down the coast. Dad's got a beach-house down there.'

'I'd like that Oliver. It would be wonderful to just get out of town and not think about business for an afternoon. I'm off to Indonesia next week and the following week I'm at Ascot Downs. Also, with the court case coming up I daresay the lawyers will want some of my time. I'll have a look at my diary and give you a call. In the meantime, I must thank you for your invaluable help and please thank Melissa again for a superb meal. Why don't we skip the fish restaurant and check out the beach-house. We've obviously got similar intent in mind. I trust your father is not going to be there?' She left him grinning from ear to ear as she accelerated away.

He walked slowly back inside and shut his office behind him. His father was awaiting his call.

'So, she swallowed it? That's great news boy. You can pull your affidavit next week and finish her off once and for all. The media will have a field day when I leak it to them.'

'No, don't be so hasty. I'm want to have a bit of fun first. She wants to drive down the coast to the beach-house before the appeal hearing. It's too late to break her in – you stuffed that up long ago when I took her to your birthday party. Anyway, I don't want to miss this opportunity – she's still a smashing looking bird. If I rescind the affidavit beforehand, it will be game over. Let's wait until the day of the hearing.'

There was a bellow of laughter. 'Jeez boy, you haven't changed, still trying to get into the knickers of any woman who crosses your path. And you say she put the hard word on you? Yeah, I say go for it while she's on heat - sounds like a real fire cracker to me, you lucky devil. And you will pull your affidavit before they put you in the witness box, but I daresay you're going to be able to explain that? It's going to give me a great deal of pleasure to see the look on the face of that smug bitch when you reveal the DNA samples don't match. It will teach her a lesson she won't forget. The media will have a field day with it all over again. Not only will she lose the appeal, but all that mud about Hanna's affair with Gould will be be rehashed along with her father's criminal background. Then there's the juicy reference to her being mixed up with a paedophile who tried to rip her off for millions. Boyce won't be able to find a large enough rock to hide under. The media will also bang on about her wealth, and as we both know the public laps up the crap about the rich not paying enough taxes. They salivate at the sight of a tall poppy being hacked down.'

'I hear what you're saying Dad, but there's something about her reaction tonight that's got me concerned. She initiated the drive to the beach too easily - I didn't suggest it. What if she already somehow knows the DNA results are going to be negative?'

'How could she? That's impossible from what you've told me. You even had to make some excuse to justify taking a sample off a cadaver.'

'That's what's worrying me. I have an image and professional standing to protect. I have a prestigious position here and I can't afford to have it challenged. It would mean the end of my appointment in England if that happened. I'm already up to my neck in agreeing to help you. An associate of mine, Tim Barrett, had to witness me taking a sample from her aunt, just in case I had to back up my affidavit. What he didn't see was me was swapping it for another sample off another cadaver during a class the following day.'

'I was wondering why you dragged someone else into this. Why didn't you just take a sample off a patient in casualty? No one would have known the difference with what you've got in mind. Sometimes I wonder how you made it where you are today.'

'Dad, that's why you're a politician – you sit on your brains and talk bullshit all day. Hasn't it struck you Professor Oliver Spencer-Gibbs is presenting an affidavit supporting an appeal by Chloe Boyce while the opposition is in effect his father, the Premier of the State. That's what I would call a conflict of interest, if ever I've seen one. That's why I had to get one of my colleagues to sign off on the affidavit as well. Your barrister will most likely avoid the conflict by calling Barrett rather than me to testify.'

'But you're going to withdraw the affidavit, aren't you?'

Oliver shook his head in frustration. 'Of course I am, but Barrett will know immediately what I've done and Boyce's counsel will recognise a stitch-up. Barrett will not say anything, but I will have lost the professional confidence of a good friend. It's one thing to keep a score-sheet of our conquests, but it's another to pervert the course of justice. No doubt your barrister will also realise what has occurred, but will keep his mouth shut. Oh God, this could end in disaster. What have I been dragged into?"

'You're worrying too much. You just do what you've told me and everything will work out. At this moment Boyce has lost and you're in the clear.'

'I'm not in the clear Dad – I won't be until the appeal judgement is handed down. If Chloe does know something, it could have a severe impact on me and my career. Maybe she has found alternative grounds for appeal And what about Melissa and her family? The mud will stick.'

'You know what I think of your wife and her family, they're your problem. Why the hell you ever married her is beyond me. The bitch is barren. Now get off the bloody phone, I've got an urgent call to make.'

Oliver was stunned by his father's debasing remark. He had looked up to his father all his life, but now he realised Jack Gibbs had only two purposes - the lust for power and opportunism. He had not noticed his wife standing in the doorway as he put the phone down and buried his head in his hands. She had followed the conversation, her father-in-law's voice so penetrating.

'What are you going to do Oliver – you can't possibly go through with it?'

He looked up angrily. 'That was a private conversation behind a closed door. I resent your eavesdropping like that - it had nothing to do with you.'

'Oliver, the door was ajar and I couldn't fail to hear what you and your father were discussing. And I believe it does affect me. You could destroy your whole career with the fraud you are intending to perpetrate. And for what? Just to satisfy your father? You've been living under his shadow all your life. Don't you think it's time you severed the link?'

'It's not going to affect either of us. Chloe's appeal will be dismissed.'

'Which is a gross injustice, which you intend to perpetrate. From what I've just heard, you swapped the samples which will show it's incompatible with that which your colleague

Tim Barrett put his name to. I heard him briefly mention it to you tonight, before you shook your head to cut off any further conversation. Your father wins and steals what rightfully belongs to Chloe. Can't you see you are committing a crime?'

'That's where you're wrong – there was no guarantee the aunt's sample would match Boyce's DNA.'

'Then why did you swap it? But let me guess – you did submit both samples and the aunt's sample matched perfectly while the substitute sample did not?'

Oliver stood and reached out for his wife. 'Melissa, why don't you forget about what you heard? We're off back to England and away from all this. This is the last time I will have to put up with my father's demands.'

She pulled away and sat down. 'Is Barrett aware of the subterfuge? If not, he's going to wake up very quickly. If Chloe Boyce does have something up her sleeve and he's called to explain what has happened, you'll be tossing him to the lions – you drag a highly qualified and respected pathologist down with you. You trash two careers.'

Gibbs poured himself a scotch and sat down. 'He's old enough to look after himself. He may guess, but he will never ask. It will never be mentioned again once Boyce's appeal is dismissed. Anyway I can't pull out now – I just cannot let my father down. It would cost me too much.'

'I know what your father is – he's an avaricious, scheming womanising louse, just like you. You're scared he will disinherit you because you married me and I'm unable to have children. And please don't deny the womanising because I'm well aware of your reputation amongst the medical interns and nurses – *Ollie the Slick*, I believe? And where did I hear that term used? Why, it was right here tonight when Barrett was having a private laugh with some of his colleagues comparing their latest conquests. You are in the lead, but Barrett is close behind. And just now I did hear you discussing your intended conquest of Chloe. You really must believe you're irresistible. I maybe wrong, but I believe she's way ahead of you - she's got your measure.'

He drained the glass and poured another. 'You are my wife and I love you. I don't believe you would do anything to jeopardise our reputation or that of your family.'

'Oliver, I gave up my career as a highly paid London lawyer to follow you out here. It was a decision I've never regretted until tonight. If I was still practising I would have no second thoughts about phoning Barrett and telling him of the deception, or likewise Chloe. But Barrett has gone down in my estimation so can look after himself and take the consequences – he's no better than you. As for Chloe Boyce, it's just possible she's fallen for your charms, so I'll also leave her to fight her own battles – collateral damage as it's referred to in military terms. As for me, I'm divorcing you Oliver. I will catch a flight out tomorrow. If and when you take up the appointment in England, please change your title to plain Professor Oliver Gibbs and save my family the stench of association.'

52

Alex was walking quickly towards the court. He had guessed the identity of the person in front. They both took the steps two at a time leading up to the entrance. He saw the microphones and cameras thrust into the face of the person just ahead.

'Any comment professor? Is it true you're appearing as a witness supporting the Boyce appeal? Have you discussed this with your father? Don't you consider your appearance presents a conflict of interest?'

'No comment,' was the reply as he brushed past.

Alex waited for him as he picked up his shoulder bag on the other side of xray security. 'Are you Oliver Gibbs-Spencer?'

'I am, but I'm in a hurry.'

Alex blocked his path as he began to walk around him. 'Oliver, I need to talk to you now.'

'Get out of my way before I call security. I'm late for a court appearance.'

'I know what you're late for, but I suggest we talk before you get charged with perverting the course of justice. And that wouldn't be good for you or your father's image.'

'What the hell are you talking about?' He swung around to summon security.

Alex stepped back from the stale smell of alcohol. It was apparent Oliver Gibbs-Spencer had been fighting more than one demon overnight – the demon of his conscience of what he was about to do and the demon drink.

'What I'm talking about Oliver is that Chloe doesn't need your testimony – she already knows you're about to do a back-flip.'

Gibbs stopped and sneered. 'Who the hell are you anyway? I'm going to have you charged with attempting to intimidate a witness. That combined with a charge of contempt of court should see you put away for a stretch.'

'I'm Alex Hammond, Chloe Boyce's stepson. And yes I'm taking a very grave risk in approaching you like this, but you're about to make a big mistake if you proceed. You see, Chloe already knows you are going to retract your affidavit supporting her application. In fact she's known for weeks.'

'She can't have.' He tapped his bag. 'I've only just signed off on it – that's why I'm running late. Her appeal is shot to bits.'

'That's where you're wrong professor. The State's barrister is going to hit the roof when he's handed your latest version. Boyce's barrister will no doubt make an application to have you declared a hostile witness and that's no laughing matter. You can't screw the court around and not expect the consequences.'

Gibbs' face went ashen as he tried to fit the events into a time-frame. 'You say Chloe has known for weeks now. In that case she must have known when she came to my home for dinner – that's impossible.'

'Oh, she knew alright professor. Her barrister is inside all smiles, just waiting for you to take the stand. He can't wait to rip the credibility of Professor Gibbs-Spencer to shreds, along with the integrity of a certain Tim Barrett.' Alex looked at his watch. 'Half an hour to go before the balloon goes up professor. Are you ready for it?

'Why d..did she do it?'

'Because she wanted to see how you played out the charade. Do you remember how she postponed a dinner engagement with the excuse she had business to attend to in Indonesia and then moved it to the following week. She wanted to make sure the person who told her what you intended was prepared to sign an affidavit and then stand up in court to testify. It's unfortunate Barrett will also be forced to resign because of your duplicity – two brilliant careers and reputations trashed. She also wanted to meet your wife, who by the way she thinks is charming. Of course she led you on about the excursion down to your father's holiday shack on the beach. You've failed twice in regard to that conquest.' Alex grabbed his arm as he began to sway. 'Sit down over here prof – you look as though you're about to pass out. You should really keep off the bottle and stick with medicine – court's of law are very dangerous places for the unwary with hangovers.'

Gibbs sat down with a glazed look of shock, the sweat glistening on his forehead. 'Is that it? I don't know that I can go in there now.'

'You could apply for an adjournment on medical grounds. I daresay you would get it considering the circumstances and your standing – all professionals of your rank like to piddle in each other's pockets – judges included. By the way there is one final bit of advice you should impart to your father – tell him to start putting fire retardant in his underpants, because a blow-torch is about to be applied to his backside, courtesy of not but one, but two of his former employees.' Alex patted him on the knee as he stood. 'And I make no apology for stuffing up your day prof.'

'Fuck you to Hammond. You're bluffing – I've got to go in there. I can withdraw my affidavit by stating I've just found out the samples were contaminated. Bang goes Boyce's grounds for appeal – she loses as she can't produce any new evidence.'

Alex shook his head. 'Chloe has got other confirmed samples of her aunt's DNA which match hers. You withdraw yours and she presents hers and your father and the State lose. Checkmate. You go in there and I guarantee your status here, your marriage and your new appointment in England will be short-lived when the media finishes with you. You saw them when you came in. They can smell blood because they've already been tipped off something big is about to break and while not giving the game away entirely, I did hint Gibbs was about to suffer a setback. Get out while you can now and save your reputation. Catch a plane out tonight.'

'But, I can't just abandon my father.'

'Professor, your father is finished – you can't save him.'

Alex was about to walk away when he was pushed aside. 'What are you doing Oliver? I've been in there waiting for you. The barrister wants to see you now – I've told him you're going to retract your affidavit. He's bloody furious as the hearing is about to start and he wants to know why the sudden change. If you're explanation is not good enough he's going to make application to withdraw, so don't let me down.'

Alex waited for Oliver to obey, but he remained sitting as he shook his head. 'I'm not going in there to perpetrate a lie Dad. I've had enough of your demands and overbearing control. Melissa has left me and I'm going to follow her just as soon as I finish up at the hospital and clear the decks – I won't be coming back.'

Jack Gibbs grabbed the front of his son's shirt, pulling him to his feet. He instantly gained attention of security who moved towards him hesitantly, having recognised his identity. 'You're not going to do this to me Oliver – I've got too much to lose.'

'So have I Dad, but you can wash your own dirty laundry from here on.' He shrugged himself loose and glared at his father. 'Alex has just told me you're about to have some heat applied to your arse and I believe him. I don't want to be around when that happens.'

Jack Gibbs swung on Alex. 'Who the hell are you and what's this about heat? What have you telling my son? You're in deep shit if you've been trying to tamper with a witness.'

'Leave him alone Dad. I think you've done enough damage.'

Gibbs glared at his son. 'Just get in there and tell the barrister you're changing your testimony – there's been a mistake and the DNA samples don't match.'

'I'm going in there Dad, but I won't be withdrawing my affidavit. The samples do match and there's no doubt Chloe Boyce is Henry Boyce' natural daughter. She has title to what you've attempted to confiscate.'

Jack Gibbs was left standing as he watched his son disappear into the court. He did not look at Alex as he walked through the foyer and out onto the street.

Alex reached for the remote and switched off the news. 'So much for Jack Gibbs. How humiliating for him to be shown being arrested in his office and marched out. The allegations and evidence of corruption are mind-blowing if the videos and tapes are to be believed. Someone really must have had it in for him to have leaked those to the media. The cops didn't have to commence an investigation based on rumours – they had the evidence served to them on a plate. Of course they will claim all the credit, which is only to be expected.'

'And I won my appeal thanks to you Alex. Mind you Peter Ellis nearly had a fit when I told him how you had approached Oliver Gibbs in the court foyer. If Oliver had complained you would have likely been serving a stretch for witness tampering. Were you aware of the danger, or were you just playing fast and loose?'

'I realised the danger, but I thought Oliver would buckle and he did. Mind you, when Jack appeared on the scene I was reconsidering my folly. I thought for a moment he was going to have me arrested by security as they were right behind him when he grabbed Oliver. I was lucky. Which brings me to your luck – how did you know about the sample switch?'

Chloe laughed. 'That was a real stroke of luck. Jack Gibbs made the mistake of telling a bedtime story to a certain secretary. Unfortunately, he then decided to stop telling stories in bed and terminated the arrangement, which upset the secretary no end. She accosted me in the street and told me what Oliver Gibbs was going to do. That really pulled the rug from under, but by then I was at the stage I no longer cared – I would stick to cattle rather than fight with Gibbs. However, it occurred to me there could be remaining DNA samples in Liz's apartment which had been vacant the whole time she was in the care home. Sure enough, Ross Dibley was astute enough to call in the experts who recovered any number of samples which matched my DNA. I had to get Ross involved because he was able to swear an affidavit that he alone had retrieved the sample and had it tested. I had gone to Ross to ask him for a key to Liz's apartment as I'd misplaced mine. I told him what I was looking for. Being the astute lawyer he is, and me being ignorant, he told me I couldn't personally look for a sample as the court would likely disregard my evidence as being tainted. I thank my lucky stars Liz had insisted the apartment was not to be sold because she planned to return. Dementia is a terrible mind-destroying disease.'

'So who was the person who tipped you off?'

'I won't name names at this point, but you'll all soon get to know her as she now works for me. I owe her a big debt. Jack Gibbs must have sensed she represented a real threat as she started getting menacing phone calls and complained of being followed. I immediately had her flown up to Ascot Downs well away from danger. She's due back tomorrow.'